Heaven®

Susi Rajah trained as an art director and worked in advertising until she was fed up enough to attempt a novel. She is also the co-author of two serious non-fiction books, one of which is *How to Spot a Bastard by His Star Sign*. Susi wrote this novel in Los Angeles, but has since moved to New York City where she lives with her first husband. She likes people who buy her cocktails, plane tickets and Manhattan real estate.

# Heaven®

SUSI RAJAH

PENGUIN BOOKS

PENGUIN BOOKS

Published by the Penguin Group
Penguin Books Ltd, 80 Strand, London WC2R 0RL, England
Penguin Group (USA) Inc., 375 Hudson Street, New York, New York 10014, USA
Penguin Group (Canada), 90 Eglinton Avenue East, Suite 700, Toronto, Ontario, Canada M4P 2Y3
(a division of Pearson Penguin Canada Inc.)
Penguin Ireland, 25 St Stephen's Green, Dublin 2, Ireland
(a division of Penguin Books Ltd)
Penguin Group (Australia), 250 Camberwell Road, Camberwell, Victoria 3124, Australia
(a division of Pearson Australia Group Pty Ltd)
Penguin Books India Pvt Ltd, 11 Community Centre,
Panchsheel Park, New Delhi – 110 017, India
Penguin Group (NZ), 67 Apollo Drive, Rosedale, North Shore 0632, New Zealand
(a division of Pearson New Zealand Ltd)
Penguin Books (South Africa) (Pty) Ltd, 24 Sturdee Avenue,
Rosebank, Johannesburg 2196, South Africa

Penguin Books Ltd, Registered Offices: 80 Strand, London WC2R 0RL, England

www.penguin.com

Published in Penguin Books 2007

1

Copyright © Susi Rajah, 2007
All rights reserved

The moral right of the author has been asserted

Set in 12.5/14.75 pt Monotype Garamond
Typeset by Rowland Phototypesetting Ltd, Bury St Edmunds, Suffolk
Printed in England by Clays Ltd, St Ives plc

Except in the United States of America, this book is sold subject
to the condition that it shall not, by way of trade or otherwise, be lent,
re-sold, hired out, or otherwise circulated without the publisher's
prior consent in any form of binding or cover other than that in
which it is published and without a similar condition including this
condition being imposed on the subsequent purchaser

ISBN: 978-0-141-02521-6

For Corey

It's a typical LA story. Girl meets actor. They keep meeting. Relationship summits are held. But before they can walk, hand in hand, towards a scenic solar event, another girl-meets-actor story begins. Another girl. Same actor.

She turns out to be the dreaded triple threat – large breasts, small vocabulary, no visible panty line. He turns out to be looking for exactly those traits in a partner. And I, it turned out, got dumped with a weak improvisation on the 'it's not you, it's me' speech. So weak it confirmed what I'd suspected all along. He wasn't a very good actor.

Days passed before I found someone else – a writer. Now I get to enjoy being with someone with even higher levels of self-obsession and insecurity than an actor, only without the hindrance of nice pecs and a cute butt.

Charles is the perpetrator of a newspaper column. A day or so after I was dumped, and still sore at men in general, I read his column and knew he was the last man on earth I wanted to be involved with. It followed that a relationship was on the cards.

The column went on and on about how girls are doing better in school than boys, due, I suspect, to girls now being allowed to attend school. What annoyed me – along with the pie charts – was the way the column ended, with the recommendation that something must be done to help the poor boys.

I found it so annoying I wrote a letter to the newspaper, suggesting alternative uses for the column and its author. Knowing how these things work, I doubted the letter would get read. I certainly didn't expect Charles to answer me with a letter of his own.

He didn't expect it, either. He has a policy of only answering letters from readers publicly, within the safety of his column. There are, apparently, sick people out there who, given the encouragement of two-way communication, will stalk anyone possessing a modicum of fame, even a newspaper columnist. Charles said he knew he was making a mistake answering a letter written by someone so clearly disturbed, but he couldn't help himself. I'd pissed him off in fewer words than anyone ever had before.

He wanted to know if I was one of those bitter career women without a life, who sat home nights writing letters to newspapers and talking back to the television because there was no possible way I could get a date. He asked if my take-out menus were arranged in alphabetical order, and how many cats I owned, or would I prefer that he called them my familiars?

My take-out menus aren't arranged alphabetically. They're sorted by cuisine.

I replied: I wrote that letter at work, hence the letterhead, idiot, and I have a fabulous life because I have a career and the good fortune never to have dated a newspaper columnist. If I'm at all bitter, it'd be a result of dealing with misogynists like you, and, no, I don't own any cats, but, if you don't like them, I'll go out and get one immediately.

He wrote back with the guess that I last had sex a decade ago. In return, I sent him a note suggesting his penis was small. From there, we started to correspond regularly.

He wrote: You wouldn't know a penis if you sat on one. Besides, I've never had any complaints, and, unlike you, I've had sex this century. My girlfriend is extremely happy, thank you.

I wrote: I admit it. Women aren't as penis-fixated as men fantasize we are. I can't name a woman who wouldn't trade one for its weight in chocolate cake. That said, I know enough to sense you don't measure up. By the way, it must be a dreadful inconvenience to have to inflate your girlfriend every night.

He wrote: An inflatable doll would be preferable to someone as cynical as you, depending, of course, on what you look like. What do you look like?

I wrote: I agree. The doll would be the better intellectual match. Women with IQs this side of 75 would have men like you scratching your heads – that is, if you could tear yourself away from scratching your balls. I can't believe you asked me what I look like. How would your girlfriend feel if she found out? It'd take the wind out of her and then where would you be? You're very lucky she can't read.

He wrote: I take it from your answer you're not even remotely attractive. Munchkins must run screaming whenever you appear. Do you like scaring the little guys? Or do you force them to date you? No doubt your last boyfriend was chopped up into pieces and buried in your backyard when he tried to escape. And, please, tell me, what makes you think my girlfriend can't read? Is literacy not a trait you demand of your partners? You can't afford to be that picky?

I wrote: If she could read, she'd read your column and wouldn't be able to bring herself to sleep with you, even if she thought as much of your penis as you do. However, I agree with you on one point. Literacy is an overrated ability. Men only misuse it. You're a shining example of this. And, for your information, I'm extraordinarily good-looking from certain angles, I'm kind to munchkins and, no, my ex-boyfriend isn't fertilizer in my backyard, but that's an excellent suggestion, thank you.

Our relationship blossomed from there. We may have started out disliking each other, but, over time, we found we liked disliking each other more than we liked disliking anyone else. We've been involved for a little more than a year now. Of course, Charles and I have never had sex. For that to happen we'd have to actually meet.

I've never suggested to Charles that we meet up, mostly because he's never suggested it either. He writes to me every week without fail, but I don't know if he's ever considered taking it further.

Anyway, if we did meet, the relationship would be over. I'm pretty sure of that. Charles is too conservative for me and I have it on good authority – his – that he thinks I'm impossible. Also, there's the girlfriend to consider. He hasn't mentioned her for months, but, if I had to guess, I'd say she's still around. I'll even go so far as to concede she's not inflatable, is probably capable of reading and doesn't require the lobotomies I've recommended for her on several occasions.

So, apart from the time it takes every week to write a short letter, fold that page into an envelope and place the envelope on top of the outgoing mail, my love life is no great burden on the rest of my life – which is less fabulous than I make it out to be in my letters. Charles is right. My descent into crazy cat-lady-hood is only a kitten away.

In any romantic film, the more two people hate each other at the start, the more probable it is they'll be together by the time the credits roll. Following this logic, I think Charles is the person I'm destined to be with. I also think he'll marry his girlfriend. They'll have two or three little misogynists, and he'll be too busy indoctrinating them to write to me. Our correspondence will dwindle to the occasional Christmas card, which, if I become more sentimental as I get older, I'll keep in an old shoebox – so the cats can't shred them – and we'll lose touch.

If that was the worst my future held, I was content. Who really ends up with the person they're meant to be with, anyway? The idea that you can live in harmony with someone for a lifetime is frighteningly optimistic. Most relationships are mistakes. Successful relationships happen when the two people concerned both stubbornly refuse to admit they made a mistake. Yet this doesn't prevent most women from actively searching for their next mistake.

Not me. I know better. Kiss a frog and he doesn't morph into a guy in a Gap ad. He stays a frog. Or becomes something slimier. I think that going senile in the company of cats is more desirable than living life with a rat.

If I get bored, this is LA; there are always plenty more

rats to go out with. Los Angeles is a rodent Mecca. Once here, the rats are all willing to date woman-with-steady-income until fame or fortune allows them to move up the food chain to date the girls who ignored them in high school. Of course, rats don't date the women who personally ignored them in high school. After all these years those women are too hard to track down. So, symbolically, rats date the girls who would ignore them now if they weren't rich rats. Only by sheer coincidence are the majority of these girls still in high school.

I wasn't unhappy with my life. There were actually some aspects of it I was pleased with. When you stop believing in things that don't exist, life becomes a lot less complicated. I had no desire to change a thing. That was when something happened to change everything.

I found God.

To be precise, He found me. I don't think He was looking for me. I was just in the wrong place at the wrong time. There was no shaft of light, no angel chorus, no trumpet herald. Nothing. He just showed up one day at work and ruined everything.

FROM: Sydney Welles <s.welles@fbmm.com>
TO: God ourfatherwho@inheaven.org
DATE: Monday, May 16, 7.40 p.m.
SUBJECT: Hi

Dear God (And not just any old God. I want *the* God. The one everyone prays to: the one in charge of the California Lottery.),

You haven't heard from me before. There's a reason for that. To simplify my life, I made a decision not to become involved with you, or your affiliated organizations. Up until now, my soul has been Switzerland. Not much has changed in that respect. I'm not writing to you because I've suffered a conversion to faith. I'm writing to you because, if we're going to have an effective working relationship, you should know where I stand.

I don't believe in you. Let me clarify that. I'm not talking about whether or not you exist. That's beside the point. Even if you burnt my bushes, shouted from the sky in a booming voice or glowed before me as a gigantic, disembodied head, I still wouldn't believe in you. I don't think you're worth believing in.

You are, after all, the greatest warmonger of all time. Presidents, generals, dictators – all claim you put them up to it. Especially when they're on opposite sides of the same war.

People, even very good people – who if left to their own devices would do nothing wrong – will murder, steal and commit horrific crimes in your name. Your religions and representatives on earth have a dirty, bloody history of being sexist, racist, oppressive, hypocritical, corrupt and power-mad.

By the way, just what are you doing with yourself these days? Judging from the number of people who thank you personally at music award ceremonies, you seem to be spending the majority of your time overseeing the production of rap music. Perhaps, if you spent a little less time on your recording projects, the world wouldn't be in the mess it's in.

You and I have managed to get this far without getting personally involved. That suited me fine. Suited you, too, I think – one less soul to worry about, when you've got billions on your plate who aren't doing so well.

However, you've seen fit to change the status of our relationship. So, from now on, I'm going to be in your face like the rest of your flock. I expect the basic package. You have to micromanage my days, look out for me, supply the stuff I want and accept blame for whatever goes wrong in my life. It's only fair. If you take up my time, I'll take up yours.

Yours – if not faithfully then at least – sincerely,
Sydney Welles (When you look down at Sunset Avenue, Venice, California, I'm the ant who lives in the cottage with the blue roof.)

PS I'd prefer it if you didn't reply directly to this note. These days, the people who claim you talk to them personally . . . well . . . they're not exactly Solomon and David any more, are they?

The only problem with the perpetual sunshine in Southern California is you can never rely on the weather to be ominous, even on the day you find out the world is going to end.

Monday had started like any other day. The sun was shining, the sky was blue, the smog was in the valley and I was in bed well after I should've been up. It didn't become apparent the end was nigh until I was well out my front door.

Californian bungalows and Hockneyesque swimming pools abound in Venice, only not on my street. Welcome mats aren't big here; high fences and concrete walls are. When the affluent and the homeless choose to be neighbours, this is the result. Those with homes design them to discourage visits from those without. It's the same architectural style used to great effect by the US government overseas. Nothing says 'fuck off' quite as effectively as a US embassy in a Third World country.

My home is out of place and style. A tiny demilitarized cottage in a yuppie combat zone.

Keeping within the under-siege theme, all my neighbours – except the homeless – drive cars originally designed to transport troops into battle. The fortified street is lined with these tanks, making it impossible for me to park anywhere near my front door.

Not that I minded much that particular Monday morning. That morning, with the bounty of vitamin D from above, and the birds twitting rather than shitting in the trees, I didn't mind much of anything at all.

It was one of those days when you feel, if you believe in that kind of thing, that the world has a baby-sitter: an old guy with a long, white beard, watching over us from his invisible house in the sky. And, for once, he wasn't as pissed at us as he normally is, and might be persuaded to give us all cookies.

I was willing to believe this was the case even after I noticed the rabbit in my front yard. Easter was only a month ago. A spontaneous bunny, while a few weeks late, was in keeping with the season.

People never recognize life's most significant moments at the time they occur. At least, people like me never do. It's only in hindsight that I see the arrival of the rabbit for what it was: a herald of disaster to come.

Unlike the articulate, impeccably dressed bunny that led Alice to her fall into Wonderland, my rodent on the run was an ordinary rabbit. He didn't even have the distinction of being white. His coat – the standard untailored rabbit kind – was patched grey. He wasn't fluffy; he was scraggly and scarred. If bunnies could be street thugs, he was one.

'Is that your rabbit? What's wrong with it? Why don't you keep it in a cage?'

Standing at my open front gate was the small demon son of my across-the-street neighbour. Five days a week he's sent out into the world, disguised as a normal child, to torment the teachers and students of the nearest Montessori school.

The evil spawn leaves home about the same time I do in the morning. Every time I see him, I wonder what new weaponry is concealed in his backpack, and hope, sincerely, that his parents are now using a reliable contraceptive.

'That's the ugliest rabbit I've ever seen,' Cupid said. 'What do you call it?'

His parents named Cupid for the equally armed and dangerous cherub, the little nudist who flits about inflicting love. There's a strong, pink-cheeked resemblance between the two. It's an apt name, but Damien or Beelzebub would suit him just as well.

I had to come up with a plausible rabbit name. Letting Cupid know the rabbit was a stray would give him the incentive he needed to torture it to death.

Bugs? Brer? What kind of a name is Brer? Peter? Roger? Thumper? Hazel? *Watership Down* was full of bunny names. What were they? That invisible six-foot-tall rabbit in that old Jimmy Stewart film, what was –

'Harry,' I said. Not quite it, but close enough, though it was possible it needed elaboration. 'Harry Rex.'

'That's a really stupid name.'

'It's not the only one.'

Keeping his gaze fixed on the rabbit, Cupid picked up a stone from under my hedge, weighing it in his hand.

'If you throw that at Harry Rex,' I said, 'I'll do the world a favour and castrate you.'

Cupid obviously had no idea what castration entailed, but he sensed its unpleasantness. Making a fist around the rock, he filed it away in his pocket and faced me, crossing his pudgy arms in front of his chest.

'My mother says you're a lesbian.'

I had no ready comeback, but was saved from further conversation by the mother herself.

'Cupid?' Her screech carried across the street. 'Come on, angel. It's time to go.'

The angel stamped his feet. 'No, I want to play with the bunny.'

I was pleased to note a look of horror taking over his mother's face.

'Cupid. Get over here at once. Or there'll be no PlayStation. For a week.'

Cupid screwed up his face to scream, then thought better of it. His features resettled into their usual cherubic curves, and he dutifully trotted across the narrow road separating his house from mine.

His mother ran a smoothing hand through his perversely angelic curls.

'You know how I feel about you petting strange animals,' she said, in her normal voice, a melodious shriek I could still hear clearly. 'That animal could have rabies.'

I had no idea what a rabid rabbit looked like, but that didn't prevent me from speaking up.

'He doesn't have rabies.'

Her answering glare could not be interpreted as friendly. She took Cupid by his shoulders, turning him about to face her. 'Now, this is very, very important, darling. You must promise Mommy. We don't go near animals we don't know.'

He must have agreed, as his golden head bobbed up and down in a good impression of obedience.

His mother fell for it. True, she could not, as I could,

see the crossed fingers behind his back, but her failure to notice the fiendish nature of the smile lighting up his chubby face proved that a mother's love is as blind as any other kind.

I can't blame her for her lack of judgement. I've dated far worse than Cupid.

'If I were you,' I said to Harry Rex, once Cupid was safely restrained in the back seat of the family assault vehicle, 'I'd be long gone before the Antichrist gets home from school.'

Harry Rex cocked a disfigured ear, seeming to give the suggestion due thought. He hopped to the hedge and slunk into it – apparently taking my advice. He left behind the piece of paper, a flyer, he'd been nibbling on. The part of it he hadn't eaten announced that the end of the world was taking place the Sunday after next at exactly 8 p.m., Eastern Standard Time; 5 p.m. local time.

✝

The sense of impending doom brought on by the discovery that the world had a rapidly approaching use-by date abated when I reached the normalcy of my office. On my computer was an urgent all-staff memo calling for the owner of the dog which left a trail of poops on the floor near the library to come forward, presumably with pooper-scooper in hand. On my sofa, someone was snoring under a newspaper. Outside my door, our agency president, Larry Crawford, strode by having a loud, one-sided debate with an entity only he could see. Just another day at the office.

By the time the priest stopped at my door and asked

the way to the bathroom, I felt like myself again. Only after I'd pointed him in the right direction did it hit me I'd seen an unusual sight.

Larry was here and it was barely five past nine. I've known him to show up before noon only in cases of emergency, or when he knows cocktails are going to be served. No celebration was slated for this morning. Which meant an advertising emergency was in progress.

I peeked out of my office to see what was going on, planning to pull my head in before anyone could involve me. I'm the most senior woman in the planning department. That means I get all the shitty jobs the guys don't want. There'd been rumours flying around the agency for weeks. Members of the clergy showing up at work had to mean trouble. Unless I was careful, I'd be landed with it.

'Just the cranium I wanted to see,' Larry said.

I jumped, for good reason. Larry's normal speaking voice is the sort usually reserved for getting the attention of someone standing on the other side of Wilshire Boulevard during peak-hour traffic. I'm accustomed to it, but he can still scare the crap out of me if he sneaks up.

My office faces the agency bar, a relic of a more prosperous, decadent time in the agency's history, but a relic kept fully stocked and in constant use all the same. Larry was filling a frosted glass with one of the three beers on tap. He offered to pour one for me as well.

'It's nine o'clock in the morning,' I said.

He checked his watch. 'So it is. Beer?'

'It's kind of early.'

'For what?'

'Beer.'

'Oh, I see.' He turned to survey the top shelf, selected a bottle of Scotch, splashed some into a glass, topped it up with a little water and, with the two glasses in hand, cautiously approached my office door, where he stopped to scan the room.

'Where's the General?'

'He must be here somewhere.' I pointed at a neat pile of papers on my desk awaiting my signature. 'They weren't there Friday night. But I haven't actually seen him this morning.'

Visibly relieved, Larry came forwards to place the Scotch in front of me, on top of a briefing document on my desk. He walked over to the couch, and lifted the corner of the newspaper, nodding to himself when he saw who was sleeping under it. Replacing the paper gently, Larry found a spare chair and folded himself into it, regarding his beer in an amicable way.

'Out somewhere practising his goose step, is he?'

'Patton's the best assistant I've ever had,' I said. 'He's just a little uptight, that's all.'

'I still can't understand why you hired him.'

'Nepotism. He's your nephew.'

'Purely by accident. They weren't planning on having him, I can tell you that.'

On the sofa, Noah, roused by Larry's not-so-dulcet tones, raised himself up on his elbows to look around. He lay back down and pulled yesterday's news back over his head as soon as he spotted Larry.

In a chair too small for someone of his height, chugging beer first thing in the morning, swiping foam from his upper lip between chugs with a monogrammed handkerchief, Larry still looked like the president of a large corporation. He's always expensively and correctly attired. You can see that he started out in a state of elegance at some point, even if he was unable to maintain it.

Silver hair makes a person seem more respectable than they are, and Larry has plenty. Most notably in important eyebrows and a handlebar moustache, which, legend has it, wilts into a Fu Man Chu when exposed to undue heat or exercise.

I leaned in to sniff the Scotch in front of me. The smell alone made breakfast turn over in my stomach.

'Enough pleasantries,' Larry said, half his beer having been guided down his throat. 'I've got a job for you. You're not going to believe who just walked in the door. I don't know if I believe it myself.'

'Why, who walked in the door?'

'The Catholic Church.' Larry crossed himself using his beer glass. 'They need our help. They want the works. Complete image overhaul.'

'The paedophile thing isn't working for them?'

Larry thumped my desk with the hand unencumbered by beer. A little Scotch and water escaped my glass, finding a new home in my in-tray.

'I love sarcastic women first thing in the morning – or maybe I've just gotten used to them. What a pity you don't have bigger breasts. You'd be the perfect woman. Once you learned to hold your beer.'

'Are we going to do this Church thing?'

'Yes, that's where you come in. The Church are afraid people may see advertising as inappropriate or, worse, opportunistic. That's why they've asked for our help. They want to float the idea, to gauge the reaction.'

'A research project?'

'That's right. You're going to find out how the plebs feel.'

'You mean consumers.'

'OK, find out how they feel, too.'

'About being sold Catholicism?'

'No, definitely not. If people hate the idea, then the Church looks bad. We can't have that. They look bad enough already. We keep things general. We don't ask: Can we sell Catholicism? We ask: Can we sell religion? Can we sell God?'

'What if people ask why we're asking?'

'We tell them it's a privately funded study, purely academic at this stage.'

'We do it secretly?'

'No, right out in the open. Pass it off as an intellectual exercise. It's good PR for the agency. Should get a lot of press.'

'OK, but why me? I'm not the most senior planning director avail –'

'No, but you're the third choice. If you don't do it we're fucked. We won't hit our number for the year.'

'I thought we'd already made the number. We had a great start of the year. Two new –'

'We hit it too early in the year. The corporate bean counters at Megacom just raised the figure again. What do you say? The guys won't touch it. Too volatile. They think if it blows up in their faces their careers will be over. They're not keen to jeopardize things just when they're on the verge of being able to afford trophy wives.'

'What if it blows up in my face?'

'I wouldn't worry. You still have time to marry rich. You're a relatively young woman.'

'And you're a sexist pig.'

'What are you talking about? I'm a feminist from way back – ever since I found it could get me laid. I supported that jobshare thing for the working mothers.'

'Yes, you did. I remember. And that was good, but –'

'Good for the agency, too. I'd rather have a smart woman three days a week than a dumb man for five, especially if she's good-looking. So, how about it?'

'I've got a lot going on right now. I don't know if I can take on something this size. What about my other accounts?'

'Let them slide.'

'Let them slide?'

'This is advertising. We don't care about the clients we already have; we care about the ones we might be able to get. Haven't I taught you anything?'

'Do I have a choice in this?'

'You could always go back to wherever it is you came from.'

The Scotch and soda on the table suddenly seemed appealing. The industry was depressed – hence the never-ending scrabble for the few new advertisers out there – and I was at that difficult age in advertising: too old to be a wunderkind; too young to have my name above the agency door.

'When do I start?'

'Good girl. That's the attitude. Of course, it's in our best interests if you deliver a positive result.'

'What are you saying?'

'Prove people will buy God and we land the most lucrative new account out there.'

'What if people won't buy God?'

Larry twisted one end of his moustache, a silent-film villain. 'Rephrase the question.'

'How much money does the Church have to spend?'

Larry leaned over the desk and dropped his voice to his version of a whisper. People more than twenty feet away would now have some trouble hearing him clearly.

'More than God,' he said.

'How much is that exactly?'

'In this country? About eight billion a year, and that's revenue alone. Then there's the real estate and –'

'Then why do they need to advertise? What? They need more money?'

'Our job is not to question why. Our job is to make our twenty per cent. If we could get them to spend what they spend settling lawsuits, we could turn the agency around. And there's always the potential this could go global. If it does . . . well, let's just say, the Vatican has its own bank.'

'What's in this for me if I pull it off?'

'The usual. A good bonus, a meaningless promotion, people kissing your butt for a week or two. You know the deal.'

'I'm already due a good bonus.'

'Well, you pull this off, you won't be the token female planning director any more.'

'What will I be?'

'The only female planning director.'

'What's the difference?'

'Nothing really.'

'What's my budget?'

'Whatever you need. And all the help you need. Hire if you have to – get him to help you; he's not doing anything.' Larry picked up a stress ball someone had left on the edge of my desk and pitched it at the outstretched form on my couch. The pitch was on target.

'What?' Noah peeped out from under the newspaper.

'Good, you're awake. You're going to save the Catholic Church. It's all up to you. Don't fuck it up.' Larry stood. 'That's today done, then.' He picked up the empty beer glass and took it back to the bar, to rectify its emptiness.

Noah sat up. On his crumpled T-shirt, 'Peace is for Pussies' was printed.

'Help,' he said.

I pushed the glass of Scotch a few inches in his direction, leaving staggered watermarks on the document it rested on.

'Drink that,' I said.

'Why do you let him get away with all that sexist crap?'

'Larry isn't sexist. He judges people on their work irrespective of the crap that comes out of his mouth. Anyway, I prefer my sexism in my face. It's the guys who say all the right things then skewer you in the men's bathroom you have to watch. All this political correctness hasn't made sexism go away, just underground. You don't see it until you step on it. Like a land mine.'

Noah made a feeble effort to smooth down his hair,

which, no matter what is done to it, always looks like a fierce sort of excrescence growing out of his head. 'This is one hell of a project,' he said.

'I know. But we'll humour them until someone in a position to do something about it realizes what a bad idea it is and pulls the entire thing.'

'And if they don't?'

'Let's hope they do.'

My computer made the sound it makes when new mail comes through. I opened the note marked urgent. Again, it called for the owner of the defecating dog to turn himself in and clean up the shit. In the past thirty minutes, three people had stepped in it.

I knew exactly how they felt.

FROM: Sydney Welles <s.welles@fbmm.com>
TO: God headgardener@gardenofeden.com
DATE: Tuesday, May 17, 9.02 a.m.
SUBJECT: Apocalypse Now?

Dear God,

Is the world going to end?

I don't usually pay much attention to any of the literature put out by the burgeoning Doomsday industry, but the end-of-the-world brochure I picked up looked as if it was published by the sort of people you like to associate with these days. It said everything would be all over by Sunday after next. Is that the plan?

This is merely an opinion – and I'm aware you like to move in mysterious ways – but, even given the problems in the world today, don't you think the Apocalypse is an extreme management solution?

Isn't it a little like stomping on the model airplane you made because it didn't turn out exactly like the picture on the box?

Sincerely,
Sydney Welles

I met Jake a few days after I met God, and liked him better. He was celebrating his thirty-fifth birthday in a bar decorated to look like a large public toilet. What passes for cool these days is so inexplicable it's impossible to tell whether the interior design was intentional or accidental. In either case, a row of urinals would've looked right at home against one of the tiled walls.

The place was two-thirds full of the usual mob: film, music and media people, out for the purpose of being seen out. Men wore the Friday-night denim and leather uniform. Women exposed as much skin as you can expose without getting arrested.

Jake was with a large noisy group standing in the centre of the floor, but I can't say that I noticed him when I walked in.

Anna, I spotted right away. She's hard to miss – a redhead so tall all skirts are short on her. She scares most men. All men if she's wearing six-inch heels.

In the five minutes Anna had been waiting, she'd secured the best seats in the bar by one of her time-tested methods: hiding the sign reserving the VIP table – always empty on the off chance of an unexpected celebrity appearance – in her bag.

'So,' she said, after I'd taken a fashionably uncomfortable seat, 'how did it go with the model?'

'Model-slash-poet. He was quite insistent on the "slash-poet" part of the job title.'

'Whatever. You went out?'

'We did. It was tragic.'

'I thought you said he was gorgeous.'

'Oh, he was. Still is. Looks like Jim Morrison at his peak. No . . . closer to Val Kilmer playing Jim Morrison at his peak.'

'What was wrong with that?'

'He had a vocabulary of twenty-five words. Must write very short poems. Haiku, maybe?'

'There's nothing wrong with the strong, silent type,' Anna said.

'Sure, unless you like men who actually speak to you.'

'I ordered you a vodka. We need to put you in a more reasonable mood before you meet anyone tonight.'

'I'll need more than one drink before that'll happen. Do they have anything to eat here?'

Anna made a disgusted face. 'The usual.'

For a place like this, the usual means fusion food. One-of-a-kind fusion. Cuisines combined not for culinary compatibility, but, rather, for no good reason. Alaskan-Korean-Scottish or some other synthesis allowing 'Haggis of Moose, served on a bed of Kimchi, with Mashed Potatoes and Bulgogi Sauce' to appear, in all seriousness, on a menu.

'Gee, I'm glad we chose this bar over the other one,' I said.

'You know I can't do that place. It's full of right-brained people. Too many drugs, not enough deodorant.'

'Doesn't matter. Food only slows the effects of alcohol down, and I need to get drunk.'

'That'll be attractive.'

'Don't worry,' I said. 'I'm never going to date again.'

'Of course you will. How else will you get even?'

'Well, no more model-slash-poets, then. Or actor, artist, writer-slash-anything.'

'Which leaves you with about ten guys to choose from in this city. That's keeping your options open – hey, wait, I know that guy that just walked in.'

'Who is he?'

'Tony-somebody,' she said.

'Who is Tony-somebody?'

'I can't remember his other name. Vince knows him. He's a banker. That's all, no slash, only one occupation that pays. No sense of humour, but filthy rich. I could introduce you.'

'That guy? The one in the pinstripe suit?' Tony was greeting someone he knew by winking, making his hand into a gun and pretending to shoot them. 'No. Thanks.'

'It won't hurt to meet him.'

A second glance revealed Tony pumping all his acquaintances full of imaginary bullets from his right hand, while his left formed a permanent shield over his genitals.

'I think it will hurt.' I closed my eyes to try to erase the image of Tony, gunslinger. 'A lot.'

Anna means well, but she thinks love is distributed by a lottery system. The more tickets you buy, the more chances you have of winning. Substitute dates for tickets, and you get the idea. Dragging me out to increase my chances of meeting potential jackpots has been her self-appointed task ever since I broke up with Matt, actor-slash-asshole.

That was over a year ago. Her desperation on my behalf has grown exponentially. She's now diabolically helpful in securing dates for me. Anna doesn't know about Charles – nobody does – but she won't be assured about my romantic future because I have a pen pal who happens to be a boy.

I go out with Anna for the company and the alcohol. I don't subscribe to her romantic-roulette theory. Anna tells me this is why I'm single and she's engaged to a multimillionaire. I remind her Vince was a client she met at work, not some random guy she picked up in a bar. We meet up almost every Friday to continue the argument over loud music and overpriced drinks.

Since her engagement, Anna spends most of her days shopping, but she continues her career vicariously, through me. I tell her what I did at work during the week, and she points out what was wrong with what I did at work during the week.

That night in the bar, I tried to scribble on a napkin to explain a concept to her, but my pen, a promotional ballpoint with the agency's name embossed on it, refused to work.

Frustrated, I threw the gimmicky piece of plastic over my shoulder.

Thirty seconds later a man approached our table. He was attractive in both the ways men can be attractive. Sexy enough to send warning pains through the scar tissue of broken-hearts past, yet somehow still giving off a trustworthy, potential-first-husband vibe. For a breath, I entertained the possibility that Anna's love raffle had delivered a prize. Then I noticed he wielded my pen.

'Does this belong to one of you ladies?'

I pretended I couldn't hear him over the bar noise, but Anna nodded and pointed at me.

'This pen hit me in the head,' he said.

'Really?' I slid several inches down in my seat.

He placed a hand on the arm of my chair and leaned over until our faces were almost level.

'Did you throw it at me?'

I could tell by his eyes that he wasn't angry. 'No. Yes. I mean . . . I wasn't aiming at you.'

'Who were you trying to hit?'

'Nobody in particular. I just wanted to get rid of it. I was mad at it.'

'Why?'

'It wasn't working.'

'So you threw it over your shoulder in a crowded bar?'

I began to see where he was taking the conversation.

'Do you know how dangerous that was? You could've taken someone's eye out.'

I counted his eyes. 'But I didn't.'

'That's hardly the point.'

Across the table, Anna was not being helpful. Instead, she carried out complicated manoeuvres with her eyebrows, and made jerky motions with her head towards my new friend.

Admittedly, the guy had a legitimate complaint. Even after two-and-a-half vodkas, I could see he was right.

I hated myself for being so reasonable.

'I'm sorry,' I said. 'I'm sorry you got in the way of the pen and got hit in the head. I hope you'll be more careful in future.'

'That's an apology?'

'How about if I promise never to throw a pen at you in this bar again?'

He smiled. A smile I could get used to. 'What about other bars?'

'Or in any other bars.'

'And restaurants?'

That was taking it too far. 'You can't have restaurants as well.'

'I guess it's enough I'm safe here for the moment.' He eyed the one empty chair at our table.

Anna stopped wiggling her eyebrows and found her voice. 'Would you like to sit down?'

I kicked her under the table.

'I'm Anna.' She crossed her legs out of kicking range, causing her skirt to get shorter and two men at the next table to spill their beers.

'Jake.' He sat, placed the pen on the table, and turned to me expectantly.

I would've supplied him with my name then and there except I couldn't remember what it was.

'Jake, this is Sydney,' Anna said.

I wondered if he'd heard Anna over the noise; Anna must have wondered something else entirely.

'You can call her Syd – if two syllables are too much for you.'

'I can cope,' Jake said. 'Syd-ney. See. Hi.'

'Hi,' I said. And it took effort to come up with that.

28

Anna could see I needed help, but, as usual, she overestimated the amount required. 'Syd-ney is single,' she said, 'and has no plans for next Saturday night.'

I kicked her under the table again. Harder.

Jake clutched his shin. 'What'd I do?'

Anna sniggered; I covered my face with my hands.

'I'm beginning to think you don't like me.' Jake winced, rubbing his leg.

'I'm sorry. I was aiming for Anna.'

'Your aim is off tonight.'

I wanted to tell him he was fortunate I wasn't wearing my steel-capped boots, but decided he might like me better if I showed compassion instead.

'Does it hurt? Maybe we can order some ice for it? Should I call 911?'

'Maybe Syd can kiss it better.' Anna again.

I glared at Anna until I realized Jake was looking at me as if I were dessert. I felt distinctly uncomfortable. It wasn't an entirely unpleasant feeling.

'I need another drink.'

The others agreed with me. Jake made a movement with his hand and a waitress materialized at his right elbow. That annoyed me somewhat. I have to tap-dance on a table to get a waitress to notice me in a place like this.

'Champagne,' Anna said, when Jake asked what we were drinking. She orders champagne when a man is buying drinks and cheap white wine if a woman is paying. It's her contribution to gender equality. As long as men are getting paid more than women are for doing the same jobs, they have to pay more for drinks when Anna is around. If you spend enough time drinking with her, it makes perfect sense.

Until the bottle arrived Anna and Jake talked. About me, and the damage I could do if someone gave me a pen made of metal. They promised each other never to give me one as a gift, finding themselves extremely amusing in the process.

I sat, mute and stupid, wondering why I'd lost the ability to speak.

Champagne came, was poured, and I faced a different problem. The bar served it in an old-fashioned glass, a wide shallow bowl on top of a tall glass stem, like the ones in old Hollywood movies. I have trouble keeping the champagne in those glasses on the way to my lips. Spill your drink and people think you're a drunk. Nobody stops to consider that you're far more likely to be a drunk if you can get the alcohol into your mouth.

On first impressions, Jake was going to think I was a violent drunk. But, as it turned out, I needn't have been concerned about what he thought of me.

'Jay-ake. There you are. What are you doing?'

Jake raised his gaze to a point above my head. I turned around. A woman was standing behind me. She was attractive – if you find outstandingly beautiful women with long, blonde hair attractive. In particular, that soft butter blonde that's impossible to achieve in a hair salon without a Beverly Hills zip code.

I ventured a tentative smile in her direction. She looked me up and down as if I were a stain that had appeared on her wedding dress an hour before the ceremony.

I was tempted to offer her food. She was the size of

your typical Hollywood starvelet. Not having eaten this month was probably what was making her irritable. I could see, however, that such an offer might make me look like a bitch. I tried thinking charitable thoughts instead. Perhaps she'd had a few too many Botox injections and could only smile on the inside.

'Jay-ake, come on. Everyone's here for your birthday. Why are you with these people?'

Why indeed? 'You have to go, Jay-ake,' I said.

'I should go.' He made no move to get up.

'Jay-ake?'

'I'll be right there, Kim. Could you give me a minute?'

Clearly, Kim was more inclined to leave Jake in the clutches of the Swedish Bikini Team than in our company, but she turned and stumped her way back towards the bar. In awe, Anna and I watched her go, the poster girl for a carbohydrate-free world.

'Your pen.' Jake held it out to me.

'No, it's your birthday. Keep the pen. We've millions of them at work.'

'Really? Gee, thanks.' He slipped it into his pocket all the same.

'It's the least I can do. I didn't get you anything for your birthday, and the pen doesn't work, anyway.'

He laughed and, soon after, was gone.

'He left the bubbly. A true gentleman.' Anna lifted the bottle out of its ice bucket to show me it was half full. 'So what about him? He was nice. And he liked you.'

I shrugged.

'Don't tell me you don't like him. He spoke in complete sentences.'

'I'm trying to figure out how you failed to notice his girlfriend.'

'I'm not so sure they are together. And, if they are, it may not be terminal.'

'It's terminal,' I said. 'You saw her.'

'OK, then why was he talking to us?'

'I don't know – to collect enough personal information about me so he can sue for hitting him with the pen.'

'I see. You're in one of your glass-is-half-empty moods.'

'Whether the glass is half empty or half full, it's still only half a drink.'

Anna's eyes became narrow. 'You did like him.'

'It doesn't matter,' I said, even though, for the first time in a long time, it did.

FROM: Sydney Welles <sydneywelles@yahoo.com>
TO: God c/- moses@askmoses.com
DATE: Friday, May 20, 11.57 p.m.
SUBJECT: The Disgraceful State of Urban Dating Today

God,

Must you dangle intelligent, good-looking men in front of me, then have them whisked away at the last minute by Baywatch extras? Out of curiosity, when you made the girlfriend, how much silicon did you use?

Dating is hard enough without you having fun with it.

While we're on the subject, tell me, why has urban dating for women over twenty-eight come to resemble a Road Runner cartoon? You get the cartoon channel, right? I see so many normally sane women devising elaborate plans to trap men. Yet, in spite of genius-level plotting and state-of-the-art accessories, the man, no matter how dumb, gets away, even though there are usually three or four coyotes after each road runner.

What is going on? Who is writing those books telling women how they ought to behave on dates? Is it Satan?

Sincerely,
Sydney

PS If you think I haven't noticed the priest you've installed in the office, think again.

Advertising is a particularly secular industry. Some would go so far as to describe it as godless. I've always considered that a perk of the job. So, the idea of a marketing priest – a priest who secured an MBA before he decided never to have sex again – wasn't one I warmed to right away.

Father Giuliani is the business end of the Church. All business. But he's still a priest. Put me in front of a priest or nun, every inoffensive word I know flees my brain and I can't open my mouth without imperilling my immortal soul.

When I found myself waiting for the elevator with Father Giuliani, I was worried about what to say to him. He was completely at ease; he strikes me as one of those people who remain calm even when those around them are hysterically running around, yelling 'Avalanche!' or 'Giant person-eating lizard on the loose.'

On the priest's face was the slightest suggestion of a smile. That's the way he smiles, in hints. It seemed to me he was almost smiling because he somehow knew I had no idea what to say to him.

He remarked that it had been yet another nice day. I said it was a pity we were indoors for almost all of it. He said the irony of life is that, for all our complaints about it, most of it slips by without our noticing. I wasn't sure what to say next, as the only thing that came to mind was, yeah, life sucks like that.

Luckily, the elevator arrived. Everybody knows it's against the law to talk in moving elevators. I was safe. I'd managed to exchange the word or two required by politeness without a hitch. All I had to do now was stand next to the priest. Easy.

Until the elevator made a sick mechanical sound like a robot vomiting and crunched to a dark, silent halt.

'Holy shit,' I said. I hit what I judged in the dark to be the open-door button several times to no avail. 'What do we do now?'

'Pray,' the priest said.

I could just make out his silhouette. 'Really?'

'It was a joke. We need earthly help. A little light to work by would be –'

Dim lights flickered on around the roof of the elevator, casting a ghastly glow and turning our skin an unwholesome green.

'That was neat,' I said.

Father Giuliani examined the panels on either side of the door. 'There must a switch in here that gets the ventilation system working again.'

As soon as he said that, I began to feel desperately short of breath. Then gears clicked in place; a low humming began. I felt a stream of fresher air on my face. I could see the benefits of having a holy man around in an emergency.

Father Giuliani read that in my face.

'It was a coincidence,' he said.

'Two coincidences. First, you said, "Let there be light," and there was light, then –'

'The emergency system kicked in.' He opened the little door to the phone and picked it up.

'What are you going to do with that?'

'Make a phone call. Sorry to disappoint you – hello? Yes, hello, we have a problem.'

While he conversed with elevator central, I helped. I pushed all the buttons several times.

I don't have much experience with the priesthood, but I'm sure that if every priest looked like Father Giuliani the Catholic Church would sell itself. Even tinted green by the unflattering overhead light, it was apparent God was this man's personal cinematographer.

Once he'd hung up, I followed his example, and sat on the elevator floor opposite him, a little ill at ease at being alone with a priest in a confined space. I was also beginning to feel cold. My cardigan was hanging on the back of my office chair. I shivered.

The priest reached inside his jacket and produced a large hip flask made of dark leather and steel. Pouring colourless liquid into the miniature steel tumbler fitting over the lid, he handed it to me, indicating I should knock it back all at once.

It seemed like a good idea at the time.

Running down my oesophagus like liquid lava, it danced a heated conga a couple of times around my stomach, then sped warmth to every cell in my body in a billion microscopic ambulances.

'Christ,' I said, when I was capable of speech again. 'What was that? It's fucking great.'

✝

Everybody goes to hell. At least, all Catholics do. I gleaned that much from the priest in the elevator, with whom I drank grappa and discussed the selling points of Catholicism – not too many that I could see. To prevent the enclosed space becoming a confessional, I kept the conversation confined to work.

'That is not precisely true,' Father Giuliani said. 'They go to purgatory, not to hell.'

'Do they still get tortured?'

'Purged of their sins, yes.'

'Then how is purgatory different from hell?'

Father Giuliani offered me the hip flask. 'Hell is for eternity. Purgatory is only temporary.'

'How temporary is "temporary"?'

'It depends on the extent of your sins.'

'Give me a ballpark figure for the average sinner.'

'Some believe it could be centuries, or longer.'

'You and I have very different ideas of "temporary". Hundreds of years of torture? What does Amnesty International have to say about this?'

'They don't have an office in the afterlife.'

'What about confession? All the Hail Marys and Our Fathers? What's the point of doing all that if you go to purgatory anyway?'

'You have to confess and repent your sins. That's essential – remember, the unrepentant go to hell – but sins have to be paid for.'

'Is there parole in purgatory? Time off for good behaviour – that sort of thing?'

'It is believed your suffering can be shortened if friends and family offer masses and prayers for you.'

I took a sip of the grappa, waiting for the kick-ass afterburn to subside before handing the flask back.

'Doesn't that mean a person who committed lots of sins, but has lots of friends, could get out before someone with fewer sins and fewer friends?'

'That's possible,' he said, 'but a person must have done some good to deserve so many friends.'

'What if they were just rich and bribed a bunch of people to pray?'

'In those cases we refer to the "bunch of people" as a "congregation" and the "bribe" as a "legacy".'

'I think, if I were Catholic, I'd want to stay alive as long as possible.'

'That, I believe, is the general idea for everybody. However, purgatory does add incentive.' Father Giuliani smiled, sort of. It hardly broke the surface at all, doing little to the flawless topography of his features. His amusement was iceberg-like; a small part of it was clearly visible in his eyes, the rest hidden, in what I suspected was a mountainous mirth inside.

'What about people who are very bad — just under the hell requirement — with no friends or money, do they stay in purgatory indefinitely?'

'Purgatory ends for everyone on Judgement Day,' he said.

'Even more unfair. Some people will get off lightly by virtue of dropping dead just before Judgement Day ... that's the end of the world, isn't it?'

The priest nodded.

'I hear the world is going to end this Sunday,' I said.

'Ah, yes, according to that doomsday sect all over the news. Do you believe them?'

'Not really. I don't know. I guess it could happen . . . nothing surprises me any more. It's all arbitrary, anyway.'

Father Giuliani was silent.

'You're looking at me funny,' I said.

'I was wondering what it must be like to live like that, believing that everything that happens is arbitrary. It must be confusing.'

'Life is confusing,' I said. 'So, what about very good people? Do they get to skip purgatory?'

'Trust me. No one is that good.'

A knock on the doors, the sound of metal on metal, was followed by a voice too faint to understand.

I knocked back from the inside. 'Hello? We can't hear you.'

The emergency phone in the elevator rang.

After a long explanation – involving facts about elevators I didn't even know I never wanted to learn – a painfully cheerful technician imparted the information that there was nothing wrong with the elevator, except it wouldn't go.

'Never seen anything like it,' the elevator technician said. 'It's in perfect working order, but it won't work. Interesting, isn't it?'

'Yes, very interesting,' I said.

'I won't be able to repair anything until I find something to repair. There's no one in there holding down the emergency stop button is there?'

'No, there's not.'

'Thought I'd check. I guess I'd better work on getting the doors open for you.'

'That'd be nice.' I hung up, and relayed the information to Father Giuliani.

Catholicism 101 was a congenial experience under his tutelage. Unlike most men, Father Giuliani became more attractive when he spoke – without any accent that could geographically place him – in a sexy, sinister voice that made me think of fast women, hard liquor and novel ways to dispose of dead bodies.

I learned that purgatory has changed a great deal since the first pope put on the first pointy hat. Even hell isn't like hell any more.

'The idea of a demonic hell is still popular,' Father Giuliani said, 'but we tend now to believe in an abstract rather than a physical hell.'

'What's abstract hell?'

'It's a state of being without life and without joy, as God is the source of these things. Hell is the absence of God.'

'The absence of God. That's all? No torture, flesh-eating worms or fires that burn but never consume?'

'No,' he said. 'But there is pain to endure.'

'What kind of pain?'

'Mental and psychological torture. Much worse than fire and brimstone.'

'I don't know. Mental and psychological torture is not that much different from normal life for most people.'

'I hope that isn't what life is like for you.'

'I . . . Is there more grappa?'

He handed me the flask.

'Why is the fire-and-brimstone version still doing the rounds if you God guys believe it's another thing entirely?'

'It's hard to let go of an idea you grow up with. It's also an easier concept for some people to grasp.'

'I see. To reach the greatest amount of people, aim for the lowest common denominator. Tap into what people already believe. Like advertising.'

'Something like that.'

We were both silent for a moment.

'You know,' I said, 'purgatory makes other religions look like Club Med.'

Father Giuliani shrugged, Italian-ly. 'That is why we are here talking to you.'

This struck us both as rather funny. Not a roll-about-the-elevator-floor-clutching-our-sides funny, but more a we-understand-each-other-and-can-appreciate-the-odd-situation-we-are-in funny.

'I think,' I said, 'we should play down the purgatory thing, along with that pesky theory of evolution. We'll put it in the disclaimer.'

Light taps sounded on the door before it was wrenched open against its will. The lower third of the technician appeared through the partially open door. The elevator had come to a halt between the two floors of the agency.

The technician got down on his hands and knees to poke his head into the elevator.

'Hello,' his large, square head said, 'we're going to have to hoist you out from here. One minute, I'll be right back. Just want to make sure these doors won't shut on you.'

We got to our feet.

'Well, that's the last time I take the elevator instead of the stairs in a two-storey building,' I said. 'We've been punished for our sloth-like ways. But I'm glad I wasn't alone. Thanks for keeping me company.'

Father Giuliani placed a hand on my shoulder. I found

myself staring into the most empathetic eyes I'd ever encountered.

'You will not always be alone,' he said.

My shoulder must be connected directly to my tear ducts because I felt my eyes fill up.

'What do you mean?'

'You are more alone than anyone I have met.'

The tears he was squeezing out of my shoulder slid down my face. 'But I'm not –'

'Right, who's first?' The technician's head was back.

'After you,' Father Giuliani said.

The elevator guy held out a hand to me, and a Catholic priest grabbed my butt. It was only briefly, to give me the shove I needed, but, not being Catholic myself, I never expected to be groped by a priest. Nor did I expect him to say, 'You made a choice to be alone; you can unmake it,' even though I imagine it's just the kind of thing that priests like to say, to mess with your life.

The elevator technician had mysteriously disappeared by the time we dusted ourselves off. The mystery was how he did it in a vast open-plan space without us noticing.

It was past seven-thirty. But we didn't have the place entirely to ourselves.

Julie Ryan and Brad Pitt were waiting for us. Brad Pitt is a squat, ugly dog. His silhouette resembles a very large brick on legs. If he's built up enough speed, he's just the right height and consistency to take you out at the knees.

Brad Pitt is an English bulldog, but, in many ways, he's more qualified than Julie is to be Director of New Business Strategy. I'd say that even if I knew what a Director of New Business Strategy does.

Rumour has it Julie was promoted well beyond her capabilities because she's in possession of compromising Polaroids. I don't care why she was promoted. I'm just happy she was.

You can find quite a few women at the top these days. The problem with them is they're all smart, talented, hard-working women who deserve to be there. Julie is all incompetence, yet still holds a senior management position.

Things won't be truly equal until the world hands out as many high offices to stupid women as it does to stupid men.

My feminist icon sidled up to Father Giuliani and asked him where he got his loafers. Brad Pitt tried to determine their origin by licking them. Once it was established which Italian leather designer was responsible for the priest's shoes, Julie plucked imaginary fluff from the shoulder of his suit, also expensively Italian.

'You're working late tonight.' She executed a series of eyelash acrobatics. In less celibate circles they're quite effective. Julie's appealing if you like perky.

'I had not realized the time. If you both will excuse me, I must make a phone call.' Father Giuliani gave me a surreptitious wink. He was ditching us.

'He's so hot,' Julie said.

'For an older guy,' I said. But she was right. The priest's sexual magnetism could be felt through walls.

'What happened with you two in the elevator?'

'Nothing.'

'Nothing? You were in there nearly two hours and, nothing? Geez. You had your chance.'

'Oh, God, please tell me you're not going to come on to a priest.'

'Why not? I didn't see a wedding ring.'

'That would be because he's a Catholic priest,' I said.

'What do you mean? He's either married or he's not.'

'Listen to me. He took a vow of chastity.'

Julie blinked, rapidly. 'Is that bad? Did they catch him taking it? Can't he just give it back?'

I made eye contact with Brad Pitt. He didn't think it was worth an answer, either.

'Think about it,' I said. 'This is a Catholic priest we're talking about. You don't stand a chance. He's either gay or a paedophile.'

'He's into guys?'

'Or kids.'

'Kids?'

'Look, whatever he is or isn't into, don't try to sleep with him. Remember what happened the last time?'

'That was different.'

'Yes, it was different,' I said. 'He wasn't a Catholic priest. This time, the pope is going to be really pissed.'

She blinked again.

'I'm going to wear my short grey dress tomorrow,' she said. 'The one that looks like a school uniform.' Giggling in a decent imitation of a schoolgirl, she headed off in the direction Father Giuliani had gone.

I told myself the priest was safe. He had God on his side. I hoped that would be enough.

Brad Pitt knocked his dense head against my knees and waggled his ears, sticking out his tongue a little to show he was listening.

I told him I'd just learned purgatory is the all-expenses-paid vacation in hell you receive for being a good Catholic. He wasn't impressed. I couldn't imagine any sane person willingly converting to Catholicism.

All in all, my life was not going very well. I was telling my problems to a dog. I had to convince the Catholic Church to sell itself. Then, I had to convince people to buy it. My most significant romantic relationship was with a right-wing newspaper columnist I'd never met. I was also slightly in lust with a guy I met in a bar whom I was unlikely ever to see again. Both these men were romantically involved with women who weren't me. And if that weren't enough, I was now developing a mild crush on a Catholic priest.

I think I could've coped with it all, unscathed by any inadvisable romantic attachments, if only there wasn't something about being privy to the knowledge that the world will end on the weekend which encourages behaviour more reckless than usual.

FROM: Sydney Welles <sydneywelles@yahoo.com>
TO: God c/- presidentoftheunitedstates@thewhitehouse.com
DATE: Tuesday, May 24, 8.12 p.m.
SUBJECT: The Easter Bunny

Dear God,

I recently acquired a pet rabbit. It's unfriendly and mangy, but even so its coming has raised my level of rabbit-consciousness. It struck me as odd that rabbits are included in the most Christian and, if recent cinema is to be believed, most bloody of holidays. See, from an outsider's point of view, Easter seems to be all about persecution, betrayal, crucifixion and resurrection. The bunny is not a natural fit.

At first I thought it was yet another marketing device foisted onto the unsuspecting public to sell something – chocolate was the first product that came to mind. It wouldn't be the first time the advertising industry has been guilty of messing with Christian holidays – under the radar, of course. Putting Santa Claus in a red suit with white trim is still one of the biggest branding coups of all time, pulled off so well by the Coca-Cola Company that everyone thinks that's what Santa always looked like.

I did a little research on the subject of Easter. I was curious to see which multinational corporation was the culprit – the bunny inserter – but I found that the bunny wasn't added to Easter at all. No, instead it turns out the bunny was there all along, and Jesus was added.

Well before the one-God-fits-all concept was adopted, back when people thought the coming of spring each year was a miracle – it must have been a hell of a lot easier to be a deity back then – there was a goddess called Eastre, who was credited with the miracle. This goddess liked bunnies, and they, being very fertile, were celebrated as an embodiment of spring.

It's funny that the two biggest pagan celebrations of the year, Christmas and Easter, are also the two biggest Christian celebrations of the year.

It's also funny that a pagan custom from tens of thousands of years ago, older than the Passion play, older than Passover, older than the Bible, older than you if we take the Bible literally, has survived and is handing out eggs today.

Regards,
Sydney Welles

PS You'd better look out for Father Giuliani. Julie is not as stupid as she seems.

There are places in the world where cars are considered utilitarian. This isn't one of those places. So much time is spent on the road in LA that getting from A to B is incidental. A car's primary function is to tell the world who you are. Cars announce your socioeconomic group, provide personality and character for those who have none and, in the case of some men, also compensate for below-par penises.

The Germans and Italians, Porsche and Ferrari, make the classic compensation cars, but there are more reasonably priced American and Japanese versions for less well-off, less-endowed men.

SUVs are usually just the result of bad judgement, but they can also double as compensation cars. For instance, any guy who drives a Hummer is compensating like crazy.

BMWs aren't, strictly speaking, compensation cars, but it's a well-known fact that, nine times out of ten, guys who drive them turn out to be assholes sooner or later.

Some women I know won't even date a guy unless his car costs a lot of money. That's stupid. If you want to be with someone with money, why choose a man who's spent all of his on a car?

I avoid dating the owners of compensation cars. Relationships are hard enough without starting with a partner who brings so little to the party. Otherwise, vehicles don't factor into my choice of a partner.

When Jake picked me up for our first date I was grateful I didn't judge people on their cars. If I did, I'd have to conclude Jake was a pimp by profession, although he claimed to be a television producer. And that'd be unfair, considering he'd gotten everything else right.

The cosy French bistro on Beverly Boulevard was the kind of place I'd nominate if anyone had asked me what sort of restaurant was right for a first date. It had authentic food, reasonably priced wine, and bossy Gallic waiters. Real waiters. Not actors playing waiters, as is usually the case in LA.

Jake had chosen the place without any prompting from me – a point in his favour. He'd also sent me flowers at the agency. Another score. Getting flowers from a guy is pointless unless there are envious eyewitnesses to the event.

A regiment of crimson tulips in a square glass vase was delivered to my desk. On the accompanying card, beneath a phone number, was written:

*This is an invitation to dinner. Considering the head injury you caused, it's only fair you call and say yes. Also, you kicked me in the shin. If you don't come, I'll press charges.*

*Jake Reed*

Tulips are my favourite flowers. Another point to add to Jake's aggregate, even if awarded for a lucky guess.

Noah, who was loitering in my office when they arrived, said maybe it wasn't a coincidence. Maybe men are more perceptive than I give them credit for.

I told him to be serious.

All the same, I was impressed. With Jake's florist and his creative use of the Zagat guide. The only blemish on the evening was that he casually handed me a single orange gerbera when he came to pick me up. That was too much. Men in LA don't try that hard. They don't try at all.

The restaurant choice was probably a fluke. The tulips I could understand. Some men think a big, floral first impression gets them to the sex part faster. However, on top of the tulips, the gerbera was sweet and unnecessary. I had to suspect Jake was overcompensating because:

a) He was a pimp as his car suggested.
b) He was gay, but needed a womb-bearing beard to take to family functions.
c) He was two-timing the blonde from the other night.
d) He had a wife and family tucked away somewhere.
e) He was two-timing the blonde from the other night and he had a wife and family tucked away somewhere.

It occurred to me at this point that perhaps I was being too cynical, suspecting he was hiding something from me before we'd even been on a date. I decided to give him the benefit of the doubt – for the moment.

After we were seated in the restaurant, I ordered a glass of water for my gerbera.

'I think you should know,' the waiter said, in a thick French accent, 'that I was born without a sense of humour. Do you want the water with gas?'

I consulted the gerbera. 'Sans gas,' I said, giving our waiter the benefit of my most charming smile.

He stared at me for several seconds, dazzled, I suppose, by my smile, before saying, 'You are making me afraid,' and leaving to fulfil our liquid needs.

'He's very droll,' I said.

Jake didn't even glance up from his menu. 'Stop flirting with the waiter.'

'You have nothing to worry about. In this part of town, there's a good chance he'll like you better than me. Shall we ask him?'

'Let's not.'

Our waiter returned with a bottle of mineral water and an extra glass for the flower.

He also carried a bottle of Beaujolais and a terra-cotta pot filled with ice. The Beaujolais was good, he said, but better after it had been chilled a little. The wine was a couple of degrees too warm. He allowed us a scant quarter glass each, promising we could have more once it hit the appropriate temperature – room temperature in France.

'Well,' I said, once the waiter had taken his straight face away again, 'if I can't flirt with the waiter and you won't either, what are we going to do all night?'

'We could try the first-date routine. Ask questions, get to know each other?'

'Fine, but, I should warn you, I'm not very good at first dates.'

'Perhaps you should let me be the judge of that.'

'Oh, no. It's a well-known fact. I've not had a second date in over a year, nor wanted to. I think I'd be much better at this if I could just skip the first two dates and start with the third.' I downed the pathetic portion of wine in my glass. 'I'm ready. Ask me a question.'

'What do you do at Fisher Bennet McMahon & May?'

'That's easy. I'm a planner. Ask me a harder one.'

'What does a planner do?'

'Plan things. Is it my turn?'

'Sure.'

'Do you think we'll get married one day?'

Jake choked on his wine.

'Not a first-date question, huh?'

'No,' he said.

'We'll move on. Do you feel comfortable going out with a woman who earns more than you do?'

'What makes you think you earn more than I do?'

'That programme you produce for, it's quite worthy. People never get paid a lot of money for doing worthy things, only for un –'

French Poker Face, the waiter, was back, to pour the wine, call out the specials and tell us what we should eat. For the most part we agreed with him. If this pleased him, we couldn't tell.

'Why do you think you earn more than I do?'

'I earn more than just about anyone I've dated,' I said. 'And it's not just because they've been losers. I actually get paid a lot. It bothers more men than you'd think. Also, there's your car.'

'My car is a classic.'

'From when exactly?'

'1989.'

'No. There were no classics made in the 1980s. Taste skipped that decade entirely. I have the photos to prove it.'

'You don't like my car?'

It's important to men that you like their cars. Even the men who don't drive compensation cars feel this way. All men see their vehicles, if only subconsciously, as extensions of their penis. If you don't like a man's car, but like the man, you lie.

'I like your car.'

'What do you like about it?'

'Well . . . it has a lot of buttons to push. I'm looking forward to pushing more on the way home.'

'You don't know much about cars, do you?'

'Not true. I know it's important that a car has chrome wheels. And . . . and I know that you use the steering wheel to aim it . . . OK, I don't know much. I've tried to learn, but anytime someone talks about cars I fall asleep. But I bet I know stuff that you don't know. For instance, did you know there's a pina colada season?'

'No. I didn't.'

'It's true, pina coladas are good only from the first of July until the end of August. If you order one out of season, they don't taste right. You really ought to know stuff like that.'

'Why don't they taste right out of season?'

'No idea. It's just the way the world is. Who was that girl the other night?'

'Kim?'

'Yes, that's the one.'

Jake took my left hand in his right. My own fault. I'd been careless, leaving it resting on the table well within his reach. He seemed reluctant to answer the question. The answer was going to be bad.

'She's . . . we used to go out.'

It was as bad as I'd thought. 'How long did you go out?'

'About two years.'

Correction. Worse than I thought. 'Who ended it?'

'I did.'

'When?'

'Just under a month ago.'

Wrong answer. 'Why did it end?'

'Many reasons.'

'Give me the top two.'

At first I thought he was going to refuse, but then, 'We want different things out of life. I want a family, she doesn't. And . . .'

'And?'

'She was convinced I was having an affair.'

'Were you?'

'I'm not sure that's a first-date question.'

'It isn't, but, if you don't answer it, I'll be keeping up my poor second-date rate.'

'I didn't have an affair,' he said. 'Not technically.'

'What does that mean?'

'It means I wasn't having sex with anyone else.'

'But?'

'But, in a way, there was someone else.'

'In what way? And where is that – no, wait, that's probably enough detail for me at this point. I'm hungry. I want the date to last until the end of dinner. Your turn to ask a question.'

'Are you always like this?'

I patted his hand, the one holding my left hand captive. 'I'll calm down once I eat something.'

On cue, our waiter appeared at our table with his arms full of our first course. The steaming bowls of mussels kept us occupied, for a while.

'I have one more question. It may not be a first-date question, either,' I said.

Jake had made a small mountain of empty shells in rapid time. He ceased adding to it long enough to say, 'All right.'

'Do you still want a family?'

'Yes, I do.'

The odds on a second date were getting longer all the time.

☦

Later that night we found ourselves in a small, unfashionable bar we'd chanced upon on the way home. It was a Brad and Chad bar, a place full of people named Brad and Chad, wearing button-down shirts tucked into jeans worn high and tight.

A dark corner by the bar had both privacy and a full view of the Brads, Chads and their main activity. Standing on a chair in turn, they'd drink a glass of beer while the rest of the bar cheered with a level of enthusiasm that suggested the task must've been more difficult than it looked to be or, more likely, that these guys didn't get out much.

'What are we up to? My religious beliefs or the number of sexual partners I've had?' Jake handed me the dirty vodka martini I didn't really need, before putting his arm around me.

'The time has come, the Walrus said, to speak of many

things,' I said. 'Of shoes and ships and sealing wax – why, how many sexual partners have you had?'

'You're a Lewis Carroll fan?'

'Of Wonderland, yes. But the guy was a pervert.'

'A pervert?'

'Well, you see, he was one of the first photographers ever.'

'And . . . photographers are perverts?'

'No. Well, OK, yes, the ones I know are. But Lewis Carroll, he was a pervert because he had a thing for the real Alice. The one the book was written for. He was kind of obsessed with her. And he took pictures of little girls naked.'

'Where were the parents of these naked girls?'

'They were around. He'd ask their permission, but not all at once. First he'd ask to take normal clothed portraits of the girls, then move on to pictures in costumes, and, finally, pictures without clothes.'

'Their parents allowed this?'

'They must have. The photos exist.' I chased an olive around my glass. 'Photography had just been invented. It had yet to evolve into a way to meet and date supermodels. Getting a photo taken must've been a huge novelty. Maybe the parents thought it was art. Or maybe they just wanted to have photographs of their daughters.'

'In the nude?'

'Yes, well, this all happened before Freud. Until Freud pointed it out, we didn't know how sexually perverted we were. These days, paedophiles are all over the news, so, if some guy asked if he could take a soft porn picture of our eight-year-old, we'd have him locked up.'

'Probably why paedophiles no longer ask for parental permission. Lewis Carroll wasn't actually a paedophile?'

'I don't think he was out in a raincoat, molesting kids, if that's what you mean. But he probably was a paedophile – a repressed one. All Victorians were repressed. Isn't that what made them Victorian? He was also a mathematician.'

'Now that is unforgivable,' Jake said.

'Do you know "Lewis Carroll" was a pseudonym?'

'That I do know.'

'Do you know what his real name was?'

'I do.'

'Do you know one of your hands is on my ass?'

'I'm aware of it.' Jake squeezed a cheek for emphasis.

'Have you been at sea for a year?'

'No.'

'Well, I have a problem with being groped in public.'

'We could go somewhere private.'

'There's no point. I'm not going to sleep with you tonight.'

'You forget. You have to sleep with me. I paid for dinner.'

'Very funny, but I can't. Anna told me not to.'

'Why would she go and tell you a thing like that?'

'Oh, everybody knows. You should never have sex on the first date because men are like dogs.'

'I know I'll regret asking this. Why are men like dogs?'

'They try to hump everything.'

'Harsh. So when does Anna say we can have sex?'

'It depends. It's all about obedience training. Sex is like a doggy treat. If the dog gets the treat before he's earned it, you'll never be able to train him. It's best to wait. At least until the dog learns to beg.'

'Is that what you think?'

'Not really. I think if someone is an asshole, he's going to be an asshole whether you sleep with him on the first date or the tenth. The trick is to avoid dating him in the first place.'

'Sounds logical.'

'Only, it's not that easy. For instance, at this stage, I've no idea whether you're an asshole or not.'

'When will you know?'

'Probably not until it's too late.'

'I'm not an asshole.'

'That's what all the assholes say.'

'I see. I can't win.'

'No, that's not true. It works the same way the judicial system is supposed to. You're innocent until proven an asshole. Sex is the litmus test. It shows up the inner asshole in otherwise nice guys. It's the only way to know for sure.'

'If it's the only way, I guess I'll have to go along with it.'

'That's another thing. Men are always ready to have sex. What is that? What would you think of a woman if she wanted to sleep with you on the first date?'

'I don't think I'd be doing all that much thinking.'

'Would you think less of her than if she'd waited until the customary third date?'

'Sex on the third date is customary? I have to get out more.'

'You haven't answered the question.'

'I don't know. It depends on the woman concerned.'

'What if I were the woman? If we had sex right now, would you think I was a slut?'

'Only if you wanted me to.'

'Be serious.'

'OK.' Jake looked down into his Scotch and smiled. 'I think it'd be better to wait.'

'Why?'

He put his glass on a table, took mine from me and put it down, too. His free hand linked up with his occupied one, behind me, south of my waist.

'It's not a good idea to have sex with me on the first date,' he said.

'Why not?'

'I'll respect you less.'

'You can't be serious.'

'Deadly.'

I took a protest step backwards, but Jake held me in place. I didn't really make much of an effort to put distance between us. Being chummy with Jake was no great hardship, but he was so perilously close to kissing me that I had a little trouble keeping up my end of the conversation.

'You'd think less of someone because they slept with you on the first date?'

'Yes,' he said.

'But you're sleeping with them, too.'

'True.'

'So what if they judge you the same way?'

'It's all right for me. I'm a guy.'

'Obviously.'

'You asked the question. You can't now complain because you don't like the answer. If a woman sleeps with me on the first date, I'd be unlikely to want to continue the relationship.'

'You can't be this backward without a reason. Were you frozen in the last ice age? Did they only just find you and defrost you?'

'I think you'll find my views aren't uncommon.'

'I think you have appalling views.'

'What is so wrong with them?'

'They're just . . . wrong.'

'I'm being honest. No one appreciates something that comes too easily. It's basic human nature.'

'What? This is really annoying me. You can't get away with perpetuating this primitive macho crap. I can't let you. I won't. I'm going to have to sleep with you tonight.'

'You are?'

'Yes. I have no other choice.'

'Your place or mine?'

'Whose is closer?'

'Mine.'

'Your place, then,' I said.

To make my point, I went with Jake to his place and slept with him. Twice. I did it mostly to do my part in the fight to change the double standards in dating. To take a stand – well, in this case, a recumbent position – for single women everywhere. But there were a couple of other reasons for my actions. That martini I had in the bar was one. Also, I wanted to sleep with Jake and not only because the world was ending the following day.

FROM: Sydney Welles <sydneywelles@yahoo.com>
TO: God c/- pope@thevatican.com.it
DATE: Sunday, May 29, 8.15 a.m.
SUBJECT: Omnipresence

Hey God,

I know you're meant to be everywhere at once, but you can't be absolutely everywhere, right? For example, you weren't at Jake's last night, were you?

I'm finding the idea of you being omnipresent disturbing. You're the ultimate voyeur. A great, cosmic pervert. Why does the creator of the universe have time to watch my sex life? Which, let's face it, was a non-event before last night. Surely you have something better to do? There are children starving in Africa, you know.

By the way, I think I've found a loophole in this no-premarital-sex business: if I don't have any intention of marrying the guy, then it isn't premarital sex, is it?

Best,
Syd

The sun dangled above a pointy tree in Vince and Anna's back garden, a lone, angry-orange ornament abandoned by celestial tree trimmers. Even with the glare in our eyes, I could see that behind her sunglasses – weighted down with designer logos so large they could double as anchors in a yachting emergency – Anna was in mild shock.

'You slept with him?' she said, for the second time.

'He tricked me into it. Did this whole reverse-psychology thing. It was quite clever. Anyway, he told me I had to sleep with him because he bought dinner.'

'You said that?' Vince said.

Jake grinned. 'I believe I did.'

'I'm impressed.'

Anna chose to ignore Vince, shifting in her seat to turn on Jake across the table. 'How much was dinner?'

'About a hundred and fifty bucks.'

'I have a feeling that won't be enough,' I said. 'You should've picked a more expensive restaurant.'

'Did that include the tip?' Anna wanted to know.

Jake inclined his head to indicate it did. 'She was cheap.'

'I prefer the term "on special". Don't forget, he did send me flowers beforehand, so you have to factor in the cost of those, too. But you're right. I should've held out for more.' I squinted sideways at Jake. 'How much would you have paid?'

62

'My entire net worth.'

'How much is that?' Anna's voice held a shade too much innocence for it to be genuine.

'Why is sex a financial transaction, even when there are no hookers involved?' Vince said. 'And why are men always the ones expected to foot the bill? What happened to gender equality?'

'Nothing happened to it,' I said. 'Something has to exist before anything can happen to it. I know patriarchal propaganda says otherwise, but gender equality hasn't been invented yet.'

'Due in no small part to closet chauvinists like you, darling.' Anna patted Vince on the forearm.

'Yes, look at the unfair double standards we all cling to. Case in point.' I waggled a finger at Jake. 'I didn't tie him up and force him to have sex with me, but you aren't judging him.'

'He scored,' Vince said. Though they refrained from high-fiving across the table, I sensed Vince and Jake shared a covert bonding moment.

'Yes. Exactly. I'm cheap, I mean, good value for money, while Jake here gets inducted into the stud hall of fame. If men are going to frown upon women who sleep with them on the first date, then they shouldn't go around sleeping with women on the first date. It's so hypocritical.'

Everyone was silent for a moment, digesting the brilliance of my argument.

'So,' Jake said, 'you think I'm a stud.'

'I think it's possible you missed the point I was making.'

'You were saying that you're a slut and Jake here is a stud – well done, son,' Vince said. 'Was there something else?'

'Yes. No. I give up. Could I have some more champagne, please?'

†

Jake told the truth last night. His house was closer to the bar than mine, two streets closer. I'd known we both lived in Venice, but I had no idea we were almost neighbours. I found it worrying. With the exception of urban wildlife and demonic children, I don't really get on with my neighbours.

'What if we have a horrible break-up? It'll be awkward if we keep bumping into each other,' I said. 'Maybe it's best we part on good terms now.'

'We've never bumped into each other before.'

'How can you be sure about that? We didn't know what we looked like before.'

'Are you always this pessimistic at the start of a relationship?'

'Only if there's a guy involved.'

Early this morning I found that Jake's fridge, though well stocked for a guy living on his own, held nothing resembling breakfast. I seized the chance to cite hunger as an excuse for a getaway. Leaving quickly was the polite thing to do.

Also, if the Final Judgement was going to take place at the end of the day, and cleanliness really is next to godliness, I had some tidying up to do that couldn't be delayed much longer.

I invited Jake to breakfast at my place, expecting him to refuse and mumble something noncommittal about calling me – the correct etiquette after you've had sex with someone you barely know. Jake was either ill-mannered or hungry. He accepted the invitation.

Found-food omelettes are the breakfast special at my house. They're omelettes filled with whatever I find in the fridge. Today it gave up green onion, prosciutto, cheddar and shiitake mushrooms. The cheddar, from Vermont, is especially good. The cows there must be very sane.

Some friends are so familiar with the found-food omelette concept they've taken to slyly stocking my fridge with their favourite fillings. That's cheating. The challenge and charm of a found-food omelette lies in letting fate decide what you eat for breakfast.

I was sliding his omelette onto a plate when Jake wandered in from the street, clean and dressed as promised.

'I'm starving,' he said, by way of greeting.

His appetite confirmed his words. It was so hearty it reminded me of a character in a movie: *Tyrannosaurus rex* in *Jurassic Park*. I donated half my omelette to the giant lizard, topped up his coffee, and toasted bread marginally faster than it disappeared down his throat.

'Do you have to rush off?' I said.

'No.'

'Oh.'

'Do you have other plans?'

'No. No plans.'

'Is something wrong?'

'It's just that . . .' I decided to be honest about the way I felt. 'It's just that I don't think I have enough food.'

For reasons clear only to the scientists who study the male libido, and then only vaguely so, this admission made Jake want to kiss me. The kiss was just getting interesting when the phone rang.

On the other end, Anna said, 'You haven't forgotten about today, have you?'

'Of course I haven't.'

'When will you be here?'

'At your place?'

'Uh-huh.'

'When do you want me?'

'How's ten-thirty?'

'Ten-thirty this morning?'

'When else? Can you still pick up the wings on the way?'

'Sure, no problem.'

I put down the phone, checked my watch and turned to Jake. 'I'm not sure why, but I have to be at Anna's in under an hour and I have to pick up wings.'

'Chicken wings?'

I considered chicken wings. Raw chicken wings? Fried chicken wings in a bucket? Spicy buffalo wings? 'No, I don't think so.'

Then my brain kicked in. I hit my forehead with the heel of my hand. 'Fairy wings.'

'Naturally. I don't know why I didn't think of them.'

'I have to go. I have to get to the Enchanted Grove on Robertson before ten to catch the fairy lady. Are you coming or staying?'

'I'll come. I think I should see this.'

I saw him glance suspiciously at the bottle of multi-vitamins on the table as I opened the kitchen window and threw a piece of toast through it – for the rabbit.

'Harry Rex hates carrots,' I said, to explain matters, but Jake looked more confused as I rushed out of the room to find my shoes.

✝

We found Anna sitting sideways on a steamer chair by the pool, gripping a gin and tonic, and an unlit cigarette, looking as if the world was about to end. A state in which she was best left alone.

Vince had greeted us at the door, relieving us of two sets of glittering pink fairy wings and two wrapped boxes from the trunk of my car, each containing a plastic, Barbie-sized Volkswagen Beetle.

His house, on the outside, is a replica of Tara. The interior is altogether different – it's Rhett and Scarlett's house in Atlanta after the Civil War. A splendid staircase confronts you in the foyer; perfect for grand entrances, climactic tumbles or any kind of drama requiring steps. After the staircase, the ornate chandeliers are the next most dominant decor feature. They're everywhere, and of the sort you'd imagine Michael Jackson would buy on a whim. Everyone agrees they're well preserved, very valuable and truly ugly.

Inside, the house looked as it ever did. It was the garden that was transformed. It'd been a normal garden – normal for a neighbourhood where everyone has a full-time gardener. Now it looked like a theme park without a theme. In which two catering vans were starting to unload what looked like enough food for two hundred people.

'You have a housekeeper and a private chef, and yet you've hired a caterer –'

I squinted to read what was written on the side of one of the vans.

'– and a very good caterer at that. Whatever happened to birthday cake and pin-the-tail-on-the-donkey?'

'When in Rome,' Vince said.

'Or Beverly Hills.'

'Right. Here every kid's party is a major social event, each bigger than the last. If you don't try to outdo everyone else, your kids are social outcasts before they start school.'

A large pink-and-white striped, fairytale-castle-shaped marquee had been set up on the lawn. Every tree was decorated; most with balloons or paper lanterns. One large tree was hung with wrapped gifts. Another dangled piñatas, low enough to be within reach of the average stick-wielding five-year-old – judging from the vast number of piñatas hanging there, the children attending the party weren't good at sharing.

'Syd-neeeee.' Audrey and Lexie tumbled out of the marquee in perfect little fairy costumes needing only wings to complete them.

Audrey launched herself at me from about three feet out, with as little regard for gravity as a character in a Chinese martial arts epic. Once I'd caught her and restored her to the ground, both the girls doled out hugs, twirled so I could get the full effect of the tutus, and allowed Vince and me to help them on with their wings. Vince then left us in a hurry, to cut off a tray-laden man from the catering company heading in a dangerous direction – towards Anna.

'Who's this?' Audrey held her arms up and in due

course was picked up by Jake. Audrey is an accomplished five-year-old flirt.

'He smells better than the old boyfriend,' she said.

After that auspicious announcement, I made the necessary introductions.

'What did the old boyfriend smell of?' Jake said.

'Smoke. He smoked – not just pretend like Anna. He's an actor. Anna says a bad one.'

'Matt was pretty.' Lexie, Audrey's younger sister by fifteen minutes, tugged on one of Jake's trouser legs. He put Audrey down, crouching so both girls could admire him.

'Was he prettier than me?'

'Yes,' Lexie said. 'Are you going to marry Sydney?'

'Do you think I should?'

'Do you have a house and a car?'

Jake nodded.

'Are they nice?'

'Very nice.'

'Do you have a dog?'

'No, but I can get one.'

Audrey and Lexie held a telepathic twin conference, coming to a quick decision.

'You can marry her,' Audrey said.

'Wait, you're marrying me off for a car, a house and a possible dog? Most serial killers have that much.'

Audrey gave me a grave look. 'You can't be picky when you're old.'

'How old is Sydney?' Jake – the sly bastard – asked.

'Very old,' Lexie said. 'About nineteen or twenty.' I'm thinking of adopting her.

'How old do you think Jake is?'

Lexie shook her head, the bearer of bad news. 'Forty-six or fifty-three, I think.'

Adorably identical, the twins are in demand as flower girls. In their experience weddings mean new dresses, being petted and admired, and cake. They try to arrange one for me at every opportunity. The girls also approve of divorce. They don't get to participate, but they've learned every divorce means there's a good chance of two new weddings.

Anna joined us on the grass, gin and tonic drained, cigarette soggy. Audrey wrapped herself around Anna's legs.

'Poor Anna, she's having a bad day.'

Me, too, if I had to live in a mansion and throw kids' parties on a competitive basis against Stepford mums armed with bottomless bank accounts. OK, the mansion – apart from the chandeliers – isn't so bad if you have Southern belle delusions, but the mothers are terrifying.

I can't tell them apart. They all look like variations on the same woman. As if they got a group discount for going to the same dermatologist, beautician, hair colourist, plastic surgeon, personal shopper and personal trainer. Their constantly serene expressions don't help. These women hold Brows & Botox parties the way other women used to have Tupperware parties. Only there's a limit to how much Tupperware a household needs. Botox falls into the rich, thin category. It has no saturation point.

Most of the mums are failed actresses and successful second wives. For them parenting is about redecorating a couple of spare rooms in pastels, producing a trophy child without it impacting their figures, and spoiling that child until the chances of it ever being able to do anything useful with its life are virtually nil.

Anna, on inheriting Vince's daughters, is three years and a pound or two of collagen behind the crowd when it comes to parenting. But, for someone who never planned on being a mother, she's come a long way.

The first time she and I had taken the girls out without their nanny, a Saturday not long after Anna and Vince became engaged, Audrey and Lexie grew restless and grouchy around noon. After a while I guessed what was wrong with them.

'I think they're hungry. We should feed them.'

Anna nodded in agreement, then asked in a small, terrified voice, 'What do they eat?'

✟

The birthday party was over by the time we'd gotten around to discussing how much I should've charged Jake for sex.

Audrey and Lexie, in spite of eating enough sugar to fuel them for a week, were upstairs taking a nap. The rest of us collapsed on chairs around a table set up on the grass. Vince broke out monk-made champagne and an elderly single malt to celebrate the end of the party and, possibly, the world. We made our way through remnant pink-frosted silver-sprinkled cupcakes. Calories don't count in the face of Armageddon.

After debate, the general consensus was that the price for a night with me was somewhere between four hundred and one thousand dollars. If I had not been in Beverly Hills, I dare say I'd have been priced somewhat lower.

Anna, proving her friendship, argued for the high end of the range. Vince was for the low end because of my amateur standing.

'That's the reason she should cost more,' Anna said. 'Guys get off on inexperience. Didn't virgins used to fetch the highest prices back when it was OK to sell virgins?'

'She's hardly a virgin,' Vince said.

'That's nice,' I said.

'You go to a professional for their experience and expertise. That's what you're paying for,' Vince said.

One of Anna's eyebrows jumped up by a couple of inches. 'Really?'

'Well, that's what I've heard.'

'Can't I at least get the hourly rate I'd earn if I were doing my job freelance?'

'No,' Vince said. 'You're a much better planner than you are a prostitute.'

'How do you know that?'

'I'm your client. You work on my account.'

'I could be even better as a prostitute.'

'I'd need to see references.'

'I could be a natural.'

Vince thought it over. 'Jake's the only one here who can tell us if that's true.'

Jake, displaying the wisdom of a man who'd like to get laid again, declined being dragged into the discussion, leaving Anna and Vince to haggle over my exact worth while the sun dropped behind the trees.

In the twilight, three ponies, coloured soft pink, lemon and baby blue, grazed peacefully under a tree, waiting for the float to come take them back to wherever it is pink, lemon and blue ponies come from. They, a stray gutted piñata oozing candy entrails onto the grass, a deserted cotton candy machine and the sagging marquee were the party carnage.

The cars I'd given the twins, now with plastic limbs and nylon hair poking out of the windows, were the girls' favourite non-requisitioned gift of the day, which, though not all cupcakes and perfection, had been a great success.

The mothers snorted champagne, wolfed down then purged the food prepared for them according to the latest diet taking Hollywood by storm, received manicures, gossiped – not always viciously – and went home clutching vouchers for twenty-five per cent off the procedure of choice from a well-known Beverly Hills plastic surgeon who happens to be one of Vince's friends.

Under the piñata tree, twenty or so daytime nannies took cover without the benefit of champagne, dishing the dirt on their employers and taking mental notes for future tell-all memoirs masquerading as popular fiction.

Every child left, tired, cranky and a little sick from too much cake and ice cream, with a piñata, a large stuffed toy from FAO Schwarz and whatever else they could get their sticky little hands on.

There was a Teletubby incident. Tinky Winky wouldn't stop hugging me, Jake threatened to snap off his antennae and Laa Laa, the yellow one, had to intervene.

Griffin, the little boy who'd arrived all by himself in a white stretch limo, snuck off with a bottle of champagne and was not found, asleep on the back seat of Princess Barbie's car, until a search was mounted two hours into the party.

The English boy, Frederick Bamford, after spending the entire party reclining in a steamer chair sipping a milkshake, said to me as I was passing:

'Go down to the store and buy me a Snickers, will you?'

I gave him the best precocious-brat-squelching stare I could muster. He stared back, bored, then reached into his pocket, pulled out a wad of money, peeled off a couple of twenty-dollar bills and tossed them at me.

'Go on,' he said.

Then SpongeBob SquarePants arrived. If I needed a sign the world was about to end, this was it – a celebrity sponge. I don't understand the appeal. He's a sponge, for God's sake, and he might live under the sea, but he doesn't look like sea sponge. He's more like a sink sponge, and a used one at that. He was a sneaky sponge, too, who crept up behind me to ask if the kids were ready for him, startling me into dropping a plate of heart-shaped ice-cream sandwich cookies.

It didn't matter. A dozen kids swooped on the cookies anyway. Their mothers were too liberally doused with champagne to notice their million-dollar babies were eating food off the ground. I felt guilty all the same, for introducing dirt into otherwise pure all-sugar diets.

Everything had gone well. Anna was no longer hyperventilating, having pulled off the most successful party of the year to date, in the six-years-and-under category. She also had the distinction of throwing the first kids' party of the year to provide valet parking. The twins were happy and even when Arabella, a very sophisticated six-year-old, pointed out my nail polish didn't match my toe polish and asked, in a kind way, if I was a street person, I had to agree with Jake when he said, 'Well, it's not the end of the world.'

He was remarking that it was past sunset and the world had not gone poof, exploded cataclysmically or whimpered to its end.

I was surprised. Given the right kind of scholarship and enough time spent with the Book of Revelation, the plagues, pestilence and conflict predicted to herald the end of time were there at the party for all to see – if you were open to substituting Teletubbies for the four horsemen of the Apocalypse, and myself for the whore of Babylon.

On some level I registered disappointment. After all, the end of all things would've been something to see. Also, a timely Apocalypse would have saved me from having to work on the Catholic Church account. And it would've meant I didn't have to face the consequences of a relationship I'd leapt into without much thought, with a guy who, so far, was so absolutely perfect that there had to be a skeleton the size of King Kong in his closet.

At the time, however, in the beauty of the garden and the glow of fine champagne, I was pleased we'd all survived.

FROM: Sydney Welles <s.welles@fbmm.com>
TO: God c/- thequeen@buckinghampalace.co.uk
DATE: Monday, May 30, 1.38 p.m.
SUBJECT: Plague of Botulinum Toxin A

Dear God,

I'm still here and, as far as I can tell, so is the rest of creation. The usual shortage of Botox and Restalyne that occurs around the Hollywood award season is well and truly over – I saw proof enough yesterday – and the world seems to be functioning as normal.

What is it with Botox? Is it here to explain the state of the world today? That is, if people will pay to have a paralysing poison injected into their faces, it follows that they will pretty much buy anything (this is a good thing if I have to sell you).

Or is Botox a plague sent to punish us? Or worse? As I stare into the blank faces of Botoxed news anchors and actors, or people I know, unable to tell how they're feeling behind the mask of their faces, I have to wonder if – combined with reality television – it's a part of a bigger plan to turn us all into zombies.

I'm beginning to suspect the Apocalypse is not about annihilation. Instead, it's about inducing a planetary coma to see us through eternity. Has the end of the world already come and gone, the virtuous saved, while the rest of us were far too busy smoothing our foreheads and voting each other off the planet to have noticed?

Speak soon,
Syd

# FISHER BENNET McMAHON & MAY

4848 Abott Way Los Angeles CA 90066 USA
310-807-3000 t   310-807-5000 f

Charles Turner
Los Angeles Times
202 W. 1st St.
CA 90012

Dear Charles,

The only redeeming feature of a conservative male is that he tends to be a creature of habit who rigidly sticks to routine, if only because he lacks the imagination to do otherwise. He is reliable the way a Honda is reliable; reliable the way a bank is reliable. Boring, yes, but reliable all the same.

In view of this, I'm at a loss as to why you haven't replied to my past two letters after fifteen months of weekly correspondence. I can't imagine that I've offended you in any fresh way, not now, not after I've spent more than a year insulting you. So, I'm assuming that one of the following has taken place:

a) You've run out of sexist ploys with which to put me in my place.
b) Your girlfriend – the absolute doll – discovered our correspondence and, in spite of her frontal lobotomy or because of it, can't believe it's an innocent

pen-and-paper affair and is forbidding any further exchange of fluids, inky or otherwise.
c) You believed me when I told you the world was going to end and ran off to bungee jump off a bridge or to do whatever happens to be at the top of your to-do-before-Armageddon-list.
d) You've joined a monastery and aren't allowed contact with the outside world.
e) You are dead and your last couple of columns were published posthumously.

There is some evidence to support this last theory. Your columns did read as though a dead person wrote them. Only in the case of c), and perhaps e), will I forgive your neglect.

Yours (on paper),
Sydney

FROM: Sydney Welles <s.welles@fbmm.com>
TO: God c/- theforce@lucasfilm.com
DATE: Monday, May 30, 7.40 p.m.
SUBJECT: Advertising is not going to work

Dear God,

Of all the gods available off the shelf today, how did I get landed with you? I'd have preferred the elephant-headed Hindu god, Ganesha. That religion offers yoga, curry, reincarnation and Bollywood. And Ganesha is a remover of obstacles, a good-luck god. What's not to like?

Blessed with facial features only a pachyderm could love, encumbered by extra arms and relying on a mouse as his only means of transportation, it's clear Ganesha doesn't go around taking himself too seriously.

A lack of pompous self-importance is so refreshing in a supreme being. Ganesha, I could sell.

You on the other hand are a bad-tempered old man who sends people to hell. You're impossible to please. You've been pissed off with us virtually from the moment you created us.

And that's just the Christian version of you. The Catholic version is worse. In your Catholic mode you don't allow contraception or divorce, and you don't allow priests to marry or be women, though, admittedly, it seems you have no problem with them having sex with children.

There are so many reasons why, for you, advertising is a bad idea, not the least being that a good deal of a product's success lies in its name.

You are called 'God'.

Even as a proper noun, 'God' is not a good brand name for a god. A good brand name for a god is Nike – Greek goddess of just doing it – or Mars or Mercury, or anything short, memorable and powerful. 'God' is a no-name name, ambiguous at best. It's generic. Say it, and people immediately think of the one they're affiliated with.

To successfully be the generic name in a product category, as Xerox is to copying or Kleenex is to tissue, it helps to be the first product of your kind to appear on the market.

You're far from the first. By the time Catholic God appeared there were already plenty of gods in existence. And, strictly speaking, Catholic God is a brand extension of Christian God, who is a brand extension of Jewish God, and Jewish God is a repackaged, re-launched version of a bunch of earlier pagan deities.

As a rule brand extensions are unsuccessful and tend to eat into the market of the original brand, thus weakening it.

Sincerely,
Sydney

A Hindu, a Muslim, a Buddhist, a Jew, an atheist and a born-again Christian were sitting around a large table in a room in an advertising agency.

It was no joke. It was my job. I, a non-practising agnostic at best, had the job of moderating the group.

Religion was the topic they were being paid to talk about. Not surprisingly, it was the main topic of contention.

BORN-AGAIN CHRISTIAN: You people are ruining this country.
ATHEIST: Yes, I've heard that one before.
BORN-AGAIN CHRISTIAN: You're trying to take out God.
ATHEIST: That's illogical. You can't kill something that doesn't exist.
BORN-AGAIN CHRISTIAN: I was talking about the Pledge of Allegiance. What you're trying to do to it is evil.
ATHEIST: What am I trying to do?
BORN-AGAIN CHRISTIAN: To take out 'under God'.
ATHEIST: It's not something I'm personally seeing to. Anyway, it should come out. It was inserted in the first place. It wasn't in the original pledge.
JEW: I remember when that happened. I was in the third grade. My teacher told us they put it in to remind us that there's a power greater than a nation. She said they did it so that what happened in Nazi Germany could

never happen here. I always thought it was a good thing.

BORN-AGAIN CHRISTIAN: We are one nation under God. No two ways about it.

ATHEIST: Whose God?

BORN-AGAIN CHRISTIAN: There's only – Jesus Christ – it doesn't matter.

ATHEIST: The 'any god is better than no god' argument. I'm familiar with that one. Let me just point out that people who don't believe in God don't fly planes into buildings on purpose.

MUSLIM: Why is everyone looking at me?

MUSLIM: Now you're all trying not to look at me. I'm not responsible for the acts of a handful of extremists just because they claim to have the same faith I do. No more than he [nodding at born-again Christian] is responsible for the Christian groups who go around shooting doctors.

ATHEIST: I wouldn't be too sure about that.

BORN-AGAIN CHRISTIAN: What are you trying to say?

ATHEIST: You wouldn't understand.

BORN-AGAIN CHRISTIAN: Oh, yeah? I understand you people all right. Hitler was an atheist, just like you.

JEW: Hitler was raised as a Catholic. He was even an altar boy in his youth.

MUSLIM: I've heard that, too. Do you know he was never excommunicated? Don't you find that strange after everything he did?

BORN-AGAIN CHRISTIAN: Bullshit.

ATHEIST: It's true. Excommunication is reserved for pop stars.

BORN-AGAIN CHRISTIAN: Catholics are worse than atheists, anyway.

ATHEIST: I'm touched.

BUDDHIST: Please remember, we're here to [pointing at me] answer her questions, not to argue amongst ourselves. Perhaps we could all try showing more tolerance for other people's points of view.

ME: Well, if we could move on to the next –

BORN-AGAIN CHRISTIAN: Yeah, well, you know where you can stick your tolerance and peace and Dalai Lamas and movie stars. You Buddhists are a bunch of wimps. Yoga makes you weak.

HINDU: Er, yoga is more my department.

BORN-AGAIN CHRISTIAN: Keep your unnatural practices to yourself. If God had intended us to do that crap, he'd have put instructions in the Bible. Where are you from? China?

BUDDHIST: Orange County. My racial heritage is Korean, if that's what you're asking. My parents are from South Korea. They moved here before I was born.

BORN-AGAIN CHRISTIAN: Korean, huh? You people should stop eating dogs.

BUDDHIST: I'm a vegetarian.

BORN-AGAIN CHRISTIAN: Well, tell your dog-eating friends back home to stop.

HINDU: Why should she?

BORN-AGAIN CHRISTIAN: You're not supposed to eat dogs.

HINDU: According to Hinduism, you are not supposed to eat beef, but I'm not telling you not to eat steak or hamburger.

BORN-AGAIN CHRISTIAN: That's different. Dogs are pets to us. You can't eat them.

HINDU: Cows are sacred animals to us, but we accept that your beliefs are different to ours.

BORN-AGAIN CHRISTIAN: A cow is not the same as a dog.

ATHEIST: It's different only to you.

BORN-AGAIN CHRISTIAN: Dog is man's best friend.

ATHEIST: In some cases, the only friend a man can get.

BORN-AGAIN CHRISTIAN: Why is he here?

ME: There's no need to shout. He's here for the same reason you are. We're interested in getting as wide a range of perspectives as possible. All opinions are welcome. Why don't we all take a short break to calm –

BORN-AGAIN CHRISTIAN: This is about God. Why have someone here who doesn't believe in God? The rest of them I can understand. They believe in something, at least. But him?

ATHEIST: Wait a minute. Do you believe in his god [pointing at Hindu]? Sorry, I mean, his gods?

BORN-AGAIN CHRISTIAN: Of course not.

ATHEIST: What about hers [pointing at Jew]?

BORN-AGAIN CHRISTIAN: The only way to salvation is through Jesus Christ.

ATHEIST: What about his [pointing at Muslim] god?

BORN-AGAIN CHRISTIAN: You've got to be kidding. He's at war with Christ.

MUSLIM: I can't be at war with him. He's dead already. They [pointing at Jew] and the Romans killed him. We had nothing to do with that one.

JEW: Hey, that's unfair.

MUSLIM: Sorry, didn't mean to add to the persecution. I was just making a point. This guy doesn't seem to understand that, to me, he is the disbeliever.

BORN-AGAIN CHRISTIAN: Christianity is the only religion based on history and fact. Everything else is mumbo-jumbo.

ATHEIST: Well, I happen to agree with both of you on one thing. For all the same reasons you don't believe in each other's gods, I don't believe in yours.

BORN-AGAIN CHRISTIAN: Yeah, well, you can say whatever you want. It doesn't matter in the end. Who do you think is going to get the last laugh?

ATHEIST: You born-agains are all the same, you do whatever you want to – things others wouldn't dream of doing – then as soon as you get that first taste of mortality, you run scared and get your slate wiped clean. Then you miss the fact that Christianity preaches humility and become the most self-righteous people on earth. Me, I happen to think you have to live with whatever you've done, good or bad, for the rest of your life.

BORN-AGAIN CHRISTIAN: You're going to hell.

ATHEIST: Yeah, yeah, I know. How does that old saying go? Choose heaven for the scenery and hell for the company? Well, for the record, I don't want to go to your heaven. I can think of nothing worse than having to spend eternity with narrow-minded idiots like you.

BORN-AGAIN CHRISTIAN: You're doing the devil's work. You just don't realize it.

ATHEIST: Look, if I don't believe in God, it logically follows that I don't believe in hell or Satan. He's your guy, not mine.

BORN-AGAIN CHRISTIAN: He's not my guy. The Lord is my shepherd.

ATHEIST: Sheep need shepherds.

BORN-AGAIN CHRISTIAN: You shouldn't be allowed to call yourself an American if you don't believe in God.

ATHEIST: Look, I don't care if you believe in fifty gods. So, why does it matter to you if I believe there are none?

BORN-AGAIN CHRISTIAN: Because you're wrong. You're all wrong. You people are ruining this country. This is a Christian country. Only Christians should be here. You shouldn't be allowed to live here unless you accept Jesus. Jesus is the only –

BUDDHIST: Oh, for Christ's sake, shut up.

FROM: Sydney Welles <s.welles@fbmm.com>
TO: God c/- toptengods@godchecker.com
DATE: Tuesday, May 31, 5.50 p.m.
SUBJECT: Catholicism has no sex appeal

Dear God,

Nothing about Catholicism – with the exception of Father Giuliani – is sexy. This is very unfortunate, as it's true what they say: sex sells.

Christianity has only one sexual position and you have to be married to use it. If you're Catholic, you also have to produce one new Catholic each time you use it. In any case, God forbid you enjoy it.

The most honoured of Catholic figures, Mary, managed to get pregnant without having sex. Childbirth is incredibly painful for women who've had plenty of sex. What must it be like for a virgin? Nothing has ever been in that vagina, but suddenly, lo and behold, there's an eight-pound baby to push out of it. Words do not exist to describe the unfairness of the situation.

Not only does the Catholic Church forbid birth control, but also, ideally, it would like women to get pregnant without having sex. Two thousand years ago, women may have gone along with this. However, it won't go down well with women today.

Let's not forget that women make up 51 per cent of the population and make 80 per cent of all purchasing decisions.

Syd

It's a great wonder that those working in the field of anthropology don't set up research camps in Los Angeles. The advances in human development originating here, spreading to the rest of the world through film, television and celebrity magazines, are astounding. For instance, a completely new breed of woman has appeared in this city, within the space of only one generation.

In the absence of qualified anthropologists, Noah is studying this divergent species, and has classified them as 'Inverse Camel Girls'.

Inverse Camel Girls are created when Hollywood starvelets hit puberty by way of breast implants. This kind of puberty occurs at the age when a starvelet realizes she's never going to be the next Julia Roberts, and lowers her sights to non-speaking parts in B-grade films – Dumb, Big-breasted Girlfriend of Lesser Villain comes to mind – or accepts the real-life role of Old, Ugly, Rich Guy's Girlfriend, which has very similar requirements.

These girls never weigh more than a hundred and twenty pounds, carrying half that weight in their breasts. They defy gravity as well as anatomy, not falling on their faces every few steps, as anyone with their weight distribution should.

Like camels, Inverse Camel Girls can survive without food for long periods of time because of the stores in their breasts. Noah puts this down to evolution: 'We live in the desert, where natural food supplies are low. It was only a matter of time before these superior creatures developed. This is natural selection at its finest.'

Inverse Camel Girls are so evolved they have a small secondary food store in their lips, which get plumper, holding more each passing year. The combination of toothpick-thin bodies, obese lips, and breasts the size of their heads makes these girls singularly attractive to the opposite sex. Men desperately want to mate with them. Proving Noah is right. Sexual desirability is up there with adaptability in the natural selection process; they must be the next step in the evolutionary chain.

Whenever we begin a new qualitative research campaign, Noah rounds up flocks of Inverse Camel Girls, taking great pleasure in moderating the groups personally. He has a special wardrobe for the job. A choice of two T-shirts: 'I Love Big Fake Tits' or 'Free Breast Exam'. Noah will hold these groups for as long as it takes me to notice what he's doing and tell him to stop. The purpose of consumer research is to find out what people are thinking, and thinking is not, generally speaking, an Inverse Camel Girl's forte.

Noah gets revenge on me by organizing interesting groups for me to moderate. The last-minute inclusion of an atheist in a group of mixed religionists was a Noah classic. But his revenge can be subtler. The Jesus-Christ-lookalike group of long-haired surfers he'd assembled first thing this morning, who referred to me as 'moderator chick', is a fine example of why someone of Noah's intelligence is wasted in advertising.

The only group of women more anthropologically remarkable than Inverse Camel Girls is that which Noah calls 'Permanently Startled Women'. From an evolutionary standpoint, they're the forerunners of Inverse Camel Girls.

The difference between the two, apart from age, is that Permanently Startled Women don't carry food stores in humps out front; breast implants were after their time. Permanently Startled Women are old-fashioned. They stay emaciated by cutting out all food groups. As far as they're concerned, Atkins is for amateurs.

Like Inverse Camel Girls, they also hang out with old, ugly, rich men, but, unlike the girls, their physical appearance is the result of being the wife of an old, ugly, rich man, not the reason they got to apply for the job.

Permanently Startled Women are permanently startled because they went on 'vacation' and came back 'refreshed' when it was still the done thing for plastic surgeons to lift all the skin off a face, stretch it taut and snip off the excess around the edges. Lift, stretch, trim; repeat every few years. A couple of decades go by and life is forever surprising you.

In meeting room number five, a group of extremely slim women, wearing outfits in the same price bracket as a new Toyota Corolla, clustered around the light refreshment table showing their backs to me.

I glanced at my notes. 'I thought I was doing a seniors group?'

Patton consulted his ever-ready electronic diary. 'Yes, ma'am, you are, ma'am.'

'Which room am I supposed to be in?'

'This room, ma'am.'

'This one?' I pushed the door. It slid open a little wider. The group's attention was still engaged at the table. They were audibly growing more excited.

'What are they looking at? What's on the table?'

'Oreos, ma'am.'

I opened the door all the way.

Eight shocked expressions below eight extreme coiffures turned to greet me.

'I'll be right with you,' I said, sliding the door shut.

'Who screened this group?'

Patton communed with his electronic diary. 'It was Noah Glaser, ma'am.'

'Of course it was. I'm going to go talk to him. Go in and make sure they have everything they want.'

'Me, ma'am, by myself? With them?'

'All right, just stand guard. Make sure none of the Chanel suits wanders off.'

'Yes, ma'am.'

Noah was, as I'd suspected, snugly ensconced in the observation room, mightily pleased.

'What is that supposed to be?' I pointed at the women on the other side of the glass wall, a mirror if you were looking at it from their side.

'Our two o'clock group.'

'Where did you find them?'

'Would you believe all in the one spot? Rodeo Drive, outside the very plush consulting rooms of doctors Williamson, Stafford and White, plastic surgeons all. Lucky, huh?'

'Very funny –'

'You can't complain. Every one of them passed the screening test. The right age group, the right income bracket, all church-going folk, or so they claim.'

'They belicve in God? Are you sure? Church attendance usually drops off once you reach that socioeconomic group. Maybe they have Him confused with Karl Lagerfeld?'

'Religion is the opium of the people. The masses are indoctrinated young, or else they turn to religion at a low point in their lives, instead of resorting to drugs, alcohol, sex or food, like normal people. Rather than face the fact their lives are shit, the world is shit and they are shit, and trying to do something about that in the here and now, they buy into the idea that everything will be perfect once they drop dead.'

'These women are hardly representative of the people.'

'I found them on the street.'

'You're getting back at me for sending you out there, aren't you?'

The research firms we hire for projects such as this provide all the screeners and moderators we need. But I believe it's good for us to get in amongst it, to hear firsthand what people are saying, rather than relying on reports.

'My parents paid two hundred and fifty thousand dollars for my education. I shouldn't be standing on a corner with a questionnaire and clipboard. However, as it so happens, I've got a talent for screening. You should see some of the other groups I put together.'

'I'm sure I will. You really think we'll get anything useful out of this one?'

'We want to prove that people will buy God, right? Stick a couture label on Him: they'll snap Him up.'

'I'm impressed with one thing. You got them to admit they're over sixty.'

Noah held up his right hand and rubbed his fingers briskly against his thumb.

'They came clean for seventy-five dollars apiece?'

'That's why they're here,' he said.

'What is it with rich people and free money?'

A skeletal woman, all big hair, pearls and pink tweed, detached herself from the group and stood in front of the one-way mirror applying powder to her regularly tightened face.

Noah inclined his head towards her. 'You think all that comes free? That stuff she's putting on her face is probably ground from the bones of a sacrificed sixteen-year-old virgin. Do you have any idea how hard it is to find a sixteen-year-old virgin these days, let alone one you can sacrifice?'

'We should get back in there.'

Noah stood; on his T-shirt was printed 'Jesus Hates Your Face Lift'.

'I don't know if that's appropriate.'

'You kidding? It's perfect.' Noah prides himself on his wardrobe. It has something to offend everybody.

'They're senior citizens. Show some respect.'

'Here, I've a spare T-shirt in my bag. In case one of the babes from the media department drags me home for sex and I haven't time to go home before work in the morning.'

'That ever happened?'

'There's a first time for everything. What do you think?'
He held up the T-shirt he'd pulled out of his bag, which, as well as boasting severe creases, said 'Religion: keeping the poor from killing the rich for 2,000 years.'

'Do you even own a plain shirt?'

'I'll put on my jacket.' He pulled something black and hooded on, and zipped it. As he preceded me out of the room I saw that the words 'Babies Are Assholes' were sewn across his back in inch-high letters.

Patton, who appeared to have the same unreasonable fear of Permanently Startled Women that we knew he suffered from when faced with Inverse Camel Girls, took up position cowering behind me, as we entered the room.

'What are you doing?'

'Protecting your flank, ma'am.'

'Well, it's very annoying. Why don't you go to the observation room and make sure the video camera is working.'

'Yes, ma'am. Thank you, ma'am.'

I surveyed our group, lined up in front of us like so many deer in the headlights.

'Do you want to moderate or shall –'

Noah got down on his knees and clasped his hands together. 'Let me do it,' he said. 'Please, let me. I'll be good from now on. I promise.'

With Noah steering it, the group progressed smoothly through the two hours allotted for it. Our Permanently Startled Women were, to a woman, quite prepared to purchase God, religion and anything else we had for sale, but I couldn't help but feel that, for these women, heaven would be a bit of a comedown.

'A rating,' the woman name-tagged 'Heloise' said. She was a dazzling woman who was the group leader in the if-you've-got-great-big-diamonds-wear-them-all-at-once category. 'I think every church should come with a rating or something. Someone ought to go out there and review all the religions. Put it all in a Michelin guide.'

'Yes,' Jackie said, 'otherwise how can we be sure we're getting the best?' Jackie, according to the information I had in front of me, was sixty-two, thrice-divorced and the possessor of an annual household income of over $650k, all of it alimony.

'No, no, no, hon, what we need is not a rating,' Victoria – at seventy, with a 1.8-million-dollar annual income, the oldest and richest of the group – said. She turned to me. 'You see, honey, what we need is a guarantee of some kind. A rock-solid lifetime warranty.'

This met with general agreement from the group. God needed to come with a guarantee.

'OK,' said Noah, 'one more question. How would you describe your relationship with God? For instance, would you say God is a friend, a companion? Or would you say God is an authority figure, a judge, someone you have to please?'

The answer was 'none of the above'. To the best of my understanding, to this group God was, first, a kind of senior flight attendant who checked your tickets and made sure that coach-class people didn't get into the first-class heaven. Secondly, He was the universe's greatest host, and heaven the house party to end all house parties.

'Unless there are any questions you'd like to ask us . . . we are just going to do one last exercise. This is heaven,'

I said, indicating a large piece of white board propped up on an easel behind me on my right. 'And this is hell.' I pointed to a second piece of board, also on an easel, next to the first.

Noah placed a large pile of glossy magazines on the table, heavy on travel and fashion, along with several pairs of scissors and sticks of glue.

'I'd like you each to go through these magazines,' I said, 'and pull three or four pictures that make you think of heaven and three or four which make you think of hell. We'll stick all the heaven pictures to the heaven board and all the hell pictures to the hell board.'

The women, on their feet instantly, buzzed between the magazines and the boards like expensively attired, anorexic mosquitoes. Soon the magazines were drained, the two large pieces of cardboard swelling with pictures.

Heaven looked like a tropical island. A tropical island lousy with Tuscan villas and five-star holiday resorts, under blue skies dotted with fat, fair-weather clouds, oversized Cartier diamonds and thin, tanned, blonde people in skintight white Versace. Also readily available in heaven were cocktails, cabana boys and several versions of George Clooney.

Hell was a dusty Third World landscape with tract housing, budget hotels, a couple of game-show hosts, two or three politicians, several children who looked as if they could use a sponsor, and other people wearing chainstore clothing.

FROM: Sydney Welles <s.welles@fbmm.com>
TO: God c/- anyresident@texas.com
DATE: Thursday, June 2, 4.32 p.m.
SUBJECT: The Ultimate Velvet Rope

Dear God,

The Bible goes to great pains to stress that rich people will have a hard time getting into heaven. Over time, that seems to have changed. Today, the people who claim to have a monopoly on heaven are all rich.

It's fairly clear that in heaven things are pretty much going to operate as they do on earth. It'll be yet another private playground where all the rich and powerful – and the best-looking corpses – get in for free. The wealthier and more connected you are, the more chance you stand of getting past the velvet rope. And to be admitted into the VIP room, you'd better be the son of the president, the president, or both if possible.

Heaven was once the great equalizer (that job is now done by the DMV). According to the Bible, all those richer, luckier and prettier than you got their comeuppance in the end. The virtuous got into heaven by virtue of being poorer, less lucky and less good-looking, while the rich – and their camels – didn't pass the eye-of-the-needle test.

These days, however, the merely virtuous will have to queue, trying to look cool enough to get in without money or connections, while agonizing over the eternal question: What if you get to heaven and the door bitch won't let you in?

Syd

Anna and I were in a bar in Venice. A bar styled like a bar in a Bond film from the 1970s. In any other place the mirrored decor would've been considered hip, in a retro way. In this bar, the decor was not considered any such thing. It actually was from the 1970s.

The bar is a classic midlife-crisis bar catering to men of a certain age and socioeconomic group. Poor men can't afford to indulge a midlife crisis with money; there's no point catering to them. Women, given the gender difference in maturity levels, reassess their lives while there's still time to do something a little more constructive about it than mope around in a bar.

Wealthy men in midlife crisis rarely do anything constructive. Instead, they purchase convertible sports cars, which they speed around in, top down, hoping the G-forces will smooth their wrinkles and make them look younger.

It was just after opening time when we arrived, but three typical crisis cases – a ponytail, a comb-over and a toupee – were already propping up the wood-veneered bar. By the way their reflections in the mirror behind the bar perked up when we walked in, we knew at least three rounds of drinks were headed our way.

Anna and I ordered Bellinis, requesting they be made with fresh, out-of-season white peaches, crushed by hand into the most expensive prosecco available. The bartender, with a nod of conspiracy, complied on the house.

An MLC bar survives by ensuring its wealthy male patrons spend their wealth over the bar. But these men, even in the throes of middle age imbroglios, can drink only so much on their own, and though they're incapable of fidelity in other areas of life they remain faithful to the unimaginative, inexpensive drink they've been drinking since youth – commonly known as beer.

The bar's financial success requires a steady flow of cocktail-drinking female customers. Women, as long as they're young enough, don't pay for a thing. Your first drink is on the house, and after that someone will buy you drinks. What patrons of an MLC bar lack in youth and hair, they make up for in a willingness to part with money.

Anna and I are exactly the right age for a midlife-crisis bar. Old enough to know better, to understand our complicit role in the bar's success, but young enough to look as if we don't know or understand anything at all.

'So, let me guess. Is this about Jake?' Anna said, as soon as we'd settled in at a table, at the start of the evening.

'How did you know?'

'Let's see. You call me and tell me you have a problem you need to discuss. At the moment you're interviewing religious nuts for a living. For the past two years you've worked for a company that treats you like a highly paid errand girl, with male colleagues who take your ideas and pass them off as their own. You have no life outside of work except when I drag you out. You use alcohol as an emotional crutch – not that I'm hypocritical enough to judge – and you've been on six failed dates since you broke up with Matt the Rat. Despite this, recently, through no real desire or effort of your own, you meet a nice, intelligent, good-looking guy who is crazy about you. It's obvious he has to be the problem.'

'Christ, you know me too well. I have to get some new friends.'

'This is LA. The only friends you'll find here are on TV. You're stuck with me.'

Our Bellinis arrived. Anna took a short break to taste hers, pronounce it not nearly as good as the original served at Harry's Bar in the other Venice, the one in Italy, and was immediately back on my case. 'So, what is the problem, exactly?'

'I don't know, not exactly.'

'I'm finding it difficult to see any problem. What? He wears women's underwear to bed?'

'That kind of stuff doesn't come out for months.'

'Any disgusting personal habits or Freudian complexes?'

'No more than the next guy.'

'Small dick, huh?'

'No.'

'Well, then, I don't know, either. He looks like good raw material to me. I like him. Vince likes him. The girls like him – that doesn't count; they like everybody.'

'He's likeable, I'll give you that.'

'He was really good with the kids at the party.'

'Why do we always assume that a guy who gets on

with kids is a great catch? Why don't we assume he's a paedophile?'

Anna put her glass down and gave me the look she gives me when she thinks I've left my brain in a jar by my bed. 'The kids liked him. You're going to hold this against him?'

'I'm not holding it against him. I'm just not holding it up as a sign that he's the world's greatest guy. When a man gets on with a bunch of small children, it's usually because they're all mingling at the same maturity level.'

One of those cartoon light bulbs appeared above Anna's head, or, rather, it should have, to add the finishing touch to the expression on her face. She said, 'I get it. I get what the problem is. It's obvious.'

'Do you think you could explain it to me?'

'Your problem is there is no problem. Don't you see? It's because there's no problem you think there's a problem when there's not.'

'I think you may have to speak slower so I can understand you.'

'Look, with every guy in LA, every guy you've dated, anyway, there's always some insurmountable issue that prevents any relationship they're in from getting off the ground. Right?'

'I guess.'

'I'm right. At the very least, it's the Hollywood seven-week itch. You know, that "How can I commit to you when every week there's someone younger and better looking, struggling to make it as an actress and therefore desperate enough to date me, coming along?" Don't you see? You're so used to dealing with guys with issues that, when you come across one without any, you think it's a problem. That's the problem.'

I tipped the rest of my Bellini down my throat. 'How do you know an issue won't kick in as soon as the next Hollywood starvelet crosses his path?'

'It won't,' she said.

'How do you know?'

'I just know.'

'Right.'

'OK, I know because of his ex.'

'Because of Kim? I'm not following your logic.'

'Well, she proves he's not in thrall to the seven-week itch. He didn't move on to a much younger, better-looking, bigger-breasted version of her, now did he? He moved on to you.'

'I see what you're saying. Thank you. I feel so much better now.'

She waggled a hand at me. 'You know what I mean.'

'I do. And, that's weird right there. Between Kim and me, he chooses me. He's either insane or a typical guy, wanting whatever he doesn't have. Neither bodes well. And how can she and I both be his type?'

'I think she may be everybody's type,' Anna said. 'Even so, you're not exactly chopped liver.'

'I think Jake's too sure of himself.'

'Well, he seems confident, yes –'

'No, I meant that he's sure about us, me and him.'

'This is a problem?'

'I know, I know,' I said. 'But it is. It's too good to be true. It makes me suspect something else is going on. I'm killing myself trying to figure out what it could be.'

Anna looked at me archly, like an actor in a BBC adaptation of a Jane Austen novel. 'You might find out if you returned one of his calls.'

We were no longer alone. The bartender was standing by our table with brand-new Bellinis. Going by the smarmy smile aimed at us by the man with the ponytail sitting at the bar, he was guilty of paying for them.

'Incoming,' Anna said. She picked up her new glass and raised it to its sponsor, who immediately slid off his barstool, to ooze on over. 'Look, this is all very simple. It's that Groucho Marx thing – that I-don't-want-to-belong-to-a-club-that'll-accept-me-as-a-member. Jake is sure about you, so you're unsure about him. It's your own self-worth issue. You just have to get over it. Which is why we're here. Therapy.'

Mr Ponytail stood by our table, trying to look casual, as if he were just passing our table and happened to notice the people who occupied it were in possession of drinks he'd paid for. Even by the low standards of a midlife-crisis bar, it was a little pathetic.

I'd called Anna earlier in the day to switch Friday-night drinks to a Thursday-night crisis summit. We chose the bar for the free therapy: spend five minutes with a man going through a midlife crisis and you'll feel great about yourself simply because you're not him. The free drinks are just an added bonus.

MLC bars, like all natural resources, should be used sparingly. In the past three years we've visited only a few times. There was the 'men in advertising are so sleazy I'm running out of agencies to work for' disaster that turned into 'the payout they gave me to avoid legal action means

I can put a deposit on a little house' celebration. Those were and are my issues.

The problems Anna brought to the bar were the 'Vince has two kids – I can't be with a man with two kids' crisis, which, after a month, developed into the 'I'm meeting his kids on the weekend – what if they don't like me?' meltdown. Then the 'Vince is never going to ask me to marry him' plight was followed closely by the 'Vince asked me to marry him' dilemma.

Most recently, but over a year ago now, it was me who called a meeting for the 'soap star left me for someone named Bambi – or was it Bimbo?' catastrophe.

'Let me guess,' Anna said. 'Your wife doesn't understand you.'

Mr Ponytail was genuinely surprised. 'How did you know?'

'A lucky guess,' I said. 'How long have you been married?'

'Three months,' he said.

'And this is your . . . second marriage? Third? Fourth? Say when.'

'Second.'

'Just a beginner, then,' Anna said.

'We got married in Vegas, when my divorce came through.' He sighed. 'I was sure this time it would be different. Women are all the same. They change as soon as you marry them.'

Anna and I traded looks, but said nothing. I desperately wanted to point out to Mr Ponytail that he was making a generalization about all women based on the only two stupid enough to marry him, but I restrained myself.

Experience has taught me that irony is often lost on men in midlife-crisis bars.

'The whole time you're going out with them, they let you think you're in charge. You think you're calling the shots. Then you get married and, bang, you find out she's been in charge all along. She only let you think you were in charge while you were dating.'

'It can't be all that bad,' I said.

'It was great before we were married.'

'Nothing's really changed,' Anna said. 'She was the boss then. She's the boss now.'

'She just tells me what to do now. She doesn't even pretend any more.'

'Does she make good decisions?'

'Well, yeah, she's smart. Smarter than me.'

'Then what's the problem?'

'I'm the man. I'm meant to call the shots.'

The old I've-got-a-penis-therefore-I-should-get-to-be-in-charge argument is an oft-repeated one in a place like this.

'Let me get this straight. You don't really want to call the shots. You just want her to pretend that you're calling the shots, like she did before you were married,' Anna said, gently. I'm beginning to suspect her upcoming nuptials are softening her.

'Is that too much to ask?'

Anna was being indulgent with him. That meant I was the bad cop in the situation. It was time for bad cop to intervene.

'Oh, cheer up already. So you're number two on the totem pole, so what? It could be a whole lot worse,' I said.

'How do you figure that?'

'Christ, think about it for a minute. You could actually be in charge.'

Mr Ponytail was clearly overwhelmed by this perspective. He gulped and blinked several times in terror of the sheerest kind.

'You're right, that would be worse,' he said. It came out in a whisper. He glanced at his watch. 'I have to get home. It's getting late.' It was a quarter to seven. 'Bye.'

'Bye,' Anna and I said in unison.

Mr Ponytail was already halfway to the door.

We grinned at each other. Our first crisis case of the evening was a success. Every time we've visited, we've scared at least one guy back to his family. We like to think we perform a community service in return for the money we save on therapists and cocktails.

An MLC bar also provides complete anonymity for our sessions. Unless all your friends are wealthy, middle-aged men with maturity problems, you're unlikely to bump into anyone you know. Until that evening we never had.

The comb-over was next in line bearing Bellinis. He turned out to be Dr Comb-over, a fifty-six-year-old veteran of five marriages and six children, who lived in a compound in Saudi Arabia. It was the only country willing to pay a general practitioner enough to cover child support in five countries. Back in California to visit his eldest child, he was leaving next week for Thailand to find the sixth Mrs Comb-over, preferably not much past her sixteenth birthday.

'You've been married five times,' Anna said.

Dr Comb-over concurred with her diagnosis.

'I don't suppose it's ever occurred to you that perhaps you might not be very good at marriage.'

Dr Comb-over agreed with this also. That was the reason he was going to marry a Thai teenage prostitute this time. She wouldn't have had the time or opportunity to develop high expectations of men.

'You're looking for a bride forty years your junior with whom you don't have a language in common,' I said. 'That might just be the reason why your next marriage won't work out either.'

No, he said, the reason marriages don't work out was because American women had taken this women's liberation business too far. Now that women expected not to be treated like shit, men just didn't stand a chance with them – and the same thing applied to women from Mexico, Malta, the Philippines and the People's Republic of China.

'It may also apply to girls from Thailand once they get past their eighteenth birthdays,' I said.

He said my attitude just proved his point about women like us, but that, in spite of that, he would be quite willing to have sex with either one or both of us. At which point we asked him to leave. Unlike Mr Ponytail, who was just a Cro-Magnon man needing to be dragged into a more recent century, Dr Comb-over was beyond help.

After the briefest of intervals, a fresh round of drinks arrived courtesy of Mr Toupee, who got up to follow them to our table. A courageous move on his part, after he'd seen us dispatch both of his fellow bar flies.

However, his courage had limits. He never made it to

our table, stopped in his tracks by another who reached our table first. Judging from the guilty look that appeared on Mr Toupee's face – he blushed to the glue of his hair – and the speed he used to propel his portly body out the door, I assumed the man was Catholic, scared away by the spectre of a priest in a place where he was hoping to sin.

I was a little startled myself. I managed to offer Father Giuliani a seat at our table, and to blurt out something stupid like, 'What's a nice priest like you doing in a place like this?'

Anna didn't say anything at all. Although I'd previously described him to her in some detail, it was the first time she'd seen Father Giuliani in person. She was busy trying not to drool.

'Hello, Anna. How do you do?' he said to her, after I'd introduced them. She managed only a squeaky sort of noise in reply that could have been 'hi' or 'fine' or 'eeee'.

Beauty, like everything else, is relative. In a room with the men on *People* magazine's Sexiest Man Alive list, Father Giuliani would be only slightly above average – perhaps not in the number-one position, but certainly well ahead of the Scientologists. In an MLC bar, it was hard to accept he was the same species as the other men present. No wonder Anna was taking it hard.

Spending more and more time with him, I was beginning to get used to his looks, but I still couldn't help but feel ridiculously pleased when he said, 'I've been looking for you.'

'For me? How did you find me?' I hoped I wasn't simpering.

'I asked your Patton. He told me you were here, then supplied me with a map, a car and a driver to get me here.'

'Sounds like Patton.'

The place had filled since Anna and I had come in. It was a far more crowded bar Father Giuliani faced when he took in his surroundings: the Sean-Connery-as-James-Bond era furnishings; the abundance of middle-aged, hair-challenged men, all dressed as if they imagined they were twenty years younger; and an odd assortment of younger women scattered intermittently here and there, who were now all staring intently at our table.

'What kind of place is this?' Father Giuliani wanted to know.

I explained the concept of an MLC bar to him and the role it played from time to time in our lives, taking care to dwell on the charitable work Anna and I perform here. Anna was, for all intents and purposes, mute.

Father Giuliani gave me the benefit of his warm, steady gaze. 'That explains a good deal. I have never seen so many obviously lost souls gathered together in one place like this.'

I laughed, but it did cross my mind that he might have been including me in their number.

FROM: Sydney Welles <sydneywelles@yahoo.com>
TO: God c/- professordumbledore@hogwartsschoolofwitch
    craftandwizardry.co.uk
DATE: Friday, June 3, 1.23 a.m.
SUBJECT: Hair loss

Dear God,

The more time I spend researching religion, the more apparent it is to me that the male sex invented it. Pinning the blame for the fall of mankind on the first woman they could find was only the beginning of religious gender discrimination.

Ever since, every job opening above middle management level – disciple, ark builder, Red Sea parter, wise man, saviour of mankind, etc. – has gone to a man. It's plain sexism and, in at least one case, also nepotism.

Even today, a woman cannot become a Catholic priest, even though it's a job routinely given to male paedophiles.

But by far the most convincing evidence that religions are man-made and made-for-men is that religions seem to have been invented to cover the signs of male pattern baldness. Two major religions both require men to wear little hats designed to cover bald spots. Both also encourage the growth of abundant facial hair to distract from receding hair at the temples. Thus allowing balding men the illusion of hair as well as piety. When in fact, they, along with their secular counterparts, are probably praying for their hair to grow back.

The evidence is overwhelming. There is only one way that

religion could get away with such flagrant sexism for so long. You, too, must be a man.

Sydney

If the midlife-crisis bar was a gathering place for lost souls, then American Airlines Flight 582, nonstop to St Louis, was hell.

I'd endured the LAX security measures requiring every reasonably attractive woman under the age of fifty to remove her jacket – even if the jacket was made of the lightest and sheerest of fabrics and would be classified, by the garment industry, as a blouse – while ugly men, wearing jackets that could hold enough arsenal to take out a dozen planes, strode through without being asked to disrobe.

The process had been slower than usual. I'd been stuck behind a heavily pregnant woman and her one-year-old baby, a round-headed, smiling boy, who fitted the day's terrorist profile. He was separated from his mother and thoroughly searched, during which he stopped smiling to scream like an infant banshee. The search turned up nothing; his diapers were clean.

Now, in a quiet area of the Admirals Club lounge, I nursed my sore head and a water bottle, alternating between curling up in a leather armchair and stretching out on the carpet while waiting for boarding time. Occasionally I'd take the time to glare at the people in suits invading the lounge. They had no right to look so pressed and fresh at five o'clock in the morning or to make cell phone calls when my head hurt. Who did they have to talk to at this time, anyway? Even on the East Coast it was only eight o'clock. Didn't these ignoramuses know people were trying to be hung over in here?

I'd spent the past three or four hours lying prone on my bed without falling asleep. At least then I was drunk and when I shut my eyes my bed seemed to pick up its feet and tiptoe around my room, which though slightly nauseating was also strangely lulling. Now, I felt as if I'd spent the past few hours wrestling with myself. The only bright side was that I was now too exhausted to think. It was thinking that had kept me from sleeping, and it was Father Giuliani who had started me thinking, though Anna and Larry had also inconsiderately gotten in on the act.

Father Giuliani had sought me out at the bar last night to tell me that some urgent Church business was calling him away and he wouldn't be able to accompany us on the trip. He could've just called or left a message with Patton, but he wanted to tell me in person. He's gracious and old-fashioned that way, preferring his human contact to be human. It was no big deal; it didn't affect the work as he was on the trip only as an observer.

The priest had ample opportunity to exercise his observation skills in the bar last night. He seemed intensely interested in its customers. I guess if you save souls for a living, then being in the midst of so many who needed redemption would make you itch to exercise your professional skills. In retrospect, I think he exercised those skills mainly on me, and quite efficiently, too, in the few minutes while Anna was being accosted by an ageing former child star, who'd managed to corner her on her way back from the bathroom in spite of being at least two feet shorter than she was.

'I've encountered men like this before. They are lost because the things they have based their lives on are things which essentially don't matter,' Father Giuliani said. He's not much of a one for gossip or small talk.

'What do you mean?'

'Judging from the cars parked outside they're all financially well off. They must have all the material things they could want. The boats, vacation homes, home theatre systems . . .'

'Is this the rich-man-getting-into-heaven and camel-passing-through-the-eye-of-a-needle thing?'

'In a way. My guess is these men have everything you can buy, but nothing of real worth. No purpose, no real relationships, nothing that means anything. They've spent their lives collecting the outward trappings of success without a thought for life's inner requirements. Going through the motions of life, but never getting to the heart of it. They own a hundred times more than most people in the world will ever have and yet, here they are, miserable.'

Call me paranoid – Anna does – but sometimes Father Giuliani, even when he's referring to others, makes me feel he's talking about me. 'Yes, here they are. In a bar avoiding their problems,' I said.

'We all do that to a certain extent.'

That, no doubt, is true, but did he have to look at me that way when he said it?

'People living in this country today have more than previous generations could've imagined, yet most feel lost and empty whether they admit it or not,' he said. 'But they fill the emptiness with diversions or material things, so they never see the real problem. They want love, so they read romances. They want a full life, so they watch others living on television. They want to impress others, so they buy a car they can't afford. We live in a time where who we are is defined by what we watch on television and what we are worth is calculated by the sum of our purchases.'

'Well, overconsuming is the national pastime,' I said. 'You know what's funny?'

He didn't know.

'From what I can tell, religion, in its purest form, has a great deal to do with being grateful for what you have. Recognizing that everything, even life itself, is something we've been given. Just about every religious belief system expounds gratitude as a virtue. You're expected to focus on what you have and be grateful. Right?'

'I would go along with that.'

'And advertising, in any form, exists solely to show people all the things they don't have, all the things they should want. It tells us that we need more, that we should never be satisfied. There's always a newer, bigger, smaller, better version we have to have. Advertising is in the business of whetting the appetite, of awaking greed. You can't deny that.'

'I do not intend to.'

'Well, don't you think that a religion wanting to advertise is, well, kind of incongruous? It's like . . .'

About then, I realized a few things:

1 I was about to tell a potential client of the agency that, if he gave us their business, it would be akin to God appointing Satan heaven's general manager.
2 The not-so-light tapping I had been feeling on my shoe for the past thirty seconds, since Anna had returned to the table, was Anna warning me to shut up.
3 I was, most probably, drunk.

'Sorry,' I said, 'I'm waffling. I think it's the champagne talking.'

Father Giuliani took a slow sip of his Negroni, his face not betraying any of the bitterness of the drink as he showed me the subtlety of his subterranean smile. 'I do not believe that. I think this may be the first time you have told me what you really think. Alcohol can do that. It is better than truth serum for some people.'

'It also makes me dance on bars and do other inadvisable things – do you know what I most like about Catholicism?'

The others assured me they didn't.

'I like that Catholics don't seem to have an issue with drinking, even though they have an issue with just about everything else. It must be because they can't be hypocritical about it, not when they serve wine in church.'

'It must be,' Father Giuliani said. 'After all, religions are never hypocritical.'

When he said that, I knew, in spite of the truth-inspiring abilities of alcohol, I'd lied. The thing I most liked about Catholicism was not the drinking. The thing I most liked about Catholicism was Father Giuliani.

He stayed for one drink, plenty of time, for a seasoned

operator like him, to make me suspect that I may have spent thirty years of life missing the point.

It wasn't something I wanted to dwell on. What I needed was a reprieve from my suspicions in the form of lighter company and more alcohol. I got both.

Larry strode into the bar at about ten o'clock. More accurately, he waddled in. At a certain blood-alcohol level, about .18, Larry moves as if his hands and feet have enlarged to twice their normal size. He walks like a cautious duck, his feet splayed out. It's slow going on flat ground, but he can waddle pretty fast downhill.

He waddled over to us.

'Girls! Girrls! Girrrls!' he said, not unlike a spruiker in front of a strip club.

Standing before our table, he was contemplating Anna and me as if we were drifting pleasantly in and out of his focal range. Larry is a notoriously happy drunk. His face begins smiling halfway through his second drink of an evening and doesn't stop unless LA County runs out of beer.

'Why don't you sit down and have another drink, Larry?' Anna said.

'Don't mind if I do. Don't mind if I do. I'm too old to be coy.' Larry slowly lowered himself onto a chair. He relaxed into his seat, but kept a sharp eye on his hands and feet, as if he suspected they'd lead him in a Ukrainian Cossack dance if left to their own devices. Once he was sure his extremities were behaving, he squinted at Anna until Anna came into focus for him.

'It's the lovely Ms Perry. Where the fuck have you been? I haven't seen you for . . . it's been so long, I don't remember how long it's been. Too long. Have you been on vacation?'

'No.'

'Then why haven't you been in at the office?'

'I don't work for you any more. I haven't for over a year now,' Anna said.

The ends of Larry's moustache lowered in surprise. 'No, not that long? What happened? Why wasn't I invited to your going-away party?'

'You were the life of the party.'

'I was?' Larry's moustache cheered up. 'Good party, was it? Don't seem to recall it.'

'Don't worry, it's a credit to your memory that you remember me at all, considering that you mass-murder brain cells every day.'

'My memory is perfect. My liver may be fucked, but my brain is in prime condition. I can recite the first poem I ever learned – in the first grade. Don't believe me, huh? Well, I can.'

'Go ahead,' Anna said.

'What? Oh, all right.' Larry paused, leaned heavily to his right for several seconds, stood up, almost straight, and cleared his throat.

'"If I Were King", by Alan Alexander Milne.' He paused for effect, and to treat us to a beery grin, then proceeded to recite the poem as if he'd spent the better part of his life touring with the Royal Shakespeare Company.

The whole bar took notice as he declared his sovereignty in the last three words of the poem – oratory rifle shots that ricocheted around the room. Larry sat down, pinkly triumphant.

'How was that, then?' he said to Anna.

'Pretty good.'

'Used to bring the house down. My parents dressed me up in a little suit with a little bow tie – made me recite to the dinner guests. Served me up just before my bedtime, between the second course and third course, along with a melon sorbet to cleanse the palate. Rotten people, my parents, torturing a kid like that. You see, I remember it all.' Larry tapped his finger against his skull. 'Nothing wrong with the old head.'

'You're very impressive,' Anna said.

Larry was still tapping his head with his finger, but the action had taken on an absent quality. 'Like it was yesterday . . . of course, I have no fucking idea what day yesterday was.'

'Wednesday,' I said.

Larry looked puzzled. 'What?'

'Yesterday was Wednesday.'

'It was? Why the hell didn't you say so sooner? This is a celebration. I've always liked Wednesday. Come on, we've wasted ten minutes already.'

He caught the attention of a waiter, ordered a cleanser for himself – Larry-speak for a beer – and 'more of that sweet crap the women are drinking' for us. Admonishing the waiter not to be shy, Larry gave him temporary custody of a credit card so major it could purchase the place.

Larry surveyed the room. 'What are you girls doing in this dump? You might be past your prime, but you can do better than these guys.'

'Thanks,' Anna said. 'But it's you we ought to be worried about. Why are you here?'

'Ah, well, that depends on where I am.'

'You don't know?'

He beamed at us affectionately, Larry, the beeriest of them all. 'No fucking clue,' he said, falling into a pleasant, private reverie until the alcohol arrived. He came to in time to frown at the bartender who had brought our drinks, which by any standards but Larry's were normal-sized. 'These are on the small side. You may as well start pouring the next round as soon as you get back.'

Larry then frowned at me. 'What's wrong with you? Why are you so quiet?'

Just sitting here wallowing in existential angst in the wake of a priest who knows just how to get me to take a step back and notice how futile life is, or, at least, how futile my life is. 'Not much to say, I guess,' I said.

'I know what's wrong with you. It's the damn Church. If I had to come up with a way to sell them, I'd be crying in my champagne cocktail, too,' he said.

'I'm not crying. It's not the Church.'

'It should be. We don't land the account, we'll be fucked for the year. The vultures at Megacom will eat us for breakfast. I'll have to sack everybody. You know what the corporate boys are like.'

I didn't know. I'd never met a soul from the Megacom Group, the holding company that owned our agency network and about a third of the other advertising agencies on the planet. But I did know, from experience, that the minutest of changes in figures, made by a faceless number cruncher at the Megacom level, could upset my life entirely.

'OK, now I'm worried.'

'Good,' Larry said. 'Worry a lot. You'll have it sorted when I get back, won't you?'

'Where are you going?'

'Switzerland. It's that time of year again.'

Larry meant it was time for his annual detox at an exclusive Swiss clinic, catering to well-heeled addicts the world over. The staff-to-patient ratio is incredible – twenty-to-one or close to it – and the facilities on a par with the three or four hotels regarded as the best in the world.

Larry is only moderately wealthy as a result of his career in advertising. He can afford the clinic because he's obscenely rich in his spare time. He's been afflicted with money since birth – the scion of an old tobacco family with numbered bank accounts to pay his respects to in Geneva, on his way to the rehab clinic in Zurich.

'Couldn't you wait to go until after this Church thing is over?'

'Nope, can't wait. Doctor says with any kind of delay there's a slight chance of death.'

'Will you be back before they make a decision?'

'I think so. Depends how long it takes to dry out this time.'

'What do I do if I run into trouble?' Larry might be drunk most of the time, but I operate effectively within the agency only under his aegis; according to general agency opinion, I'm a little too young and a lot too female for my position.

'Do what you can.'

'I've no idea how we're going to approach this,' I said. 'But at least the questionable morality of selling religion doesn't seem to be an issue.'

'That was never going to be an issue. We ought to have seen that from the start. People will never see the real issues, not when they can focus on the things that don't matter. Have you learned nothing from presidential election campaigns? Getting Joe Public to agree that God can be sold is the easy part. If you don't say it's an issue, he doesn't know it's an issue. Getting him to buy our brand of God is the trick. What have you tried?'

'All the usual ways of positioning it. Nothing's working. We've tried appealing to guilt, the need to belong, the need for pleasure, the need to escape, everything. Even tried drumming up a sense of entitlement about it all, but that didn't work even though it always works in this market. No one's biting at anything.'

'What do you think the problem is?'

'I think the problem is advertising. As an industry, we've trained consumers to look for a product benefit, and we've trained them to be sceptical about that benefit, unless we can provide them with a reason to believe it. You just can't sell snake oil any more. Religion, as a product, is snake oil. The product benefits are all things that can't be proven or demonstrated. How do you package heaven when no one has ever seen it?'

Larry was nodding in agreement. 'You're going to have to pull something out of your ass.'

'Maybe we should recommend a brand campaign. Take the spiritual high road; forget about product benefits.'

'That works for Nike and only Nike. Besides, the Church wants measurable results. They need to put butts on pews, especially after all the scandal. They won't buy a campaign that's too hard to monitor.'

'Maybe you just can't sell religion.'

'Not true. Thank God. There are TV evangelists flying between their mansions on Lear jets because people are buying what they are selling, which, essentially, is nothing. You can sell religion. It's just that no one has figured out how to do it with integrity.'

'I don't have a working hypothesis to take into quantitative research yet. And I've no idea when I'll have one.'

'Hell,' said Larry, 'don't look at me like that. I don't know either. This wise old guy exterior is just a facade. I look like Methuselah, but only because I drink too much. I'm just a normal guy. I get up every morning. I shave. I have a beer. I go to work. That's all. Just a normal fucking guy. I don't have any answers.'

Neither did I.

☦

'Just call the poor guy,' Anna said, as Larry's car – sans Larry, as he was visiting another bar while his driver dropped us home – pulled up in front of my place. She was, of course, referring to Jake. She seemed to have appointed herself head of his fan club.

I looked around at the tan leather and burled wood interior of the golden Rolls-Royce we were in. 'I wonder how much this set Larry back?'

'Call him.'

'Can't. It's too late to call him now, and I'm getting on a plane at six o'clock in the morning, which is too early to call him.'

'Where are you going?'

'It's that research thing I told you about, the three-city sample tour – St Louis, Houston and Vegas.'

'I thought you said you didn't have to go on that trip.'

'I did say that. Strictly speaking, I don't really have to go, but I thought I'd keep my hand in . . . keep an eye on things . . . this is a really big project . . . if anything went –'

'You're running away. From Jake.'

'You know, the world does not revolve around Jake. I'm not running away from anyone. It's work. Unlike those in the back of the car who are marrying money, I have to work for a living.'

'You're running away.'

'I am not.'

'Are too.'

'Am not.'

'You are. And you know it.'

'I'm not.'

'Are too, are too, are too, are too.'

'Am not – it's too late in the evening, I mean, early in the morning, for this. I have a cab picking me up in four and a half hours. I have to go.'

'Call him from the road. They have phones where you're going, right? Your cell phone still works?'

'I will if I can. If I'm not too busy.'

'Yeah, right,' Anna said. 'Let me just say this for the record. You're making a big mistake. You'll regret this. I'll be saying "I told you so" just as soon as I possibly can.'

'That certainly gives me something to look forward to.'

'Me, too,' she said.

✝

My frequent flyer status is such that I automatically get upgraded if there's a seat available in first class. The lady who sat behind the desk in the lounge, her hair in the smoothest French roll I'd ever seen, had accomplished the upgrade with a remarkable lack of fuss. I guess that if you can do something like that with your hair, then everything else is easy.

I looked forward to taking an uninterrupted nap in that slightly larger seat, in the part of the plane where the flight attendants don't scowl at you for existing – well, not as much, anyway.

The early morning flight to St Louis did not yield any sleep. A woman seated behind me, with an especially loud, nasally voice, made the confines of the plane seem even smaller. Everyone breathed a sigh of relief when she announced she would don a pair of headphones and watch the movie. That just made things worse.

Five minutes into the film, she declared, and most of the occupants of both cabins heard, that it was the worst film she'd ever seen in her entire life. That didn't prevent her from watching it, and providing running commentary for those of us trying to sleep.

Trafalgar Square appeared on screen, complete with a subtitle that stated it was Trafalgar Square, and she said, 'It's Trafalgar Square.'

There was no answer from her husband. That didn't deter her.

The pigeons of Trafalgar Square were pictured. 'Birds,' she said.

And in case some of us missed that: 'It's birds.'

Still no answer from her husband, but it was becoming

apparent she was quite content to carry on the conversation at full volume, all by herself.

'There are a lot of birds.'

Pause.

'It's just like that Alfred Hitchcock movie.'

Pause.

'*The Birds.*'

Pause.

'I hate this film.'

Pause.

'Hilary Swank is in this. I said Hilary Swank is in this.'

Pause.

'Why did she do this film?'

Pause.

'She has an Academy Award, for goodness sake.'

Pause.

'For that other film, the one where she's a boy.'

Pause.

'What was it called?'

Pause.

'This is the worst film I've ever seen.'

Pause.

'Doesn't she look just like my cousin Sue?'

Pause.

'Don't you think she's the spitting image of Sue?'

Those of us who had never seen Sue could not agree or disagree.

'She looks just like her. They could be twins.'

Pause.

'Or cousins. Maybe Sue is a relative. That means we

could be related, too. Did you hear that? We could be related to Hilary Swank.'

Finally, the air stewards began plying the woman and her husband with the Napa Valley sparkling wine they'd offered us with breakfast. I'd refused it, having gotten my drinking out of the way the night before.

Saturating the woman in alcohol did not shut her up; it only caused her to change subject, to her son, whose twenty-one years of life kept her vocal cords busy for the next hour.

Five minutes before we landed, the woman berated her husband for spilling some of his drink, 'Free champagne. Who spills free champagne? I'm married to the stupidest man on earth. The stupidest man on earth.'

The stupidest man on earth didn't seem to mind his moniker. He'd kept his equilibrium the entire trip. He even seemed happy, though that could've been the champagne.

I guess that's the way most people get through life. They don't realize, or refuse to realize, they're living in hell.

FROM: Sydney Welles <s.welles@fbmm.com>
TO: God c/- god@google.com
DATE: Monday, June 6, 8.02 a.m.
SUBJECT: Compatibility

Dear God,

I told your priest that advertising and religion are incongruous partners, but I've been thinking about it since and, when you really look at them, advertising and religion have a lot in common. Both:

1 have their fair share of false prophets
2 are in the business of getting the public to part with their money
3 distort the truth as it suits them
4 have no basis in science
5 claim miracles do occur
6 want you to believe their version of the truth is better than the other guy's version of the truth
7 use fear, uncertainty and doubt as marketing tools
8 are fond of making exaggerated claims
9 promise acceptance and validation by your peers if you buy what they're selling
10 offer intangible promises that can't be proven one way or the other

If you drink this sacramental wine you'll go to paradise, or, if you drink this beer, women barely in bikinis will wrestle each other in front of you, and this, for some reason, represents paradise for most men. What's the difference, really?

Best,
Syd

PS How is Elvis? Everybody wants to know.

One of the peculiar things about the United States is that fun is distributed on a geographical basis. It's contained entirely in a number of designated sites.

Childhood fun is enclosed in a series of artificial worlds, or theme parks, where junk food and rides – which cause you to vomit junk food – equal a good time.

Adult fun is allocated space in the real world. At times it has entire cities at its disposal. In the real world, fun is all about giving your money to a casino or giving it to a stripper. An adult good time always involves alcohol, which also causes vomiting. It also sometimes requires a silly item of clothing, so that those around you will be able to tell that you're having fun.

People behave so badly in fun places you'd think they didn't have any fun at home. This is probably true. For example, there's no fun in Houston. That's understandable. They keep NASA and oil companies there. If they had fun, something would be bound to blow up.

The reason adult fun is restricted to certain areas is because fun, in the adult sense, is equated with sin, in the mortal sense. God doesn't like it when you have fun. So, to avoid the wrath of God, people don't want to live in fun places. They don't want them anywhere near their homes. But even God understands that a person has to work, so all business conventions are held in fun places.

While there are other notable repositories, Las Vegas is the main US storage facility of fun for grown-ups, especially ageing frat boys, conventioneers and anyone who thinks getting a hotel room at a cut rate and then losing thousands of dollars in that hotel's casino is a good deal.

In spite of being in a casino, in Vegas, I wasn't having fun. The joy that comes from depositing a mortgage payment into a slot machine eluded me.

'What about a show?' Noah pointed at an indoor billboard featuring several women wearing only strategically positioned rhinestones and feathers. 'They seem to be very talented dancers.'

'They're topless dancers,' I said.

'They're not,' Noah said. 'They're wearing – things.'

He was right. They had rhinestones where their nipples should have been.

We watched security guards round up a nearby man, who didn't meet the dress code, and escort him out of the room. While the official dress code was more or less anything goes, the man in question was barefoot, claiming to have lost his shoes and socks somewhere near the blackjack table. According to one of the security guards, several people had complained about his foot odour.

'Amazing,' Noah said. 'You can piss in a plastic cup in here, but you can't go barefoot.'

'The irony,' I said.

'It would've been more ironic if he'd lost his shirt. What about a magic show?' Another poster featured a man with a supernatural tan, wearing a sparkling white suit. He was holding an orb of light in one hand, staring out from the wall in that intense, maniacal way only magicians can.

Both Patton and I pulled faces.

'We're not going to get into anything good at the last minute,' Noah said. 'We must accept this and choose from the available crap.'

'It's all class,' I said, 'but I think I'll give it a miss. You guys go ahead.'

'You're being such an old woman,' Noah said. 'You didn't come out in St Louis, either.'

'I had to have dinner with my parents. They drove in from Chicago. I couldn't very well blow them off.'

'Sure you could.'

'I'll see you back at the hotel,' I said.

A waitress bearing a tray walked past in what would have been a toga if it were a lot longer, taking all of Noah's attention from me.

'OK, then,' he said. 'See ya.'

'I'll come with you, ma'am.' Patton was trying to take up as little space as possible, uncomfortable in this den of iniquity.

'No, you stay,' I said. 'You and Noah have a good time. Befriend one of these poor women who can't afford tops.'

'I'd rather come with you, ma'am.'

'You're old enough to drink and gamble, aren't you?'

'Yes, ma'am. As of January, ma'am.'

'Then go drink and charge it to the project. Tell you what, if it makes you feel better, I'll give you a research assignment. Find out how many of these people will be in church on Sunday.'

'All of them, I bet,' Noah said. 'Hypocrites.'

'We're here,' I said.

'We're here,' he said, 'but we don't go around thinking we're better than us because we spend an hour a week sitting in a building with a bunch of other hypocrites, wishing we were some place else –'

The T-shirt Noah had picked out for the evening read: 'Remember that Jesus loves you. Because the rest of us think you're an asshole.' He was clearly in an aggressive mood.

'OK, I get the point,' I said.

'What are you going to do?'

'I'm going to head to my room,' I said.

'Do you want us to walk you?'

'It's in the building. I'll be fine. Take care of the little one.'

Patton drew himself up to his full six foot three and a half at being thus addressed.

'It won't kill you to have a good time,' I said.

He looked pained, as if it would.

✝

I walked around for a while looking for the elevators to my room. They proved elusive, shrouded by the noise, lights and garish decor of the casino. Instead, just past the high rollers' room, I discovered a bar. It was dark, quiet and all but empty. I needed to escape the desperate atmosphere of the casino – the collective delirium of hundreds of people, each believing wealth would be theirs in the immediate future, despite the overwhelming odds against that ever happening, even in the infinite future. I escaped into the bar.

Ignoring the crunchy quality of the tired carpet under my feet, I made my way over to the bar, perching on a sticky stool. The barman, looking as if he'd shaved for the very first time that evening, hovered behind the bar polishing a glass. He asked what I'd like to drink as soon as I sat.

I've noted, on more than one occasion, that my alcohol consumption has gained in momentum since I broke up with Matt the Rat. Actually, the escalation may have dated from the time I started going out with him. But now that I was in a town where everybody seemed to be drinking – that is, when they weren't busy throwing away their life savings or spending quality time with sex industry employees of their preferred gender – I didn't feel like drinking at all.

'I don't know. A Coke?'

The bartender showed his disappointment in me. 'We can do better than that.'

The bar had three other customers, one sitting at the bar, like me. In a corner, at a table, two middle-aged, moustached men, dressed like cowboys, were arguing. When their dispute became louder for a moment, the snippet I overheard made me think that they were disagreeing about the respective quality of two racehorses, although, in retrospect, they could also have been discussing two fast women.

The bartender put a martini glass in front of me, and filled it from a little jug, which he also put in front of me. The liquid in the glass looked as if it could be the world's dirtiest martini, but tasted just like fresh apple juice.

The bartender, once I was served, did not appear to

be the chatty sort. He went back to polishing the same glass he was polishing before; the glass he'd continue to polish for the rest of the evening. I was therefore forced to attempt conversation with the other person seated at the bar. He was the sort of guy for whom a light blue button-down shirt worn over a white T-shirt and teamed with jeans and sneakers would always be the height of fashion.

'So,' I said, 'are you here for a convention or something?'

Brightening, he said, 'No, actually. It's a funny story. An old college buddy of mine — he's a vacuum cleaner salesman — rang me out of the blue and told me he'd won a trip for two to Vegas. It was for selling more vacuum cleaners than anyone else in the whole region for all of February. That's a tough month to win. On account of it has less days in it to make the numbers.'

I nodded, to show I was impressed at the February showing.

'Anyway, he didn't want to bring his wife — she didn't want him to come at all — so he asked me. I'm waiting for him now. I haven't seen him since college. Can you believe that? We're going to have so much fun.'

'This is where they keep it.'

He nodded in a way that made it clear he wasn't exactly sure what he was agreeing to. His left hand was curled around his glass. I checked his ring finger. It was occupied.

'What about your wife? Is she here, too?'

'My wife? No, she's home. She didn't want me to come, either.'

'And, yet, here you are.'

'I'm going to do cultural things, too. Going to see the Eiffel Tower tomorrow.'

'Isn't that in France?'

'They have one here. Why go further?'

'Why, indeed.'

'You going to head out?'

'Me? No. No fun for me. I'm here for work – ostensibly. My best friend thinks I'm here because I'm running away from my life. She thinks I'm running away from someone, actually. This is my third city in four days, so I guess I'm doing a pretty good impression of being on the run. It's one of those if-it's-Tuesday-I-must-be-in-Texas trips.'

'Er . . .' he said.

'Problem is, she's right. I am running away from him. Not just by taking this trip, either. Since he and I, you know, got together, I've been on my way – this trip is just a kind of a physical exclamation point to the journey. You know what I mean?'

He didn't answer, but that didn't really matter. I was on a bit of a roll.

'The thing is – well – Jake seems just about perfect. But, you and I both know there's no such thing. I mean, look at you. Your wife married you in good faith, and here you are about to play poker with your kids' college funds – or to get friendly with a lap dancer. Either way, I'm sure it's not what she had in mind when she got dressed up in that white lace airship, floated down the aisle, and said I do.'

'I –'

'The world has unrealistic expectations when it comes to love. I, on the other hand, don't. That's why I prefer dating people who wear their flaws on their sleeves. It's better to know upfront. However, if I continue dating the seemingly perfect Jake, the unrealistic expectations will set in. I'd just be setting myself up for a fall. What's the point? It'll end, anyway. This way, it ends quickly. No one gets hurt. No one gets left at home while others go to Vegas.'

'Er ... um ...' He glanced around the bar for a way out of the conversation.

'It's just like you said. Why go further? Although, in the case of the Eiffel Tower, it may be worth seeing the real thing over a replica in Vegas – but that's just my opinion.'

He was cheerful again when he spotted someone outside the door of the bar, looking in. 'Here's my friend Richard.'

Richard approached us. He was dressed in the same fashion as his friend, but, unlike his friend, had gone to the effort of combing his hair. Slicked down with a sticky-looking substance, it featured the most severe side part I'd seen outside of grade school.

The two men greeted each other not as old college buddies who hadn't seen each other in years, but in an apprehensive way, as if any minute someone would tap them on the shoulder and tell them they had to go home.

'Are you ready to go?' Richard said.

His friend obediently stood up and, together, they scampered out of the bar as if a thousand disapproving wives were after them.

The bartender had discovered a whole pineapple somewhere under the counter and was holding it up to show me. 'Pineapple juice?'

'Hit me.'

A man in a tuxedo blew in the room. He took the seat on my left, placing a violin case on the bar.

'The usual, Nick,' he said.

I was immediately impressed; I've always wanted to be able to walk into a bar, plop myself down, spout 'the usual' and have the bartender produce it.

The newcomer was a clean-shaven, slightly slimmer version of Santa Claus. He had merry eyes, pink cheeks and a smile powered by the same batteries they put in that toy bunny that plays the drums.

The usual turned out to be a tall pink drink adorned with a slice of pineapple, a plastic flamingo and a pink-and-white striped straw.

'Pink lemonade,' the man said. 'I don't drink.'

I motioned my head towards the violin case. 'Are you a gangster?'

The man clapped his hands together. 'Oh, you think I'm wicked. I love it. I'm afraid I'm nothing so exciting. Just a violinist.'

'Have you been out violin-ing?'

'I'm part of an eleven-piece orchestra for the lounge act – a tribute show.'

'Who's the act a tribute to?'

'It varies. Depends who died.'

I pointed to myself. 'I'm Sydney,' I said.

'Hello.' He slid off his stool and bowed. 'I'm Bartholomew. Bart, if you like.'

We shook hands.

'Do you want me to play you something?'

'You take requests?'

'Naturally – only don't ask me to play "La Vie en rose". Everyone always asks me to play "La Vie en rose". I'm sick to death of it. I never want to play it again as long as I live.'

'Go on, play "La Vie en rose".'

'Oh, all right.'

The men in the corner sidled two tables closer to us while Bart played. Everyone in the bar was silent until he finished.

'Where does one learn to play like that?'

'Boston Philharmonic. Played with them for years and years, until I came out of the closet, left my wife and Boston, and came here. Now it's weddings, parties, bar mitzvahs and playing the dinner show for people who don't know the difference between a violin and a viola.' Bartholomew put down his violin. 'But enough about me. What about you? What ails you?'

'How'd you know that anything ails me?'

'You're in this place of your own free will, aren't you?'

'Good point.'

'I've changed my mind. Let's talk about me some more. How old do you think I am?' Bart said. 'How old?'

I squinted at him. 'Forty-nine.'

'No!' He laughed, thrilled with my guess. 'I'm over sixty.'

'Are you sure?' I squinted at him again.

Bart was so pleased he wanted to perform again. He picked up his violin and tucked it under his chin in one smooth, well-rehearsed movement. His bow danced to the theme from *Carmen*, which he followed with a series of show tunes, each gayer than the last. The bar filled with people, all drawn by the spontaneous concert. How they had heard the sound of a lone violin above the din of the floor of a casino I'll never know.

'You know, Bart,' I said, when he took a break, 'if you weren't already married, over sixty, gay and a teetotaller, I'd marry you in a minute.'

Pleasure tinted his round cheeks. 'Oh, you're just saying that.' He patted my knee. 'You know why else you ought not marry me?'

'Why?'

'No life insurance. No point marrying an old man if there's no life insurance. I don't have any kind of insurance at all. Don't believe in it.'

'Why not?'

'I love to gamble, but I gamble to win. Insurance is gambling to lose. You're putting money on yourself to lose. Life insurance is the worst. You bet money on yourself to die. You live, you lose. The only way to collect big is if you die young and, then, you're not around to collect it. It's a hell of a scam. The only thing we know for sure is that we'll die. Why bet money on it happening sooner rather than later?'

Bart picked up his instrument again. He placed the bow between his knees, holding it so it stuck out in front of him at a 45-degree angle, turned the violin upside down and began to play a tune he claimed was an Irish jig by rubbing the fiddle against the bow.

I sat there stunned, not because of his unorthodox

violin playing, but because he'd just inadvertently told me how to sell the Catholic Church.

I found a pen and envelope in my purse and jotted down the outline of the idea, then, realizing that there was something in the envelope, I peeked inside and found fifty unspent per diem dollars. I tucked the money into Bart's violin case, while he was busy fiddling between his legs.

FROM: Sydney Welles <s.welles@fbmm.com>
TO: God c/- info@hollywoodjesus.com
DATE: Friday, June 10, 12.32 a.m.
SUBJECT: Celestial Incompetence?

Dear God (Christian God to be precise),

The Bible claims you created the earth, the sun, the stars and the universe for the benefit of humanity, making us the most significant citizens of the universe. It claims this even though:

1 You gave us our own planet and we've already nearly ruined it and are now poised to destroy the only ecosystem we can actually survive in.
2 You tell us we're the only occupants of the entire universe, yet all we seem to do is squabble viciously over bits of oily desert.
3 You made us in your own image, yet you have us tucked away in a backwater solar system in an unfashionable galaxy, as if you're embarrassed by us.

But, according to the Bible, we are your greatest achievement, the pinnacle of your creative power, your magnum opus.
If we're really the best you can do, you ought not to give up your day job.

Sincerely,
Sydney

# FISHER BENNET McMAHON & MAY

4848 Abott Way Los Angeles CA 90066 USA

310-807-3000 t    310-807-5000 f


Charles Turner
Los Angeles Times
202 W. 1st St.
CA 90012

Dear Charles,

Thank you for your profuse and abject apologies. Consider them accepted and yourself forgiven, even though they could've been a little more profuse and a whole lot more abject.

It does sound as if you've been busy.

It is a good feng shui practice to get rid of old, unwanted things on a regular basis. I'm pleased that you're doing what you can to unclutter your life and allow your energy to flow freely. But I'm curious. What exactly made you dump your girlfriend?

What happened? Did you just turn forty? Did she just turn twenty-six and become too old for you? Or did you see a more recent model of her and decide to upgrade?

For your sake, I hope you find a new girlfriend who:

a) likes your new Porsche
b) likes your new Ferrari
c) likes your new Harley-Davidson

d) is too young to recognize any of the above as midlife-crisis accessories

If the answer is d), you can use one of those accessories to take her to her high school prom. Personally, I'd go with the Harley. You'll be the envy of all those teenage boys.

Yours (but only in theory),
Sydney

In spite of arriving in the office just before one o'clock after a turbulent flight, only to face what looked like ten hours of back-to-back meetings, I was so cheerful and efficient at work that several people complained to management.

Everything concerning the Catholic Church account is supposed to be top secret, even within the agency. Any information regarding it is shared on a need-to-know basis, only with those directly working on it. This means that everyone who works at Fisher Bennet and its subsidiary companies knows more about the project than I do. The whole agency was keen to find out how our research groups had gone.

I left most of the recounting up to Noah, as recounting is one of his favourite things to do at work – that, taking naps, and eating plain Saltine crackers, starting at a corner and nibbling his way through like a hamster, one after the other, for hours on end. I had work to do or, rather, I had meetings to attend, but I stuck around long enough to listen to the retelling of a couple of trip highlights.

In Houston Noah had trumped himself, producing a focus group made up entirely of society matrons and their debutante daughters. He did so at extremely short notice, too, after I'd decided to make the trip at the last minute. The group was convened to cheer me up, as in Noah's opinion I'd been as depressing as shit the past week or so. In that group, I did see some of the biggest hair I'd ever seen in my life.

Another notable session of the trip was also in Houston – a one-on-one interview with a motherly, middle-aged woman who'd driven into town for us. She brought a small basket of freshly baked home-made cookies with her, most of which she fed to Noah, whom she took to straight away. Mostly because his T-shirt du jour read, 'Jesus Votes Republican.'

'You're a good boy,' she said. 'Your mama must be proud. My eldest is your age, but he didn't turn out so good. He went to college, become a lawyer and got all kinds of liberal ideas. He's one of them en-viron-mental-ists. He married a foreigner. We all know why she married him, don't we?'

Noah and I looked at each other before I asked why.

'For the green card, what else? That's what all them foreigners want, to come to this country and live off social security. She's Italian, from Queens. She says that's in New York. Bet she still needs a green card, though. She's one of them lawyers, too. Why did he have to go and marry her? After what them Romans did to Jesus, too.' She sniffed and shook her head.

'A lawyer working to save the planet doesn't sound like such a bad thing,' I said.

Trying to console her was a mistake.

She sniffed at me. 'If God didn't want us to make things outta wood, he wouldn't have given us the forests. Look at Jesus. He was a carpenter. Are you telling me it's wrong to do what Jesus done?'

'No, of course not.'

'It just breaks a mother's heart when her boy grows up wrong.' She sighed, rather melodramatically in my humble opinion. 'The Lord gives us our crosses to bear. I just don't know why I have to bear so many.'

She pulled out a tissue and dabbed at her eyes.

'John Thomas, that's my son, he shamed us all when he and his lawyer friends kicked up a big fuss about them drilling for oil in the swamp over there in Louisiana. Went to court and everything. Upset over an ugly swamp. I mean, where are we going to get oil from if we don't get it from the swamp? We need our own oil. Everyone knows that. How else are we going to run our cars? Otherwise we got to buy it from them terrorists over there in the middle of the east.'

Noah coughed violently. She turned to him with concern. 'Are you all right, honey?' She gave him a couple of thumps on the back before continuing.

'Now, my other boy, James Edward. We wanted him to join the army, but he won't do that on account of they don't take homosexuals in the army. There, I went and said it. That's what he is. As soon as we found out we kicked him outta the house. And ain't spoken to him since.'

'You kicked him out?' I said.

Noah was having another coughing fit.

'There, there, dear,' she said. She poured him a glass of water from the jug on the table. 'Drink that up. Have another cookie.' She looked pleased when he took a cookie. She forgot to offer me one.

'No, he ain't my son no more. The Lord ain't gonna let him in his house, so I don't gotta let him in mine.'

I thought it wise not to say anything more. Noah was concentrating on his cookie.

'I pray for James Edward every day. I pray that he don't become Catholic as well as homosexual. Them Catholics take all the homosexuals in. Maybe this advertising business might help him. Maybe when they show Jesus talking on the TV, Cricket – that's what we call James Edward at home – will see he was wrong. Maybe then he can come visit with us. If he gets saved by Jesus from being a homosexual, I'll forgive him. That's the Christian thing to do.'

She patted Noah on the hand and put the basket with the remaining cookies down well within his reach, well out of mine.

'But I can't let him back in the house if he's ever been in one of them Catholic churches.'

✝

The rest of the day passed in a blur of meetings. I attended meetings that couldn't start because half the agency was supposed to be in attendance and most of them were late; meetings that were really just group therapy for those who called them; meetings that were ego exercise sessions for those so senior in management they no longer had any kind of function to perform; and meetings with no discernible purpose at all.

All the meetings had two things in common. They all ran overtime, and no food was served. I found both annoying, as I'd been up since six, had spent my time with some of Nevada's oddest Catholics, and had had nothing to eat except for a couple of Saltines filched from Noah's supply.

When I'd escaped the final meeting of the day, a brainstorming session to which most of the attendees forgot to bring their brains, it was late and I was tired. It was almost ten o'clock on a Friday night and about a quarter of the agency was still here working. That was not surprising. As well as the Church project, two other new business pitches were under way, and all of them were conducted over and above the normal workload for the clients we did have. At the agency, 24/7 is merely the starting point for a typical working work.

I was heading back to my office, to gather up my things and leave, when a voice called out my name from the office that had temporarily been assigned to Father Giuliani. It was Larry's voice, but it sounded thicker, higher than usual, as if it came from a Muppet of Larry, rather than Larry himself.

The priest's office is a small meeting room, made over. The remarkable woman who manages the agency's physical space and is in charge of assigning offices had obviously assigned this one for the benefit of the whole agency. The priest was displayed like some precious artefact under glass, clearly visible from hip-height to ceiling. In his office, privacy, like God, could be found only on your knees.

His feet on the footstool, in one of a pair of original Eames lounge chairs, Larry, using both hands, held on to an unopened bottle of beer as if it were keeping him afloat in the sea of whatever it was he was swimming in.

He was helplessly happy. Squinting at me, he said, 'Why are you fuzzy around the edges like that?'

'I'm not – in this case, I think fuzziness is in the eye of the beholder,' I said.

'Oh, OK, fair enough. Do you have a bottle opener?'

'Not on me. Where's Father Giuliani?'

'I don't know. Does he have a bottle opener? I need one.' Larry held up his beer and tipped it upside down. 'It doesn't come out otherwise.'

'Give it to me.'

Face pickled in a smile, he clutched the bottle to his chest. 'It's mine.'

'I'm not trying to steal it from you. If you give it to me, I can go open it and bring it back.'

Larry looked at his bottle, at me, and at his bottle again. 'No.'

I picked up the phone on Father Giuliani's desk. Through it I asked Patton to find and bring a bottle opener to me. To the credit of his training, he asked only, 'Wine or beer, ma'am?' before hanging up to execute the task.

Gratitude glowed on Larry's face – very pinkly in his nose and cheeks.

'You'll go far,' he said. Then he blinked rather slowly. Five minutes passed between his shutting his eyes and opening them again, during which time I visited the bathroom and Father Giuliani returned to his office.

'When did you get back?' He half-sat on the edge of his desk, speaking quietly so as not to disturb Larry.

'Around lunchtime. And you?'

'About half an hour ago. I came by to pick up a few

papers I'd forgotten. I didn't realize my office would be so lively at this time of night. How was the trip?'

'We got some interesting stuff. I'll take you through it first thing next week.'

'And you? How are you?'

'Fine.' Convincing, I thought, but the priest didn't buy it.

'Do you want to tell me about it?'

I wasn't surprised to find that I did. Ever since the elevator incident, he had that effect on me.

Patton tapped at the door, three bottle openers and one Swiss army knife in hand. Larry opened his eyes.

'Good work,' he said, when Patton was close enough for Larry to make out the tools he brandished. 'You look familiar.'

'It's me, Uncle Larry. Patton.'

'General? Is that you? Are you sure?'

'Yes, sir.'

'You never used to be so much taller than me.'

'He's not,' I said. 'You're sitting down.'

'That explains a great deal.' Larry stood and, after swaying for several seconds in a violent wind not felt by the rest of us, reached out to put an arm around Patton's shoulder. 'Let's go get a bottle of beer for each of these fine devices you've found. Don't tell your mother.'

'No, sir.'

Larry took one of the bottle openers, a waiter's friend, from Patton and handed it to me, saying, 'Hold on to this for next time. For when I get back.'

I put it in my pocket for the time being. 'Have a good time in Zurich.'

'It's not fucking possible to have a good time in Zurich. That's the point.'

'You take care, Larry,' I said.

'You take care of my agency.'

'I'll do my best.'

'S'all you can do. See you when I'm sober. You, too, priest.'

Together, Patton and Larry toddled out of the office, tall, slim versions of Tweedledum and Tweedledee – before Dee spoilt Dum's nice new rattle.

Father Giuliani settled back behind the desk in his chair, a black leather swivelling affair, his elbows on the armrests and hands constructing a pyramid below his chin. From there he studied me. Honeyed light, from a recessed setting directly above his head, created dramatic highlights and lowlights all over his person, and a filler light, source unknown, made sure his facial features were not obscured by shadow. He was a still from *The Godfather: Part II*.

'What?' I said, though he hadn't said a thing.

'Do you want to tell me about it?'

'About what?'

'What it is that is upsetting you.'

Whether it was his posture or the lighting, I don't know, but I felt confident he could solve any problem put before him with or without God's help.

'No. Not really. OK.' I perched one knee on the footstool Larry had vacated. 'There's this guy.'

'In my experience, there is always a guy.'

'Well, actually, there are two guys.'

His Corleone composure trembled faintly. 'You believe this to be a problem?'

'The problem is one guy is interested in me and the other one isn't – or if he is he's doing a great job of hiding it.'

'The situation inverted is preferable?'

'No, I'd like them both to be interested.'

I thought I caught the inkling of a smile in his eyes.

'You sound undecided,' he said.

'Tell me about it.' I wondered what to tell Father Giuliani. That I sort of got involved with Jake, then got cold feet, as he seems to be perfect and the sex was, well, pretty good, which makes me think that there must be something that's not quite right because nobody is that perfect and good, and I don't want to spend the next few months waiting for the other shoe to drop. And now that Charles is single for the first time since I've known him I'd really like to meet him. Only problem is that he hasn't expressed a similar desire to meet me. It seems as lost a cause as ever and yet a part of me thinks he's the one, even though that's completely irrational and I don't really believe in the whole notion of 'the one'. Of course, I haven't returned any of Jake's calls, so I've probably blown that. And in spite of my doubts about him, I have a feeling it might have been a huge mistake to ignore him, and Anna is going to say 'I told you so' until I'm eighty.

'Dating is complicated these days,' I said. 'I'm beginning to think I'm just not meant to be in a relationship at all.'

'I am sure it is not as bad as that.'

'I think it might be.'

Father Giuliani spoke as if he was considering every word. 'A person's pain is always as great as the difference between the way things are and the way they want them to be. Happy people are not happy because of wealth or beauty or power. What makes them happy is acceptance. The key to happiness seems to be not about getting what you want, but about wanting what you can get.'

'You're a walking Hallmark moment,' I said. 'But I think that was exactly what I needed to hear. Thank you.'

I paused, on my way out of his office. 'Don't take this in a *Thorn Birds* kind of way, but it's a great tragedy for women everywhere that you're celibate.'

'Thank you,' he said.

As I walked back to my office I realized what I needed to do. What Father Giuliani was talking about had to do with that bird-in-the-hand-is-worth-two-in-the-bush business. Birds in the bush crap in the bush, and that seems better than having one crap in your hand, but it really isn't because they all crap anyway. The priest tried to put a more positive spin on it, but he was still right. I had to go see a man about a bird before it disappeared into someone else's bush.

FROM: Sydney Welles <sydneywelles@yahoo.com>
TO: God c/- Secretary-General@UN.com
DATE: Friday, June 10, 5.41 p.m.
SUBJECT: American God

Dear God,

Up until this week I was under the impression that *the* God and American God were the same guy. Now, after two weeks of research groups infested with his followers, I'm convinced American God is a deity unto himself.

This is a very religious country; perhaps that's why it's been allocated its own God. American Christians have a somewhat confused relationship with American God. It's not entirely clear just who created whom. Either way, there's more church going, Bible thumping, Jesus freaking and born again-ing going on here than anywhere else on earth.

I was aware of that before I went into the fray. Now, I've actually experienced it. I've spoken to people who believe American God superintends every minor detail of their lives down to the quality of their bowel movements; people who believe American God speaks directly to the President of the United States on some sort of bat phone to heaven installed in the Oval Office, which works only for Republican presidents; and people who believe American God wants them to foist their own personal version of morality onto the rest of the country and, if possible, have their opinions become the law.

Apart from the obvious geographical bias, and a fear of cities – American God doesn't exist in urban centres – American God has a couple of other unique features. He is so transparent that everybody can read his mind, and he's so adaptable that he's somewhat of a chameleon. The way that works is simple. For example, if you're bigoted, American God is bigoted, too.

The wonder is that people I've spoken to don't see the absolute miracle, the cosmic coincidence, of American God hating all the same people they do, disapproving of everything they disapprove of, and possessing exactly the same political convictions.

Although America and Americans don't get a mention in the Bible, American God has made it clear that we are the chosen people – chosen to have bigger cars and more stuff than anyone else in the world. No wonder he's the most popular god in the country (though it has to be acknowledged he enjoys little acclaim outside of it).

However, if I were American God I'd be worried. One day, lawyers will find a way to prove, on some technicality, to the satisfaction of the American justice system that he exists and is legally responsible for everything in creation. That day, American God will see that he has chosen for his flock the people in the world most likely to sue him for everything that has ever gone wrong in their lives.

Sincerely,
Sydney

Small armies have defeated great ones, armed only with surprise. It can be a formidable weapon. But outside the battlefield, surprises, especially if anyone involved has a weak heart, are generally not a good idea.

Of all surprises, surprise visits are the worst. They're always ill timed, and half the time the surpriser ends up more surprised than the surprisee. I was fully aware of this and yet it didn't prevent me from paying one.

At just after ten-thirty on Friday night when Jake opened his front door to me, surprise wasn't just written all over his face, it was tattooed on his forehead. I'd materialized on his doorstep without warning, well past normal visiting hours. His surprise was understandable.

What was disconcerting was that once the shock on his face subsided it was replaced by another emotion I couldn't identify. I was sure of only one thing. Jake wasn't pleased to see me. Every self-preservation instinct I had screamed at me to turn around and leave.

'Hi,' I said.

It took him fifteen abnormally lengthy seconds to respond.

'Sydney.' There wasn't a great deal of enthusiasm behind it.

'Oh, good. You remember my name.'

Given the lack of warmth in his welcome it was better

that I waited for him to say something next. At least, in hindsight, it would've been better had I waited.

'I was hoping you'd be home.'

I paused to allow him time to invite me in. He didn't.

'I tried calling your cell phone,' I said. 'I only got your voicemail.'

'I've had my phone turned off.'

'Which would be why I got your voicemail. I didn't have your home number at work or I would've called before I came – I just thought as you're on my way home, well, you're practically a neighbour and everything . . .'

Jake continued the man-of-few-words routine. The next thirty seconds went by like a snail with no sense of direction.

'OK. Now I'm feeling that this is one of those ideas,' I said. 'You know the ones. They seem good at the time you think of them, but go bad as soon as you try to execute them.'

'Why are you here?' Not the most convivial thing he could've said, but that he spoke at all was encouragement enough for me to plough ahead.

'I wanted to see you . . . I was under the impression you might want to see me, too.'

Jake closed his eyes as if in pain, massaging his temples with his thumb and fingers. I seemed to be giving him a migraine. I didn't take it as a good sign.

'It's your turn,' I said.

He opened his eyes. 'My turn?'

'Your turn to add to the conversation.'

The strong, silent act was beginning to get on my nerves.

'The way it works is I say something, then you say something, and we keep taking it in turns to say things. Otherwise, it's more of a monologue than a dialogue.'

Judging from the expression on his face, his migraine was getting worse.

'Have I called at a bad time? I can leave –'

'Your timing couldn't be worse.'

'Oh . . . OK. No problem. We can do this some other time – but, of course, only if you want to. It's not compulsory. We don't have to do anything at all. It's not like we're actually doing anything now. I'm just kind of occupying your stoop. Next time we could even go somewhere – or not – whatever you prefer. I'm going now. Bye.'

I turned to face the street and wondered, in an out-of-body kind of way, if it would be possible for me to feel stupider than I did at that moment. It was.

A voice, calling out to Jake from inside the house, made me halt at the top of the steps.

'Who was at the door –' Kim stopped when she saw me.

At first I thought she was going to retreat into the house, but she only moved back a foot or so to rest a hand on Jake's shoulder, standing by her man just as the song advised. Jake didn't fling her hand from his shoulder like a hot coal. I had to assume he didn't mind it being there.

My mind, traitor that it is, registered that they were wearing matching robes, but, instead of thinking this was contrived and tacky, it thought they could pass for the kind of couple you see in catalogues, surrounded by things to buy so your life looks as good as theirs. Fleetingly, the idea I'd stumbled onto a catalogue shoot occurred to me, but my mind rightfully dismissed this as a desperate, silly notion. Then it thought: wow, their kids are going to be really good-looking. Then it decided it might be a good idea that I give up thinking altogether.

I took a deep breath and, foolishly, stood my ground.

'Right,' I said to Jake, 'this is the part where you tell me this is not at all what it looks like.'

'I can't do that. This is exactly what it looks like.'

'Well.' I examined the finish on my boots and tried to remember the last time they were polished. 'If that's the best story you can come up with, I'm afraid I have to suspect that there's something going on here.'

Nobody laughed.

'So,' I said, 'it's been lovely catching up with you, but, um, I need to polish my shoes, so I'll say goodnight. Have a nice life, both of you.'

Jake caught up with me at the bottom of his front steps, blocking the path in front of me.

'I called you eleven times,' he said. 'You didn't return a single call. I thought you weren't interested.'

'You seem to have gotten over it.'

'If you'd just picked up the phone –'

He broke off as he glanced over my head. I turned to follow his gaze and was surprised by a surge of empathy for Kim. She was standing half-in, half-out of the doorway, watching us, chewing a thumb, looking more like a normal woman and less like the pictures plastic surgeons show you, to help you pick out new facial and body parts, than I imagined she could.

'The strange thing is I think I do understand. If you

guys have worked it out, that's great. Really. I should've called, but . . . that's now irrelevant . . . I have to go.'

'Syd, wait.'

'Why? Is something more going to happen? If you don't mind, I think I'll skip the second act.'

I skirted the outer extremities of Jake and took off as quickly as I dared to in high-heeled boots. I wanted to make it to the confines of my car in case I started to cry, and the sidewalk in front of his place is a little uneven. A pratfall was the last thing I wanted to perform in front of the happy couple.

'Shit,' Jake said.

It summed up the way I was feeling precisely. I'd not felt so depressed since the time I was too lazy to go beyond the D section at the video store – it's right by the front door – and I'd rented *Deliverance* and *The Deer Hunter*, and watched them one after the other, in the same Saturday evening.

I headed straight home, deciding on the way I'd spend what was left of the evening in close consultation with the bottle of vodka in my freezer. Other occupants of my freezer, Ben & Jerry, would also be consulted.

Vodka would help me to see that I had no use for men like Jake and convince me that what just happened was not the result of my own stupidity, but a blessing in disguise, albeit an exceptionally good disguise.

Vodka is a greatly underrated beverage. However, my plans to spend quality time with a bottle of the stuff changed dramatically when I reached home.

It's always quiet on my street at this time of night. The muffled sounds of HBO, the flickering glow of plasma screens in windows above the high walls, the only indication my neighbours are home and awake.

A vacant parking space right in front of my house was waiting for me. In the entire time I've lived here, there has never been a place to park in front of my house this late at night. I should've known something was up, but I was too busy – too busy thinking up things I could have said to Kim and Jake instead of the things I did say. Somehow believing that, if only I'd been more of a smart ass, I'd be feeling much better now.

It was better than wondering if Jake and Kim had ever been apart at all. Wondering if I'd been as much of a surprise to her as she'd been to me. Or asking myself why I was surprised, when a part of me always suspected, as soon as Jake asked me out, that this was how it was going to end.

I took the parking space, not acknowledging the miracle of its existence at all. Nor did I spare a thought for the white van, the one double-parked nearby with its motor running and back doors open. I didn't notice anything until I got out of the car, and all I saw then was Harry Rex, sitting in the middle of the road, smoothing down his ears with his paws.

'What are you doing? You're in the middle of the road, you dumb bunny. You'll get run over.'

He blinked and twitched his whiskers, giving the impression that he was surprised, pleasantly surprised, to see me.

'I live here, stupid. Come on, come into the yard.' I took a couple of steps towards the gate. 'Come on. I'll give you a cookie.'

Harry Rex didn't budge.

A vodka-and-ice-cream-induced stupor was beckoning, and I felt too drained of energy to continue arguing with a rabbit in the middle of the street in the middle of the night. It wasn't my night. First Jake had ex-sex, and now my pet rabbit was trying to commit suicide.

Out of habit, I glanced up at one of the second-storey windows of the house across the street. It was Cupid's bedroom window. I've gotten used to seeing the little guy's silhouette framed in it when I arrive home. He's taken to spying on my comings and goings. He wasn't there tonight. It was too late; even demon children need their sleep. Not seeing the imp up there, plotting my demise, made me feel lonelier.

I returned my attention to Harry Rex. 'Fine. Be road pancake. See if I care.' Problem was I did. 'If you don't come now, I'll give you away to some rotten kid who'll hug you every day.'

I opened my white waist-high front gate to encourage him. The gate chose that moment to fall off one of its hinges, hanging, useless, from the other. It really wasn't my night.

Harry Rex wiggled his ears as if to say 'whatever'. Obviously, he preferred being road kill to hanging out with me. I wondered, idly, if I'd have any ego left by morning, consoling myself with the thought that my life couldn't get any worse. The thing about getting dumped is that, once it happens, you don't have to worry about getting dumped any more. It'd all be on the up and up from here. I wasn't being optimistic. I was being realistic. Everything that could go wrong tonight already had.

That was when two men sprang out from behind the front hedge, plucked me off my feet and threw me, not very gently, into the back of the waiting van.

FROM: Sydney Welles <s.welles@fbmm.com>
TO: God c/- billgates@microsoft.com
DATE: Sunday, June 12, 3.30 p.m.
SUBJECT: Rewrite

Dear God,

I read your book. OK, I admit, I didn't read all of it. To tell the truth, I skipped over most of it. It's not exactly a page-turner, is it?

Yet, it's still the bestselling book of all time and has been since Gutenberg first printed it, back when it was the only published book in existence. It even outsells Harry Potter and The Lord of the Rings. That could have something to do with the fact you don't go to hell if you haven't read those other books.

The threat of eternal damnation is compelling, but just think how many more copies you'd sell if it were actually readable.

Sydney

PS For people who are supposed to love their enemies and neighbours, Christians sure do seem to hate a lot of people.

I made a mental note to cut my hedge back so it no longer provided cover for people lying in wait for me. I was on my hands and knees on the floor of a strange van, taking a spontaneous trip with a couple of guys I hadn't been formally introduced to, and who, quite significantly, were wearing ski masks. It could mean only one thing.

I was being kidnapped.

Not a deduction worthy of Sherlock Holmes, I know. I'm usually much quicker, but my head still reeled from ocular proof that my new, sort-of boyfriend was still involved with his ex, a woman who made Malibu Barbie look homely. Although my life of late has been more eventful, getting dumped and kidnapped in the space of half an hour still constitutes a big evening for me.

Of the emotions ricocheting inside me, at first masked by shock, frustration was the first to make itself known. Life was very unfair. Being kidnapped threw my romantic problems into comparative insignificance. Five minutes ago I'd hoped never to lay eyes on Jake again, but now I'd be quite pleased to see him, or Kim for that matter.

Self-pity replaced frustration and produced tears, but they didn't help the situation any. I tried to think of what I should do. Stay calm. Think. The kidnappers had taken my bag, but except for bruised knees I wasn't hurt. The important thing was not to panic. Why is it they always tell you not to panic? In the given situation it seemed the most appropriate thing to do.

I became aware I'd stopped breathing. The lack of oxygen to my brain had tipped me off. I added to my mental note:

1. Engage gardener to cut back hedge.
2. Remember to breathe. It's important.
3. Escape.
4. Given current circumstances, get priorities in order. Oxygen is first priority. Escape is next. Gardening can probably wait.

We sped up to at least twice the speed we'd been doing. The van maintained the higher speed. We had to be on a freeway. This time of night is the time LA freeways work the way they're supposed to. We could cover a lot of ground in a very short time.

I once read about this kind of thing in a magazine. It was coming back to me. When you find yourself in the trunk of a car involuntarily, you pull out the wires connected to the tail-lights, or else kick the lights out. The cops will pull the car over because it has no tail-lights, you make more noise than a car trunk is supposed to make, and you are saved by the California Highway Patrol.

Crawling to the back of the van, I looked for wires to pull or lights to kick out. There weren't any. Those who make up advice in magazines really ought to take all kinds of vehicles into consideration.

My only plan had failed, but I'd seen enough movies. I just had to wait until a chance to overpower or outsmart my kidnappers came up.

Meanwhile, I tried the doors. Locked. The van was empty of crowbars and useful things for prying locked doors open. It was empty of everything except me, and a few bumper stickers on the floor. I folded one, putting it in the back pocket of my jeans with a vague notion that, if my lifeless body was discovered dumped in the middle of nowhere, an ambitious young detective could use the sticker to track down my killers.

Waiting until after my death for something to be done seemed a little passive-aggressive. I always thought I was one of those people who, when faced with danger, would spring into action like a Marvel superhero. Apparently, I was wrong.

The van slowed right down. It was exiting the freeway we'd been on.

I had no idea how much time I'd wasted. No obvious opportunity to escape had presented itself, so I did the only thing I could think of. I sat behind the back doors of the van and, using both feet, tried to kick them open.

The doors didn't budge, but my kicking slowed the van down, causing it to pull over to the side of the road. Doors opened and closed; footsteps approached the back of the van. I wrapped my arms around my legs and sat still, once more forgetting breathing was necessary.

The van doors, though easily withstanding my physical assault, were not very soundproof. When my kidnappers began to speak to me, I could hear them clearly.

'Hey, you, girl, why're you kickin my van?' said a voice.

I didn't dare answer.

'You stop doin it, OK.'

Another, deeper voice spoke: 'Yeah, you stop or . . .' There was silence for several seconds. 'Or we have to . . . do somethin . . . to stop you . . . yeah.'

'Yeah, shit,' the first voice said, 'be nice.'

'Be nice? You're kidnapping me.' It must have been me who said that.

'It ain't personal. It's a job. Only part time, so course they don't pay for damage. It won't do you no good doin that. Doors only open from the outside.' He paused. 'Come on, I only got the van last month.'

Now that he mentioned it, the van did seem new. 'What are you saying? I'm supposed to sit here and allow myself to be kidnapped?'

The first voice brightened considerably. 'That'd be good, yeah.'

'What are you going to do to me?'

'Us? We ain't gonna do nothin.'

'Then why are you kidnapping me?'

'Don't know.'

'You don't know?'

He hesitated before he said, 'That ain't part of our job. If it ain't part of the job, we don't know nothin bout it. We just doin our jobs. Nothin more.'

'What, is there a union?'

There was another silence. The first voice broke it, sounding defensive. 'This ain't what we do for a livin. We got other jobs.'

'Really? What do you usually do?'

'We're locksmiths,' said the second voice. 'That's how

come we got this freelance work, on account of we can pick locks. Me and Joe work for his stepdad in Culver City – hey, man, what the ... why'd you go and hit me for?'

'Look, girl,' the voice named Joe said, 'you ain't gonna kick my van any more, got it?'

'Oh, I don't know.'

The two outside spoke in low tones, but I could tell they were debating. The voices became a little clearer, as if they'd moved closer to the back of the van. The tiny windows in the back of the van were the kind that didn't open. They were also blacked out. I went to peer out a tiny eye-sized hole scratched in the black paint-like substance that coated them.

'We shoulda tied her up,' Joe was saying.

'They gotta pay extra for that.'

'We shoulda done it on our own account. That's my van.'

'I didn't bring no rope.'

'Jesus, Eddie, you gotta always bring rope. It's not professional we don't got any.'

'They don't order the tie-up service, I don't bring the rope.'

From what I could see we were in a well-lit but deserted business district. It was unfamiliar to me. Somewhere in the Valley, maybe. My kidnappers were huddled together behind the van. They'd taken their ski masks off. In the bright streetlights I could see one of them wore one of those trucker caps that guys wear to be ironic, or to look stupid. I haven't figured out which. The other had hair that looked suspiciously as if it were styled in a minor mullet. Otherwise, they looked more like secondary members of a boy band than hardened criminals.

'Joe? Eddie?'

'Shit,' Joe said, 'how she know our names?'

'She psychic or somethin?' Eddie found three syllables in the word 'psychic'.

'You could just let me go,' I said. 'Then your van will be safe.'

'Nah, we ain't gonna do that,' Joe said, after a minute. 'It'd be what you call defeatin the purpose.'

'What she say?' Eddie said.

'Nothin. She sure talks a lot. Most these guys real quiet. Come on, we gotta go. Gettin late. She does somethin to my van, I'm claimin it and you back me up.'

I heard them get back in the van. It started up and we pulled onto the road again. I wasn't exactly relieved, but somehow I felt better learning of their part-time status as kidnappers. I was the prisoner of a couple of locksmiths who were unlikely to become members of Mensa anytime soon. I wanted to laugh. I also wanted to cry. I did neither.

The thick black-tinted glass window separating the front of the van from the back, which for some reason I had not noticed until now, opened.

'We're stoppin to get coffee,' the three-inch strip of Eddie visible through the opening said. 'Don't be making no noise. No one'll hear; we're parked aways from the shop. You got that?'

I nodded.

'You want somethin?'

'Sorry?'

'Coffee or somethin?'

'Coffee would be good,' I said.

'Milk? Sugar?'

'Just black. Please.'

'Joe? You want anythin else?'

'Yeah. Get me a couple of doughnuts. And see if they got *AutoTrader*.'

'OK.' Eddie shut the door a little more firmly than necessary and was gone.

Joe opened his side of the window to look at me. Whatever he saw caused him to say, 'We shoulda tied you up.' He shut the window between us.

I peered out the back peephole again. We were on a dark road, surrounded on both sides by trees and shrubbery so profuse, so natural-looking, it had to be nature. We could be out in one of the canyons. Topanga Canyon?

Eddie was gone a while. When he got back he handed me my things from the driver's seat through the window dividing us. He'd bought me doughnuts and a magazine, too.

'Don't you think about spilling anythin,' Joe said. 'I find shit, I know who did it. Don't think I won't figure it out. You're the only one back there.'

The magazine, when I unrolled it, was *People*. Even if there were enough light to read, I can't read in moving vehicles, but I was strangely touched Eddie had thought to buy it for me.

I noticed how cold it was in the back of the van for the first time. It was cold and dark, and no one I knew had any idea where I was or what was happening to me.

Out of the peephole in the back window all I could see was a long, unlit, deserted road stretching for miles behind us. If I had to, I'd guess we were somewhere on the Pacific Coast Highway, heading to Malibu. I thought I could smell the ocean. There were no buildings. No friendly headlights to break the monotony of the road. It was then it really hit me. I was being kidnapped.

'Help,' I said. But no one heard.

In less than half an hour the van slowed to a stop on a crunchy gravel road. Joe and Eddie exchanged a few words with a third person outside. I heard activity outside the back doors when the engine stopped. The doors opened without warning and a powerful flashlight shone in, temporarily blinding me, so all I could make out were shadowy figures grouped at the back of the van.

I was taken out of the van and escorted by each arm towards what looked to be a large house. I suddenly felt quite attached to Eddie and Joe.

'Bye, Eddie. Bye, Joe.' I said.

'Bye,' Eddie said. Joe grunted.

'Thanks for the coffee . . . and stuff.'

'You have a nice time,' Eddie said.

My new captors weren't talkative – not so much as a hello escaped them. Leading me through the house to the doorway of a room, they pushed me inside, locking the door behind me. I tripped over my boots and sent myself sprawling onto the floor. Being kidnapped is hard on the knees.

I was in a whitewashed, windowless room. To one side was a small sofa, upholstered in a daisy fabric that made your eyes hurt. An old-fashioned iron bed stood against a wall, covered with a hand-stitched quilt. It, too, festered with daisies. Above the bed, mounted on the wall, a large, wooden Jesus was miserable on his cross.

On either side of the bed, little tables stood. One held a glass and a jug of water. On the other was the frilly lamp responsible for the room's golden glow. The drawers of the faux French provincial bedside tables proved to be empty except for a King James Bible – those Gideons sure do get around. Through a door was a standing-room-only bathroom where towels and toiletries had been neatly laid out.

It wasn't to my taste, but I could see it was better than being tied to a chair in a deserted warehouse – the usual quarters assigned to kidnappees according to Hollywood.

Unable to think of anything else to do, I sat on the bed and pulled the quilt around me. I tried flicking through the magazine Eddie bought me, but found I couldn't focus on anything.

I decided that whatever happened I'd blame Jake. Then again, if it weren't for Charles, I probably would've called Jake and he might not have gone back to Kim, so maybe Charles was more to blame for my current predicament. And if Matt hadn't broken up with me I may never have been pissed off enough to write to Charles in the first place, so it was Matt's fault first. I saw that I could keep going backwards until eventually I'd run out of men I've been involved with and have to blame myself.

It was God's fault. He was responsible for creating two genders and allowing them to mingle. Having arbitrarily assigned blame I felt better, even though I didn't know at that stage that I'd assigned it correctly. After deciding to stay on watch all night to prevent anyone from sneaking up on me, I fell asleep almost immediately.

FROM: Sydney Welles <s.welles@fbmm.com>
TO: God c/- headsheep@sheepusa.org
DATE: Monday, June 13, 9.31 a.m.
SUBJECT: Heaven is full of dead people

Dear God,

The one prerequisite for entry into heaven that everybody agrees on is death. No one gets in without dying. You get to live in paradise and have the best of everything, but only once you're a corpse. Am I the only one who sees a problem with this?

If you applied the same principle to any other situation, you wouldn't be able to hear yourself think for the protests. Imagine a product that worked only after you were dead. Or a company that paid employee salaries or benefits posthumously. Not even Wal-Mart could get away with that – well, at least, not yet.

See ya,
Syd

I opened my eyes to the sound of a door closing. Morning had broken. Through a small skylight, an indecent amount of sunlight deluged the room. Outside, not far enough away, birds chirped joyously. Inside, a breakfast tray had been placed on the small coffee table in front of the sofa.

My bedroom does not have a skylight or a sofa, and it is a place where breakfast never miraculously appears by itself, which went a long way to prove that the events of last night were not the nightmare I was hoping they'd turn out to be.

Also on the breakfast tray was my wallet. Inside it, my cash and credit, membership and business cards were all present and accounted for. At least my kidnappers were honest.

If the kidnapping was real, my less-than-happy encounter with Jake and Kim was, too. Which was worse: being kidnapped or dating? I couldn't decide.

Sunshine and birdsong prevented me from going back to sleep – obviously some sort of sleep-deprivation torture devised by my captors. Though I was hungry, I found nothing tempting enough on the breakfast tray to risk poisoning. I freshened up in the teeny bathroom, then, for something to do, tried the room door. It opened. Whoever had delivered breakfast hadn't locked it after them.

A loud noise that sounded a lot like a breakfast tray hitting the ground made me jump. The door across the hall flew open. In the doorway stood a tall, familiar-looking blonde wearing the minimum amount of terry towelling that you can wear and still be regarded as clothed. She looked up and down the hallway.

I decided to let her break the ice. I'd been abducted; I was pretty sure the burden to make conversation did not fall on me.

'You haven't, like, seen Doctor Nicolls, have you?'

'No,' I said.

'Shit. I'm totally out of pills.' The tall blonde pulled a face. It was then I realized she wasn't tall. She was only about my height, but stood almost a head higher because she balanced on ten-inch platform heels, secured to her feet with thin straps of green crocodile skin. The green contrasted nicely against what there was of her white dress.

'You just get here?'

I nodded.

'What's your name?'

'Sydney. What's yours?'

'India. Isn't that funny? We're, like, both named after places. Wasn't being kidnapped a trip? I'm going to see if I can do it again. Did you get bound and gagged?'

As soon as she mentioned her name, I knew why India looked familiar. I'd seen her photo occasionally in celebrity magazines. She was a retail heiress, famous for having a father who had more money than she could spend. If memory served, she'd recently gone ahead and released a single, undaunted by being unable to sing.

'I didn't get the tie-up service.'

'Next time, then. It's the poo. What do you think of the place? It's so basic, it has to be, like, completely spiritual, don't you think?'

'Is there a phone I could use?'

'Oh no, no phones.' India giggled. 'There's, like, nothing, no television, no radio, no Internet. It's a total technology fast.'

India teetered across the corridor and took my arm.

'Let's go.'

'OK,' I said.

'I feel, like, naked without a bag. Hate that they always take your stuff. I was on the waiting list for two months for this purse, and I bet they've just thrown it on top of all the others like it's only a two-thousand-dollar bag or something.' She pointed down the corridor. 'We'll go this way. Do you have a boyfriend?'

'Er, no.'

'Oh,' she said, 'I know we're not supposed to, you know, date anyone while we get enlightened. But you can tell me. I won't tell. I'm, like, sleeping with several people myself.'

'I really don't have a boyfriend.'

'Oh.' India turned this over in her head, a new concept. 'Cool. So, do you get paid an allowance or something?'

'I get a salary, if that's what you mean.'

'You have a job?'

'Yes.'

'Wow.' India seemed impressed. 'I once took golf lessons every single day for two whole months. But I guess that's not really like a job, is it?'

'Oh, I don't know.'

She steered us down another long corridor. At the end was a big room, filled with tables and chairs, and shelves of books, mostly Christian romantic fiction, which, India explained, is like normal romantic fiction except no one has sex. People kissed, got married and even then they didn't have sex.

'Isn't this place so quaint? It could be, like, Amish or something. But don't worry,' she said. 'There's a full-on spa. And there's loads of stuff to buy.'

That must've been why they'd returned my wallet to me. 'Oh, good. I was worried I wouldn't get any shopping in this weekend.'

'Yeah, really.'

She opened a large door, and I found myself squinting in the bright daylight. I couldn't believe what I was seeing.

There, in front of me, exactly as though he'd been standing there waiting for me, was Matt, my ex, aka Dr John Somers to daytime soap fans, aka fireman Gray Somers to those same fans before he came back from the dead as Gray's evil twin, and aka Matt the Rat by those not in his fan club, Anna being the foremost amongst them.

Relief was not the emotion I expected to feel when I bumped into Matt again, but relief was the feeling that overcame me. So much so that my first instinct was to hug him. Thankfully, I controlled it and held out a hand instead. He took it.

'It's really good to see you.'

'It's good to see you, too,' I said. 'But don't take it personally. Right now I'd be glad to see anyone I know.'

'This is boring,' India said.

Matt gave her a look that, if not killing, was at least maiming, and she ditched us, tottering on to greener pastures, of which there were many to choose from. Around us, in a sublime and seemingly endless Japanese-style garden, a great many people were seated or walking. The view was rendered even more picturesque because everyone, except me, wore white.

'You might've let me know there was a dress code,' I said.

'You don't have to wear white your first time,' Matt said.

'First time? I'm not going to be abducted again, am I?'

'The abduction is optional. I thought it'd get your attention. Being snatched from your life is supposed to be symbolic.'

'Really? Of what exactly?'

'The control we think we have over our lives is just an illusion. Everything can change in an instant if it's the will of God.'

'God is here? That figures. I think He's stalking me.'

'God is everywhere,' Matt said – without any irony whatsoever. Either he had become an extremely good actor or he was serious. I couldn't work out which was more unlikely.

'OK. God's here, you're here and I'm here. Why?'

'It'll take a little while to explain,' Matt said.

'I don't have to rush off anywhere. Even if I did, I don't know that I'd be allowed to.'

Matt flashed his small-screen heartthrob smile at me. It was the reason he'd landed the part of Gray Somers in the first place. It also had something to do with why I'd been involved with him. Although back then it hadn't been four or five shades whiter than naturally possible.

'What is that thing on your face?' I was being facetious. I knew perfectly well the thing on his face was intended to be a goatee.

'They made me grow it. To make it easier for people to tell the difference between Dr John Somers and Gray Somers.'

'I thought Gray Somers was dead.'

'He is, but the art of the flashback is alive and well.'

'One twin is good and dead, and one is alive and evil. This isn't enough for people to differentiate between them?'

'You know what they say. No one has ever lost money by underestimating the intelligence of the American public. Or lost public office that way. If I recall rightly, it was you who told me that.'

'It sounds like something I'd repeat,' I said. 'So, you were going to tell me why I'm here.'

'Let's sit down.' Matt led me over to a stone bench under a tree and we sat. 'My guide here – she's kind of my life coach and therapist – helped me to realize that for me to move on with my life I first had to speak to you.'

'You couldn't have called me?'

'It's more complicated than that. Because of the way I treated you, I'm in debt to you; to repay that debt I have to help you in some way.'

'So this is some kind of twelve-step programme? Thank God. I thought it was a cult – what with the abduction and white clothing and everything.'

Matt gave the impression he was considering his next words carefully. 'I don't think you're happy. I don't think you'll ever be happy unless you face a few issues.'

'Let me get this straight. You had me kidnapped so you can get closure on our relationship, yet you're telling me I'm the one with issues. I wasn't the one who ran off with Bambi.'

'Berry.'

'Close enough.'

'I'm the bad guy. I know that. I don't expect you to get this straight away, but this is my way of making things right.'

I had nothing better to do while kidnapped. 'I'm listening.'

It was a very uncomfortable bench we sat on, but not uncomfortable enough to justify Matt's current squirming. 'This is going to sound bad,' he said. 'I had your chart done.'

'My chart?'

'Your natal numerology chart.'

'Oh, that chart.'

'I know, I know. I thought it was load of crap, too,' he said. 'Only, I've seen it work. I don't know why it works, but that doesn't matter. Right now I'm prepared to accept anything that might help.'

'OK,' I said.

'You don't have any twos in your chart.'

'No twos? I take it that's a bad thing.'

'The number two is the number of emotions. The number of the heart, if you like.'

'What are you saying? I have no heart?'

'That's not as far off as you'd think. The numerologist said your chart was the chart of a highly intelligent, deeply spiritual person who had a lot of trouble dealing with emotion.'

'I don't understand. How can I have trouble with emotion if I'm devoid of it?'

'It's not that you don't have emotions. You have them, but you have trouble accepting them or showing them. You reason your feelings out of existence. Kill them with logic. It's not that you're incapable of love, just incapable of allowing yourself to feel it.'

'I see.' For someone incapable of feeling emotion, I was feeling kind of depressed. So far, this weekend sucked.

'I wouldn't be telling you this if I didn't think it was important.'

'Why do you think this is important?'

'The numerologist said you're pushing people away because the person you're most incapable of loving is yourself.'

'Wow, that's deep,' I said. 'I'm guessing that you have a lot of twos in your chart.'

'Too many. That's my problem. Well, one of my problems – we're not here to catalogue my problems.'

'That's right. We're here to shed light on mine.'

'With the benefit of hindsight, I think the only reason you were happy to get involved with me was because you knew the relationship didn't stand a chance.'

'That doesn't make sense.'

'Can you honestly tell me you thought that you and I would end up together?'

'You forget; for some bizarre biological reason a man

who combines charm and a self-destructive urge is irresistible to all women. People break up. It's not like everyone goes into every relationship thinking it's the one.'

'Yeah, but they also don't usually go into a relationship because it's not the one. Look, it took me a long time to figure out my shit and even longer to accept it. I'm telling you this because I think that somewhere down the line it might help you. You've been doing this for so long, you don't even know you're doing it. Just think about it. If you come to the conclusion it's a crock of shit, fine. OK?'

'OK,' I said.

'OK.'

'Are you still with Bambi?'

'No, Christ, the woman couldn't even read a map.'

India came wobbling up to us, as gracefully as you can in ten-inch heels on soft grass. Under her arm she carried a large box of what I guessed to be communion wafers by the pictures of wafers on the box and the brand name: 'I Can't Believe It's Not Jesus!'

'You'll never guess what I found,' she said.

I was inclined to believe her. 'Probably not.'

'A whole stash of sacramental wine. There are, like, hundreds of bottles.'

'That's great,' I said, more because I felt it was expected of me than because I was impressed with her discovery.

'All I need now is a bottle opener.'

'I have one,' I said. I did. The one Larry had given to me was still in my pocket. I'd forgotten all about it until now.

India tripped off with the opener at a dangerous speed.

'So, you all take communion here?'

'You can if you want to,' Matt said. 'Any ritual that

makes you feel closer to God is encouraged. Up to and including dancing naked in the woods and howling at the moon.'

'You have no idea how disconcerting it is to hear you, of all people, talk about God like that, and with a straight face.'

'Yeah, I know. Honestly, you can't know how much this has helped me.'

'I can guess. You get paid too much money for what you do and are the fantasy boy of hundreds of bored housewives. I can see why something like this might help keep you grounded. It's certainly healthier than doing coke every night.'

'Yeah, you were right about that.'

I reached out and gave his left hand a little squeeze. Matt returned the squeeze before giving my hand back to me.

'So, what's next for the dastardly Dr Somers?'

'He devises a computer chip which he implants into the minds of several female characters who all just happen to need brain surgery at the same time – a rare but very contagious tropical brain virus that someone brings back from vacation. Then he does the puppet-master thing for a while, turns them all into his personal sex slaves, until he gets his comeuppance. They haven't figured out how that happens yet.'

'Sounds good.'

'I'm not looking forward to it – all the sex scenes.'

Loud giggling broke out, coming from the nearby building India had disappeared into with several other people.

'I don't think you should've given India that bottle opener,' Matt said.

'Why not? Aren't you guys allowed to drink?'

'Well, no.'

'Oh,' I said. 'Oops.'

'Are you seeing anyone?'

I was tempted to pour out the whole Jake saga, but suppressed the inclination when I realized it might give Matt more material for his misguided theories about me. 'Not really, no. You?'

'Sort of. We're not exactly dating or anything yet. But she's agreed to give me a chance after I sort my shit out.'

'Sounds like a smart woman.'

Matt turned to listen to squeals coming from India and company. 'I think we should get going before they discover India in the wine supply. Can I buy you breakfast? They do these great truffled eggs at the restaurant here – really pricey. And we could go over your chart.'

'Oh, goody,' I said. 'Well, as long as the eggs are very expensive.'

'Everything here is expensive. Salvation doesn't come cheap.'

FROM: Sydney Welles <s.welles@fbmm.com>
TO: God c/- thedalailama@majorlamas.com
DATE: Tuesday, June 14, 12.52 p.m.
SUBJECT: Ten Is Not Enough

Dear God,

Some of your followers believe that the only way to live life is in absolute fear of going to hell, that the Ten Commandments need to be followed to the letter and that a God who showed leniency on these matters would be a bad God, a God not worth believing in.

If you are that kind of God – the severe, unforgiving kind – why are there only ten commandments? If you're going to have a list of things we ought not do, the danger is in leaving things off the list. Omission implies that those things are OK to do.

For example, we're all agreed that rape is not a good thing. Yet, something like one in three women are raped and you do nothing about it. Less than 60 per cent of convicted rapists admit to reading porn, but 95 per cent of them admit to reading the Bible. As the Good Book is a rapist's reference, a commandment about not raping other people would go a long way.

May I suggest a comprehensive addendum?

Here are a few more just off the top of my head: thou shalt not start wars in My Name; thou shalt not enslave other people; thou shalt not torture anyone, not even thy enemies; thou shalt not abuse children; thou shalt not beat up thy wife or girlfriend; thou shalt not sell heroin to twelve-year-olds nor force them into prostitution nor exploit or oppress them in any way; thou shalt not be a racist asshole or any kind of asshole; and so on.

If you really want everyone to take everything literally, you have to get more literal.

Regards,
Syd

PS Almost forgot one: thou shalt not kidnap people, not even people who work in advertising.

It was almost dark by the time we pulled up in front of my house, but the entire trip had taken only about half an hour, even though the ride the night before lasted well over an hour. I was allowed to sit up front between Joe and Eddie. The former didn't have much to say to me, but the latter chatted happily all the way to my house.

As I waited for Eddie to get out of the van so I could get out, I noticed Cupid was sitting on the sidewalk in front of his gate. He seemed to be waiting for somebody. His attention was now focused anxiously on the van. Cupid was going to be severely disappointed when I got out. But if he was he didn't show it. Instead, he stood looking at me with something that, if I didn't know him better, I'd mistake for relief. I was so glad to be home, so glad to see even him, I blew him a kiss. He pulled a grotesque face. I was home.

'Your purse,' Eddie said, holding my bag, which I hadn't seen since it was taken from me, out of the window of the car.

'Thanks.'

'See ya,' Eddie said, as the van drove off. I gave him a half-hearted wave.

I walked over to Cupid and patted him on the top of his head.

'You should be getting inside,' I said to Cupid. 'It's dark.'

'You're not my mother.'

'A fact for which I'm eternally grateful.'

'What are you doing that for?'

I was fluffing his curls. They were hard to resist. Cupid was standing directly under a streetlamp. His curls were lit up like a halo around his head. It made him look ethereally beautiful in spite of the scowl on his face. 'I'm just checking to see if there's a three-digit number tattooed on your scalp.'

'Why do people always do that?'

'It's a reflex action. Now, get inside. There are all kinds of bad guys out here in the dark. Even the not-so-bad ones that mean well can wreak havoc.'

'You can't tell me what to do. You're not –'

'Yes, yes, I know, I'm not your mother. What I am is a lot bigger than you. Go.'

He glared at me before scooting past the gate and slamming it as hard as he could in my face.

'Such a dear boy,' I said to the gate.

I passed my own sorry excuse for a gate, still hanging limply open on one hinge, let myself in my front door, picked up the phone and dialled my own number. A recorded voice told me I had twenty-six new messages.

I was tempted to call my parents. But what would I tell them exactly – that I was kidnapped by a cult my ex-boyfriend was in, but I was OK now that the kidnappers had dropped me home? My parents think I'm still dating Matt. They get so attached to people that I find it's best not to tell them I've broken up with someone until I have someone new they can attach themselves to instead. Calling them now would mean I'd have to go into lengthy explanations, as well as ruin my policy of not telling them anything that can upset or worry them. Just calling them at all when it wasn't the time for my weekly call would send them into a panic. I put the phone back down and headed for the bathroom to take a shower.

The doorbell rang as I was running a comb through my towel-dried hair.

'There better not be Mormons out there,' I said, through the closed door. Is it just me, or do others also think it strange that some religious groups claim to revere God, but then peddle Him door to door as if He were nothing but a second-rate insurance policy?

'It's Jake.'

I opened the door. It was Jake, as promised, and he carried a large shopping bag in one hand. A bunch of daisies peeked out the top.

'I hate daisies.'

He grabbed the daisies and tossed them over the hedge into the street. 'So do I.'

'What else is in the bag?'

He reached in, rustled around and pulled out a box and rattled it. 'Chocolate. Handmade. From that little shop at the old Hollywood market – you said you liked it.'

I stood aside to let him pass.

'Where have you been? I've been trying to find you since last night.'

I sighed. 'It's a long, complicated and slightly sordid story.'

'I have all night.'

'Where's your girlfriend?' I led him down the short hall into my living room. 'I miss her.'

'That was a mistake. It's over.'

'Again? I have to start taking notes. I'm having trouble keeping up with your love life.'

'Give me a chance to explain.'

I sank into the sofa and pulled my feet up after me. 'No, sorry, I can't take an explanation right now. You can give me the chocolates instead.'

Jake knelt in front of me. 'I think we can work this out.'

'Maybe we can. I don't know. All I know is I can't deal with it now.'

'OK.' Jake's gaze shifted to what I was wearing: Marvin the Martian flannelette pyjamas. 'Nice pyjamas,' he said.

Unfortunately for Jake, it was precisely then that my body's supply of adrenalin – the only thing that had seen me through the past twenty-four hours – ran out. I burst into tears.

'I'm sorry. I like your pyjamas. I really do. Jesus. I'm sorry. Please, don't cry.' He found a box of tissues for me, then joined me on the couch and held me. In return I made the front of his sweater wet. I also built up a good-sized collection of soggy tissues.

'Are you going to tell me what's wrong?' To his credit, he'd figured out I wasn't as sensitive about my sleepwear as I appeared to be.

'No.' I treated us both to a series of sniffs, before rubbing my nose with a handful of tissues, for what I hoped would be the final time. 'What else is in that bag?' It was now sitting on my coffee table.

'Things to make you like me again.'

'Then it should be a bigger bag.'

'Is this about me?'

'You're really not as cute as you think you are. This is . . .' I didn't know where to start. 'I need to cut back the front hedge.' I closed my eyes. 'I'm exhausted.'

'I think it'd be an idea if I stayed here tonight.'

I opened my eyes. Jake held up his hands. 'Just to make sure you're OK. I don't think you should be on your own. I'll even help with the gardening in the morning. A purely practical, platonic arrangement.'

'Platonic? No, it'd never work. If you're going to stay you may as well make yourself useful.'

'I'm at your service.'

I poked him in the chest. 'OK. You need to make someone bring a very large pepperoni pizza to the house. And it has to have a thin crust. The crust is very, very important – a matter of life and death. Then you can give me whatever is in that bag. But be warned: tomorrow, when I have more energy, I'm going to kick your two-timing butt.'

'I understand.'

FROM: Sydney Welles <sydneywelles@yahoo.com>
TO: God c/-
   vicepresidentoftheunitedstates@thewhitehouse.com
DATE: Wednesday, June 15, 7.09 p.m.
SUBJECT: Science 101

Dear God,

The universe is a big old place. Big enough for you and Darwin. The idea of a divine initiative to get the ball rolling combined with evolution to keep it rolling is not incompatible with Catholic dogma. A couple of popes have even said as much.

Even if you forbid evolution from being taught in schools, everything will still keep evolving. You'd do much better to embrace Darwin and claim credit for his work.

Or, failing that, some religions avoid having to deal with the theory of evolution altogether, simply by implying that supreme beings have no concept of time. This allows you to incorporate all the sciences without having to concede a thing. Seven days to a god is like four and a half billion years to us. You know how it is. When you have stars and planets and large primates to make, and there is no one around to help, time just gets away from you.

Syd x

Detective Karl Lauderdale wore plain clothes and a uniform face. Deep lines radiating from the outer corners of his eyes were his only distinguishing features. For my sake, I hoped they were laugh lines.

In a small, airless room at the Pacific station, we sat at a table on wooden chairs so unforgiving my butt was numb within seconds of taking a seat. Soft furnishings were sorely needed. My kidnappers had provided me with far more comfortable surroundings, but, naturally, I didn't tell Detective Lauderdale that. Nor did I ask if his butt was numb. He didn't seem to be coping with me as it was.

He was Jake's brother's best friend's brother or best friend's brother's best friend or some variation on that theme. It seemed he was regretting the connection and volunteering to take me on, for the sake of his friend or brother or whatever, so that I could avoid the normal process involved in reporting a crime. I thought it'd be a good idea to avoid official procedure. I wasn't sure if what I was reporting qualified as a crime.

From the moment I'd made his acquaintance, the detective had spent a great deal of his time gazing at the ceiling. Nothing up there excited interest. It was plain, white plaster, alleviated only by a utilitarian light fitting dangling from the centre. Yet while I told my story, he kept tipping his head back, only occasionally checking to see if I was still seated across the table.

When he did look at me it was as if I were an exhibit in a roadside museum boasting a preserved alien baby salvaged from a flying-saucer wreck, or a small, mutated turnip in a jar of vinegar, depending on your level of gullibility.

'You don't believe me,' I said. 'It usually takes people several months to work out not to believe a word I say. You've known me only fifteen minutes and you've already figured it out. You must be a pretty good detective.'

The good detective glanced down at his pad and seemed surprised to find it still blank. He gave his pen an accusing look, and smiled, in a sheepish way, at me. The lines around his eyes crinkled; for a moment he didn't look so bland.

'I believe you. I don't think you could've made that up.'

'It sounds silly, doesn't it? I was in two minds about reporting it.'

'So, after going to the trouble of abducting you so that ... what was his name again?'

'Matt the Rat. Oh, you mean his real name. Matthew Kendall-Walker.'

'So that Matt the Rat could get ...'

'Closure on our relationship. He also had this idea that he had to do me a good turn. It was very important for his spiritual advancement. To clear any lingering bad energy in his relationship chakra, as a clogged relationship chakra may prevent him from recognizing his soul mate when he meets her in the future.'

Detective Lauderdale squinted at me, as if in pain.

'I'm just repeating what he told me.'

'What was the good turn he did you?'

'He told me how he thought I was sabotaging my own happiness.'

'How were – never mind. So, in the end, they just let you go?'

'Even drove me home. At least it was a full door-to-door return service kind of kidnapping.'

'Did they hurt you in any way?'

'No, not really. I nearly got baptized, but that was my fault. I stuck my feet in the font.'

'The font?'

'That's what they called the baptismal pool. Catholics normally just spritz a little water on you and, presto, you're one of them, but apparently full-body, full-contact baptism is starting to get popular again.'

'They were Catholic?' He was looking at the ceiling again.

'No. They seemed to be a bit of everything, actually, with a good deal of psychotherapy, a lot of New Age spirituality, some witchcraft and a little science fiction thrown in.'

'Did they force you to do anything you didn't want to do?'

I picked up the police doll someone had left on the table – Patrol Officer West, the LAPD's first foray into collectible action figures – and bent him into a sitting shape. I felt as if I was letting the detective down because my captors didn't perform any cruel acts I could describe to him in detail. 'Everyone was pretty decent to me, especially considering they were spoilt, rich and crazy.'

'They did abduct you and hold you against your will.'

'Yes, they did do that, didn't they?' He was good, this Lauderdale – quick with the salient points.

'Did you notice anything illegal going on at this ... place?'

I thought about it. 'There seemed to be a lot of pills freely available, but with the high psychiatrist-to-cult-member ratio, it's quite likely they were all prescribed.'

'What kind of pills?'

'Happy pills mostly, but I think there may have been some sedatives around, either that or some of those people could use a personality transplant. They weren't exactly the most self-reliant bunch on earth.'

'People who need a place like that generally aren't.'

'Yeah, but these guys ... Every time someone had to make a decision they consulted God, the I Ching, the stars, tarot, a palmist, their spirit guides and higher selves. And then, when they do finally come to a decision, they psychoanalyse it to ensure it's not a reaction to something traumatic that happened in early childhood.'

People were passing by the open doorway. I shifted in my seat, partly to try for feeling in my butt and partly to watch a group of five men walk by. Two wore handcuffs as bracelets and the rest wore guns in holsters. The ones with guns looked happier.

I returned my attention to Detective Lauderdale. He inspected the ceiling again. I looked up. We both stared for several seconds. Nothing happened up there.

'Can I call you Lauderdale?'

His eyes crinkled up again as he smiled. 'I wish I could think of a reason why you can't.'

'You can call me kid.'

'OK, kid, let's try to make some sense of this.'

'Sure thing, Lauderdale.'

'Let's start with the two guys who grabbed you. You think you'd know them if you saw them again?'

'I think so.'

'Can you describe them?'

'Yes.' I thought about it. 'Or I could just give you their names and numbers.'

Lauderdale's eyes rolled upwards. 'Yes, you could just do that.'

'The head kidnapper was called Joe Mitchell. He runs a locksmith business for his stepfather. It's on Washington, in Culver City. Or at least that's what his girlfriend told me. She's in the cult, a poor little rich kid having her blue-collar fling. Eddie works with Joe; his last name was Cameron or Connor – hang on.' I picked up my bag and started going through it. 'I have his card somewhere.'

I'd lost Lauderdale to the ceiling again. 'You have his card?'

I passed it over. Lauderdale looked at the card, then at me.

'That's his phone number there.' I pointed it out.

'I can see that. I am a detective.' He turned the card over. 'Kid, my job would be a lot easier if all criminals handed out business cards. I hope this is the start of a new trend.'

'I wouldn't call Eddie a criminal. I mean, he's not the brightest crayon in the box, but he wasn't a bad guy. He's not going to get into trouble, is he?'

'He could get three to eight.'

I tried to think of something to absolve Eddie. 'He bought me doughnuts.' That had to be a point in Eddie's favour. Cops liked doughnuts. 'I don't want anyone to get into trouble. I don't want to press any charges.'

'I understand that. I just want to take a bit of a look at this, to make sure nothing illegal is going on.' Lauderdale turned his eyes upwards again. 'You didn't happen to get a business card from this place, did you?'

'No, I didn't,' I said, staring at the ceiling to be companionable. 'But I have other stuff. They were big on merchandising.'

I emptied the contents of my bag, all purchased by Matt as a gift for me, onto the table for Lauderdale to see: a meditation CD to help release unrealistic expectations; a patchouli candle to eliminate negative energy; a bottle of drinking water, purified by blessing rather than filtering; a short piece of wool, which retails in fashionable stores for thirty-five dollars, a miracle in itself as you can buy a whole ball of wool for about two bucks in less fashionable retail outlets; and a book called *Find True Happiness and Your Life Purpose in Seven Days*, written by the founder of the place, that came with a free early episode of *Star Trek* on DVD – he had a small part in it before he gave up show business to start a religion.

'There's an 800 number to call on the back of the book,' I said. 'Does that help?'

Someone knocked on the open door. It was Jake. He had driven me to the station, but, after I'd assured him I could handle the interview on my own and insisted that his presence in the room would undermine my independence and add to the oppression of my gender in general, he'd exchanged a look with Detective Lauderdale and gone to pick up his dry-cleaning.

The real reason I hadn't wanted him in the room was because I wasn't sure how much Lauderdale would want to know about Matt. However much it was I thought it best Jake didn't hear it.

'We're almost done.' Lauderdale waved Jake in.

'Do you have someone you can stay with for the next week or so?' he asked me.

'Why?'

'I don't think you should be on your own. Don't worry, I doubt you're in any danger, but with these things there can be delayed shock.'

I nodded. 'I have friends I can stay with.'

'Good.' He handed me one of his cards. 'Let me know where, and I'll be in contact.'

'You won't be mean to Matt or the others.'

'I won't be mean.'

Lauderdale and I looked up at the ceiling one last time, for old times' sake. Jake looked to see what we were looking at, and for a moment we all stood like that.

'Is that it?' I asked. Once again the vision the detective was waiting for had failed to appear on the ceiling.

'For today.' The lines around his eyes crinkled. 'See you, kid.'

'Later, Lauderdale.'

Jake waited until we were in his car before asking, 'Why were you both staring at the ceiling like that?' and then, after staring at me dubiously while I answered, he took me to lunch at a place on Pacific Avenue, a communist-looking eating establishment that could make tofu, green beans and brown rice taste good.

I felt so healthy afterwards, I decided to walk home by myself, declining all offers of help to pack a week's worth of clothing into my car. It was something I felt I had to do on my own. It would shake the damsel-in-distress image of me Jake was currently enjoying and reinstate my sophisticated modern-bitch image, which had been obliterated last night when I'd shed rivulets of tears down his chest.

When I reached home, there were two things that caught my attention immediately:

1. The front gate, which had been barely hanging on by one hinge the last time I saw it, was now back in place, fixed and securely shut with one of the most elaborate locks I'd ever seen.
2. My two former kidnappers were standing beside their white van, parked in front of the house next to mine, and I couldn't fail to notice that one of them was brandishing a crowbar.

FROM: Sydney Welles <s.welles@fbmm.com>
TO: God c/- god1@hotmail.com
DATE: Friday, June 17, 8.05 a.m.
SUBJECT: What were you thinking?

Dear God,

'Blessed are the peacemakers'? Where are they blessed? Not in this country. Unless, of course, you're referring to firearms when you say 'peacemakers'. Then, yes, they do seem to be unaccountably blessed.

'The meek shall inherit the earth'? When exactly? And how? Will the powers-that-be and the mega-corporations just one day say: 'Here, it's yours. We've been bad and hogged it all for a very long time. Sorry about that. Now it's only fair you meeks get your turn.'

I don't think so.

You've gone about this all wrong. If you want humble creations, you don't tell them you created the universe for them and only them. You tell them all existence, as they know it, takes place within a step in a dance that you – or Shiva, in this case – is doing. In the time you take to pick your foot up off the floor and put it back down again, a universe comes into being, exists and is destroyed. Within that step, in a moment so fleeting it doesn't register on any cosmic time scale, the human race runs its course on a particle of dust. Again and again this happens. Universe created. Universe destroyed. Every time you take a step. We exist because you're out partying. The life span of our universe is the beat of a song in the nightclub of creation. We're not significant enough to be insignificant. Now, that's a humbling thought. If you're doing the macarena, it's mortifying as well.

Syd

**FISHER BENNET McMAHON & MAY**
4848 Abott Way Los Angeles CA 90066 USA
310-807-3000 t   310-807-5000 f


Charles Turner
Los Angeles Times
202 W. 1st St.
CA 90012

Dear Charles,

Last Friday night I was kidnapped by a couple of locksmiths on behalf of a religious cult. The cult has a nice sixty-acre property just the other side of Malibu.

As far as kidnappers go, mine were quite nice. Their names are Joe and Eddie, and they came back the next day to fix my gate. They were the ones who broke it in the first place. It's fixed so well that now I can't open it and have to scramble over the top of it to come and go.

The new lock on my gate was intended as a surprise, to make up for my abduction. They also wanted to avoid seeing me as they thought I'd call the police. But the guys locked themselves out of their van and were still hanging around when I got home. They'd been trying to break back into the van for three hours. Methinks they aren't very good locksmiths. In the end they picked the lock with a crowbar they'd borrowed from a neighbour's shed, without permission.

I think I can also say, even though I've only ever

been kidnapped by the one cult, that it was a better-than-average cult. It boasts an ocean view and its own spray-on-tan booth. It's mostly populated with minor television stars, the young adult progeny of the rich and famous, and others who also lead lavish lifestyles with no visible means of support, all searching for a way – other than cocaine – to alleviate the guilt of having much more money than talent. God, it seems, absolves them of responsibility for their actions in return for a generous donation.

The only really terrifying moment of my weekend away was when I realized my ex-boyfriend was also a member of the cult. I don't believe I've mentioned him to you. Suffice to say that he, even more so than you, is a good indication of my appalling taste in men.

Apart from the kidnapping, the attempted brainwashing and the police interview, it was a quiet couple of days. I did some gardening on Sunday afternoon.

How was your weekend?

Love,
Syd

The venue for the evening came down to a choice between two bars. One is popular because it's almost impossible to find. In an industrial district, housed in an unremarkable, unmarked warehouse, the only visible indication of its existence is a tiny valet parking sign stuck, seemingly, in the middle of nowhere. The second is popular because it's located far away from anything you'd want to be near. It has the added enticement of being extremely seedy-looking on the outside. No one is quite sure what the interior looks like, as no one has seen the interior.

Because the first bar is attached to a restaurant that features mediocre food at fine dining prices, we chose the second bar. As far as we know it serves only alcohol. Anna and I felt it'd be easier to manage our disappointment in the food if there wasn't any.

Still blinded by the ironically tacky neon sign above the entrance, it took a while before my eyes adjusted to the near darkness inside. Finally, I made out a soft line of light glowing behind what I assumed was the bar. I knew I'd guessed right when I heard the reassuring sound of glass and ice clinking and alcohol being poured in the generous amounts you get in LA, where bartenders never use measuring tools and everyone drives home after drinking.

Slowly, the shapes of people perched on barstools came

into view. Their silhouettes outlined the spiky haircuts and retro glasses of LA intellectuals, who go to great lengths to dress to show that they're not influenced by fashion and who each are working on an angst-ridden screenplay which opens on a depressed protagonist waking up in the morning.

The rest of the room, even more dimly lit than the bar area, held table-, chair- and people-shaped shadows. I noticed a person shape seated alone at one of the table shapes was either waving vigorously or having a convulsive fit. I made my way over to it.

'Is that you?'

'Yeah,' Anna said. 'What do you think? Is this a lighting concept or did they forget to pay the power bill?'

I groped around under the table, found a stool-like object and sat on it. 'I could go either way.'

'If I'd known, I wouldn't have bothered to put on make-up. I think there's a martini list on the table. Only you can't read it. It should be in Braille.'

'We can't read Braille.'

'A mere technicality. They have Braille on drive-through ATMs, why not here? It'd be just as useless. What do you want? I'll go to the bar. If there's table service I can't see it.'

'Vodka martini, dirty.'

The long, black shape that was Anna got up and disappeared into the gloom.

'Maybe it's a celebrity privacy thing,' I said, when the silhouette of Anna reappeared with martini glass silhouettes in its hands.

'What is?'

'The lighting. A celebrity could come in here, drink all night and never be spotted.'

'You think there could be someone here now?'

We squinted at the people at the other tables, who, it seemed, were squinting back at us.

'It's a scam,' Anna said. 'They want us to think there are celebrities here when there aren't. Cheers. Here's to the latest in the sorry tale of your romantic life.'

'Why don't we talk about your wedding instead?'

'The wedding is a full-time job for me. This is my leisure time. And, anyway, I can hardly show you swatches. I don't think we're really going to be able to tell the difference between pearl, ivory or mist in here.'

'Work is going really well.'

'I don't care. I'm ecstatically engaged, soon to be happily married. Where am I to get my fill of relationship drama if not from you?'

'You're as bad as my sister,' I said.

'I have a long way to go before I get quite as bad as that.'

True. My sister, Morgan, married her high-school sweetheart about two minutes after high school was over, then moved to a small Midwestern college town – full of other people who've had sex with only one person in their entire lives – from where she is scandalized by my life. She, of course, calls me constantly for fear of missing anything.

'Well?' Anna waved at me in the dark, or, at least, I think she did.

'Well, what? What more do you want? What could possibly top finding my boyfriend having sex with someone who wasn't me?'

'Only after you didn't return his calls for two weeks.'

'Let me just take a moment to remind you that you're supposed to be on my side.'

'I am,' she said. 'Usually, I'd be the first to say dump the two-timing rat bastard on his thick head. But in this case there are extenuating circumstances. You guys had only one official date before you stopped speaking to him for two weeks.'

'Are you going to keep bringing that up?'

'The point is you weren't exactly in a committed relationship. What he did was bad, but not unforgivable.'

'It happened last Friday night. Only a week has passed. I'm allowed to hold it against him a little longer. It's not like I've dumped him.'

'No,' Anna said, 'you are living with him.'

'Yes, even if it's a temporary, police-enforced kind of arrangement, I am living with him. I'm living with him and yet I'm not really sure if we're still seeing each other.'

'Are you sleeping with him?'

'If you're going to get technical about it, yes — but it doesn't count.'

'Why not?'

'Well, if I hadn't been kidnapped, then Jake and I wouldn't be together now, not after the Kim incident, so we certainly wouldn't be living together. Therefore any sex that occurs is purely circumstantial and not to be held against us as evidence of a relationship. Anyway, it could all be over tomorrow. I'm going back to my place. There have been no further kidnapping attempts on my person.'

'You know, he may be your last chance for a heterosexual guy with a job and a full head of hair without two ex-wives, three kids or a drug addiction.'

'Your expectations for me are so high it's touching.'

'Besides, you like him.'

'Ah, but I have notoriously bad taste. Take Matt, for example.'

'Is what he said still bugging you?'

'Oh, only all the time.'

'He obviously hit a sore spot.'

'You're really not getting the whole friendship-and-loyalty thing tonight, are you?'

'I never thought I'd say this, but, for the first time in his life, the Rat is right. Mind you, he had professional help. It's not like he figured it out all on his own with his tiny rodent brain.'

'I can't believe you're taking his side.'

'Nobody, least of all you, thought that relationship would work.'

'Everybody makes mistakes.'

'Yes, but not everybody is as determined to make them. Look at what you're doing now.'

'What am I doing now?'

'Looking for a reason to dump the only guy you ever dated who stands a chance of going the distance.'

'Looking for a reason? Exchanging bodily fluids with Ex-Girlfriend Barbie not good enough a reason for you? The visual is indelibly etched in my mind, thank you. And how do I know he won't do it again?'

'You don't. But I think this one's worth sticking around for. Trust me, I'm almost married. I know everything there is to know about men.'

'I'm so glad we're sharing like this,' I said.

'Saying "I told you so" is getting tired.'

'I'm sure that won't stop you.' I brought my glass up to my eyes to see if it was really as empty as it felt. 'I guess it's my turn to grope my way to the bar. What will you have?'

'Same again, thanks.'

'What was that? I can't see.'

✝

'Karl Lauderdale called. He wants you to call him,' Jake said, after he'd met me at the door, propped me up against the doorjamb and waved Vince and Anna, similarly propped up in the passenger seat, off. 'He said he was just checking up on you.'

'Oh, boy. More police business. Maybe I ought to call him now?'

'That's not a good idea. The morning will be fine. It's very late.'

'Were you waiting up for me?'

'I was. I have to answer to the cops if anything happens to you.'

'That's nice. I mean, that you waited up. Not that you have to answer to the cops. That's not so nice. It wouldn't be nice if something happened to me and they thought you were responsible – the cops, I mean – then the bad guys would get away and you'd be thrown in jail. And I'd have to stop seeing you because you'd be a felon. Though I guess I could learn to bake those cakes with the metal files in them. But I'm pretty sure the cake would taste metallic – and that would definitely not be nice.'

'Right,' Jake said.

'But you're nice and I like you.'

'I'm glad.'

'Do you like me?'

'Yes.'

'How much?' He needed some sort of scale with which to judge his feelings for me. 'This much?' I spread my arms as wide as they would go.

'Sure, now come on.' Jake turned me around in the right direction and prodded me in the butt to get me moving. It didn't work. With my arms outstretched I was too wide to fit through the door.

'You like me' – I assessed the distance still between my arms – 'a whole lot. And, though you have no concept of personal space when it comes to ex-girlfriends, you are an intelligent human being. So, it stands to reason. I can't be all bad.'

He pushed my arms back down by my sides and guided me through the door. 'You have one or two redeeming qualities.'

'Yes, that's my point exactly – oops.' My purse had somehow come loose from my grip and fallen to the floor. Jake picked it up and threaded it back on my arm, tucking it under my shoulder.

'Thanks,' I said. 'I like you.'

'Yes. You like me. I like you. We've been over that.'

'That's right. You like me. I'm OK. So what if I don't have any twos? Is that really such an issue? Is that why you went back to Kim, because I don't have any twos? Do you have any twos?'

'I can't say.'

'Never mind. It's OK. I'm not numberist.' I patted his

cheek. 'You're prickly. Who is he to tell me I need therapy, anyway?'

'I can honestly say I don't know.'

'The guy can't tie his shoelace without a psychiatrist in the room. The only thing he's managed to get out of all those twelve-step programmes is the ability to count to twelve. And that, it seems, makes him a numerologist. Only in LA.'

'I've no idea who you're talking about.'

'Rat. The Matt. I mean, Matt. Rat is his middle name.'

'Your ex, the cult guy?'

'That's right. My ex. My Kim . . . only without the anti-gravity breasts.'

'I see,' Jake said. 'Have you spoken to him again?'

'Oh, no. Spent an entire day with him. That's enough. Had a really nice lunch, though. Excellent foie gras. Not seeing him again.'

'OK.'

'Seriously, if anyone is incapable of love, it's an egotistical actor with the emotional range of an egg cup. How can he say that I'm the one incapable of love? I'm the one incapable of showing emotion? He can't show emotion even when they pay him to. This is all pots and kettles and degrees of blackness. And it's not true. It can't be true. I mean, what about you?'

'What about me?'

'Well, you're Exhibit A. You're hard evidence. You're living proof.'

'Proof of what?'

Really, Jake was being quite dim tonight.

'Hello? Proof that I'm quite capable of being in love with someone, thank you very much.'

The silence that ensued made me think Jake's ability to take in information dwindled drastically after midnight.

'You see,' I said, speaking slowly so he could follow me. 'Your very existence proves he's wrong. And that I'm right.'

'I'm not disagreeing with you.'

'Exactly. I have emotions. I'm in love. True, I don't think I've ever been in it before, but he's not to know that, is he? For all he knows I could've fallen in it all over the place. Right?'

'Right.'

'The guy hasn't a clue. He's on daytime television and what? That makes him Oprah? Men. They think they know it all. Like a penis is some kind of inbuilt *Encyclopaedia Britannica*.'

Looking at Jake, it occurred to me I'd said something I ought not to have said.

'Uh-oh,' I said, 'I shouldn't have said that. You're a men.'

'I'll overlook it this once.'

'Will you? That's nice. I like y– . . . oh . . . I don't feel so good.'

'We need to get you to bed.'

'OK.'

At the bottom of the stairs I motioned Jake closer to let him in on a secret.

'I'm drunk.'

'I know,' he said. But I felt I owed him more of an explanation.

'You see. I've been drinking.'

'That's the way it usually happens.'

I had plenty more to say on the subject, but, before I could, Jake had picked me up, and, judging by the way they were falling away from me in an alarming manner when I looked down, I was on my way up the stairs through no exertion of my own.

'Look, Ma, no legs,' I told Jake's left ear.

There was a lot of giggling on my part and quite a bit of patience on his when we reached his bedroom. I entered the room in a thoroughly good mood, but as I lay in bed waiting to fall asleep I felt unsettled. More unsettled than the bucket of martini I drank could be held accountable for. It was as if I'd eaten something I shouldn't have. Or said something I shouldn't have. The more I thought about it, the more I was sure it was the latter. I hadn't eaten anything. Besides, there was something suspicious about Jake's behaviour once we were in the bedroom, a kind of watchful speculation in his eyes that wasn't there before. But my mind was balancing precariously between vodka-induced paranoia and sleep, and I didn't want to nudge it in the wrong direction by recalling what it was I'd said. In the morning I'd be hung over and wouldn't remember anything at all. Comforted by this, I spent the night in fitful sleep, visited by several strange dreams, all involving me being caught flying around in public places without a stitch of clothing on.

FROM: Sydney Welles <sydneywelles@yahoo.com>
TO: God c/- satan@hell.com
DATE: Saturday, June 18, 11.01 a.m.
SUBJECT: Hung Over in Southern California

Dear God,

Who turned all the water into vodka? My head feels as if several thousand freed Israelites are holding a dance party on it. I swear I'm never ever going to drink again.

Actually, I don't swear. I know you don't like swearing and it probably isn't wise to bandy words like 'ever' about when talking to an immortal being holding absolute power over life and death, and life after death, especially one who's been cranky for at least two thousand years. So, let's just say that, in the future, I'm going to try to rethink my beverage choices.

I have to go sit on the bathroom floor for a minute now.

Bye,
Syd

FROM: Sydney Welles <sydneywelles@yahoo.com>
TO: God c/- melgibson@reformedmoviestarswithamessage.net
DATE: Sunday, September 25, 3.21 p.m.
SUBJECT: Update

Dear God,

How are you? It occurred to me today that you probably hear from people only when they need something – that is, apart from those sickeningly cheerful people who feel the need to constantly bombard you with their gratitude, which must be annoying in a different way.

I haven't been in contact for about three months, for one reason. My life has been going exceptionally well. And, as is the case for most people, when life is going well, you aren't a priority.

I'm really only getting in touch now because I have work news to pass on. You are, ultimately, the head client on the Catholic Church account, and you have a right to know. Since we hit upon the strategy of selling the Church as an insurance policy against hell – which, let's face it, is actually what it is – everything has been going right. The rest of the qualitative groups responded very well to the idea. People have health insurance, car insurance, home insurance, mortgage insurance, travel insurance, disability insurance and life insurance. Afterlife insurance isn't much of a leap. It was the only strategy we took into quantitative research.

After a sample of eight thousand people, it looks as if we're on to something. It's only a matter of time before you are available at a supermarket near me.

Being omniscient, you probably already know all this.

You probably know also, as you like to watch people have sex, that I still have the boyfriend I sort-of-had when we last spoke. He's just finished that piece on drug lords in custody. Everyone thinks it worthy of some kind of award. It certainly is very gritty and real. At the very least, Jake has a dozen new contacts for discounted drugs, should he wish to become an addict.

Life seems to be going frighteningly well. No doubt something will happen soon to mess it up. Even in California, people can only go around following their bliss for so long before it all goes to shit.

Hope everything's okay in heaven,
Syd x

# FISHER BENNET McMAHON & MAY

4848 Abott Way Los Angeles CA 90066 USA
310-807-3000 t   310-807-5000 f

Charles Turner
Los Angeles Times
202 W. 1st St.
CA 90012

Dear Charles,

I've given the question you put to me in your last letter a lot of consideration. I think it odd that you've asked me to lunch now, after all this time. Especially after you pointedly ignored the unsubtle hints I dropped in every second letter telling you where I'd be so you could easily bump into me, if you ever wanted to.

However, my answer is yes. There was a time when our letters were embarrassingly long, when we poured our insides out on paper for each other's perusal, and I wrote things to you I wouldn't dare say to anyone. It was the only time in my life I think I've ever been that open with another person – and, Christ, I put it in writing. I don't know what made me do that. If I remember correctly, that period of candour lasted about seven months before our correspondence regressed to become, more or less, what it had started out as. To this day I have no idea what happened.

It is because of the letters we wrote during that time

that I'd like to have lunch with you. I think it best to go along with whatever you say. After all, I'd hate for the world to find out what really goes on in my head, and you have the evidence in writing.

See you at there, noon, Saturday.

Syd

For most of Thursday morning I tried to shake off my conscience. There was nothing wrong with having lunch with Charles. It was just lunch, in a proper restaurant, in full view of the world. I wasn't going to have sex with him on the table between courses. I'm familiar with the restaurant. The tables are too small.

Besides, by asking me to lunch instead of dinner, Charles is indicating it isn't a romantic date. According to those dating books full of dating rules, if a man is interested in you that way, he asks you out to dinner. Preferably on a Saturday night, as Saturday night is the only night of the week that men have serious intentions towards women – those books are very specific.

If a man asks you to lunch as a first date, he's deliberately keeping things neutral. He's not sure whether he's interested in you, but would like to have sex with you anyway, or he's interested in you but only for sex, or he just wants to be friends – friends who have sex. So, in truth, it isn't a date at all. The only flaw in this logic is that there's a good chance Charles hasn't read those dating books and may not know it isn't a date.

There's also the distinct possibility Charles is unattractive; newspaper columnists, especially the humorous ones – not that his columns are always intentionally funny – aren't known for their good looks. I also have to allow for the possibility he might find me unattractive. There's no accounting for taste these days.

By all standards it was an innocent excursion. It wasn't much use telling myself this. Since being exposed to Catholicism my sense of guilt is more highly developed.

However, it's not as if Jake and I are in a committed relationship. Since the Kim-and-kidnapping episode, we see each other – to the best of my knowledge – exclusively, but, so far, have avoided any kind of serious state-of-the-union discussion.

Lately, though, Jake has been talking about future events in his life as if I'll be concerned in them. The 'we' and 'us' business of romantic partnerships has snuck into his vocabulary, and, I'm ashamed to admit, mine, and we've come to take it for granted that, unless one of us is away or otherwise engaged, we spend our free time together.

Just this morning, he'd admitted to me what it was that had made him fall in love with me. Well, actually, that wasn't exactly how he phrased it. Love wasn't really mentioned at all. In fact, I think it was me who asked him what it was he liked most about me. I was curious and only half joking.

He'd replied, without hesitation, 'Your nose.'

'My nose?' I said. 'The thing you like most about me is my nose?'

He'd said, 'I think you're underestimating your nose,' which was nice, but, even if I were underestimating my nose, it still doesn't strike me as much of a basis on which to build a relationship. I blame proximity, that consummate enabler of romance, for the ease with which we've fallen quickly into what, from the outside, looks like an established relationship. In Los Angeles, distance is the most important contributing factor – after silicon, of course – to a successful relationship.

In a place made up of a series of sprawling suburbs cobbled together by a freeway system that sometimes works, it's entirely possible to have a long-distance relationship with someone who lives in the same city. The average person spends over two hours commuting to and from work. There are not enough hours in the day to also commute for sex. I know many men who won't ask a woman out if she lives more than twenty minutes away.

When I consider the very minimal distance between Jake's house and my house, and that he has not officially declared his feelings for, or intentions towards, me, I could come to the conclusion – especially if I've just been reading one of those dating books – that, for him, the relationship is convenient rather than serious. According to the aforementioned books I'm not in a real relationship for two reasons:

1 There is a list of things, rather like commandments, that you're not supposed to do if you want a guy to take you seriously, and everything that you're not supposed to do – sleeping with the guy on the first date comes pretty close to the top of the list – I've done.
2 Until he declares himself one way or the other, he is not committed to me – these books state that only the man can decide if a relationship is serious or not – so therefore I'd be stupid to consider myself committed.

By this reckoning, I've no reason to feel guilty for agreeing to a blameless lunch with a newspaperman, but, as I strongly suspect that these dating books are full of shit, and emotions can't be reduced to a few arbitrary rules, I was wallowing in guilt.

My conscience annoyed me for the better part of the meeting I was in – a meeting held to determine the way we should run meetings. After going over it in my mind, and weighing up the possibility of upsetting my relationship with Jake against a strong desire to finally meet Charles, I knew what needed to be done.

It was obvious. I had to break the plans I'd made with Jake to spend the entire weekend together, at least for Saturday, around lunchtime. Of course, I couldn't tell Jake I was ditching him to have lunch with some other guy, so what I needed was an alibi, someone to cover for me, someone I could say I was having lunch with in case Jake became suspicious. The only question that remained was who it should be.

It had to be someone no one would suspect of being capable of deception. Someone who didn't really have any kind of moral or ethical code that I'd have to worry about. Someone who doesn't stop to think things through before they agree to them.

I found Julie Ryan in a small meeting room near her office. Her constant, constantly panting companion, Brad Pitt, was nowhere in sight. She was with Patton, who looked as if he'd dearly like to be gone.

Julie tapped the pen she was holding on Patton's notebook. 'You got all that?'

'Yes, ma'am.'

Julie wriggled around in her seat, coming to rest in what looked to be an exceptionally uncomfortable position, at the same time as spotting me in the doorway.

'Oh, hello,' she said.

'What's wrong with you?'

'New kind of pube torture.'

Patton looked to me, confused. 'Pube?'

I translated for him. 'Pubic hair. I think Julie's just had a bikini wax.'

Blushes, like concentric circles on the surface of water, spread across Patton's face, each more crimson than the last.

'I should get going, ma'am. Don't think I should be present for . . . for . . . secret women's business.'

'Fine, off you go,' then.'

Patton began gathering his notebooks together.

'Spill,' I said. 'What did they do to you?'

Julie used to be in the habit of having her pubic hair waxed and trimmed into the first initial of whomever she was dating. That fashion ended when she found she was going through men too quickly to allow time for the regrowth required between different letters of the alphabet. Seeing only men with the same first initial – she tried 'M' for six months – was too limiting.

Since then she's been experimenting with a series of pubic hairstyles and colours, all of which she's prepared to describe in detail to anyone who'll listen.

In my opinion, what she does serves only to perpetuate the grossly unfair private-parts situation between men and women. Women undergo the pain and humiliation of paying a complete stranger to rip the hair out of their genitals, to appear more attractive to men. They trim, shave, wax, dye, plait and pierce, according to the current definition of vaginal attractiveness as dictated by the old men who publish girlie magazines – who, I dare say, have never allowed hot wax anywhere near their nether regions. In return, men occasionally wash in their genital region to appear more attractive to women.

While I stand by my opinion that the excessiveness of her pubic grooming is ideologically unsound, it's still fascinating to hear what Julie's had done.

'It's called a "Tiffany's",' she said.

'Is there jewellery involved?'

'No, just the packaging. All they left is a small square, dyed the same blue as a Tiffany's box.'

Patton, on his way out of the room, walked into the doorframe.

'That must have hurt,' I said.

'No, ma'am, not at all. I'm fine.'

'I meant her, not you.'

Julie screwed up her cheerleader face. 'The bleach was the worst – I'm not going to make it to the gym tonight.'

Patton, who couldn't leave the room effectively, was blushing again. Red rose slowly from his neck and crept up his face like sunrise. The boy possessed the widest variety of blushes I'd ever seen.

'That reminds me. Patton?'

'Ma'am?' He turned back to face me from the doorway.

'Could you please call my trainer and cancel my appointment on Tuesday – I'm not going to be able to make it, not while getting this presentation together.'

'Where do I find the number?'

'It's under "E" – for "Evil Josh" – in the old Rolodex. You know, while you're at it, you may as well cancel the next week's appointment, too.'

'No problem.'

'Only don't do it until this time next week. Just make a note of it so you remember. In fact, make a standing note to cancel my Tuesday morning appointment every Thursday or Friday afternoon. OK?'

'For how long, ma'am.'

'For ever, I should think.'

Patton looked puzzled. 'If you aren't intending on keeping any of the appointments, why don't I cancel Mr Evil altogether.'

'I can't cancel him altogether. I'd have no trainer at all. That would be really letting myself go.'

Julie agreed. 'You can't not have a trainer.'

'It's true – like she says – it's much better to just cancel every week. You understand?'

'No, ma'am, not at all.'

'Will that prevent you from completing the task?'

'No, ma'am, not at all.'

Patton managed to leave the room successfully.

'There goes military training at its finest,' I said.

Julie appeared to be lost in deep thought. It's an optical illusion she performs from time to time. When she spoke, it was clear her thoughts had not strayed from the pelvic region. 'Do you think he's still a virgin?'

'Who? Patton? Don't even think about it. Keep your jewellery box away from him.'

'I'm too sore to try.'

'Stop doing this to yourself.'

'Guys really like it.'

'I'm sure they do, but there's no need to spoil them. Listen . . . I need to ask a favour.'

'OK.'

'If it's all right with you, I'm going to tell Jake that I'm having lunch with you on Saturday. So, if you should see him and he should ask –'

'Are we having lunch on Saturday?'

'Well, no, we're not.'

'You just said we are.'

'Yes, but –'

'Then why did you say we are having lunch on Saturday?'

This might be harder than I thought. 'We're not having lunch. I'm just saying that we are.'

'But if we're not, then that's a lie.'

'Yes, yes, it's a lie.'

'Why are we lying?'

'Because I don't want to tell Jake who I'm really having lunch with.'

'Who is that?'

'A . . . friend,' I said. 'It's nothing. Just lunch. I'd just prefer that Jake doesn't know.'

About then, Julie's intellect grasped the situation entirely.

'Oooh, I get it. This is like a cover-up.'

'That's right.'

'I pretend that I had lunch with you, so Jake doesn't find out you're having lunch with this friend. I can do that. Don't worry about a thing.'

'I really appreciate this, it'll – what is it?'

Concern had wrinkled Julie's usually unnaturally smooth brow. The time for another round of paralysing poison to be injected into her brain cavity must have been close at hand.

'What should I say I had for lunch?'
'What?'
'If Jake asks me. What did I have for lunch?'
'I don't know,' I said.
'Did I have a first course?'
'No. Maybe. I . . . does it matter?'
'What about wine? Did we have wine?'
'Um . . . OK, sure, a glass or two.'
'Red wine or white wine?'
'Red?'
'I can't drink red during the day; it's too heavy.'
'OK,' I said, 'white, then.'
'A Chardonnay? Or maybe I had a Sauvignon Blanc? Did I eat fish? A Pinot Gris? That's quite the thing at the moment.'
'OK, let's make it Pinot Gris.'
'What about dessert? I think it'd sound more realistic if I say we split a dessert. Profiteroles?'
I was seriously questioning my choice of accomplice. 'Fine,' I said, 'have the profiteroles.'
'Nah, I'm not in the mood for profiteroles. Can I have crème brûlée instead? With something interesting in it, like lavender or citrus. That's very trendy right now.' Alarm grew in her eyes as she blinked at me. 'Where did we go?'
'Sorry?'
'For lunch. Where did we go? What if the things we

had aren't on the menu at the place we say we went to. He'll go there and see right through the whole thing. We've got to be careful. Where did we go to lunch?'

'We're – I am going to that wine bar on Abott Kinney.'

'I know the one. I've never been there. I should go beforehand.'

'I don't think that will be nec –'

'With you. I'll have to go with you. What if he asks what you ate? Or what we talked about? We'll have to go there for lunch by Saturday.'

'But that's the day after tomorrow –'

'Good idea. We'll go today.' Julie looked at me in a satisfied way. 'This has worked out so well. I didn't know what I was going to do to fill the rest of the day and I really wanted to go somewhere nice for lunch. Are you ready to go now?'

'Where's Brad Pitt?' He was my last hope. Julie insists on taking him everywhere, and the restaurant wouldn't allow him in.

'Doggy daycare day today. For his social development.'

'I . . . I'll just get my bag.'

Not for the first time, I wondered if Julie was really as silly as we've all been led to believe.

FROM: Sydney Welles <sydneywelles@yahoo.com>
TO: God c/- thethirdman@holytrinity.com
DATE: Thursday, September 29, 6.39 p.m.
SUBJECT: Miracles Are No Longer Miraculous

Dear God,

Miracles aren't what they used to be. These days they're all about statues and some form of liquid: statues weeping, statues bleeding or statues drinking milk.

Face it, you've lost a good deal of your showmanship over the years: manna never rains from heaven and water never morphs into wine. No one is parting seas. No one is walking on water. And no one is rising from the dead.

While fairly stupid on a number of counts, the average consumer is, thanks to modern cinema, very sophisticated when it comes to the quality of their special effects. They like them big, bold and believable. They like things to blow up. They like to see tricks they've never seen before.

If you want to put butts on pews, you're going to have to do better than a leaky statue.

Sydney x

Theologians define miracles as God-willed transgressions of the laws of nature. In Los Angeles, so much contravenes the laws of nature that, God willing or not, these violations, for the most part, occur without incurring much comment. This is understandable. Miracles need to be rare to be classified as such. A surfeit of anything lessens its value, as our consumer society demonstrates on a daily basis. The supply-and-demand equation that applies to the most popular handbag of the season also applies to God's handiwork.

That is not to say that all marvels go by completely unnoticed in this town. I, personally, am witness to one on an annual basis, as are at least several hundred other people. I've seen the Crawford transformation three times before, but for those beholding it for the first time – and there are always plenty of virgins in an agency of five hundred with high turnover and burnout rates – just seeing Larry Crawford not drunk must seem quite miraculous.

In my opinion, our agency is full of miracles. After all, it is also somewhat of a wonder that Noah never seems to need to leave the sofa in my office – a sofa which I've never considered mine, as I've never had the chance to sit on it. Reclining like a Roman emperor, eating Saltines instead of grapes, Noah was distributing cracker crumbs with surprising range, still wearing yesterday's T-shirt, which still said: 'Fundamentalism means never having to admit you're wrong.'

I was at my desk, imprisoned by piles of paperwork, trying to tailor a presentation to suit men of the cloth. 'You want to take a crack at part of this?'

'As I'm paid far less than you, I feel my job is to lend moral support. That's best achieved from over here.'

'Why are you always in my office?'

'Because my office doesn't have any walls. No privacy.'

'Not much in my office, either. Shouldn't you be working on ... something?' What was he supposed to be working on? I'd lost track of all our other projects since becoming embroiled in Catholicism.

'God before Country Style Frozen Dinners,' he said. 'And, you need me.'

'Hardly. This is the easy part. The hard part begins when we're awarded the account and have to produce something.'

'Details, details. All we need to do,' Noah said, 'is ask ourselves what kind of advertising campaign Jesus would do.'

A deep, familiar voice spoke up. 'You think you're being ironic, but you're not. Jesus, ultimately, was the one who kicked off this campaign.'

The man who stood at the door of my office was almost too elegant to bear. His suit bespoke, his collar painfully crisp, his tie exhibiting equal amounts of good taste and individuality, he was too well groomed for real life, giving the impression a team of professionals had polished him until he gleamed, arranged him in my doorway, and now waited off camera for any touch-ups required.

'Larry,' I said, 'you're back.'

'Glad to see your sense of sight is still working. I was mildly worried about you. Tales of your adventures reached the Swiss.'

'Which adventures were they?'

'Your little religious experience over in Malibu.'

Noah sat up, curious. 'What experience in Malibu? We didn't do any –'

'You look famished,' Larry said. 'Go to lunch.'

'I'm not –'

'Did your mother drop you on your head as a child? Go, before you waste away.'

Noah does look undernourished, being one of those tall, skinny people who can and do eat a horse, never gaining an ounce. He eats constantly during his waking hours, so it's inconceivable he could ever be famished, but he could take a hint. Grabbing his precious Saltines, Noah threw me a look of commiseration and left.

Larry immediately took Noah's place on my sofa, first fastidiously dusting off the crumbs.

'How did you hear about that?' I'd told no one at work about my kidnapping experience. I usually keep quiet about my personal life at the office; it's more professional that way and, besides, until recently there was nothing much to tell.

'Not through the usual channels, I assure you,' Larry said. 'An old friend asked me to give his goddaughter a job. She's been pestering him to speak to me since allegedly meeting you at a weekend retreat of her spiritual-guru-of-the-month club – she got kicked out of it for drinking. I think you know whom I mean. She's a professional party girl, the daughter of –'

It all dawned on me. 'You don't mean India Walsh?' I'd given her one of my business cards, but I hadn't the slightest suspicion she'd know how to use it.

'I do.'

'Why does she want to work here?'

'She got the idea from you. Wanted to go to an office every day, carry a Gucci briefcase, help organize an office Christmas party, date men with career paths – I believe those were the reasons she gave.'

'Are you going to give her a job?'

'Sure. Her father is one of the biggest advertisers out there and not yet gracing our client list.'

'What kind of job does she want?'

'VP of Something – I think she's under the impression vice president is an entry-level position.'

'We don't have any VP positions.' Being a vice president is no longer in vogue, not since C-level jobs became the status management-job-title of choice. 'It could be an entry-level position if you wanted it to be.'

'Vice president of what?'

'I don't know – Julie needs an assistant. She's been using Patton. And he's scared of her.'

'That could work. It doesn't really matter what we give her – given what India's godfather has told me, her enthusiasm for a job may not last long enough for her to fill out a W2 form.'

'I could see that.'

'Still, we get her on the payroll, however briefly, and

next time daddy reshuffles his deck of advertising agencies – something he does fairly often – he'll have to throw us a bone.'

'Very Machiavellian of you.'

'Yes, isn't it,' he said. 'Have you solved our little Church problem?'

'As a matter a fact, I have.'

'Tell me everything.'

'Well,' I said, 'turned out I was looking in all the wrong places, trying to find something good about religion that people wanted to buy, when I should've been thinking of it as a necessary evil all along. To cut a long story short, I'm now using insurance as a selling model. It works because of –'

'Brilliant,' Larry said. I'd forgotten that Larry, sober, doesn't need anything explained to him. 'Makes perfect sense. How's it doing in research?'

'It's researching its balls off.'

'Good. Good. We're ready to go, then – on this, at least. I wish I could say the same for the rest – they're all performing to expectations, saving up the problems on their accounts all year for me to deal with post-rehab. No wonder I'm an alcoholic. At least the Church will come good.'

'Well, if it does, I hope it keeps the bean counters at bay.'

'It will, for a while, until they want more beans to count.'

'If we get the Church account, we'll have grown twenty per cent for the year, and the year isn't over yet. They can't expect more. Everyone is working well above the call of duty as it is.'

Larry shook his head. 'You seem to be under the impression that there's humanity, or, at least, consideration for human beings, involved in the running of a public corporation. There isn't. Try to get over it. All that matters is the share price.'

'It has to be enough. We've been going after new business since this time last year. If we get this one, that makes five wins in a row. Everyone is exhausted. There has to be a saturation point. They can't expect us to do this again.'

'That's exactly what they will expect. What we've done in the past year will be the new benchmark for the next.'

'Christ, it's like trying to fill a bottomless pit.'

'Exactly,' Larry said. 'Now you're getting it.'

'What's the point if nothing we do will ever be enough?'

'Can't tell you that. I know what the point is for me. It gives me something to do between cocktail hours. What the point is for you is something you're going to have to figure out for yourself.'

'Yes, Obi-Wan.'

'You jest, but this is important, life-changing shit . . . speaking of shit, I think it's about to catch up with me.'

I glanced up to see what Larry was referring to. His rather formidable personal assistant, trailed by several account management people, meekly walking in single file behind her, was on her way to my office to collect him.

'Here come the please-fix-the-mess-I-made suits.'

'Good luck,' I said.

Noah returned to take up space on my couch soon after Larry was rounded up and marched off. Noah's hair was damp and he had a fresh T-shirt on. Actually, I didn't know how fresh it was, but it was certainly a different colour to the one he'd been wearing when he left the room. He'd taken a shower. Sometimes I wonder if he lives at the agency.

Not that I can talk. Los Angeles has an indecent 329 days of sunshine a year, yet I seem to spend most daylight hours in here, basking in fluorescence.

Noah shifted into a more relaxed, open position on the couch, enabling me to read his new T-shirt: 'God Hates Homosexuals, But Lesbians Are the Shit!'

'Did Larry like the work?'

'He didn't look at anything,' I said. 'But he did say the selling model was brilliant.'

'We keep our jobs for another year, then.'

'It seems so.'

Satisfied with his tenure, Noah yawned, stretched out and settled in for a nap.

Briefly, I wondered where on earth he obtained his unending supply of sacrilegious shirts, but I soon went back to wondering what I'd been wondering before he came back into the room.

What was the point for me?

FROM: Sydney Welles <s.welles@fbmm.com>
TO: God c/- info@churchofscientology.com
DATE: Friday, September 30, 4.59 p.m.
SUBJECT: Heaven is designed to keep people out

Dear God,

More and more people now live in gated communities. I used to think it was because people like to live near other people who are scared of the same people they are.

Now I'm wondering if they're actually attempting to create heaven here on earth. After all, heaven is the ultimate gated community. It's virtually impossible to get into.

First, you have to choose – from a dazzling myriad of choices – the one true religion. Then you have to live a life devoid of sin, and do this on earth, where it's practically impossible to get through life without breaking a commandment every couple of days.

Is this because, like all gated communities, heaven has only a limited number of places for the right kind of people?

Or are you the Greta Garbo of supreme beings? Do you just want to be alone?

Best,
Sydney

Pulling up at the valet parking stand that serves several restaurants at the Main Street end of Abbot Kinney, it dawned on me I couldn't possibly have lunch with Charles. It wasn't cold feet, though mine seemed frostbitten, or my sudden loss of appetite. It was Jake at home, innocent, unsuspecting and probably trying to fix something, while I was out on what may or may not be a date with a newspaper columnist.

If I'd examined my feelings a little more closely at the time, I'd have also seen that I was terrified. Meeting Charles after he'd existed, perfect and fictional, in my imagination all this time was bound to be a disappointment. I feared he'd fall far short of my expectations, but not as much as I feared he might live up to them. Luckily, I didn't examine my feelings any more closely than was required for me to change my mind about lunch. Panic then took over, as I tried to think of a way to extricate myself from the situation.

The right thing to do was to stop in and inform Charles of my change of heart:

a) 'Hi, nice to finally meet you after all this time, but I can't stay and break bread with you. I just wanted to see whether you were cuter than my boyfriend, and, well, now I see that you're not.'

b) 'This is all your fault. If only you'd dumped your girlfriend and asked me out sooner, I'd be able to eat now.'
c) 'I've only two weeks left to live and want to eat only lobster, which they don't serve here. Sorry.'

On second thought, I could sneak around like the coward I was and leave a message with the hostess without being seen. That shouldn't be too hard. Charles didn't know what I looked like; it wouldn't matter if he did see me. It was the best solution.

Stepping on the accelerator, startling the valet parking attendant, whose feet just escaped being flattened, was the chicken-shit thing to do, but that was the choice I opted for.

I soon came to a halt, mostly because of a stop sign and partly because I hadn't any idea where I was headed. The horn of the black SUV behind me forced me to make a decision. Like most everybody on the road in LA, the woman sitting on her horn had no real idea where her life was headed, but had a V-8 engine to get her there, fast.

Turning right was easier than turning left. I turned right. That turn came off without a hitch. I turned right a few more times and after a while found myself turning into Jake's street.

Shortly afterwards, I was ringing his doorbell. He didn't answer. Odd, as he'd told me he'd be home all afternoon. He'd even told me what he'd be doing, cleaning his outdoor furniture, and assembling his new patio umbrella so we could eat outside when we felt like it – we were experiencing a bit of an Indian summer in October in Los Angeles.

Now, it struck me as odd that he'd tell me that. He doesn't usually go into details of domestic chores – it's one of the things I like about him. I began to wonder, had I been so busy deceiving him about today that I completely missed the possibility he might be doing the same to me? Telling myself I was being paranoid, I sat on his front steps and waited. And waited.

I was still waiting, nearly an hour later, and by this time thoroughly convinced something was going on, when Jake's car pulled up in his driveway and stopped just before hitting his garage door. He was whistling cheerfully, but not terribly tunefully, as he got out of his car. The whistling chafed me a little, but I couldn't pinpoint the reason why.

Walking around the back of his car, he glanced across the road, registered my car parked there, and looked around for me. I was still camped out on the steps; his search was short and successful.

'Hey,' he said, bounding up to the steps in a way I found as irritating as his whistling.

I stood up and dusted my butt. 'Where have you been?'

Jake, in a disturbingly cheerful mood, picked me up and spun me around, in the process even helping a little with the butt dusting.

Once the dizziness subsided, I tried again. 'Where have you been?'

'Getting something to eat.'

He unlocked the door, holding it open for me. 'What happened to lunch?'

'It, er, was cancelled.'

'You're all dressed up.'

'This? No, it's an old dress – I never wear it – I just thought I should this once – rather than – I never wear it – it's old.'

'It doesn't look old.'

'It looks new, but it's old. Because I never wear it.'

'You're still too well dressed to help.' Jake had begun to rummage around in the storage cupboard under the stairs. He soon found what he was looking for, a wooden, mallet-like object.

'What are you going to do with that?'

'Wait and see. Why didn't you just let yourself in?'

'Why didn't I break into your house? I didn't have one of those things.' I pointed at the mallet.

'But you have keys, right?'

I did? I'd forgotten that I did, but, when I checked, there they were on my key chain. 'I'm not staying here any more, so I can't use these keys. It's against the rules. Sorry. I should've returned them to you. It's your fault, too; you ought to have asked for them back.'

Jake headed towards the kitchen. 'Keep them.'

I followed him. 'Why?'

'They're very useful for opening the door when it's locked.'

I detached his keys from the others on my key chain, at the cost of a fingernail. I held them up. 'I can't keep them. We're not ready for this.'

'For what?'

'Keys are a commitment,' I said. 'We should wait.'

'How do they suddenly become a commitment? You've had them all this time.'

'That doesn't count. I didn't know I had them. Now I know, so now it counts as a commitment.'

Jake was looking for something under the sink. He emerged from the cupboard to squint at me. 'I think you may have a commitment problem.'

'No. I don't have a commitment problem. I'm the girl. Historically speaking, my gender does not have a problem with commitment. I just think we may be getting ahead of ourselves.'

Jake stood, brandishing the booty he'd discovered under the sink, a couple of T-shirts-turned-rags. 'You're being really silly. Keep the keys.'

'But these things snowball. Once you start, there is no turning back. I don't nip it in the bud now, and, next thing you know, I'm in Reno, waiting for a divorce, with issues that could cost me years in therapy.'

Jake put the rags down on the counter. 'You're sane most of the time, so I'm going to forget we had this conversation.' He took the keys and key chain from my hands, reattached them and put them back in my purse, on the kitchen counter. 'See, now, everything is as it was before. If it helps, you can pretend you don't know you have them. Either way, cease and desist with the commitment dementia.'

'Now I'll have to give you keys, too, won't I?'

'Syd?'

'Yes?'

'Shut up.'

'Shut up? Oh, we are definitely headed for divorce.'

'You're under no obligation to give me your keys.'

'You don't understand. I have to give them to you now. I can't not.'

'Why?'

'If I don't, I look like the one not coming to the commitment party – I'll be the bad guy. I can't be the bad guy because I'm the girl.'

Jake stared at me closely for quite a while. 'You have a real gift for complicating the simplest things.'

I did what I was taught to do when someone pays you a compliment that most likely is not a compliment. I smiled and said, 'Thank you.'

☦

Sunday morning, we were up and out of bed early. Slipping on sweats and flip-flops we set off on our usual Sunday forage for breakfast, walking down to the farmers' market on Main Street, where there were French pastries sold by Ukrainian people to be had in exchange for very little money.

Within seconds of arriving at the market I regretted setting out. There between two rival flower stalls I spotted a woman and a dog I knew. After my abrupt change of luncheon plans yesterday, quite possibly the last owner and pet I wanted to see.

Julie approached us, Brad Pitt reaching us a leash length ahead of her.

'Hi, Julie,' I said, in a way I hoped was laden with warning. 'You remember Jake, don't you?'

'Yeah, we met at drinks at the agency. Hi.' She paused dramatically. 'So, Syd, how'd you pull up after that extremely long lunch?' Her question was accompanied by an unsubtle wink.

Thankfully, Jake was crouching to take a closer look at the resplendent ugliness of Brad Pitt. I took the opportunity to give Julie a meaningful glance and a shake of my head, mouthing, 'No,' to alert her not to say anything more. It was all lost on her.

'Syd and I had the nicest lunch yesterday – went for hours,' she said.

Jake looked up with interest. 'You did? Yesterday?'

'How's the interviewing for your new assistant going?' I said.

'Fine. So, Jake, have you been there? They have eighty-five wines by the glass. I only tried five. I have to go back.'

I tried again. 'You're up early for a Sunday, aren't you?'

'What?' she said. 'Anyway, get Syd to take you there. The food was good – lots of little courses. I liked the lamb, and the ribs. All of it, really.'

Jake stood back up. 'This was yesterday?'

'Thursday,' I said. 'It was Thursday we went to lunch.'

'No, it was Sat-tur-day, re-mem-ber, Syd-ney?' She was winking again.

I cringed.

Julie went on. 'It was full, but we got a table outside without a booking. No wait at all. Turned out I'd slept with the bartender in my early twenties. Lucky, huh?'

'Very lucky,' Jake said.

I bent over and rubbed Brad Pitt's head.

'Help me, doggy,' I said.

He cocked his head as if to say he was on the job. He

started barking, pulling Julie in the direction of a passing golden retriever, who was barking in return.

'Ooooop,' said Julie, 'looks like he's spotted a friend. He goes on play dates with that dog. Wish the owner was more attractive – I could play with him as well. Gotta go say hello. See ya.'

'Play dates for dogs?' I said. 'I thought doggy daycare was excessive. What next?'

'That was odd.'

I shrugged. 'Not really, not for Julie. We had lunch on Thursday – I guess she just got the days mixed up.'

'She seemed pretty adamant.'

It was a good thing I was wearing dark glasses. 'Yes, didn't she?'

'Come to think of it, when I dropped you home Friday night, I think you said you were having lunch with Julie yesterday.'

'I did?'

'You did.'

'I lied. This presentation I'm working on is making me forget whether I'm coming or going –'

'So, who were you meeting for lunch?'

'Yesterday? Oh, yesterday. I had to go into work for a while, you know, because of this Church thing – I had lunch there – oh look, fresh chocolate croissants. Shall we get some?'

'Sure,' Jake said, and that put an end to the subject.

Jake wasn't at all suspicious – quite the opposite, in fact. His lack of suspicion made me suspicious. Not for the first time since the night I surprised him and Kim, it occurred to me that he was hiding something. Call it women's intuition, or call it paranoia, somehow I was sure there was something going on.

He was whistling tunelessly again. That's when I realized what had bugged me about his whistling the previous day. I knew why he was whistling today: sex. Men are inordinately pleased when they can put their early morning erections to use. I didn't know what caused him to whistle yesterday, except that I had nothing to do with it. I began to wonder just who did.

# FISHER BENNET McMAHON & MAY

4848 Abott Way Los Angeles CA 90066 USA

310-807-3000 t   310-807-5000 f


Charles Turner
Los Angeles Times
202 W. 1st St.
CA 90012

Dear Charles,

You may have noticed that I did not join you for lunch on Saturday. I offer my deepest and sincerest apologies, but can offer no explanation of my absence at this time – well, no explanation that you'd buy. I will explain this all to you one day, in person, if you're still speaking to me at that stage.

In the meantime, please accept one of the following pathetic excuses:

a) My house burned down.
b) My car wouldn't start.
c) My rabbit ate my homework (this one is definitely not true, as my rabbit has run away from home and I haven't seen him for a couple of weeks).
d) I was upset about my rabbit running away.

Even if none of these excuses suits, I hope you can forgive me,

Syd

FROM: Sydneywelles <s.welles@fbmm.com>
TO: God c/- ravinglunaticontheradio@clearchannel.com
DATE: Tuesday, October 4, 10.38 a.m.
SUBJECT: Discrepancies

Dear God,

Jesus Christ was Jewish. And Buddha was a Hindu. I just thought I'd point that out.

Syd

Any psychiatrist could have told me it was my own guilt over Charles that made me suspicious of Jake. They say it's always the less-than-faithful partner in a relationship who is more mistrustful, while the innocent party trusts implicitly, as each is guided in their outlook by their own behaviour. I became convinced he was hiding something from me because I was hiding something from him.

Had I a psychiatrist, he or she would have probably told me just that, but, as I'm one of the handful of people in Los Angeles not currently in therapy, no one told me anything. My paranoia, which grew rapidly the weekend I was supposed to meet Charles, was allowed to blossom without being analysed. You could say, the night I broke into Jake's house, my paranoia had reached full bloom.

Once inside the house, I slipped out of my shoes and picked them up. I'd no intention of turning on any lights. Espionage is traditionally carried out in the dark. I'd gone over the layout of his townhouse in my mind and was pretty sure I could find my way. Waiting only until my eyes adjusted, I walked straight into an armchair and stubbed my toe.

Shit.

Fortunately, I had a small flashlight in my jacket pocket. My keys and purse were in one hand and my shoes in the other, so I used one of my other hands to go for the flashlight. Everything I was carrying hit the ground.

I decided it would be OK to turn on the living-room light for just a minute. Long enough for me to gather my belongings and tiptoe to the kitchen. It was as good a place as any to start. In the flurry of planning a crime I'd forgotten to eat dinner. Investigating the fridge first, I made myself a sandwich – avocado, ham, cheese and mayonnaise – and ate it.

My search of the kitchen turned up nothing else. I moved on, taking only the flashlight with me. I was pretty sure now that the best spies didn't bring their purses along on jobs.

The only room in Jake's house I hadn't legitimately spent time in was his study. I had no reason to be in there. That's where I headed.

His desk was clean except for a pile of bills, a few charity solicitations and his computer. I opened the laptop and turned it on, looking over the desk while I waited for it to come to life.

The top drawer was full of bits and pieces – paper clips, staples, glue, tacks, scissors – it was a mess, but not an incriminating one. The second drawer held chequebooks, postage stamps, a letter opener shaped like a miniature sword, with its own little scabbard, and, in a small plastic resealable bag, a locket. It was too heavy to be silver; too silver to be white gold. It had to be platinum. A beautiful, delicate, feminine platinum locket on a threadlike chain.

I lifted it out of the drawer. I didn't need three guesses to work out who it belonged to.

The locket found its way into my pocket. I wasn't

stealing it, just temporarily seizing it as evidence. My plan was to ... well, I didn't know what my plan was, but I was sure I'd think of something.

Jake's computer made a ploink noise; the screen asked me to enter the access password. Password? Who did he think wanted to get into his computer? I thought I was paranoid.

The third and largest drawer was locked. I was paralysed by the discovery. This was it. Whatever I was looking for would be in that drawer. I was sure of it.

The phone on the desk rang, startling me so much I shrieked like a girl. This was OK as the ringing drowned out the shrieking and, well, I am a girl. After a few more rings, my heartbeat returned to normal and the machine answered the phone.

'Jay-ake, it's Kim. Please pick up if you're there.' She waited for him to pick up. He didn't. Neither did I, though I was sorely tempted to. 'Can you call me as soon as you get this? It's important. I need to speak to you. You know the number. I really need to talk.'

I bet she did.

I played the message back, listening for anything that might indicate there was still something going on between them. Her words didn't tell me anything one way or the other. It was clear she needed to talk to Jay-ake. I wasn't so keen on the idea. My right index finger liked it even less. It depressed the 'Erase' button and the message was gone.

It wasn't one of my finest moments. Then, neither was breaking and entering. If Kim needed a kidney or something, she'd call back.

I knelt in front of the drawer. If I were Jake, where

would I keep the key to a drawer I didn't want me to look in? Well away from me. He had to have the key on him. Only a complete idiot would lock a drawer, then leave the key lying around.

Defeated by my logic, I pulled myself up into the chair. And found myself staring at a key attached to the inside of the metal shade of the lamp by means of a double-sided magnet. I picked it off. It was the right size – too small for a door; too big for a padlock. I tried the key in the drawer. It slid in smoothly, and released the lock without any pressure.

A door slammed shut. It sounded like the front door. I stopped breathing. Someone was in the house, someone with a key, someone who was home a full hour before he said he would be – Jake, obviously.

What do I do? Lock the drawer. Replace the key. Hide under the desk.

Plan A: Stay under desk all night and let myself out after he goes to work in the morning.

Brilliant – provided he wasn't planning on using the study in the meantime and I didn't need to go to the bathroom during the night. It also didn't help that tomorrow was Saturday.

Jake was moving around downstairs.

Plan A (modified): Stay under desk until he falls asleep, then sneak out and blend fluidly into the night, not unlike a ninja.

Simpler. Better.

'Sydney?'

I hit my head on the underside of the desk. He knew I was here. How did he know I was here?

My purse. I'm a moron. I left it in full view on the kitchen counter. Then there were my shoes, the plate, breadknife and half a sandwich. I'd also left the living room light on.

Oops.

'Sydney?' He sounded as if he was at the bottom of the stairs.

Plan B: I needed a plan B.

Wait. For all intents and purposes, I was Jake's girlfriend.

I dashed into his bedroom, peeled off my clothing down to my underwear, and threw myself onto the bed. I shook out my hair, hoping it would look dishevelled in a come-hither way, rather than dishevelled as a side effect of turning to a life of crime. I arranged myself on my side across the bed in a seductive pose. I hoped it was seductive. It was hard to tell. It certainly wasn't comfortable. Too late. I could hear footfalls at the top of the stairs, and no other seduction positions came to mind.

Jake stopped short in the doorway when he saw me. He was grinning, and it was one of those grins that you can't wipe off.

It was just possible I was going to get away with this.

He leaned up against the doorjamb.

'Hello,' he said.

'Hi.' I tried to be casual, as if lying around in my underwear in other people's bedrooms was something I did on a regular basis.

'I thought you had to work late.'

'Not as late as I expected. I came to return that CD I borrowed.'

He glanced at the pile of discarded clothing on the floor.

'Where is it?'

'What?'

'The CD. You don't seem to have any pockets in that outfit.'

'It's, um, I think I forgot to bring it.' That sounded suspicious, even to me, and I was on my side.

'Aren't you cold?'

Freezing, actually. 'No.'

'You look cold.' He dropped his gaze, pointedly, to nipple level.

'Maybe I'm just pleased to see you.'

'Are you trying to seduce me?'

'Why, is it not working?'

'If you're going to all this trouble, shouldn't your lingerie match?'

'Oh.' There was that. I'd dressed for espionage, not seduction. People like Mata Hari must dress for both. Note to future spy-self: wear interesting underwear at all times.

My bra was the main offender, being worn thin and, worse, grey. Grey is not a colour that reminds men of sex. My underpants had potential. They were black. Black is officially sexy.

There was only one thing to do.

'Close your eyes.'

He was instantly obedient.

As all fashion editors know, less is more. I sat up, removed the bra, tossed it on the floor, then resumed the position.

'OK, you can open. Is this good?'

'Better,' Jake said.

He didn't question my presence in his house. Nor did he ask how I knew he'd be home an hour early. He didn't question anything. His complete lack of curiosity led me to think:

a) He was hiding something from me – guilty people can't see past their own guilt.
b) He wasn't hiding anything from me – innocent people can't see anything either.
c) Men are easily distracted.

While I was convinced one or two of these theories applied, I felt pretty awful about getting away with what I'd done or, rather, tried to do. Whatever his reasons, Jake trusted me. I wasn't sure whether or not he'd betrayed my trust, but I was sure, by nosing around in his office, I'd betrayed his. I began to wonder how I'd gotten worked up enough to do it. Emotions are strange things.

There was only one thing I could do to make up for it. I had to wake up before he did and steal his car. I'd been planning to do it all week anyway – as a kind of belated hostess gift to thank him for having me to stay after I was kidnapped.

FROM: Sydney Welles <sydneywelles@yahoo.com>
TO: God c/- info@kabbalah.com
DATE: Saturday, October 8, 8.12 a.m.
SUBJECT: Money Management

Dear God,

According to Larry, Jesus started all of this. Apparently, his last request to his disciples was to go out and promote the Gospel to all of creation. That sounds like a request for a national ad campaign to me.

I guess, the same way some people consider him to be their co-pilot, we can think of Jesus as our co-brand director.

Now all we need is for someone to step up in the financial department. You have serious money issues – you're always in need of it. Everyone who claims to have anything at all to do with you is in need of money. Wealthy TV evangelists need more money. If you go to church, you also get hit up. And all religions seem to be real big on tithing.

Considering that money isn't even used in heaven, it's alarming how much of it you're going through. A little money management wouldn't go astray. As Jesus is busy with brand management, maybe you can get that Holy Ghost guy onto it.

Syd

In Marina del Rey, a gold Mercedes cut me off as I was turning into the driveway on Washington Boulevard. It parked haphazardly, blocking off most of the entrance to the auto shop. Two men got out of the car. The first was a silver-haired man in a handsome silver suit, the fabric of which shone dully and expensively in the sun. Though elegant, he had a sharp edge to his polish that suggested that he did not pay much, if anything at all, for his finery. The other man was much less august, and about twenty years younger, thuggish in his appearance, slightly softened by shoulder-length hair glossy enough for a shampoo commercial.

I lowered the driver's side window to ask them to move their car, but then thought better of it. They looked like Russian mafia to me.

The older, silver man glanced at me, then at the narrow space his car had left in the driveway.

'You can fit,' was all he said to me, before entering the building through a side door, closing it behind him.

His hit man stayed behind to watch I didn't scratch anything I shouldn't scratch, and to toss his European-soccer-star hair and smoke a cigarette. To his credit, he smoked exactly the way a gangster should.

Being unfamiliar with the outer reaches of Jake's car

I manoeuvred around the gold Mercedes awkwardly and slowly.

'I know this car,' the hit man said. 'This is a good car.'

Reluctant to end up a headline on the six o'clock news, I inched by the other car cautiously, and did not answer him.

'This is not your car.'

'No,' I said, 'it's not.'

'You steal this car?'

I had managed to get past the mafia mobile alive. Relief flooded through me. 'Yes.'

He nodded. 'You want to sell?'

I shook my head.

'OK.' He flicked his cigarette butt out into the street and took up sentry outside the door the older man had disappeared into.

I parked on the other side of the building, well away from the gold Mercedes.

The old, rotund Russian who was the Pete of Pete's Auto Body Shop came out of the office to greet me loudly.

I rummaged around in my purse and produced a bottle of paint, about the same size as a bottle of nail polish, but ten times more expensive.

'Mercedes Black from the dealer, like you said. Are you sure that will be enough? It doesn't look like much.'

'It plenty enough. I make very nice touch-up for you, young lady. Like new.'

Pete was giving me a tour of the spots on Jake's car where the paintwork was not all it should've been, when the side door of the building opened and the man in the silver suit came out. He and his hit man exchanged a few words. The younger man pointed in my direction. Nodding, his boss got into the gold Mercedes and drove away, leaving him still standing by the building. Before long, he was sauntering over to us. He stopped by the car and tapped the scratched front bumper with the tip of his shoe.

'Peter, this car need new bumper bar to be perfect.' Walking around the back, he said, 'Back bumper, too.'

Pete examined the bumpers. 'You have to order this things ahead. I have not part.'

'No parts,' I said, apologetically.

'I know where are parts,' the hit man said. 'You have cash?'

'Some,' I said.

He dropped his cigarette, flattened it with his foot, opened the passenger door and got into the car. 'Come, we get bumper bar.'

I looked at Pete. He did not seem at all disturbed by the turn of events or alarmed for my safety.

'Get bumper,' he said. 'I install for you.'

New bumpers would surely make up for breaking into Jake's house. They'd probably make up for burning it down.

'OK. Where are we going?'

'My friend live very near to here. Eight blocks. He has many bumper bar. I make him do good deal.'

Less than fifteen minutes later I was the owner of two new bumpers. The hit man, who gave his name as Eryk, helped me put everything in the trunk, then stood back as I got into the car.

'I stay here,' he said. 'Visit friend. He has sister.'

So far I'd seen no friend; it was Eryk who found the bumpers in his friend's garage, after forcing the door up, and he who had sold them to me.

'You take this,' he said, handing me a card. 'You call if you need more.'

'Thank you.'

I took the card and put it in my wallet.

He tapped on the hood of Jake's car. 'You steal more like this?'

'No, probably not,' I said.

Eryk bore his disappointment stoically.

As I pulled out of the driveway, a woman in a short silk kimono and sheepskin boots emerged from the small house to watch me leave.

'Who's that girl?' the woman said.

'She is business,' Eryk said, waving me off.

Pete was waiting when I arrived back at his shop. I opened the trunk, proudly displaying the new bumpers.

'How much you pay?'

'Fifty dollars for both.'

He grinned, wide as his face. 'Normal price two hundred. You steal them.'

'No, but I think somebody might have.'

'This your car, too?'

'No.'

'This nice car. Better than your car. This real car. Your car, girl car. Your husband?'

'Boyfriend.'

'How much he pay?'

I repeated the amount Jake had told me he paid, telling

the story about the little old lady in Florida, who had bought the car new and kept it garaged in Beverly Hills for the occasions she visited LA. She didn't like to drive rental cars; they were dirty.

Pete walked around to peer in at the odometer. He tapped on it.

'Too low, not original miles. They turn it back,' he said.

'No, it's original.'

'Original? No one drive this car. No one drive it. You pay so little. You steal this car.'

'Yes,' I said. Jake was going to be so pleased that I did.

☦

Detective Lauderdale examined the crack in my kitchen ceiling that runs from the base of the light fitting to the cornice. He'd insisted on meeting me at my place, instead of the station. I suspect that was because he wanted to check out my ceiling.

'I'm not sure I understand,' he said.

'Which part don't you understand?'

He sighed. 'I don't understand any of it, kid. It's a mystery.'

'Do you want me to explain it again?'

'Go ahead. Start from the burglary.'

'It wasn't a burglary. Not precisely.'

'Yes, you said that. Something was taken?'

'A locket.'

'A locket. Good, we're getting somewhere. What was it worth?'

'I don't know.'

'What was it insured for?'

'I don't know if it was insured or not. It didn't belong to me.'

'Can you describe it?'

'Yes. It was a platinum locket, about so big. Quite exquisite workmanship – I think it may be vintage. I've never seen anything like it.' I pulled it out of my pocket and placed it front of him. 'It was like this.'

Lauderdale picked it up off the table; the locket and chain looked positively ethereal in his large, square hands.

'How much like this?'

'I'd say pretty much exactly like that.'

Lauderadle looked me in the eye. 'Is this the stolen necklace?'

'Yes.'

'Did you steal it?'

'Technically, I did, but it was an accident. I only took it out of a drawer and put it in my pocket.'

'Accidentally?'

'No, I meant to take it. Only I didn't mean to leave the house with it. That was the accidental part. You see, I got caught and I had to take my pants off –'

Lauderdale put up a hand to stop me from going on. 'This is where you lost me the first time. Back up. Where did you get this necklace?'

'From Jake's house. I broke in.'

'You broke into Jake's house?'

'Yes. I have keys, but I didn't think it was very sporting to use them for this kind of thing, so I left a window open and climbed in.'

'You broke into your boyfriend's house . . . and accidentally stole a necklace?'

'I only meant to move it around a little – actually, to tell the truth, I didn't know what I was going to do with it. Now I'm stuck. He must know it's not there. Of course, he doesn't know that I know it's gone. And he doesn't know that I know that he knows it's gone.'

'You've lost me.'

'You see, he won't be discussing it with me on account of it belongs to another woman that he doesn't want me to know about. I know – he just doesn't know that I know. That's why I took the locket in the first place.'

Lauderdale cast his eyes upwards, beseeching heaven. 'I'm not even going to try to understand. Just tell me how I can help you.'

'Well, I figure that you, being a detective, must have, in the course of your career, been in this kind of position before.'

'Not that I recall. No, I can honestly say, I've never stolen a necklace from my boyfriend's house.' The skin around his eyes crinkled in amusement.

'OK, so not exactly the same position, but there must have been times when you have acquired evidence in a way . . . well, in a way that may not stand up in court.'

'I guess I've been in that situation. What has that to do with this?'

'The necklace is evidence.'

'Evidence of what?'

'That Jake may still be involved with his ex.'

'Now you've really lost me.'

'See, I need to know how I can still use this evidence to confront Jake, without him finding out how I got it.'

'OK, I think I understand.'

'So, how do I do it?'

'Have you tried just asking him?'

'I was thinking more along the lines of making something up.'

'Like what?'

'Well, we could say that you recovered it, through quick and daring police work. I could be there when you tell him. Then I could ask him why he has it.'

'Difficult, considering Jake hasn't reported it stolen.'

'Oh. Well, this sort of thing must happen all the time, right?'

'No, not really. This is a first.'

'Maybe the thief, just before he became a chalk outline, wanted all the things he ever stole to go back to their rightful owners. He gave you the names and addresses of everybody he stole from, along with the items he stole.'

The detective was inspecting the crack in the ceiling again.

'Come on, Lauderdale. Help me out here. I don't want to mess things up. Everything has been going so well since I stole Jake's car.'

That got his attention down from above.

'I gave that back.'

'Why can't you give the necklace back and ask him why he has it?'

'There really has to be another option.'

'I could arrest the thief.'

'What should I do?'

'You want to know what I think?'

'Yes.'

'You're going to have to come clean. Tell him what you did and why. Then ask him if he's still involved with his ex. I don't know Jake that well, but I don't think he's that kind of guy. It's probably just a misunderstanding.'

'That would be even worse. He'll hate me.'

'Just pick your moment. Courage, kid. He'll understand.'

'Do you think so?'

'I'm sure if anyone can get away with it, you can.'

'Thanks.'

We both sipped our coffee. Lauderdale's gaze was drawn naturally upwards again.

'You know, I think I knew I had to tell him, but I had to hear it from someone like you; someone with a gun.'

His gaze remained fixed on the ceiling, but he said, 'You're welcome.'

I scrutinized the patch of ceiling he was staring at. 'Have you been to the Sistine Chapel?'

'No,' he said. 'Why?'

'No reason in particular. I just think you might like it there.'

That got me a crinkly smile from one of LAPD's finest.

I knew Lauderdale was right. I'd known what he was going to say before he said it, but I needed to be told to confess by a secular authority. If I'd sought the advice of a religious authority – Father Giuliani being the most likely candidate, as he is the only religious authority I know – no doubt he'd have said exactly the same thing, but I didn't go to him for three reasons:

1 If I told Father Giuliani what I'd done, God would also find out. He has a commandment against swiping stuff, and may not see the subtleties of stealing by accident, as He's old and grumpy, and has been doing this for a long time without a break.
2 It would be too easy to disagree with Father Giuliani, on the grounds that I didn't believe in his God. Besides, Catholic priests prescribe confession to anyone and everyone as a matter of course, also making it easier to disregard.
3 He is a client, used to seeing me as calm and professional – well, for the most part – and shouldn't be privy to the woeful nature of my private life any more than is absolutely necessary to win the Church account.

Furthermore, Father Giuliani's authority is good only in the afterlife. Detective Lauderdale, on the other hand, could arrest me now. I guess I chose him because I was too ashamed to tell anyone else, and I figured that, compared to the hardened criminals he encountered on a daily basis, I'd seem not so bad. Also, Lauderdale, after the kidnapping incident, had told me to keep in touch, and to be sure to report anything else out of the ordinary that happened to me, but only to him. He'd been quite insistent about that – something to do with the book he was going to write once he'd retired from the force.

I considered telling Lauderdale about the suspiciously well-priced bumpers I'd purchased from a low-ranking member of the Russian mafia, then decided against it. One crime at a time. I first had to come clean with Jake. I was going to follow police advice and tell him everything, regardless of the consequences. Well, almost everything.

FROM: Sydney Welles <s.welles@fbmm.com>
TO: God c/- australianjesus@mambo.com.au
DATE: Thursday, October 13, 6.33 p.m.
SUBJECT: He knows if you are sleeping

Dear God,

There's something that has been bothering me for a while.

You keep a book or ledger (or maybe you just have a very retentive memory) with everyone who ever lived listed in it. In this book you keep a tally for each and every one of us. You know what we've been up to. You know if we are good or bad. Naughty or nice. And you reward us or punish us accordingly.

I have to know. Are you and Santa the same guy?

Syd x

They say a woman can confess any sin to a man, and, providing she picks her time correctly, he will forgive her. Unfortunately, they never say exactly when that time is. Up until now I've always assumed the correct time was some time during sex. This is not the case. Men do not multitask well during sex. Coitus confession is a waste of breath.

Confessing directly after sex doesn't work, either. It is only in French films that men lay about carrying on meaningful postcoital conversations, smoking Gitanes. For non-celluloid, non-smoking men in Southern California, this time is naptime.

When can you admit to murder, or casually mention you were raised by wolves and, on occasion, still like to howl at the moon, and have it not affect the way a man feels about you? This magical time of assured clemency continues to elude me. I'm hoping, however, that it's around dinnertime.

After all, they also say the way to a man's heart is through his stomach. If you ignore the appalling ignorance of human anatomy inherent in this statement, it isn't so ridiculous. Most men, no matter what they may claim, do not have sex three times a day, but the majority do eat three meals a day.

The locket weighed heavily on my conscience all weekend. By Monday evening, I was bursting to confess, if not all, then at least the part about me snooping in Jake's study. He would probably want to know why I snooped, so I'd tell him why, but no more. Jake was still pleased with the improvements I had made to his car, with the help of Eryk – hit man and spare parts distributor. I wanted to strike while Jake's good will towards me was high, but I didn't want to strike too hard.

To stir up more good will, I offered to cook dinner – a shrimp and pasta dish I was pretty sure he'd like, as he seems to like most everything I like, and I like anything with vodka in it. After installing him in a chair, with beer, cheese and crackers within his reach, I beheaded shrimp in my kitchen sink. I hoped it wouldn't give Jake any ideas. He couldn't get too mad at me. I was the one holding the knife.

To say he was astounded at my confession would be a technically correct description of his reaction, but the word doesn't do justice to the full breadth of his bewilderment and bemusement. Predictably, he wanted to know why I felt the need to break into his house. I told him I'd suspected he was still seeing Kim and wanted to find out one way or another. He, quite reasonably, asked why I didn't just ask him. I said I didn't know why I hadn't just asked him. So, he asked why I thought he was still seeing Kim. By this point I was a touch defensive.

'Gee,' I said, 'maybe it's because Kim has been calling you, desperate to get in touch.'

Jake was surprised. 'How did you know that? I only spoke to her this morning. She called me at work.'

Oops.

'How did you know?'

'I . . . OK, that night when I broke into your house, she called and left a message on your answering machine. I couldn't help but overhear it, as I was in your study at the time, trying to get into your file drawer.'

'Did you get into my file drawer?'

'No, that was when you came home and I had to stop what I was doing to seduce you.'

'That, I remember,' he said, smiling a little, before frowning. 'There weren't any messages on the machine that night.'

'That's right. Her message sort of got erased.'

'How?'

'Um, I erased it.'

'You erased it,' he said. 'You erased it.' He seemed to have lost his sense of humour, as well as his ability to form interesting and original sentences.

'It was kind of an accident.'

'Why didn't you just give me the message?'

'OK, when I say it was an accident, I mean that I did it on purpose, only I wasn't fully in control of my actions at the time, due to my paranoia. I didn't pass on the message because I didn't want you to know what I'd been doing. I suppose, I also didn't want to pass it on. But you have to understand that the necklace was truly an accident. I did mean to take it, but not to take it out of the house.'

'What necklace?'

Oops.

'What necklace?'

'OK, I found a locket and chain in the second drawer of your desk and I was sort of pissed that Kim was still leaving her jewellery lying around at your house, and I . . . I took it. I don't know why. I guess I wanted to piss you off. To make you think you'd lost it. I was going to put it back. At least, I think I was, but then you came home. By the next morning, I forgot it was in my –'

'It doesn't belong to Kim.'

'It doesn't?'

'I hadn't noticed it was gone.'

Damn. Damn. Damn – wait a minute. 'I'm sorry,' I said. 'Which of your girlfriends does it belong to?'

Jake gave me a look that, well, let's just say 'loving' was not the descriptive term that came to mind. 'It belongs to you,' he said.

'I'm afraid you're mistaken. I've never seen it before. You must have me mixed up with some other girl.'

'I bought it for you. I haven't gotten around to giving it to you yet.'

'Oh.' I deserved to be demoted to the bottom of the food chain. 'Why?'

'You had a lot of trouble accepting keys. I wasn't sure what kind of scene truly precious metal would entail. Let's just say I needed to build up to it.'

I wondered if I'd be allowed to live at the base of the food chain or if the other bottom dwellers would blackball me. 'No, I mean, why did you buy it for me?'

'No reason. I thought you'd like it.'

The basement level of the food chain was officially above my reach.

Jake, seeing my misery, let me sink in it for a few moments more before saying, 'I got it at that seized goods auction we covered for the show.'

'The drug lord story?'

'I thought you'd like the fact the locket had a sordid history.'

'I do. I like the locket. Very much.'

'I guess you must. You did go to the trouble of stealing it.'

'I have it in my bag, I'll go get –'

'No, no. Now you have it, keep it. Saves me giving it you and introducing God knows what for you to worry me about.'

There wasn't a lot I could say besides, 'Thank you.'

'You're welcome.'

Jake got up to get another beer out of my fridge. I decapitated the last shrimp. I rinsed the little slimy creatures – which, considering my new status in the ecosystem, ought to be eating me for dinner – with several changes of water, before washing my hands with the toothpaste I had on hand to get rid of the smell.

'I'm sorry,' I said.

'You should be.'

'I thought you'd be angry with me.'

'I am.'

'I thought you'd be angrier. You're taking this very well.'

'There was no real harm done. If I look at it another way, it's quite flattering. Your psychotic jealousy is strangely endearing.'

'Thank you,' I said.

'You're going to be saner in the future, right?'

'Yes,' I said, 'no more paranoia.'

'Good.'

'What did Kim want when she called?' I don't think

Jake was taken in by the seemingly casual way I asked the question.

'She wanted to tell me she's relocating with a new job.'

I could live with that. 'Where's she going?'

'New York.'

Even better news. 'When does she go?'

'Tomorrow.'

Detective Lauderdale and Father Giuliani are both right. This confession business is good for the body and good for the soul.

'I hope she's happy there,' I said. I even meant it. I placed the herbs I'd been washing on the chopping block.

'So,' I said. 'You still want to go to this charity thing in Brentwood on Friday?'

'I'm not sure I'll be back in time. What time does it start?'

'Back from where?'

'I have to go away for a few days, background check on a story. I'm back Friday evening.'

'What time? I can leave your name on the door, you could come later.'

'My flight gets in at seven-forty-five. If I came straight from the airport, with traffic, I doubt I'd be there much before nine.'

'Well, come if you feel like it.'

'I will.'

'Where are you going?'

My question brought on a strange mix of wariness and amusement in Jake's eyes. 'New York,' he said.

'That's . . . nice.'

I pretended to be intensely interested in the Italian parsley I was mincing. It was taking all the self-restraint

I had to keep from commenting. Jake was fully aware of this and, it seemed, found it mildly comical.

Unfortunate, then, that I'd just confessed my dirty deeds to Jake and he'd been so reasonable. Now I was in no position to be angry with him over what was – if he was to be believed – a work trip and one of the world's most remarkable coincidences.

On the slight chance it actually was a remarkable coincidence, I didn't want to enact a jealous scene now, to make Kim, replete with a Manhattan backdrop, even more attractive by comparison. Or make Jake so angry he'd go see Kim to spite me – if there was a chance he wasn't already planning on it.

'When do you go?' I asked, when the Italian parsley could be minced no more.

'In the morning.'

'Tomorrow?' Chalk up another extraordinary coincidence. 'Well, have a nice trip.'

'Thank you.'

I didn't mention his New York trip again for the rest of the evening. No jealousy, no distrust emanated from me – at least, not that I noticed. I was proud of myself. I was so magnanimous I offered to wake up at six to drive him to the airport. An offer he refused on the grounds that it'd be easier for him to have his car at the airport, if he was to come straight from the airport to the charity auction.

'You could catch a cab to the thing. That'd be cheaper than parking your car at the airport for four days.'

'Work covers parking. Do you know how long it can take to get a cab at LAX?'

'It can take a while,' I said. His logic was sound, irritating.

Jake came over, close to me, to look me in the eye. 'It's a coincidence. That's all.'

I'll say this much for him, he had a convincing act going.

'Yes, of course it is,' I said. 'Anyway, it's a really big city.'

Was New York big enough that they could both be there at the same time without having sex? It was hard to know. I tried not to imagine the two of them strolling around Central Park together or, for all I knew, meeting at the airport and taking the same flight over, canoodling all the way to JFK. I was not going to lose a minute's sleep over this. I'd just wait until Jake got back from New York. Then I'd kill him. And dance the haka on his grave.

FROM: Sydney Welles <s.welles@fbmm.com>
TO: God c/- santaclaus@thenorthpole.com
DATE: Tuesday, October 18, 2.28 p.m.
SUBJECT: A conflict of interest

Dear God,

According to your Bible — King James Version, Exodus 20:1–17 — your commandments don't allow advertising. I took the Bible from the drawer of the room I was held in by kidnappers. Strictly speaking it was a breach of Commandment 8, but I think you can make an exception if the people you stole it from kidnapped you first. Especially if you go with the Old Testament's eye-for-an-eye thinking. Anyway, you spake against advertising in Commandments 1, 2 and 10:

1 In Commandment 1, you modestly introduce yourself, 'I am the LORD thy God.' Then you go on a bit, claim credit for getting everyone out of Egypt, parting the Red Sea and all that. Only the last eight words are an actual commandment: 'Thou shalt have no other gods before me.' If you are the one and only God, not only is there no need for this commandment, but also no need to advertise. If there is only one, people don't have a choice. By advertising you imply there is a choice.
2 Commandment 2 goes something along the lines of 'Don't make a graven image or likeness of anything in heaven, earth or the water.' That pretty much covers everything in terms of copyright. Painters, sculptors, photographers and

filmmakers are all in deep shit. It pretty much means advertising is out, too.
3 Commandment 10 tells us: 'Thou shalt not covet the cool stuff your neighbour has.' This has to be the least successful commandment of the ten. American society is based on coveting what your neighbour has. House, ox, ass, George Foreman grill, plasma screen TV, RV, SUV – all of it.

Advertising is an industry set up to tell you what stuff your neighbour is likely to have, so you can get on with coveting it.

The point of living for most people is not just to covet, but also to get the stuff their neighbour has and, if possible, get bigger, better things, and have him covet back. It's a vicious cycle ending only in death or bankruptcy. It keeps you working your entire life to earn money to stay half a step ahead of credit-card debt. If anyone paid any attention to this commandment, the country's economy would collapse.

All the same, I think it rules out advertising for you, don't you?

Cheers,
Sydney

Fear is the greatest motivator there is. Anyone in advertising can tell you that. And religion has been using the two greatest fears – the fear of death and the fear of God – to great effect for at least two thousand years. For advertising, however, using these fears is a new low.

Our spirits, before our meeting with the Church, were similarly low. With the help of a good Scotch Larry can easily forget the importance of meeting and breeze right through it, but Larry sober never forgets for a second that agency jobs may be riding on the outcome of a particular presentation. He gets so anxious he never knows what to do with himself in the last half hour before a meeting begins. Today, he was spending it making me as nervous as he was.

I'd taken the precaution of getting Patton to duct-tape all the bottles of Scotch in the agency shut. In possession of one of these sealed bottles, Larry was admonishing me in preparation for the meeting. He was wielding the bottle as if it were Excalibur, using it to punctuate what he was saying.

'Don't get sucked in by the man-of-God stuff. These people are ruthless.'

'OK,' I said.

'I mean it. The Catholic Church is the oldest and one of the most successful corporations in the world. They didn't get that way by being a bunch of pussies. Don't forget, two Borgias were popes. Nasty, nasty family. They murdered everybody they met.'

'OK.'

'Go for the throat. Show no mercy. Tell them what they need to know without any touchy-feely shit. Cold. Hard. Factual. Tough. Don't present like a girl.'

'Right.'

Larry pointed the blunt end of his bottle at me. 'These are the guys who invented the crusades – a way to rape, pillage and massacre, and still be regarded as a hero – and they got Torquemada in to run the Spanish Inquisition.'

'OK.'

'You realize the future of the agency is riding on the outcome of this presentation.'

'Thank you for reminding me.'

'Everything's ready?'

'Everything.'

'What's the time?'

'Twenty minutes to go.'

'Twenty minutes? Oh, fuck.'

☨

A corporation is an inherently male world. Having been born without a penis, the corporate rituals that all my male colleagues seem innately to understand – even when they don't understand anything else – are an enigma to me.

When you have a meeting with a client, and they are going to bring six warm bodies, you must also produce six people or, failing that, at least five, possibly seven. If they are bringing only two people, you cannot bring six.

You must scale down your numbers to approximate theirs. You cannot let the other side greatly outnumber you, nor can you greatly outnumber them.

Even if I try to think like a man, I can think of only one reason to explain this standard practice: if war breaks out in a meeting, the even numbers ensure a fair fight, provided no one is packing a weapon – which, if I continue to think like a man, is not a remote possibility.

The matching-numbers ritual was observed in this case, although everyone on the client's side was a priest or bishop or cardinal, and – despite Larry's warnings – people quite unlikely to become violent. As we needed only four people for our side, we had to find two extraneous warm bodies to drag into the room.

We'd had one body lined up since Father Giuliani told us there'd be five representatives of the Church, including himself, attending the meeting. Julie Ryan is always available to fill a seat at a moment's notice. Her job title is long and important-sounding enough for clients to believe she has a purpose, regardless that she has no visible function in the meeting.

The second body we scrounged for at the eleventh hour, after one of the receptionists reported six, not five, men of the cloth sitting in the waiting area. Noah – once we'd borrowed a tailored shirt from an obligingly dapper management supervisor, and wrestled it over Noah's embellished T-shirt, on which tiny rhinestones were clustered in letters to read 'Pimpin' Like Jesus', tamed the more energetic sprouts of hair resulting from his most recent nap, and made him promise to not speak unless directly spoken to – was ready to go.

Larry had gotten over his pre-meeting jitters, and I'd gotten over my nervousness that I'd fall into my usual trap of saying something rude in front of a man of God. That fear dissipated when I found myself faced with several men of God at the same time. In a group they seemed quaint, rather than terrifying. I managed to present the research findings and recommendations without invoking any words that could, with so many priestly ears tuned in, send me straight to hell.

It was only when I presented the strategy we would work from for the campaign, and was greeted by blank stares all around – except for Father Giuliani, who understands everything, but is not a good person for me to focus on in a meeting for fear of going weak at the knees – that it crossed my mind I may have been in hell already – in the Catholic section, of course.

'That's interesting,' Father Lauren said. He was seated next to Father Giuliani, and was the only other man of God whose name I remembered from the mass introductions at the beginning of the meeting.

In client speak, 'That's interesting' means one of three things:

a) I don't understand a thing you just said.
b) I hate it, hate it, hate it.
c) I don't understand a thing you just said, and I hate it, hate it, hate it.

'That's interesting' wasn't the reaction I was hoping for. But, then again, Father Lauren was a priest and had never been the client of an advertising agency before, so he probably didn't know any client speak and might be telling the truth.

'But . . . er . . . but . . . I'm just not sure it's right for us,' Father Lauren said.

I was wrong. Client speak is a language everyone is born with. It just lies dormant until the moment you hire an advertising agency.

'The approach is not as modern as I expected,' said the fatter of the two bishops. 'To be honest, we were expecting something along the lines of the other faith-based marketing you showed us. This is completely different.'

'It's different,' I said, 'because the Catholic Church is different. If we go hip and modern, or sophisticated and witty, it will end up working against you. Your Church is none of those things.'

'It doesn't seem very inviting.'

'Neither does Catholicism. "Open Hearts, Minds, Doors" works for the Methodists, but not for you.

'Look, it's our job to get them in the door. After that it's up to you guys and your guy upstairs. But there's no point in getting them in the door at any cost. We can't promise them a modern, forward-thinking religion when Catholicism isn't one. We are taking a hardline approach because Catholicism is a hardline religion.'

'Couldn't we soften the image a little?'

'Not unless you soften the religion. The marketing message we put out there has to match the consumer's Catholic experience. We could say anything to get people interested, but, if they find the Church isn't congruent with its advertising, they won't come back. Worse, they'll think they've been had – they'll never trust you again. We have to build a brand consistent with the product.'

'I understand your point; however, we then look like the heavies of Christianity.'

'You are the heavies – though Evangelicals seem to be giving you a run for your money these days. Look, I understand that you're afraid of polarizing the market. But you have to. Rather than trying to cover up the fact that you're an old-fashioned, hardline religion, we'll make it your strength, and build your brand around it. You're never going to get to some people no matter how attractive your ads are. You can't be all things to everybody.

'As our research shows, there are plenty of people out there who want to be told what to do and think. They are your market. Would-be Buddhists and Scientologists aren't. If you want to sell the Church, this is the way to go. If you want to be seen as nice guys, hire a PR company.'

'We did.'

'Did it work?'

'No.'

'There you go.'

'It's not a true calling to faith,' the bishop said. 'You are going to tell people that they should go to church just in case there's a God, who will send them to hell if they don't. That's not really what faith is about.'

'No,' I said, 'it's not, but neither is it about hiring an advertising agency.'

Larry threw me a sharp, pleased look that told me I was kicking bishop butt in a manner of which he approved.

The bishop with the butt in question chuckled, causing his pink and fluid chins to cascade over his collar in an oddly mesmerizing way.

'Do you believe in God?'

The bishop had a sense of humour. 'Do you believe that's relevant?' I said.

He and his chins laughed again. 'Let's just say I'm curious.'

'OK,' I said. 'If you mean a grumpy, bearded old man who watches me when I go to the toilet, then, no, I don't believe in God. But, if you mean a non-emotional creative source and balancing force, then I'm willing to consider the possibility. Unfortunately, the thing that comes closest to explaining my idea of God is the original *Star Wars* trilogy, which does nothing to up the believability factor.'

The fatter bishop nodded; his chins kept it up long after he stopped. On the agency side of the table, I could see the others exchanging looks, wondering if I'd said something to offend.

I decided to take the bishop by the balls. 'Look at it logically. It's a good thing I don't believe what you believe. The most valuable thing we can give you is our objectivity. We can sell the Church because we can separate ourselves from it in a way you can't.'

'That makes a lot of sense. It is, after all, why we're here,' Father Giuliani said. And – if he wasn't a priest, and we weren't at a crucial point in a meeting that could decide whether I had a job next year, and there weren't other priests watching – I could've kissed him.

'I suppose it does at that,' the fatter bishop said. 'You've certainly given us a great deal to think about.' A harrumphing noise came from the other, matching round bishop, indicating agreement.

'And we have the research to back it up,' Larry said.

The fatter bishop tapped the booklet in front of him. It contained all of the information we'd presented today. 'The numbers are certainly impressive.'

Somehow, that, in secret priest code, signalled the end of the meeting. The cardinal, who had not said more than a couple of words the whole afternoon, now stood and thanked us, and said his goodbyes. The priest who was his assistant, who, indeed, seemed to exist for no other reason, stood also and mimicked his boss.

By client standards they hadn't asked many questions at all. I wasn't sure if that was a good sign or a bad sign.

I began gathering my visual aids, as the others — with the exception of Julie, who was reapplying her lipstick — were shaking hands and thumping backs and doing all the things that men do when a group of them manage to get together without starting a war.

I was exhausted. I'd just outlined a plan to sell the Catholic Church as insurance against eternal damnation — in other words, a plan to scare the hell into people. I felt as if I'd spent a couple of hours handing out cigarettes to eight-year-olds, which some agencies probably do, in theory if not in practice.

It was then I noticed that the priests were halfway to the door, but the bishops were standing their ground, near me. There was fierce whispering back and forth between the two.

'There is one more thing,' said the multi-chinned bishop. 'We thought that you might . . .'

'Yes?' I said.

'Well, we thought – it's just that we heard that you could get good tickets to things – to things that are hard to get good tickets to – and we thought, if it wasn't too much trouble...'

'What would you like to see?'

The bishops exchanged looks, both shy to speak up, both hoping the other would take the matter out of his hands. I began to have serious doubts about what it was they wanted tickets for. The slightly less rotund bishop with the chipmunk cheeks finally confessed. To my surprise, the priests wanted to go, too – as did Larry, but that came as no surprise to me at all.

FROM: Sydney Welles <sydneywelles@yahoo.com>
TO: God c/- Gandalf@middleearth.com
CC: elrond@rivendell.com
DATE: Thursday, October 20, 7.09 p.m.
SUBJECT: Books & Burgers

Dear God,

If I had to back a religious group to win, I wouldn't back the Catholics. And I certainly wouldn't back the sorry lot that kidnapped me. No, I'd have to take into account the contribution made to society, which brings it down to two groups.

1 The Gideons, for the furthest-reaching book distribution system I've ever encountered.
2 The In-n-Out Burger Christians, for obvious reasons, which are more apparent when you're hungry.

Syd ☺

Down on the Venice boardwalk, you can see a man, wearing only Speedos and a coat of olive oil, walk on broken glass. In Santa Monica, on Third Street Promenade, against the backdrop of homogenized retail outlets and homogeneous homeless people, you can hear a thirteen-year-old in a tuxedo sing like Louis Armstrong and tap-dance like, well, like no one I've ever seen before. In Malibu, wild dolphins will entertain you when you eat lunch in oceanfront restaurants.

Although it's far from being a pretty city, there are amazing sights to be seen in Los Angeles. But no sight here, however amazing, is as significant as seeing a star. For Angelenos, celebrity spotting is a competitive and, at times, full-contact sport. There's a constant celebrity safari going on. A-list stars are the biggest game, but anyone remotely famous counts.

Anything you see a celebrity doing is remarkable. Anything at all, whether it's walking, talking, eating or standing. Humdrum activities become extraordinary when executed by someone famous. So extraordinary, people will pay for the privilege of watching.

Charities know and exploit this. Whenever a fundraiser is held, a collection of celebrities is rounded up and displayed like prize pigs. Here, choosing a charity to support is not about finding a cause that resonates with your soul. No, it's about deciding which celebrities you'd like to hang with.

In the terraced back garden of the Brentwood home of a former senator, Anna was doing an exceptional job of not turning her head while her eyes darted around the room in a way that made me fear for her contact lenses.

'You're doing the LA thing,' I said.

'What?'

'Pretending to listen to me while scanning the room for someone better to talk to.'

'Well, say something interesting, then,' she said. 'Is that Richard Gere?'

'Where?'

'Behind you.'

'I'm not going to look,' I said.

'Oh, why not?'

I normally avoid charity events. I'm one of the few nobodies in Los Angeles who regard the celebrities here as a kind of pestilence. There are high infestations of the famous in certain areas of this city, making it practically impossible to do anything without the head-turning, eye-popping, intelligence-reducing presence of a star nearby. It's not the stars themselves, but the gaping, blubbering twits they leave in their wake that I find annoying.

But, occasionally, when an invitation to an event for a truly worthwhile cause comes through from the media department, I accept and find myself participating in the city's favourite pastime.

'Celebrities at cocktail parties are like those Dementor things from the Harry Potter books – those creatures that suck the souls out of people.'

Anna looked at me blankly.

'Celebrities suck, too,' I said.

'You don't like Richard Gere?'

'That's not what I mean. It has nothing to do with Richard Gere. It's just that a famous person at a party like this creates a natural vacuum which sucks up everyone's attention and most of their good sense.'

She frowned. 'He's not very tall, is he?'

'See,' I said, 'you're caught in the vortex. You're staring at some actor, trying to look as if you're not staring at him, all the while ignoring your very best friend in the world, who got you tickets to this stupid thing in the first place. Now, I ask you, is that right?'

She was too busy rubbernecking to answer me.

At least it meant we were supporting a very fashionable cause. An unfashionable cause, no matter how worthy, will yield only character actors, minor politicians or people from reality television shows.

Some people think disasters present the biggest opportunity to see stars, but this is not the case. A large tragedy, natural or otherwise, does flush out equally large numbers of the famous, but tragedies of that scale tend to cause telethons, and telethons allow celebrities to appease their publicists from the safety of a television studio.

Supporting the cause or disease du jour, whatever it may be on the given day, is the best bet for a nobody-with-enough-disposable-income to rub shoulders – or any body part that can be managed – with a Somebody.

Anna poked me in the arm. 'That's Meryl Streep, over there, about to leave.'

I turned to look. The paparazzi stationed at the entrance

to the garden had recovered from the zombie-like state they'd exhibited when we walked past them, now excitedly shoving each other, cameras up, flashes popping. 'Yes, it is.'

'She's not very tall, either.'

'No one is very tall compared to you, and actors are, generally speaking, shorter than most.'

'Ooh! There's, um, you know – the one that plays the gay guy on that, what's the name of that – why is there so little wine in the glasses?' The last part was addressed to Vince, who'd returned with three glasses filled with negligible amounts of wine.

'It's a wine tasting,' he said.

'We're going to have to taste a lot of wine to even get close to getting our money's worth,' Anna said.

'You may not be expressing the true spirit of charity there,' I said.

'And what?' Anna waved her arm to encompass the crowd, dressed in their designer best to gawk at celebrities – whose presence drove all thoughts of the terminally ill children whom they were here to help from their minds. 'This is the true spirit of charity?'

'Point taken.'

'Did you invite Jake?' Vince asked, before Anna could warn him not to.

'Did I invite Jake? Well, yes, as a matter of fact I did extend the invitation to him. But he won't be attending. No, the poor boy will be too exhausted. He had a busy week in New York, visiting his ex-girlfriend. In fact, he was so busy he didn't get a chance to call me. Not once. So, I doubt very much he'll find the time to show up tonight. Why do men do that? Say they'll call, then not call? Why not just say they won't call and make it easier for everyone?'

'Maybe he was busy.'

'That's right. Stick up for your fellow man. Why do you guys always do that?'

'Why do men have to call?' Vince said. 'Why couldn't you call him?'

'Under the circumstances, I chose not to. Anyway, it's not as if I'm going to miss him. I may have waited by the phone like an idiot all week, but, let's face it, men who prefer women manufactured by Mattel are not worth missing.'

'What makes you so sure he won't turn up?'

'Look,' I said, 'women just know these things, OK. We're infallible like that. Tell you what, if he does show, I'll take back everything bad I've ever said about your gender and be a perfect geisha the rest of the weekend. It's not going to happen. Why are you asking, anyway?'

'He just walked in.'

'Oh.' I turned. Jake was at the greeting desk, waiting while they searched for his name on the list. 'What's he doing here?'

'You invited him,' Vince said, helpfully.

'You should stop talking now,' Anna said. 'Really.'

One of the hazards of having an amazon for a friend is that they're easy to pick out in a crowd. Anna's red head, sitting half a foot above everyone else's, functioned as a beacon for Jake to make his way over.

An auctioneer's voice boomed across the garden, just as Jake reached us. The voice, on loan from Christie's, herded us onto the paved terrace at the bottom of the garden. There, we were encouraged to form a tight mob by charity-committee members patrolling the area like sheep dogs.

The former senator whose current terrace we were on stepped up to the microphone, welcoming us with a few sexist remarks. It must've been acceptable to do this back in the century he was a senator; he seemed to think it funny. At his side, his wife smiled fiercely, giving us the impression she'd never had an opinion in her life.

Before long – there's only so much sexism a wealthy, liberal Californian crowd can politely laugh at – the auctioneer once again had control of the microphone and began the night's auctions, making it impossible for us to speak to one another without shouting.

Jake, who was the main person I wanted to shout at, showed no contrition for not calling me from New York, instead displaying a great deal of interest in my dress. When the first item for auction – a walk-on role in a movie and tickets to its premiere – sold for a couple of grand, he leaned over, close to my ear, saying:

'That's a different look for you.'

'What are you saying?'

'Nothing. Except that you usually wear more fabric.'

'You don't like it?'

'I didn't say that.'

'But you're implying that this dress is kind of a slut dress.'

'What do you mean, "kind of"?'

It's kind of hard to be mad at Jake when he's in formal wear and a flirtatious mood.

'You be quiet,' I said. The auction had started again.

After several spa packages, dinner packages and fine wine collections had gone under the hammer, and Jake had flirted some more with my dress, the evening was over. Now that there was no further way to extract money from us, we were no longer welcome. So much so, they turned out the lights to get us to leave.

Anna and I waited in front of the house, while Vince and Jake retrieved their cars from the valet parking service.

'You sure told him off for not calling,' Anna said.

'I'll speak firmly to him later.'

'Sure you will. You went all giggly and girlie the moment he arrived.'

'I did not,' I said. 'Did I?'

She was right. I didn't speak to Jake, firmly or otherwise. I didn't have the heart to. He collapsed in his favourite armchair as soon as we got home. The poor boy was exhausted after his trip, and, as long as I didn't dwell on possible reasons why he was exhausted, I was still in a charitable mood.

On impulse, I reached up under my dress, pulled down my panties, and stepped out of them. Jake seemed to gain a little energy at that point, sitting up straighter in his chair.

'Don't worry,' I said, after hitching up the skirt of my dress a few inches to be able to sit comfortably astride his lap, 'you won't have to do a thing.'

It was around the same time that he said he'd missed me, told me how happy he was to be home, and took the Lord's name in vain a couple of times.

I was happy, too. Maybe I'd hit upon the secret to relationships. As long as you're willing to check your brain at the door, and ignore inconvenient facts – things such as Jake not calling me from New York and that I still suspected he was hiding something from me – you can believe whatever you want to, and you can be happy. It was just like religion. I had doubts, though, about how long this kind of happiness could last. My guess was not long.

Anyway, even from a secular point of view, you're not supposed to ask men why they haven't called you. What you're supposed to do is retain mystery. If you don't ask, men wonder why you don't ask, and this makes you mysterious to them. And that makes them call you.

FROM: Sydney Welles <sydneywelles@yahoo.com>
TO: God c/- anyoneexisting@doesgodexist.com
DATE: Saturday, October 22, 10.38 a.m.
SUBJECT: Ignorance is bliss?

Dear God,

Both the Bible and Dr Atkins agree. Fruit is not at all good for you. It's forbidden on the Atkins diet and so, too, was it forbidden in the Bible. Fruit contains too many carbohydrates and, back before Christ, it also contained way too much information.

In the Garden of Eden the forbidden fruit was on the Tree of Knowledge. Adam and Eve were told not to eat the forbidden fruit, but they did anyway and were consequently chucked out of Eden for being know-it-alls.

As far as I can tell, the moral of the story is this: if only they'd followed Atkins strictly, we'd all still be gambolling about Eden. Or, alternatively: if only they'd not sought out or gained knowledge, we'd still be living in paradise, where we'd all be stupidly happy.

Is this the basic message of Christianity? The more ignorant and less informed you are, the more God will like you and the happier you will be. All those capable of reading a novel without moving their lips are not welcome in the Kingdom of Heaven.

Is that any different from our society? Where the powerful, to keep power, keep the rest ignorant, not from a lack of information, but from too much information, delivered in useless, confusing, contradicting snippets, by a corporate- and government-controlled media.

This could explain why 60 per cent of Americans are overweight or obese. Perhaps, for want of understanding of the world they live in, they're all trying to chomp their way to knowledge and enlightenment, still trying for a bite of that forbidden fruit, for the understanding that is still being withheld from us.

Is that the reason that we're fat? Or is it all, as Dr Atkins claims, merely a question of carbs?

Syd

Some hero in the media department came up with six last-minute tickets to the Saturday afternoon hockey game, courtesy of a news magazine, in that magazine's corporate seats. Thus, on Saturday afternoon, I was in an aisle seat at the Staples Centre, sipping beer from a plastic cup, and flanked, in order, by a marketing priest, a lawyer priest, a couple of business bishops and a sober boss. They were also sipping beer from plastic cups – all except Larry. His cup held iced tea; occasionally, he'd forget, take a sip of it and be exceedingly disappointed.

The clergy were too engrossed in the game, and Larry seated too far away, to make conversation with. So, when not keeping the clerics in beer by acting as the middleman between them and the waiter, I had no choice but to watch hockey. I found it about as interesting as shredded wheat – I'm not a spectator-sports person. I was here for two other reasons.

1 Attending sporting events with potential clients – as long as they are male – is second only to playing golf with them as the thing most likely to turn them into clients.
2 It gave me something to tell my father in my weekly call to the parents. Something that didn't require a lengthy explanation of my life to go along with it. Fathers like sport.

For a reason I couldn't fathom at all, play had stopped and the players were just standing around on the ice.

'Why is everything stopped?'

'Paused. Commercial break,' Father Giuliani said.

'They stop for commercials?' No wonder everybody hates advertising.

As soon as play resumed, two opposing players threw down their sticks, helmets and gloves, and started a fight. Punching each other proved to be quite difficult when they were balanced on thin metal blades, on ice. They were reduced to wrestling, while the referees – who, according to Father Giuliani, couldn't stop the fight until one or both of the players hit the ground – circled like striped sharks. The crowd, including the men of God seated beside me, cheered them on. I was wondering why, when a fight produced more delight than a goal, this crowd didn't attend a boxing match instead, when I noticed that someone in a corporate box on the next level across the way appeared to be waving at me.

Unable to figure out who it was waving or whether it really was me he was waving to, I flicked through the programme, noting most of the players had names that could only have originated in the coldest of climes – they need the extra, difficult syllables in those temperatures, to keep their tongues from freezing. When I looked up again, the man who'd waved was gone from the box across the way.

He was now walking through the restaurant on our level. As he got closer, I recognized him, even in an LA Kings hat. His gangster gait was unmistakable. It was Eryk, the only hit man I know to speak to.

The idea of introducing Eryk to the priests and bishops, and of him offering them cheap car parts – or something worse – didn't seem to me to be a bright one. I excused myself to the nearest priest and ran up the stairs, reaching the entrance to our section the same time Eryk did. Eryk looked pleased under his cap.

'I think it was you from over there,' he said.

'What are you doing here?'

'We are always here. We watch our player. That one, there, he is ours.' He pointed at one of the players in a purple jersey skimming over the ice.

'You own a player? Can you do that?'

'We can, we do.' Eryk stared curiously at the group I'd just left, clerical collars all in a row. The cameras covering the game were displaying a similar interest. Every so often the priests and bishops would appear on the big screens, and the crowd would roar their appreciation. The Catholic clergy had not enjoyed such popularity for a long time.

It was, it turned out, the coverage of the priests that had alerted Eryk to my presence. One camera had zoomed in for a closer look at the outrageously photogenic Father Giuliani and, lingering adoringly on him, gave me, or at least the right half of me, a few on-screen seconds.

I tried to divert Eryk's attention from my guests at the game. 'Do you want to get a beer at the bar?'

'Da. OK,' he said. 'You are here with many priests.' He shrugged, unimpressed. 'There is no God in Russia.'

We took our seats at the bar, and Eryk noticed the locket and chain around my neck. Wonder crept over his face.

'You steal this necklace,' he said.

'No. Well, yes. But after that it was given to me.'

Eryk looked confused. 'I know this necklace. How you get necklace?'

I told him where Jake had bought it – at a police auction where all the goods for sale had been seized from drug dealers now living in prison or, in some cases, not living at all.

Eryk nodded. 'It is only one of kind. I know who own it. I know who wear it. It has story.'

'What kind of story?'

His face became comically grim. 'Love story. Very sad. We get beer, I tell you.' Eryk rapped on the bar, which alerted the bartender, serving a long line of customers, to his needs. The bartender immediately left what he was doing to bring us two beers, free of charge.

'It is story of Ivan and Anya, and Little Lenin,' Eryk said.

'Little Lenin was their son?'

'No, he was chicken.'

'Chicken?'

'For pet. Ivan get him for good luck. When Little Lenin there, police don't come.'

'Why would the police come?'

'That is part of story.'

'Sorry. Please continue.'

'Ivan like Little Lenin very much. Let him live in house.'

'Was Anya OK with that?'

He made a dismissive motion with his hands. 'Chicken come first. Anya come second. Ivan tell cousin in Moscow to get wife for him. In Russia, easy to get good wife. Here, hard to get wife. You have husband?'

I nearly spat out a mouthful of beer. 'God, no.'

'See, it is as I say. In Moscow, where there is many good wife, cousin find Anya. He send photo to Ivan. Ivan want to marry her.'

'Did she want to marry him?'

'She want to come to USA. She want to live like the movies. So she come. They marry. They are happy.

'Then Anya become not happy. Her man fix shoe. He work in shop. He go to work, come home – every day the same. They have nice house with chicken. She not want this. She get too many idea from movie,' Eryk said.

'He bought her this to make her happy?' I touched the locket.

'This, he not buy. This, he get for payment from young want-to-be actor – who have no money for to pay. Actor get from dead mother. Ivan customers, they are Hollywood – they are all want-to-be or already-they-have-been.'

I weighed the locket in my hand. 'He got this for resoling shoes?'

'No, it is not for shoe fix. It is for drug fix. Why else need chicken?'

'Drugs?'

'Da, shoe repair is shop front for drug deal. Coke, plenty coke. Drop off shoe for resole. Pick up, pay too much, find little package in left shoe. Very good business. Also can make Italian shoe last for twenty year. But Ivan not tell Anya. He think, he get caught, she have no trouble.'

Eryk sighed. 'Anya, she say, chicken live in garden. She not understand why shoe fixer need so much luck. Little Lenin not like Anya, too. She take away his standard living.

'Anya not take care, leave gate open when she go out. Little Lenin get out and the luck run out. He go across road. No more Little Lenin.'

I couldn't help myself. 'Why did Little Lenin cross the road?'

'Everyone ask this question.' Eryk frowned at me. 'It is mystery of life, OK?'

I nodded.

'Then police come, arrest Ivan.'

'Just like that?'

'Da, like that.'

'I don't know if I believe in lucky chickens.'

'It matter not if you believe. Ivan believe. When Little Lenin go, his luck go. Poof. All gone. Ivan go to jail. They sell his things. You get necklace. End story.'

'What about Anya?'

'She go away.'

'Back to Moscow?'

'Minnesota.'

'Oh. Didn't Ivan try to stop her?'

'How to stop her from jail? No stop her. Ivan learn great lesson that day. Wife is nothing. Chicken is everything.'

'He should've told her the truth.'

'She should look at what she have, but she look at what she not have. She is happy with Ivan. She have exciting life. She just not know it. She is stupid woman.'

'That's not fair.'

'What is fair? No matter it is fair or not fair. No matter he keep secret from her. At end of every day all that matter is he like her and she like him. It is only thing that ever matter. You remember this – it is good advice for woman.'

'Is that the moral of your story?'

Eryk nodded sagely, 'Yes, you can count chicken, but only after you shut gate.'

Of course, I failed to see that Eryk was some kind of wise man of the former Soviet Union and that the odd little story he'd related contained everything I needed to know to navigate the next part of my life gracefully: all that really matters in any relationship is 'he like her and she like him'; sometimes you already have what you want without realizing it; sometimes people keep things from you for reasons that are not all bad; and whatever you believe becomes true for you because your beliefs shape your life. The man was some kind of Mafioso soothsayer. It was all useful stuff, especially considering what happened next. Or, rather, it would've been useful, if I'd taken any of it in. Problem is you have to be a lot more perceptive than I am to get that out of a story about a lucky communist chicken, on the first go.

When I returned to my seat, loud screaming broke out all around us. From what I could gather one of the purple players had shot a goal in the final thirty seconds of play, and most people in the stadium were on the side of the purple players. That was what caused everyone to spontaneously start screaming as if each and every one of them had won the lottery. It was hard not to be stirred by the spectacle of so many people so aggressively happy – even if the main emotion stirred was fear.

The final siren went. I stood with the rest of the crowd and cheered my heart out.

Father Giuliani watched me, his eyes hinting that much merriment, at my expense, was going on beneath his calm surface. 'Have you developed a passion for the game?'

'God, no,' I said, 'I'm just really glad it's over.'

FROM: Sydney Welles <sydneywelles@yahoo.com>
TO: God c/- danbrown@thedavincicode.com
DATE: Saturday, October 22, 7.01 p.m.
SUBJECT: You probably don't exist

Dear (Christian) God,

You're a cosmic Mr Snufalufagus.

You're invisible, you live in the sky and you no longer have much to say to anyone. The people you used to speak to on a regular basis are all dead. Now, all your spokespeople are self-appointed and, in most cases, self-interested. Yet, you're the ultimate imaginary friend to millions of people.

Being unseen and unheard are very common supreme-being afflictions. Deities haven't been sighted on a regular basis since the days of the ancient Greeks and Romans, when you used to come down to earth all the time to help, hinder and have sex with mortals.

Given that we haven't heard from you for so long, it's only natural we've started to doubt your existence. (However, that doesn't seem to prevent us from pitting our gods against each other, to see whose will win at war.)

Everyone wants to believe in you and go to heaven. Imagine what a depressing place the world would be if we were all nihilists. Yet, when it comes right down to it, it's doubt, not faith, which overcomes; after all, even the Vatican has lightning rods.

Sydney xxx

## FISHER BENNET McMAHON & MAY
4848 Abott Way Los Angeles CA 90066 USA
310-807-3000 t   310-807-5000 f

Charles Turner
Los Angeles Times
202 W. 1st St.
CA 90012

Dear Charles,

Thank you for your letter. As much as I appreciated getting it, especially after I stood you up, I have to ask: what has gotten into you? Did you fall into a vat of Prozac? I don't remember you ever being quite this flirtatious. But, trite as it may sound, I'm happy that you're happy, even if I can't see the reason for it.

The answers to your questions, in the order you asked them, are:

1 Eighteen.
2 No, never on a plane. But, if it counts, once on a rooftop while a plane flew overhead.
3 It was purple lace.
4 No, I can't run away to Prague. Not right now.
5 Yes, I think so. Why do you ask?

Yours,
Sydney

Larry informed me at 5.30 p.m., Friday, that he had a media interview scheduled for 6 p.m. The subject of the interview was the religious research study our agency was known to be conducting. Larry wanted me to take his place in the interview, as he had better things to do.

He often has me stand in for him when he can't be bothered. I wasn't concerned. Sure, it was a newspaper interview and print journalists love to print you out of context, love to edit any glimmer of reason or intelligence out of your words, making you sound like a fanatic or an idiot, or both. Sure, I didn't have any time to prepare, so there was a good chance I'd come off as a moron without any journalistic help, but, still, I wasn't worried.

Larry has made a habit of landing me in it at the last minute, and most of the situations are much more dire. Like the time he sent me to give a short speech in his place to 'a bunch of marketing students'. I'd walked into the ballroom of the Regent Beverly Wilshire, and found myself speaking in front of fifty MBA graduates from one of the most prestigious graduate schools in the country and more than four hundred CEOs, COOs, CFOs, CSOs, CMOs and any other C types that exist of the largest corporations in the country. In comparison, I didn't find the prospect of one newspaper journalist that daunting – a gross misjudgement on my part.

It wasn't until I was turning onto Ocean Boulevard, a couple of minutes away from the meeting place, that I realized I didn't know how I was supposed to recognize the journalist. I placed a distress call to Patton, who promised to torture Larry's personal assistant until she gave up the information. Sixty seconds later Patton called back; a table had been booked under the name of the journalist, and that name, he told me – without preparing me for the shock at all – was Charles Turner.

Patton started to tell me which paper he was from, but I told him, thanks, it was OK, I was familiar with his column. By that point I was already in front of the restaurant. The valet parking attendant was holding my door open, and there was nothing for me to do but get out of the car. A not-so-discreet cough from the valet guy made me aware I was failing to do so.

Curiosity, not courage, finally nudged me into the restaurant. I told the hostess there was a reservation under Turner. She agreed that there was, and informed me 'my party' was waiting for me. I followed her to the table, finding myself getting more apprehensive with each step. All my fantasy versions of this meeting, every hope I'd ever harboured for the relationship, all the mind portraits I'd painted of Charles, were fighting for dominance like Internet porn pop-up ads, overwhelming the meagre portion of my brain still functioning.

When she turned, smiled, and I saw Charles for the first time in person, I can honestly say he wasn't what I'd expected. He was so far from what I expected I had to hold on to the back of a chair, to ensure I didn't make any sudden dropping moves towards the floor.

My only consolation was that Charles looked almost as shocked as I felt. He'd started to get up upon my arrival and was now frozen halfway to his feet, doing a valid impression of a goldfish.

Meeting Charles would've been a pleasant experience in different circumstances. He was attractive in the way currently considered to be the thing. Blue-eyed and dark-haired, in need of both a haircut and a shave, he looked as if he went about the world doing great justice to blue jeans.

Annoyingly, he recovered himself before I did and, with litheness inappropriate for the gravity of the situation, stood and was at my side of the table in one fluent move.

'Hey,' he said, and after kissing me on my left temple, he loosened the death grip I had on my chair, guided me into it and returned to his seat. At least, there, he looked uncomfortable. He rubbed his chin with his knuckles. It's a habit of Jake's. He does it when he's not quite sure what to say.

The busy blur of a drinks waiter came into focus by our table, no doubt directed to us by the hostess after she witnessed the shock on my face. I had just enough presence of mind to order a vodka gimlet on the rocks. Jake ordered another Scotch and water. Judging from the way he was draining it, the drink he already had didn't have long to live.

'This is a . . . nice surprise,' he said.

I don't think he meant it.

We stared at each other in silence for several minutes, until my own loss for words resolved itself in one very appropriate one.

'Asshole.'

The drink-laden waiter froze on 'asshole', then thawed out just enough to deliver our order, before quickly melting away.

I embraced my gimlet and made it disappear.

'Asshole.' Vodka had done nothing to change my mind.

'You don't really mean that.'

I considered this theory. 'Yes, I do.'

'You weren't meant to find out like this.'

'Was I meant to find out at all?'

'Yes, of course.'

We stared at each other. It was evident neither of us knew what to say. It's when I have nothing to say that I usually speak up.

'So, you moonlight as a newspaper columnist?'

'I started in print. You know that.'

'When were you planning on letting me know?'

'I've been trying to tell you for a while now.'

'Can't have been trying too hard.' I checked my glass. It hadn't refilled itself.

'You'd have found out if you'd gotten into my file drawer that night.'

'How – oh, your column?'

He nodded. 'My column. Your letters.'

'You knew it was me from the start?'

'That first night.'

'That night in the bar? I'm not the only Sydney in Los Angeles.'

'The pen. The one you threw at me. It had your agency's name on it. You always write to me from work. And, I knew you'd be there.'

'That's right. I told you – I mean, Charles – that I'd be at that bar that night.'

'You did.'

'So, you came to – you came there for me. It wasn't just the pen-in-the-head?'

'Yes,' he said. 'But the pen helped.'

I didn't meet Jake by chance. For a moment I wondered what this did to my theory that life is just a series of random coincidences, and therefore essentially meaningless. Luckily, the moment passed.

'That makes sense,' I said. 'Everything makes sense. Here I thought I'd finally found someone who understood me, but that was only because I'd already explained myself to him in full, in writing.'

'I'm not the only one who's been keeping Charles a secret.'

'What's that supposed to mean?'

'Just that neither of us was blameless. Look,' Jake said, 'this doesn't have to be bad. Let's not blow it out of proportion.'

'I think it's already blown.'

I stood up. So far, I'd held it together. I felt the need to put an end to the conversation before the situation changed.

'Please, sit down,' Jake said.

'Thank you, but I should get going. It's been fun and I'd love to stay and have you fuck with my mind some more, but it's getting late. I have places to go.'

I left the table in what, at first, promised to be one of the better exits of my romantic career. It was sweeping, it was dramatic and it was only marred by one thing.

Due to its commendably clean state, I didn't notice the clear glass door of the restaurant was shut. Walking into it with a resounding thud, and having Jake, and a couple of waiters, rush to my aid, was not just one of those moments that transcend embarrassment to reach a degree of humiliation previously unknown, but also ruined the whole effect of me walking out on Jake without so much as a backward glance. Leaving him a broken man in my glorious wake was now also out of the question.

After the group of concerned waiters had offered me a glass of water, ice wrapped in a napkin and, for some reason I couldn't understand, a slice of chocolate mud cake, all of which I refused, they dispersed as quickly as they had gathered. I found myself on the side of the door I'd been aiming for when I collided with it. Jake had made it through, too, unharmed. While his concern for me, and my possible head injury, seemed genuine, even in my dazed and confused state I was aware he was having trouble keeping a smirk off his face.

'This isn't funny,' I said. I lied. I could see it was exceedingly amusing for anyone who wasn't me.

'No, it's not.' To his credit, Jake managed to keep a straight face. 'I'm going to take care of the bill. You'll be OK here for a minute?'

I nodded, then waited until his back was turned to hand the valet guy my ticket. My dramatic exit had failed dramatically. Sneaking off was the next best thing. But the way the day was going I wasn't really surprised when Jake came back just as I was getting into my car.

'Are you OK?' he asked, leaning on the open driver-side door.

'Fine.'

'Do you want me to follow you home?'

'No.'

'Are you sure you're OK?'

'Yes.'

He continued to lean on the door.

'I'm going to need that door to get home. You see, it's attached to my car.'

I pulled on the door handle. He didn't give it up.

'I'm fine. Honest.' I did my best to sound reassuringly sane, not at all like someone who'd just received a severe blow to the head.

Jake didn't look convinced, but he stopped the tug-of-war with my car door and stood back to watch me drive off. To my credit, although I was still reeling from both physical and emotional blows, I managed not to hit anything else on the way home. All I wanted to do, upon reaching that sanctuary, was to curl up in a ball and never venture out amongst people again.

What I did do was get dressed and go to a party.

From what I can recall, I had a reasonable time at Julie's birthday party.

I remember putting on a lot of glittery make-up, to compensate for the way I felt. I remember putting on a mildly sequinned top, to balance all the make-up.

I remember the bar was on Fairfax in Hollywood and that it was called a girl's name. I remember a friendly bartender who was setting me up well in the way of vodka and encouraging me to dance on the bar. Whether I danced or not is something, thankfully, I don't remember.

I remember meeting a rocket scientist and a jet-propulsion engineer, who both worked for NASA, arm wrestling with one of them, and getting them both to inhale helium from birthday balloons before singing 'Yellow Submarine'. I've always believed the secret to mixing well socially lies in the skill of bringing people down to your intellectual level.

I remember giving a phone number to a guy called Ted. Or was it Todd? He spent an hour trying to chat me up. I thought he deserved it for tenacity.

I remember ending up back at Julie's house and continuing to be well set up for vodka. I remember Julie handing me Brad Pitt on a leash and telling me I could have him to keep me company for the weekend. That way if I'd sustained a concussion from my collision with the restaurant door, and went to sleep without any idea of waking up, Brad Pitt could run around barking and save me. He had yet to perform one useful task in fourteen doggy years, had yet to obey a simple command, but I remember we felt illogically optimistic about his latent saviour skills. He needed only a life-and-death situation to nudge his inner Lassie into being.

I remember having to bribe the cab driver to take us, after Brad Pitt tried to eat one of the tyres. I remember that, after I'd spoken sternly to him for munching on the Michelins, Brad Pitt and I had a good talk on the way home. Well, I talked and gave him a snapshot of my troubles, and he licked my hand a couple of times in a supportive way, in between taking great chomps out of the seat.

By the time we reached my place we were of one mind, having decided to sleep straight through the next day, giving it a miss altogether. Today, after all, hadn't turned out that great. Brad Pitt seemed to think it unlikely that we'd be allowed to sleep uninterrupted. I put his pessimism down to him being a dog and not his own master, and dismissed it. I remember looking forward to having my bed all to myself and told Brad Pitt I wasn't going to budge from it for at least twelve hours. That was the plan we finally agreed on.

I didn't know, at the time, that what they say about the best laid plans of mice and men also holds true for those of women and dogs.

FROM: Sydney Welles <s.welles@fbmm.com>
TO: God c/- info@evangelicalsRus.org
DATE: Saturday, October 29, 3.25 a.m.
SUBJECT: Science 102

Dear God,

Science doesn't lessen you. It makes you so much greater. What science shows us, when it shows us the infinite universe, the microscopic detail of life, or the precise patterns in nature, is that creation is so infinite and so complex that we can only ever be aware of a minute fraction of it.

But if we admit we can only ever comprehend a teeny, tiny part of the universe, we then also have to admit that there is no way any of us can fully understand its creator. A person who can tell you what God is thinking is as likely as an ant that can describe how a car works. Anybody who claims to be able to speak for God is either lying or delusional.

This must be why religions denounce science. If they acknowledged science and incorporated it into their beliefs, they'd have to admit that any being capable of creating the universe is beyond their comprehension. Then they'd have to give up speaking for you, and organized religion would become far too hard to organize.

It all makes sense now.

Syd x

My life to date has been a barren one. I find babies just as aesthetically pleasing as the next woman does, but I've survived thirty years on earth without succumbing to the need to grow one of my own in my belly.

My less fortunate friends, since decanting infants into their lives, have all but disappeared from mine. So, the only regular interaction I have with anyone under voting age – with the exception of the devil's spawn across the street – is with Audrey and Lexie, Anna's steptwins-to-be.

I adore the girls. Even if a Pied Piper's train of biddable children took to trailing around after me, I'd still consider them my two favourite women-in-the-making. There's a pleasing symmetry to their twin-ness; miniature, matching human beings have a charm all their own. Mostly, though, I like them because they are unspoilt, good-natured, humane kids in spite of being born horrifically rich.

All that being so, it still came as a jarring shock to me to open my eyes and find them standing by the side of my bed at six-thirty in the morning. At first I thought I was seeing double, that there was only one small, pigtailed girl, wearing a pink one-piece pyjama suit with feet attached, standing in front of me. Then the two remaining brain cells I owned collided, and I recollected the girls were identical twins.

I tried, as far as my eyelids would allow – they'd been

weighted down with sandbags overnight – facing the girls with what dignity I could muster. They were, after all, of an impressionable age. Not yet ready to discover I wasn't always the sophisticated woman they knew and looked up to, if for no other reason than that they're really short. I must've succeeded in gaining my composure, as the twins regarded me for several seconds in what I'd like to assume was respectful silence. Lexie was the first to break it.

'Who hit you?'

'What?' I said.

'Who hit you?' She considerately raised her voice twenty or thirty decibels so I could hear her better.

'It wasn't a "who". It was a "what". A bottle of Absolut ... or maybe it was Grey Goose. I can tell you which when I see how much money is left in my purse. Why do you ask?'

'You have black eyes. Like the panda in the zoo.'

I ran my little finger under my left eye and found it gained a substantial black smudge.

'That? Don't worry about that. It's the slutty eye make-up I had on last night. It'll come off.'

Audrey seemed to doubt my claim, but the question she asked was, 'Can we get into bed with you?'

'Depends. Is there anyone else in the bed?'

'Just him.' She pointed past me to the foot of the bed.

Brad Pitt had snuck onto the bed during the brief time I'd been asleep, even though we'd discussed the different designated sleeping areas for dogs and human beings at some length before retiring. A large, ugly dog was already in my bed. Adding two gorgeous little girls to the mix wouldn't make much difference. I told them to get in.

The most direct route must've been over the top of me, as that was the path trodden. I had to clutch the edges of the mattress as the bed began to tilt and heave. The girls, and Brad Pitt, who awoke to join the fun, bounced, squealed and barked. Their joy reached a crescendo of brain-mincing yelps all round and caused the room to sway in a way I found distracting. After what seemed like several long hours, the other occupants of my bed calmed down, the world levelled out and my nausea eased slightly.

'What's "slutty"?' Lexie asked.

I tried to come off as a stern authority figure while also toying with the idea of vomiting. 'Where did you hear that word?'

'From you.'

'Really? Oh. OK. Well. Um. You know the way you two just jumped into bed with me?'

'Uh-huh.'

'Well, in different circumstances, jumping into bed with someone like that would be considered to be slutty. Do you understand what I mean?'

'No.'

'I'm very glad to hear it. Where's your wicked stepmother?'

Both girls glanced towards the kitchen. A loud smashing sound came from that direction. I sat up in bed.

'Anna?'

'Sorry, sorry. But, really, it was ugly anyway.'

Anna's voice was followed by the rest of her, and, once I saw her, with two steaming mugs holding what all my barely working senses told me was freshly brewed coffee, I forgave her for entering and breaking. Anna placed the mugs on the chest of drawers, pulled a pint-sized bottle of Scotch from the pocket of her green Chinese silk dressing gown and showed me the label.

'Want some?'

'Will I need it?'

'Very likely.' She doused the coffee and handed me a mug. I took it gratefully. A sip or two and I felt better. Not like my old familiar self. That was impossible because there was still at least half a bottle of vodka diluting my blood, but at least now I felt like someone I was vaguely acquainted with.

Anna, after shucking off her fluffy stiletto mules, had settled herself at the end of the bed and was absently drumming her fingers on Brad Pitt's flat head.

'Nice shoes,' I said. I didn't think anyone actually wore shoes like that outside of 1940s movies, and then only in mysterious places called boudoirs.

'You look like shit. What did you do to yourself last night?'

'Serious damage, obviously. Why are you here?'

'I don't think I can go through with this wedding.'

It is my duty as chief bridesmaid – and only bridesmaid over the age of six – to remain calm in the face of bridal wedding nerves, even before seven in the morning, the day before the wedding. 'Oh, really. Why is that?'

'I shouldn't have gone strapless. My arms look too fat in the dress. I can't wear it.'

'Trust me, if you lost any more weight off your arms, you'd look like the Venus de Milo.'

'I left Vince.'

My white sheets nearly acquired a striking café noir stain. 'But . . . the wedding . . . it's tomorrow. You'll lose your deposit. You can't have left him. Not now.'

'She did,' Lexie said. 'We all did.'

I placed my coffee carefully on the bedside cabinet. 'You left your daddy?'

'Yes. He's nice, but he's a boy. He can't take us to the bathroom at the mall.'

The girl had a point, but still. 'You can't just take off with the girls like that,' I said.

'Why not? I'm keeping them as my share of the settlement.'

'This isn't a joint property issue. And it's . . . it's not fair to Vince.'

'I know. I know. The fair thing to do would be to get one each, but could you separate them? They're a matched set.'

'Wait. Wait. Don't you have to carry them around in your uterus or raise them from seed, or something of that magnitude, before they'll grant you custody? How are you going to take care of them? Are you getting Louise in the settlement, too?'

'Lulu didn't want to come,' Lexie said.

'True,' Anna said. 'She didn't think it was a good idea. Strange, she's normally quite sensible. It doesn't matter. We'll do without a nanny. Lots of people do, you know, and I'll have plenty of help from my best friend.'

I glanced around the room. 'You mean me, don't you?'

'Of course I mean you. Who else?' Anna leaned forwards, placed her coffee mug on the bedside table and grabbed me by the shoulders. 'You have to promise me something.'

'OK, what?'

'If anything happens to me, you'll take care of the girls.'

'But they have Vince –'

'No, I mean, should anything happen to the both of us, you have to take the girls. Promise me.'

'Me? You want me to take the girls? What about Vince's parents?'

'They're too old. Promise you will.'

'Yes, OK, I promise. Of course I will. Of course.'

Anna calmed down a little – enough that I thought it was safe to ask, 'What's really wrong here?'

'It's all so final, this marriage business. And the thing is, it's not just me and Vince. What about the girls? What happens to them if we fuck it up? They've already lost one mother.'

'So, what are you doing? You leave now, you'll definitely fuck it up. Kids are a consideration in most marriages – just not usually at the wedding stage.'

'How can I know for sure that this is the right thing to do? The best thing for everyone?'

'You can't know for sure. No one can – have a little faith. It'll all work out.'

'You're telling me to have faith? Christ, now I know I'm in trouble.'

'It's just nerves. Getting married is a big deal.'

'Whatever. Look, we'll stay here until we get on our feet. The house seems a lot smaller than the last time I was here ... but it'll be fun. I'm almost sure of it. We could become one of those non-nuclear families that conservative politicians get so upset about. Though I suppose Jake mightn't like it, either.'

'Well, actually, Jake and I, we kind of broke up.'

'That's great. See, it's all working out already.' Anna got up, gave Brad Pitt's left ear a gentle yank, and went to see who was at the door. For some reason, my doorbell was ringing at twenty to seven on Saturday morning.

'Don't worry,' I said, 'they'll get back together. This is just a pre-wedding episode. That's probably your daddy trying to break my doorbell now.'

The twins didn't seem at all worried. If anything, the whole affair was putting them to sleep. I decided to join them and was rearranging myself in the space left to me when Anna came back into the room with Jake Reed, aka Charles Turner, in tow. I hid under the covers, hoping he'd go away. No such luck. He unearthed me by folding back the comforter.

'You look like shit,' he said.

'Charming. No wonder she broke up with you,' Anna said.

'She broke up with me?' Jake was concerned. 'When?'

One of the twins turned over and said, 'Shit, shit, shit, shit,' in a sleepy voice.

'I think you forgot to tell him something,' Anna said.

'Yeah, you did,' he said.

They were ganging up on me.

'I can't be expected to let everyone know everything right away. It must have slipped my mind – I might be concussed. How come you let him in? You're supposed to be my best friend.'

'He had a key.'

'Does everybody have a key to my house?' I pulled the comforter back over my head as the doorbell rang again. I peeked out at the alarm clock. It told me seven o'clock was still fifteen minutes away. I had a feeling it was going to be a long day.

'Who'd be calling so early on a Saturday?' Anna was on her way to the door again.

'I have no idea,' I said. 'All the people I know who'd do a rotten thing like that are already here.'

It occurred to me that if Anna left the room I'd be more or less alone with Jake; the short people in my bed provided no protection. I sat up. 'Wait, don't go . . . whoever it is probably has a key as well.'

Anna was gone. The doorbell continued to sound, rather more violently than necessary, I thought.

Jake had seated himself in the chair under the window.

'Please, make yourself at home,' I said.

He leaned back in the chair, propping his feet up on the foot of the bed. He didn't seem to be at all aware of the awkwardness of the situation — of him being in my bedroom now we were no longer together — and had somehow acquired my cup of coffee and was taking a sip.

'What's in this?'

'Scotch. If you want something else, you have to get it yourself.'

'I'm not here for the coffee.'

'What are you here for?'

'What do you think I'm here for?'

'This isn't a good time. I'm very busy. As you can see, I have a lot on this morning.'

'You don't look as if you have that much on at all.'

I followed his gaze down to my nightgown. A couple of buttons had come undone, and it wasn't doing a brilliant job of protecting my modesty. Unable to think of anything to say, I strategically withdrew under the covers to do the buttons up.

Raised voices came from the front-door region of the house.

'Vince must be here,' I said, to my comforter.

'Sounds like it.'

The argument escalated. Judging from the stomping going on, the conflict went free-range, taking in most of the rest of the house and ending up in the kitchen, where it was enhanced by the sound effects of cupboard doors being opened and slammed shut. I wondered what it was they were looking for.

'Tell them they're going to wake the twins,' I said.

'The twins aren't in any danger of waking.'

I propped myself up on my elbows. Jake was right. The girls were profoundly asleep. The battle being waged in my kitchen needed to reach an all-out nuclear assault before it'd disturb them.

'I guess they have a few things to sort out before the wedding,' Jake said.

'I guess so.'

'Are we going to talk about it?'

'Vince and Anna?'

'You know what I mean.'

Exhaustion made me honest. 'I do,' I said, 'but I've had about two minutes' sleep and, I promise you, you don't want to talk to me right now. I am not a reasonable human being. Could we please sleep on it?'

'We'll talk later?'

'Yes, sleep first, talk later. An excellent plan. Thank you and good night or morning or whatever it is.' I closed my eyes.

Drowsiness came in an instant; the world receded into the ether. In a kitchen, in a galaxy far, far away, an argument lost intensity and became quiet. Closer, somewhere in this solar system, someone dropped shoes on the floor and got into bed beside me. I tried to tell him no, no vacancy, bed full of small identical pink space invaders with feet built into their garments, no possible room. Especially not for him, as he was actually two people in one, making a total of five people and one dog in the bed.

Jake felt warm and comfortable when he wrapped himself around me, so I let the matter rest for a second and sleep got to me first, well before I could warn him about Brad Pitt's proclivity for nibbling on exposed toes.

FROM: Sydney Welles <sydneywelles@yahoo.com>
TO: God c/- god2536@yahoo.com
DATE: Saturday, October 29, 2.54 p.m.
SUBJECT: Rinse & Repeat

Dear God,

With its confession-and-absolution system, Catholicism, as a product, reminds me most of a cleaning product – washing detergent comes first to mind. Catholicism is in the business of cleansing. Go out and sin. Confess. Repent. Be absolved. Repeat the process.

Can you imagine the ads if we sold the Church like detergent?

While we see before and after shots of a sullen, taciturn kid transforming into a beamish, bouncing boy, much to the joy of his stereotypical soccer mom and business dad, a female voice-over says: 'We thought our son Henry was beyond all help. At times we were sure he was possessed by the devil. Then a friend recommended Catholicism. We tried it and it started working right away. After a year, it got all of the sin out. We still can't believe it. The results are truly miraculous. Now Henry is a good boy. He's an altar boy and the priest's favourite. We're so proud of him.' Insert the appropriate before and after pictures, and finish with the deep male voice-over they use for all commercials of the kind: 'The Catholic Church: gets out even the most stubborn of sins.'

Maybe all religion is a kind of soul soap. Perhaps that's why they say cleanliness is next to godliness. Some people do a little light cleaning once a week, while others wait for a lifetime of muck to accumulate before undergoing a dramatic cleansing. The latter tend to be the most annoying.

Me, I think that life leaves stains. Some wash out, but others are there for good, no matter how long you soak.

Sydney x

I awoke to the sound of an ambulance siren, disturbingly loud and close, before it abruptly stopped, leaving me wondering if I'd dreamt it. The room was cool and quiet. I was alone. The clock by my bed showed noon. No one rang my doorbell. No one hogged my sheets. No one smashed my plates. My head no longer felt like a small grenade had gone off inside it. Gratitude for my complete reversal of fortune propelled me out of bed into the shower.

Moisture in the tub indicated someone had been there before me. My hot-water system is continuous and, provided they hadn't used all the clean towels, I didn't care if an entire basketball team had dropped by to shower, which, considering the events of the early morning, was likely.

I stood under the water until my fingers and toes were pruney and I'd run out of shower activities to perform. It then took half a bottle or so of eye make-up remover to remove most of the black under my eyes. Some of the black, it turned out, was natural.

My reflection, resembling something vaguely human once more, reminded me I was human, and that for all human beings, except those who were models and actors, food was necessary for survival. The kitchen, then, was my next port of call, and what I found there made me glad I'd bothered to get partially dressed, albeit in an old Bert and Ernie T-shirt and equally vintage underpants announcing, incorrectly, it was Tuesday.

Brad Pitt was asleep in a strip of sunlight on the floor, in his usual position of repose. His big, baggy head rested between his front legs, stretched out straight in front of him. His back legs were stretched out straight behind him. He was sleeping like Superman in full flight, but he wasn't even close to being the main event in my kitchen.

Seated at the small table was a godlike creature, wearing a towel in the most casual of arrangements around his waist. The vision was bending sunlight to his will. It glinted off bronzed skin, highlighted damp, tousled hair and added a dangerously sexy gleam to his eyes.

In other words, it was Jake, sitting there, looking hot.

A newspaper was open on the table in front of him, but his attention was fixed on a spot of vacant wall. A spot that, in spite of appearances, was so interesting it took him several moments to notice I was in the room. I managed to sidle over to the fridge, open the door to discover it had been filled with an array of omelette fillings, all of them known favourites of Anna's, before I gained his attention.

Upon divining my presence, he did display definite signs of being pleased to find me within arm's length, instantly inviting me to sit on his lap. In light of my having broken up with him, I felt obligated to refuse. My lack of compliance with his preferred seating plan caused Jake to go all alpha male on me. I ended up on his lap anyway. He offered to show me what was under his towel and continued the dominant male behaviour until I gave up wrestling him and agreed to look under the towel.

Not long after that we came to a mutual decision to have sex up against the fridge. Other than that slight transgression and the one that followed about half an hour afterwards on one of my kitchen chairs – which, by the way, are a lot stronger than they look – I was in complete command of the situation and unrelenting in my decision that things were over between us.

Jake, for some reason, seemed to think he could convince me otherwise. He had the nerve to say, 'I don't see the problem.'

'That would be because you're using boy logic.'

'Well, I am a boy.'

'I can see that. There is, in fact, such a thing as too much evidence. Put your towel back on.'

'I'll get dressed – unless . . .'

'I don't think so,' I said. Though his suggestion was not without merit, having sex with him for the third time in the one afternoon might give him the impression I wasn't really over him.

I followed him into the bedroom, where he pulled on socks, boxers, jeans and a long-sleeved T-shirt, in that order. I took the opportunity to gain a sweater and a pair of jeans of my own.

'Why do you use a pseudonym for your column?'

Jake settled himself on the bed. 'I like the freedom it gives me to say whatever I want without having to answer to too many people.'

'Why Charles?'

'Jake didn't sound like a writer's name.'

'Chuck does?'

'Think Chuck Dickens.' Jake patted the space beside him. 'Come here. Promise I won't seduce you. Scout's honour,' he said.

'You were never a scout.' I sat anyway, figuring I could quickly dampen any ardour he felt by asking the right questions.

'It's my middle name,' Jake said.

'Charles?'

'Old family name. Someone in every generation gets stuck with it. I'm lucky my parents took pity on me and didn't give it to me as a first name.'

'Very lucky. I had doubts about dating someone named Chuck. It's not a name I can imagine myself even uttering during sex – although, it does rhyme with . . . um, what were we talking about?'

'Todd wants to ask you out.'

'Who is Todd?'

'That's the same question I was going to ask you. He called my place late last night wanting to speak to you.'

'To me?'

'Yep.'

'Are you sure?'

'You're the only Sydney I know. Besides, you fit the description he gave.'

'Todd?'

'That's what he claimed.'

'Why did he call you?'

'That I can't tell you.'

'Oh?' I said, then, 'Oh.'

'I take it the penny has dropped.'

'He's this guy I met at Julie's party . . .'

'Go on.'

'I had to give him a phone number, for trying so hard to pick me up. And, well, I didn't want to give him mine.'

'So you gave him mine?'

'OK, when you take it out of context like that, it sounds bad. But, you see, when you give a guy a number to get rid of him, it has to be one you know in case they ask you to repeat it. I guess your number was top of mind. That he called and annoyed you late at night is really just a happy coincidence.'

'Poor guy. Must be tough, paling in comparison, next to me. I'll be nicer to him next time he calls.' Jake stretched out on my bed, grabbing a couple of pillows to prop up his big head.

'Please don't encourage him.'

'Are you going to tell me why you think we've broken up?'

'You lied to me,' I said.

'I didn't exactly lie. I withheld information.'

'It's the same thing. Why didn't you tell me about Charles?'

'I could ask you the same question. And another. Why didn't you tell Charles about me?'

I could see the point he was making, but I wasn't ready to admit it. 'I asked first.'

'I did try to tell you. I would've told you if your behaviour hadn't been so erratic.'

'You're saying it's my fault you didn't tell me?'

'I didn't want to scare you off.'

'I don't scare all that easily.'

340

'Come on. We had an amazing thirty-six-hour first date, which we agreed at the time was something special. You were as happy about it as I was, and yet you disappeared for two weeks. If I'd told you I was Charles, you'd have been so thrilled that I'd probably never have seen you again.'

I hate it when people have reasonable answers for everything.

'What's the big deal? You like Charles. You like me. Now you have both of us in one neat package. You should be twice as happy.'

'You're using boy logic again.'

'I don't get it, Syd.' Jake sat back up on the bed. 'We seem to be getting on just fine.'

'Getting on has never been our problem. Our problem is . . .' What was the problem? I was having trouble defining it.

Jake didn't seem to have the same trouble. 'This isn't about Charles at all, is it?'

As soon as he said that, I felt very exposed.

'You know, not every woman's goal is to end up some guy's handmaiden for the next fifty years. Some of us want more out of life.'

'We're not living in the dark ages. You can have a relationship and a life.'

'It's not the same. Men have an unfair advantage. You're allowed to make more mistakes. You can still start a family at age fifty.'

'This isn't a gender issue.'

'Fine for you to say when your gender doesn't have a use-by date.'

'None of that matters with us.'

'If it works out,' I said.

'Are you so sure this won't work out?'

'Why are you so optimistic? You fell out of love with Kim.'

'I don't think I was ever in love with Kim.'

'You dated the girl for two years. It proves my point exactly. What were you doing? Killing time until the girl you're supposed to marry graduates high school?'

I thought I was going to hear his 'not every guy is an asshole' speech, but instead Jake answered the question. 'I was with Kim because I wanted to be with someone, and I guess I thought, maybe, that was all there was.'

'OK.'

'You have to remember, I hadn't yet met you.'

That just made me feel worse. Tears, of their own accord, started to roll down my cheeks. I tried to blink them away, but that seemed only to increase the flow. I used the sleeves of my sweater, pulled over my fists, to stem the tide.

I could see Jake was making an effort to be patient. 'Why can't we just see where this goes?'

'I don't want to see,' I said. I'm sure it sounded as petulant to his ears as it did to mine.

'Why not?'

'I just don't believe in happily ever after.'

'I'm beginning to think you don't believe in anything at all.'

Now he was angry, and my sleeves were soggy enough without having to take that statement into consideration. True, I didn't believe in what Jake seemed to believe in, or what most other people believed in, but there had to be something I believed in. If I could only think what it was. I changed the subject.

'Anyway, how do I know for sure you never saw Kim in New York?'

'I guess you can't know for sure. But you could try having a little faith in me.'

'Faith? I should believe whatever you say because believing it makes my life neater and easier? That's what you want me to do?'

'I think the work you've been doing has made you very cynical.'

'I'll take cynical over stupid any day.'

'Sometimes,' Jake said, 'people believe in something or somebody because the belief itself, regardless of whether it's true or not, makes their lives better.'

'Not me. I'm sorry. You've put your faith in the wrong person.'

'I don't think so.'

'Trust me, there's a twenty-two-year-old out there waiting for you who'll believe anything you want her to believe. When you find her, you'll thank me for this.'

'You really have issues, don't you?'

'If you've only just realized that now, you're in serious trouble. Look, I'm sorry, but this is . . . I can't pretend that I believe in something when I don't.'

'Then why start this in the first place?'

'I didn't think it'd get this far. I thought that because of Charles . . .'

'You'd always have a way out.'

'Yes,' I said.

Jake stared at me. He stared for a full minute, almost without blinking, but whatever it was he was trying to see eluded him.

'Are you sure this is what you want?'

I wasn't sure, but I said I was.

'So, that's it?' Jake stood and looked out the window. He didn't appear to see anything of interest, but he kept at it for a while, before he picked up his shoes and slipped them on, not bothering to do up his laces.

'I wish I knew why you won't let yourself be happy,' he said.

Happy? Christ, I wasn't trying for happy – just for manageable.

At the bedroom door, he paused, looking back. I thought he was going to say something more, but he was silent. I wondered if I could stop him from going if I said the right thing. I was sorely tempted to try. Only, I had no idea what to say.

'So, I guess this means I'll be going stag to the wedding.'

'I'll call and give them my apologies,' he said.

Brad Pitt eagerly followed Jake to the front door, then returned to glare at me reproachfully when it slammed in his face. That's why I don't own a dog. They have no discernment whatsoever when it comes to whose side they should be on in a fight.

'Trust me, it'll be easier this way,' I said. 'It was already getting too hard and it was definitely taking up too much time. I want my old, uncomplicated life back.'

Brad Pitt did not look convinced.

'Oh, what do you know? You're a dog; you love everybody. It's really quite pathetic.'

I had a funny empty feeling inside me. It turned out to be hunger, but, even so, I was aware I'd lost a lot more than an argument. Knowing that I was self-reliant and capable of leading a relatively enviable life not dependent on any other person wasn't the consolation it used to be.

There was nothing to do about it – nothing to do but try to hold it together. All the same, all I wanted to do was to keep crying into my sleeves. What I needed was outside intervention. The only thing that can save you from drowning in the murky self-pity of your own tragedy is someone else's greater tragedy.

FROM: Sydney Welles <sydneywelles@yahoo.com>
TO: God c/- specialfxdepartment@universalpictures.com
DATE: Saturday, October 29, 5.33 p.m.
SUBJECT: Heaven & Other Unrealistic Endings

Dear God,

I like a happy ending as much as the next Hollywood studio exec, but I suspect that, when a film ends on a soaring, impossibly happy note, nobody in the audience is crying from happiness. No, they're genuinely crying because they know nothing like that will ever happen in real life.

For most people, happily ever after is shelved, alongside Santa, the Easter Bunny and the Tooth Fairy, well before adolescence. We soon learn there's no such thing. Yet as soon as people stop believing, they become part of the great conspiracy. They lie to little kids, elaborately, at considerable expense and trouble, to keep these myths going.

Why is it that adults feel better if children believe in fairy tales and bogeypersons and happy endings? Why is it that no matter how much gritty reality people have endured, no matter how dire the circumstances of their lives, no matter what mistakes they've made, they still want to believe that life works out in the end, just like a fairy tale? After all, isn't heaven the ultimate fairy-tale ending? It's the only story of its kind to survive the end of childhood. The only one that becomes more popular the older people get.

How can we still believe in heaven when all the other happy endings we were promised turned out to be lies? Are we the most gullible race in existence? Or just the most tenacious? Or both?

Sydney

When the doorbell rang two hours after Jake left, I only fleetingly indulged the thought that it was Jake ringing it. Really, he was the last person I expected, or, rather, the next to last. The people on my doorstep were the least expected of all – Cupid and Cupid's mother, the incongruously named Sunny.

From what Cupid has told me of his maternal grandparents, I've gathered that his mother was the offspring of proper hippies from the 1960s, who gave their five children natural names: Sky, Sunny, Sandy, Meadow and River. Sunny had disappointed her parents by embracing capitalism, but had continued their tradition of choosing children's names that guaranteed the kids who bore them get beaten up at school.

Sunny appeared to be quite beat up herself. Her normally not-a-hair-out-of-place coiffure was seriously awry, her mascara worn two inches below the area usually recommended for the application of that product, her shoes and purse mismatched. Though, her shoes, if you weren't too fussy, matched the small, ugly leather suitcase she carried in her right hand.

More than her dishevelled appearance and Cupid's disquietingly waif-like demeanour, it was the little suitcase that disturbed me – the suitcase and the bulging *Spiderman II* backpack on Cupid's back.

Deathly pale under her fake tan, Sunny began to speak rapidly, breathlessly and slightly hysterically – I managed to catch only every other word. I made a little sense of what she was saying. Something of a serious medical nature had happened to her husband. It required her to spend the next few days at Cedars-Sinai. Cupid's old nanny had the flu, and his baby-sitter wasn't allowed to stay out all night. Sunny's brother was overseas, and her younger sisters were irresponsible – free-range nymphomaniacs attracted to men with questionable grooming habits – and very likely to leave the kid somewhere and forget about him. Her husband had no brothers and sisters, and being an only, late child, his mother was too old to look after Cupid. Certain friends she'd normally turn to were nowhere to be found. And the mothers' group she belonged to was composed of a bunch of calorie-deficient cows. I was wondering why she was sharing all of this information with me, until I clearly heard her say, 'The thing is, he said he wanted to stay with you.'

'With me?' I looked at Cupid. He looked at his mother's shoes. It was hard not to stare at them. They were a truly hideous mustard leather.

'My parents will pick him up first thing in the morning. They're driving through the night to get here. They can't get here any sooner.' Sunny shook her head. 'It's an ideological problem: economic inequality. Until we reach a time where everybody in the world can afford to travel by plane, they refuse to fly.'

'I see,' I said.

'Do you think we'll be able to make this happen?'

'I'd like to think so, but, realistically, I don't think that we will ever reach that kind of economic equality until we can manage to curb corporate greed and –'

'No, I meant is it OK for Cupid to stay with you tonight? Or, if you prefer, you can stay at our place with him.'

Cupid had transferred his attention to my shoes, which were pink fluffy slippers with a cheeky monkey's head embroidered on the front of each, but, even so, not at all deserving of the scowl he was treating them to.

'Yes, of course he can stay. I'd be happy to have him. Please, come in.' Someone had said that out loud. It had sounded a lot like my voice.

Brad Pitt, who'd been standing quietly behind me all this time, barked his welcome. Sunny flinched when she noticed the dog, but visibly steeled herself, prodding Cupid through the open doorway before following him in.

Ten minutes later, Sunny was gone, and Cupid and I were seated at my kitchen table engaged in a staring contest.

'Do you have PlayStation 2?'

I shook my head. 'Not even PlayStation 1.'

'X-Box?'

'I don't think so, but I can't be sure. I don't know what it is.'

'Nintendo 64?'

'No. And none of the other sixty-three, either.'

'Sixty-three what?'

'I've no idea.'

'I brought my GameBoy. Do you want to play?'

'Maybe later. Have you had dinner?'

He shook his head.

I got up, pulled open the fridge door and stared at its contents, hoping they'd add up in my mind into something easy that'd appeal to the appetite of a sad seven-year-old boy. I wondered how close that appetite would be to that of cheerful five-year-old twin girls with a live-in cook. I spied a hunk of cheese that needed only to be melted in a pan with a knob of butter, seasoned and mixed with a little milk to become a sauce.

'How about Gorgonzola pasta and arugula salad?'

'What's that?'

'It's a mild blue cheese – wait, no, you won't like it. I didn't like blue cheese when I was your age. Too stinky.'

Cupid perked up. 'My dad eats stinky cheese.' His face returned to its forlorn expression. 'Maybe I'll like it, too – like him. Do you think I'll like it?'

'No,' I said.

'What is ar-roog-goo-lah?'

'Oh, arugula salad. You won't like that either, come to think of it. It's kind of bitter.'

'I don't like salad.'

'Neither did I when I was your age. Hated the stuff. What do you like?'

He sighed. 'All the things I like, I'm not allowed to have.'

'Is that so? Well, tonight is different. Tonight, you are allowed to eat what you like.'

Cupid regarded me with suspicion. 'Anything? No broccoli? You won't tell.'

'I won't tell.'

'Promise, cross your heart, hope to die?'

'Yes. All of the above.'

He was not convinced of my good intentions, but he

said, 'I want a cheeseburger, but not a junior one. I want a grown-up one.'

'OK.'

'With big fries.'

'OK.'

'And a strawberry milkshake. The biggest one.'

'OK.'

'Really?'

'Really.'

'What will happen if I don't finish my food?'

'Nothing at all. If you don't, Brad Pitt will. Do you want to eat out or bring it back here?'

He thought it over. 'Here. Do you have any PG movies?'

'I do, or we could go to the video store if you like.'

'Can we go in your Mini?'

'Yes.'

'Can I help drive?'

'No.'

☦

Long after Cupid's appetite for junk had been sated and we'd watched two films that fulfilled his mental junk requirements – they both provided more evidence for my theory that almost all mainstream Hollywood films are made for seven-year-old boys – I heard a muffled noise coming from my second room, where Cupid should have been asleep on the day bed. I listened for a few minutes; the low noise continued steadily.

By the light in the hallway, which Cupid had insisted I leave on in case I was scared, I could see his golden head was face down on his pillow, into which he was sobbing as if all the PlayStations in the world had suddenly stopped working. Comfort was required and, as there was only me or Brad Pitt – who'd been standing sentinel by Cupid's bed all night – around to give it, I turned on the lamp and sat on the side of the bed next to Cupid's prostrate form. Brad Pitt, in his Superman position on the floor, considerately became a footrest for me.

I reached out and softly touched the mop of curls on the pillow. 'Well,' I said, 'look who's had too much sugar.'

He lifted his head and glared at me defiantly through tears. 'I feel sick.'

'OK. Where do you feel sick?'

He pointed vaguely in the direction of his stomach and chest.

'Kind of a general middle-bit sick, is it?'

He made a snuffling sound in agreement.

'I've heard it's going around. Does it hurt?'

'It feels funny in here.' Sitting up, he pointed to the space between his chest and stomach. 'Maybe it's a heart attack like my dad's.'

'Trust me, you're in the low-risk category for heart disease. Maybe your tummy is a little unsettled from all that food.'

He nodded, miserably. I was compelled, by the mysterious magnetic force sad little children have surrounding them, to put my arm around him.

'Your dad is being taken care of by some of the best doctors in the world. Everything is going to be OK. You'll see in the morning.'

A flood of fresh tears and snot broke through. I placed

the tissues from the small side cabinet on the bed beside him, hoping he was old enough to blow his nose on his own. He ignored the tissues, using his sleeve and my sheets instead.

'Your TV isn't very big,' he said.

'No, it's not. But I'll let you in on a little secret. Bigger is not always better. When it comes to television, the bigger the screen, the less interesting the life of the person who owns it. You'll work this out as you get older.'

Cupid sniffed. 'Your dog is ugly.'

'He's not my dog. But, you're right, he's very ugly.'

'You don't have any toys.'

'I know. It sucks. But I'm going to get some, and you can help me choose them. Are you tired?'

'No,' he said.

Then he yawned three times in a row, laid his head on my shoulder and cried himself to sleep.

☦

Morning Star – I suspect that wasn't the name on her birth certificate, as her husband Frank had called her Maureen a couple of times – stared at me, or, rather, at the air around me, with such concentration I wondered if she'd slipped into a trance.

'Lovely,' she said. 'Frank, come take a look at this.'

Frank, who in the short time I'd known him did everything he was told to, came to have a look.

'Very nice,' he said, after a minute or two.

'What is?'

'Your aura, honey,' Morning Star said. 'You have a very powerful aura.'

I looked around, seeing nothing at all where they both had stared. 'I do? What colour is it?'

'Why it's golden, of course.'

'Of course.'

Frank had returned to carrying out a previous order he'd been given – to gather up Cupid's belongings – and was helping Cupid to put his bag on his back. 'Are we all ready to go?'

'All set,' Morning Star said, holding out her hand for Cupid to take.

His grandparents had no idea what Cupid was talking about most of the time, but it was clear they adored their only grandchild and that Cupid, equally perplexed by them, adored them in return, although he did his best to hide his affection in front of me.

The morning had begun well, with a call from Sunny to tell Cupid his father was in a stable condition and the doctors were optimistic about a full recovery. Shortly afterwards, Sunny's parents had arrived in, of all things, a brand-new Lexus. I later discovered Sunny leased it for her parents, as she didn't want them driving Cupid around in their beat-up old van when he visited.

While his grandparents refreshed themselves, Cupid and I went for a walk along the beach to watch the passing parade of the weird, wonderful and terrifying on Venice boardwalk. Cupid had his photo taken with the aliens set up on chairs for the purpose and his head patted for free by the guitar-playing, roller-skating, turbanned man who's been rolling up and down the boardwalk for as long as anyone can remember. After watching a man with no shirt on – and not much in the way of pants, either – walk on his hands on the sand, we took his idea and improved on it. Veering off the path, taking off our shoes, squishing our toes in the sand, making footprints all the way down to the Santa Monica pier, where we rode the Ferris wheel.

Upon our return, we made an early lunch of lentil patties and bean sprouts at the nearest vegan restaurant I knew of. Or, at least, Frank and Morning Star did. Cupid and I merely pretended to, having taken the precaution of bolting down hot dogs and chicken nuggets while we were on the pier.

Now, as we stood by the Lexus in which his grandparents were already seated, Cupid was shuffling his feet in an embarrassed way in front of me.

'Where is your rabbit?'

'I don't know. I haven't seen him for weeks now. I think he's run away. So, road trip, huh? Should be lots of fun, especially with those guys.'

'They sing all the way. They don't even turn on the radio,' Cupid said. He didn't seem unhappy at the prospect, even though he had a television screen and DVD player in the back of the SUV his mother drove.

'Do I get a goodbye kiss?'

'Yuck! No. No way.' He shook his head violently, making vomiting noises, with his tongue hanging out in disgust, in case I missed the gist of what he was saying.

'All right, then, so I'll see you in a week or so.'

Cupid and I solemnly shook hands.

He paused, just before getting into the car. Putting his knapsack on the ground, he rummaged around in it and produced a complicated piece of red and grey plastic about the size of both my fists together. He handed it to me.

'You can keep this until you get some toys of your own,' he said. 'Because we're special friends now.'

I blinked back sudden tears. 'Thank you.'

'It's my fifth favourite toy.'

'I'm honoured.'

'You have to take care of it.'

'I will. I promise. What is it?'

'It's a Transformer – don't you know anything?'

'Apparently not.'

As the car drove away, I glanced at my watch, then down at Brad Pitt, who was stolidly enduring the departure of the little human being who had pulled his tail and won his fickle canine devotion, to the point that he'd foolishly ignored the only person in the house capable of using the can opener.

I nudged him with my foot. 'I have to get ready,' I said. 'I have bridesmaid duties all afternoon and a wedding to attend at the end of the day. At least, I hope I do. I better call and check.'

FROM: Sydney Welles <sydneywelles@yahoo.com>
TO: God c/- info@weather.com
DATE: Sunday, October 30, 1.02 p.m.
SUBJECT: Give me a sign

Hi, God,

If you think that breaking up with Jake was the wrong thing to do, could you give me a sign? Only don't make it rain. Anna would never forgive me – the wedding ceremony is a sunset special, on the beach. Thanks.

Syd x

'One Love', the original Marley version, was playing, but my progress down the aisle was much slower than the beat dictated, a request from the nervous bride. I was easily outpaced. Lexie and Audrey skipped ahead of me down the sand in a wild zigzag pattern, pelting everyone within shot with blossoms.

As far as bridesmaids go, I didn't fit the part. My dress did not make me look twice my size and age. Instead of shoes impossible to walk down the aisle in, I had jewelled flip-flops on my feet. I'd even escaped big bridesmaid hair. A large orchid had been tucked behind my left ear by a West Hollywood hairstylist, but otherwise my hair was allowed to do what it liked.

Along with a bouquet of more of the orchids – Cattleya orchids, according to the overpriced, overbearing Beverly Hills florist who made it up – I held a leash, at the end of which was Brad Pitt, who, even with his coat brushed by the aforementioned hairstylist and a floral garland around his collar, was not a pretty sight.

Brad Pitt was my date for the evening. To cut a long story short, I told Anna I'd rather date a dog than call Jake, beg his forgiveness and ask him to reconsider attending the wedding – I wasn't ready to admit I was wrong yet. An unfortunate choice of words as she knew I was dog-sitting Brad Pitt for the weekend, and included him in the bridal party. I think she did it out of spite. She'd been counting on Jake to dance with some aunts at the reception.

The twins wore dresses in the same fabric and colour as mine, but with skirts pouffy enough to satisfy little-girl notions of high fashion. They wore their orchids in top knots and were barefoot, having abandoned their miniature versions of my slippers once they found their feet preferred the feel of cool sand to that of expensive, custom-made leather.

Vince and his business partner and best man, Michael, were watching our progress down the aisle. They were dressed in white linen suits, mirrored sunglasses and candy-coloured shirts, and they were smoking cigars. It was a good facsimile of the Miami gangster look. Vince must've been allowed to choose the outfits himself.

I was over three-quarters of the way down the aisle when I was brought up short by what I thought was a shriek from the tent where I'd left Anna. It could also have been the wind. The twins had already reached Vince and Michael, and were attempting to scale them. I was unsure as to what to do.

A smart ass in the crowd said, 'I think they're waiting for you up there.' Brad Pitt seconded this, by tugging on his leash. I cranked my face back into a smile, allowing him to drag me the rest of the way to the floral archway, set up in the middle of the small Malibu beach, where the others had arranged themselves in the usual wedding formation.

There we waited for Anna to appear. And waited. And waited. Two minutes passed with no sign of a bride. I started to get worried. The song ended and, after a short silence and some furtive whispering in the crowd, it began to play again from the start. Still no bride.

I caught Vince's eye and inclined my head towards the tent, silently asking if he wanted me to go back and get her. He was considering the option when we heard, 'Sorry, sorry. Damned hem got caught on a tent peg. We had to pin it. Thanks for waiting. It's not like you can start without me, anyway.'

Anna appeared at the bottom of the aisle. Her wedding gown was a strapless sheath in the shade of emerald green that looks stunning on women with creamy skin and red-red hair – both of which Anna has – but is avoided by everyone else outside of a leprechaun colony for good reason. A white orchid was tucked behind her left ear, a stray from the cluster she was carrying. There was no doubt that Anna made a beautiful bride, but she was glowing in a way she had not been when I left the tent. Her serenity, as she sweetly smiled her way down the aisle, made me suspicious.

As she reached us, I leaned in to whisper, 'What is it?'

'Gin,' she said.

The marriage celebrant stepped up and began the ceremony.

✝

The reception, as well as the ceremony, took place on the beach, in the huge marquee set up for the purpose. Once my official duties were over, and the photographer could not coax any more light from the setting sun or smiles from the bridal party, the rest of the evening passed in a pleasant blur. I diligently performed my unofficial bridesmaid's duties. I drank as much champagne as I could, flirted with everybody – man, woman or dog – within striking range, and checked my cell phone for non-existent messages from Jake only every two or three minutes. He'd left one, during the ceremony, when my phone was turned off, but that was only to point out my hypocrisy in being maid of honour at a ceremony I didn't believe in. I couldn't tell from his tone whether he was angry or teasing.

However, it wasn't as if I spent the whole night dwelling on the Jake situation. I managed to forget about him for the time I had to get up and give my speech. About four minutes in total.

Besides, other people kept bringing him up. At one point in the evening, I had an interesting conversation about him with Anna's cousin Brigid, a financial wizard and complete slut. She cornered me halfway through dinner, by the champagne bar.

'Anna said you're seeing Jake Reed,' she said.
'Not any more. Why, do you know him?'
Brigid nodded. 'Not half as well as I'd like to.'
'Really?'
'Why'd you guys break up?'
'Just a guess, but I'd say it probably had something to do with him being gay.'
'No.' She rolled her eyes. 'No – so typical. It figures. No one cute is straight any more.'
'Isn't it always the way? Champagne?'
'Yeah, why not. Funny. He didn't register on the old gay-dar. I'm usually infallible.'

'He's not fully out of the closet. Still dates girls, you know, for appearances.'

'Oh, God, one of those –'

'Tell me about it. A real waste of time. I mean, you could invest years in someone like that . . .'

'You poor thing.'

'Excuse me, I have to go see what Brad Pitt is up to.' He was sniffing the main tent pole to see if it was worthy of his pee.

Brigid scanned the room excitedly. 'Brad Pitt's here? Where?'

I pointed him out.

'That's a dog,' she said.

'Yes.'

Much later, after the twins had gone home to bed, I caught the bouquet in spite of myself. I'd separated myself from the little horde of squealing single women and gone to sit in an out-of-the-way spot at the bar to watch the scramble and tackle. A wedding really isn't the best place to go directly after you've broken up with your boyfriend. I'd been sitting by myself for just long enough to recognize that, although two people I loved had just gotten married and I had a terrific champagne buzz going, I was miserable, when the bouquet sailed through the air in a high, graceful arc and landed in my lap. It's not widely known, but Anna played basketball at college. She's still a good shot, even backwards, drunk and wearing a strapless dress.

We saw Vince and Anna off, pouring them into the car that was taking them to a hotel on the beach in Santa Monica, where they were to spend one night before their flight to Spain. By this stage the band members had drunk enough to be in their ballad phase, and a man who looked vaguely familiar to me walked up and introduced himself.

'I'm Tony,' he said, 'and, baby, I think I'm in love.'

He struck me as the kind of guy who wears sunglasses at the gym so he can stare at women's body parts without anyone knowing what he's up to, or so he's stupid enough to believe.

'Tony,' I said, 'Who do you think you're in love with?'

'You, babe.' He winked at me, made his right hand into a gun and shot me.

'Don't I know you from somewhere?'

'Hey, that was supposed to be my line.' He shot me again, making a clicking noise with his mouth as he pulled the trigger.

I remembered him. He was the guy from the toilet bar going around shooting all his friends, the one Anna had threatened to introduce me to, the night I met Jake.

'It's not possible we've met before,' he said, finger cocked and ready to fire once more. 'I'd remember you.'

'Is that some kind of affliction?'

He glanced around, confused. 'What?'

'That thing you do when you pretend to shoot people with your hand. Is it some kind of disorder?'

'Whaddya mean? It's my thing.'

'Trust me. You'd be much more popular if you stopped doing it.'

'I'm popular now.'

'OK. Look, why don't you go shoot someone else. This isn't a great night for me.'

He winked and made the clicking noise. 'Don't be too sure about that, babe. Your luck is about to change.'

'Please don't talk to me any more.'

'Right,' he said, uncertainly, before regaining his seemingly indestructible confidence, 'I get it.' He pulled his hands out of imaginary holsters on his hips and let both barrels off, point blank, in my face. 'You want to dance?'

'With you? No, not if my life depended on it.'

'Hey, come on. I think we, you and I, the two of us could be good together.'

'It's late and you're desperately trying to score before you leave the party.'

'You want I give you a ride home?'

'I really think you should go and bother someone else,' I said.

Brigid, with another of Anna's red-headed cousins, caught us on her way out, another bottle of champagne the worse for wear.

'Hey, you need a ride? We've got a cab waiting,' she said.

'That'd be great,' I said.

'Hey, babe, you got a ride.'

'You be quiet, Tony.'

'Well, come on, then,' Brigid said. Then she passed out.

By the time we'd laid her, face down, on the back seat of the cab, and her cousin was installed in the front seat, there was no room left in the cab for me.

'Your friend has great tits,' Tony said, using his hands to emphasize his words.

'Thank you.'

'I gotta tell you, I don't like it when women drink that much. A drunk woman is just not sexy.'

'Oh, you mean in the way a drunk man is?'

He seemed confused.

'You said something about a ride,' I said.

'Stay right where you are, babe. I'll get the Corvette.'

'You're kidding, right?'

'About what?'

What the hell. It was late, I needed a ride and I wasn't planning on getting anything more. 'Fine. Get the Corvette.'

I was pleased to see Tony's face fall when he saw Brad Pitt, waiting with me, after he brought the car around. He clearly didn't want the dog in his car, but also didn't want to ruin what he thought were his chances with me. In the end his libido won out and Brad Pitt was ensconced on my lap, where, I was proud to see, he drooled liberally all over the leather upholstery whenever he had a chance.

The conversation was a little stilted on the way home, as I answered Tony only when he didn't say something that offended me in some way, but because of the lack of traffic on the road the trip passed quickly enough.

'So,' I said, as we pulled up outside my house. 'Thanks for the ride.'

'No problem, baby. You gonna invite me in?'

'Don't be ridiculous.'

'It's only a quarter to twelve. The night is young and so are we.'

'I'm much older than I look. And, I'm really tired.'

'You sure about that? You sure you want to let me get away? It's a big, lonely world out there tonight.'

Obviously, Tony was God's way of telling me what He thought of my breaking up with Jake. I knew I deserved it, but I think I'd have preferred a natural disaster.

'I'm not sure about anything any more,' I said. 'But I'm willing to take my chances on this. Goodnight. And thank you.'

Tony reached into his inside jacket pocket, and produced a small bottle of breath spray. He squirted it a couple of times into his mouth.

Brad Pitt saw it coming before I did and started barking loudly in alarm. I was struggling with the dog and the car door, so it took a few moments more before I realized Tony was swooping in for a goodnight kiss, rather than leaning in to help me with the door. I moved my head, but not quite swiftly enough. The kiss landed on the corner of my mouth.

Then the earth moved, but not in a good way. It registered four-point-six on the Richter scale and distracted Tony from his task long enough for me to make a dignified escape. Thank God.

FROM: Sydney Welles <sydneywelles@yahoo.com>
TO: God c/- jesus@jesusmaryandjoseph.com
DATE: Tuesday, November 8, 3.35 p.m.
SUBJECT: The Religious Right

Dear God,

I read about a Mormon fundamentalist who killed his sister-in-law and her baby in your name. When they asked him what the difference was between him and Osama Bin Laden, he said, 'I'm right and he's wrong.'

I've come to a conclusion that I think holds true for all religious beliefs (and most everything else in life):

The more convinced you are that you're right, the more likely it is that you're wrong.

Faith, it seems, needs a little doubt mixed in to remain healthy.

Perhaps this is why you remain a mystery. If people will kill in your name and on your behalf when your existence can't even be proven, imagine the wholesale slaughter that'd occur if you came out of the celestial closet.

Speak soon,
Sydney x

Brad Pitt had sniffed and rejected twenty-two potential peeing places and was in the process of dismissing the twenty-third. If the number passed twenty-five, this, I decided, was the last time I was taking him for a walk.

'Come on, boy, does it really matter where you pee?'

Brad Pitt looked at me in a way that told me how little I understood the business of pissing. How little I understood most things that were important in life.

'Well, you'd better decide soon. I have to get back to work.'

We both knew that was a lie. Bishop Fullerton – he of the many chins – had called Larry this morning to tell him we'd been awarded the Church account. And I'd been drinking beer all afternoon – I was incapable of work. Not that I was drinking to celebrate. No, that was work – research for our beer client. A bar crawl of the worst sports bars on the Westside, which for some reason were the only bars with the beers we required on tap.

Even if I weren't toasted, I could get away with taking it easy for a while. With the Church account in the bag, I could spend the rest of the year in the Bahamas and still collect my salary. I was the goose that laid the golden egg.

As Brad Pitt investigated a letterbox, a small bush and the rear tyre of a convertible BMW, and found them all wanting, I wondered why I wasn't happy with my success. I suspect the problem was that, golden egg or not, it made me a goose.

By this time we'd reached a church situated down the street from the agency. A sign in front of it said 'Jesus Saves' and underneath, in smaller type, told that Tuesday-evening bingo would commence at six, with a grand prize of two hundred dollars, which I assume was the amount Jesus had saved.

There was still half an hour before four, but we had company. The large square front lawn of the church was split equally in two by a path. Two little old ladies occupied one side of the lawn. They were the kind of comfortable old ladies with old-fashioned breasts like large loaves of unbaked bread, who filled out the rest of their flower print dresses in the same dough-like manner, balancing rose-covered straw hats, brims the size of Australia, on their heads. In addition to these considerable feats they were gossiping at the speed of sound, and setting up a table for cake and the makings of coffee at almost as great a rate.

Brad Pitt sniffed the air with joy. He took off at a gallop, a bulldog's version of a gallop, involving a torrent of drool. The leash jerked out of my hand and, barking like he'd discovered the Promised Land, Brad Pitt ran up the path. The church, it seemed, met with his approval as a urinal. I ran after him, catching up with him at the front double doors of the main building.

'Oh, God, why here? Do you have to pee on holy ground in front of the ladies' bingo committee?'

He lined himself up to christen the church's steps. The

ladies stopped arranging cupcakes on paper plates to point and shake their continent-sized headgear in disapproval. I picked up the end of the leash, giving it a tug.

'Don't pee on the church. Don't pee on the church. Please, don't pee on the church.'

To my amazement, Brad Pitt complied. He walked away from the stairs with great dignity, once again taking the leash out of my hands, and made his way to the flowerbeds at the side of the building, where he lifted a leg to piss on God's roses.

I threw an apologetic look at the little old ladies. They looked as if they'd like very much to take me behind the church and beat me up.

Praying for Brad Pitt to hurry up, I couldn't help but notice a man emerging from the church dragging a rectangular folding table behind him. When he had the table outside, he sent it clattering down to the bottom of the stairs with a shove. He followed slowly, step by step, and picked it up again before he became aware of me.

The man grinned at me as if he'd never have another chance to grin again. 'What a day, huh? What a day?'

'It's some day all right,' I said.

'Makes you happy you're alive, don't it?'

I made a noise to indicate I didn't disagree with this statement in principle.

The man looked to be about a hundred and twenty-five years old and shuffled along, dragging the table, at the rate of twenty inches a minute. He was wheezing heavily, and his face had turned the same shade as my nail polish, Starlet Scarlet. I estimated he had approximately thirty seconds to live.

I glanced at Brad Pitt, still watering the roses, in what was shaping up to be a marathon pee. He was doing fine without my help. I couldn't say the same about the old man.

My heavy-lifting skills being less rusty than my resuscitation skills, I bent my knees and picked up the other end of the table as it inched by. The load lighter, the old man picked up the pace by a couple of yards per minute. Eventually, we made it to the shade of a large tree in front of the church, as far away from the cake stall as you could be and still be on the lawn. Under the tree, several boxes were piled. I winced, imagining how long it would've taken for him to move them there.

When he turned around the old man was surprised, but not unhappily so, to find me on the other end of the table. I helped to set the table up. We spread an old fitted sheet over it. He had carried it concealed inside the beige, zip-front jacket all men over seventy wear. The sheet was decorated with faded Winnie-the-Poohs, dipping their paws into jars of honey, causing envy in the equal number of worn-out Piglets looking on. Although the breeze was moving slower than traffic on the freeway where the 10 feeds the 405 South, at the man's request, I duct-taped the sheet to the table legs while he kept up a continual stream of bright conversation.

Brad Pitt, having finished sprinkling the roses, came over to see what I was doing on my hands and knees, and sniffed interestedly at the table legs, seeming quite put out that he had no urine left. He tried to eat some duct tape, until a slight lift in the breeze alerted him that there was a vast amount of sugar and flour nearby.

Immediately, he trotted back to the church stairs and climbed to the top, to survey the lay of the land.

'Have you seen it?'

The old man was referring to a current film.

'No. Not yet.'

'You'll love it.'

'You seem to see a lot of films.'

'I go to the movies all the time. On Tuesdays I go with my movie buddy, on Thursdays by myself and on Sundays with my girlfriend. Thrillers and action on Tuesday, independent on Thursday and whatever she wants on Sunday.' He winked at me.

'Your girlfriend?'

He beamed pinkly and proudly. 'Had the same one for sixty-five years.'

'That's nice,' I said, surprised to find I meant it.

'What about you? You got a fella?'

'No.'

'Why not? Nice young girl like you? I bet there are a lot of young men keen on you? If I wasn't already spoken for, I'd take you out myself.'

'I wouldn't be able to keep up with you,' I said.

'Well, I keep in shape. I keep in shape.'

This guy was definitely the survivor of something, of a stroke, cancer or heart attack. He had that second-chance-at-life, every-day-is-a-bonus cheerfulness that I normally find annoying. Today, I found it soothing.

I studied the chipper old man before me. Did he just decide one day that he was going to be happy for what was left of his life? Was it that easy? Were the rest of us just complicating everything? Missing the point?

He was unloading boxes, producing the usual garage-sale fare that provides proof beyond doubt that, no matter how we try to dress it up with more meaning, life is merely a series of bad purchasing decisions. Yet, he was happy.

He fished out a nearly new teddy bear from a box. He sighed, losing a good deal of his aggressively chipper manner, though he was still brimming with joy if compared to a normal person.

'Some little boy or girl . . . they probably begged their parents to buy this for them, probably gave them hell until they did . . . and now they don't want it any more . . . now you can buy it for a quarter.' He sat the bear carefully on the table, so its feet dangled over the edge.

Out of the eye corner I was keeping on Brad Pitt, I saw he had abandoned his command position atop the stairs and was now making a wide circle around the ladies and the cakes. The ladies, spilling over the edges of their folding beach chairs beside their table, were taking a break, as yet unaware of the advancing canine threat. It was time to get going. In five minutes I'd have to buy every cake the stall held.

Picking up an ornate teacup and saucer, the old man examined them closely before putting them down on the end of the table where the better junk was going.

'You know what the matter is with the world today?'

I have several hundred theories, but I kept them to myself. 'No, what?'

He spread his hands, indicating the flotsam and jetsam of people's lives that he was arranging on the table.

'Nobody values anything any more. They buy, buy, buy, but it's just for the sake of buying. What do you expect? These days, everything is for sale.'

The guy had a point. And it was the same point I'd made with months of research. You can sell anything. But what did that prove exactly?

'I'm sorry,' I said. 'I missed what you said.'

'I said, the best things in life are free, not because they aren't worth anything, but because you can't buy them with money.'

I felt a sudden chill. I put my hands in my pockets to wrap my jacket around me. My right hand closed around a folded piece of paper. I pulled it out. It was a dollar note. I unfolded it and looked into the solemn face of George Washington. The first president gave me an idea.

'Can I take the bear off your hands for a dollar?'

The grin-to-end-all-grins reappeared on the old man's face, just before the first of the little-old-lady shrieks reached my ears. 'Sure,' he said. 'You need a receipt?'

✝

Father Giuliani was an instant favourite of the local Protestant Ladies' Social Club. They regarded him as a hero, without the need for any special effort on his part. In the course of his usual afternoon stroll he merely reached out, grabbed Brad Pitt's leash, and became one.

True, he checked the dog just as Brad Pitt had been preparing to launch himself at the table holding cake and coffee for the evening's bingo enthusiasts, but I think it would be fair to say that, had I been the one to get there first, had I been the leash grabber, the disaster averter, it wouldn't have resulted in quite so many dewy-eyed, gushing thanks, and certainly not as much free cake, if any.

A newly minted Congressional Medal of Honor winner could not have been made more of, even if he'd single-handedly subdued a misbehaving Middle East nation and handed these ladies title deeds for oil wells liberated in their names.

I arrived on the scene with the same heroic intentions just a few seconds after the priest, and received nothing but glowering looks, and those only when eyes could be spared from Father Giuliani, who, after soothing the savage beast, also managed to convince our ladies of cake to embrace the menace. It was settled within minutes. Beaming and blushing, the ladies were to watch Brad Pitt, while the priest explored the church.

As his guest in his expedition, something that Father Giuliani quickly assured the women I would be, I was officially noticed and treated to smiles and floppy nods of their hats. Those same smiles, passable as friendly when pasted on the faces of respectable senior citizens in the light of day, would've sent me scurrying in the other direction if I'd encountered them in a dark alley. I knew not to push my luck. I stood silently by while Father Giuliani finished playing priest-in-shining-armour.

After he politely refused four more offers of cake, I followed the priest into the church. The last time I'd been in a church was – I don't remember exactly when it was. A spate of big, white weddings amongst my acquaintances about five years ago had made me a fairly regular church-goer, but, since then, I remember attending only one christening. I have visited a few European cathedrals since, but only for tourist purposes.

There was something immediately familiar about the cool, dark hush of the place. It occurred to me that all the places of worship shared a similar stillness, no matter what the religion or denomination. God, it seems, is the universe's head librarian, shushing everyone who enters one of his houses.

Our peace lasted several seconds before it was shattered. An organist, unseen by us, began hammering out a series of pompous, wrathful chords, which I assumed formed a battering song of praise to the glory of God.

I stood, flinching in time with the music, in the aisle, while the priest made a round of the room. I joined him when he'd chosen a pew to sit on.

'Not very catchy, is it?' I had to practically yell to make myself heard.

'Nice bear,' Father Giuliani said. He didn't raise his voice, but somehow I heard him through the dissonant sounds made by the invisible organist.

I'd forgotten the teddy bear I was carrying in a headlock under my left arm. I sat it on the bench between us.

'I promised my neighbour's kid I'd get some toys. He was probably expecting something more sophisticated, but it'll give him something for his battle toys to maul and decapitate.'

'A sacrificial bear?'

'Should you be in this church? Isn't it sort of like being unfaithful?'

'The ecumenical movement used to be quite strong in the Catholic Church. I am a practical rather than academic theologian. Ecumenicalism is easier for everyone. I stand by the one light, many lamps ideal.'

'Except that what you're doing now isn't exactly going to foster a very ecumenical attitude, is it?'

Father Giuliani's undivided attention, when bestowed on me as it was then, makes me feel the need to explain myself, and I always become more loquacious than I plan to be.

'Well, once you start advertising,' I said, 'all the others will jump on the bandwagon and it's going to be a free-for-all. All of you, out there, claiming to be the One True Faith. It's hardly going to promote unity amongst the churches, is it?'

'Our mandate is to save only one Church.'

'And in doing that you could seriously damage religion as a whole.' My voice was beginning to get hoarse from yelling.

Father Giuliani waited for me to go on. I waited for the organist to finish a very loud passage in a particularly nasty hymn.

'It's like you said at that midlife-crisis bar that night,' I said. 'Everyone is acquiring more and more stuff, yet they're more and more stressed. And things are getting worse.

'Our culture is becoming shallower. There's a kind of mindless greed in the choices we make. Nobody wants the standard issue American Dream any more. They want American Dream Deluxe – Dream Plus, Plus, Plus – bigger, better, more. Nothing they get will ever be enough.

'And people are willing to sacrifice everything else in their lives to make these purchases, even though anything we purchase is something that we'll replace as soon as they make a better model. That's the irony. We sacrifice things that can't be replaced – our time and personal relationships – for things that are easily replaceable, things we'll actually want to replace.'

'You seem to be very lucid on this subject today,' Father Giuliani said.

'I had about twenty beers this morning – research. The thing is, if you sell religion the way you sell everything else, it becomes a commodity. Faith becomes upgradeable and, therefore, disposable. Is that what you really want?'

'I'm curious. Why does it matter to you if religion becomes a commodity? You are not religious.'

'You're right,' I said. 'I don't believe what you believe, and I don't think I ever will. But it should matter to you. Consuming is about getting the goods, having the goods, then getting more, better goods. It is never about doing good. It's at odds with the spiritual values you believe in.

'Don't you see? If you advertise, people will rationalize their choice of religion the way they rationalize any purchase: What's in it for me? Correct me if I'm wrong, but I don't think this was quite the message Jesus was trying to pass on.'

The hideous hymnal chords had stopped abruptly – apparently proving too much even for the organist – leaving me shouting over the silence in their wake. In the temporary void, I again felt the empty calm common to all places of worship. It was the emptiness not the calm I noted this time. Whatever people find in here must be whatever it is they bring in with them.

After a moment, a cheering rendition of Mancini's

'Baby Elephant Walk' started up. The unexpectedness of the tune made me laugh out loud.

'Why are you so upset about this?' Father Giuliani wanted to know.

'I'm not ups –' But I was upset. I shouldn't drink during the day; it makes me far too emotional. I shifted in my seat, wondering why they don't install comfortable seating in churches. Does God have something against upholstery? Are cushions the work of the devil? It was impossible to get cosy on the hard wooden pew. My new teddy bear, for one, looked decidedly unhappy. It was in the process of sliding off the bench. I reached out to straighten it up, while the priest waited patiently for an answer. Around us, the church was filling up fast with the happy noise of immature ambulant elephants.

'I don't know,' I said. 'I guess . . . I guess that I don't think what we're doing is right.'

Father Giuliani seemed to consider this for a moment. 'Why is that?'

The priest was the gentlest interrogator I'd ever encountered, but the question made me a little angry. I poked at my bear, forcing it to sit up straighter.

'Because . . . because there has to be something that can't be bought or sold,' I said. 'There has to be something to believe in. There has to be something that's worth believing in, whether or not I personally believe in it. There has to be more to life than who wins the SuperBowl. There has to be.'

The expression on Father Giuliani's face was enigmatic. He produced a real cloth handkerchief from a secret storage place on his immaculately tailored person and handed it to me. I stared stupidly at it until I realized he must've given it to me for a reason. I made a quick swipe across the moistness leaking onto my cheeks. I really shouldn't drink during the day.

Having vented my feelings – beer-fuelled or not – I felt foolish. It was not an unreasonable feeling to entertain when you realize you've been preaching to a priest in a church. I looked to my teddy bear for a little solidarity. It stared straight ahead, pretending not to know me.

'What do I know?' I said. 'I don't know anything.' I gave the bear a prod in the head, more sharply than I'd intended. It flopped towards Father Giuliani. 'I've only ever been to church to see what the bride wore.'

The priest picked up my bear and placed it on the other side of him, safely out of my range. 'A person's faith is not determined by where they sit for two hours a week,' he said. 'It is determined by what is most important to them. If that is money or power, I assure you, they will never reach true understanding no matter how long they sit in church.'

I remembered something I'd heard once about hospitals being full of sick people and churches being full of sinners. I decided this was not the time to bring that up.

'There are people who are capable of believing only what they were brought up to believe,' Father Giuliani said. 'You are definitely not one of those people. There are also people who refuse to believe in anything. You think you are one of these people. I think you belong to another group of people entirely.'

'What do you mean?'

'There are people who believe only what they find

agrees with their reason and common sense, what they understand in their hearts. This, I think, is the only way for beliefs to be wise, for them to last. It is, of course, the hardest way, the bravest way, because sometimes you will be alone in what you believe — but it is also the best way. You are one of these people, whether you think so or not.'

The organist switched from 'Baby Elephant Walk' to the *Peter Gunn* theme, though this wasn't immediately obvious. We both stopped to listen, until it dawned on us exactly what the organist was trying to play.

'You are a lot closer to understanding than you think,' Father Giuliani said.

'I don't understand a thing.'

'That is all you can understand,' he said, looking more Sphinx-like than ever. What was odd was that, for the first time, I thought I felt a glimmer of understanding.

FROM: Sydney Welles <sydneywelles@yahoo.com>
TO: God c/- info@freemasons.com
DATE: Thursday, November 10, 11.23 p.m.
SUBJECT: I Resign

Dear God,

Please accept my resignation.

In spite of my general agnosticism, Dadaist tendencies, depression-induced bouts of mild nihilism, and general cynicism, I'm pretty sure that no one should be able to buy salvation in three easy payments of $49.99.

I no longer wish to work for you. I don't even know if I have been working for you. After all, you don't organize religions; people do. And they're still organizing them. Religions aren't static things. As the world changes, as people continue to change, religions will change, too. Anyone who says otherwise, anyone who tries to claim the word of God has never been rewritten to suit a particular agenda, is trying to sell something. I should know.

I've been thinking about mortality recently. A lot. I don't know if it's an afterlife or another life, heaven or hell, nirvana or nothing that awaits us. I don't think anyone knows for sure.

As far as I can see only one thing is for certain: we all die. And while I don't know if there's life after death, I do know, beyond doubt, there's life before death. The only logical reason I can find for being here on earth is to live.

I think you put us here to do that – to eat and drink with people we like, to dance, to sing, to laugh (mostly at ourselves), to work, to play, to be kind to each other and, at some stage, to make something out of popsicle sticks.

I have faith in that much.

Yours faithfully,
Sydney Welles

To cope with the stress and disappointment love and religion had introduced into my life, I'd taken to having a beer or glass of wine on the front porch at the end of the day. A reckless choice of porches as it leaves me in full view of Cupid's second-storey bedroom window. More often than not – since he came back from his stay with his grandparents and his father came home from hospital – Cupid comes to join me on the porch. We've settled into a kind of routine. What passes for civil conversation with Cupid always starts the same way.

'Why can't I have a beer?'

'Because.'

'Because why?'

'Because if you do you'll stay the height you are now for ever and your hair won't go curly any more.'

'Is that true?'

'I don't know. But I can't give you beer. You wouldn't like it, anyway.'

'How do you know?'

'I didn't like beer when I first tasted it. I still don't, really.'

'You drink it all the time.'

'I don't drink it "all the time" – just "all the time" the past couple of weeks. It's just something you have to do when you're grown up. You're too short to understand.

You can have juice or flavoured milk. Those are your choices.'

'I have no choices.'

Once he knows he won't get a beer, Cupid tries to graft a taste of mine, then gives in to the inevitable and disappears into my house, returning with a non-alcoholic drink from the fridge, a straw from the top drawer and a scrounged snack from the pantry. I frisk him to make sure he didn't get a beer after all, and we settle in for a chat until his mother wails for him to come inside. Most days, he unfailingly introduces a topic of conversation in some way painful to me.

'What happened to your boyfriend? Why doesn't he park his car here any more?'

'He's . . . actually, I'm not exactly sure where he is.'

'What did you do?'

'What makes you think I did anything?'

Cupid raised a cynical and weary eyebrow. He'd seen it all before it seemed, several times. 'Cheese puff?' he said, holding out the bag.

'Where did you get those? I didn't know I had any.'

'Behind the cans of tomatoes on the top shelf.'

'How did you reach the top shelf – no, never mind, don't tell me. What I don't know, your parents can't sue me for.'

'What did you do?'

'I didn't do anything. He pretended to be someone he wasn't. No, actually, he pretended not to be someone he was – oh, never mind. The point is it was his fault, OK.'

Cupid's face took on its dubious one-eyebrow-lifted Jedi-master-Yoda expression again.

'OK, OK. It was my fault. It had nothing to do with who he was or wasn't. I just got scared.'

'I get scared sometimes when I wake up in the middle of the night and I think there's something there, in the dark.'

'That would be scary.'

'But I can turn on my lamp and see nothing's there.'

'That's very brave and clever of you, but my situation is slightly more complicated than that.' Or was it? 'Anyway, what's the point of investing everything in one person? What if doesn't work? What do you do then?'

'You have a do-over,' he said. He inserted several cheese puffs into his mouth, holding them all in his left cheek, where the collection formed a large, irregular hump.

'How old are you?'

He filled his other cheek with cheese puffs, before answering my question. His mouth was too full to speak, but he held up eight fingers when he spoke, making me afraid I'd end up with cheese puffs all over my porch, as it left him with only two fingers to hold on to the bag.

'I was being rhetorical.' And he was lying. He was seven.

Cupid placed the bag next to his soda on the floor, raised his hands to his face and squashed his cheeks flat, opening his mouth afterwards to display the orange goo within.

'Gross,' I said. That was the reaction he was after. I was rewarded with a very cheesy grin.

'Still gross.'

'Are you going to get a new boyfriend?'

'No, I'm not going to get a new boyfriend –' Cupid's

concern for my romantic welfare suddenly struck me as aberrant. Concern for anyone or anything is not normally a part of the demonic child's oeuvre.

'Why are you so worried about me?'

'I don't care. But Mommy does.'

'OK, why is your mother concerned about me?'

'She said that, if you mess this one up, you'll never get married and move away. And we'll never get a nice family living across the street to fix up the house.'

'I see.'

'But she said it's OK for you to be my friend.'

'She did?'

Cupid nodded. He was starting to refill his mouth.

'So, we're friends.'

'Yeah,' he said. 'But you're not my girlfriend or anything.'

'Got it.'

'What happens on *Sex in the City*?'

'Why do you ask?'

'I'm not allowed to watch. Mommy says it would bruise the fragile bud of my blooming sexuality.'

'That's just the kind of thing I'd imagine she'd say.'

'What does it mean?'

'It means she doesn't want you to turn into a pervert before the age of eight.'

'What's a pervert?'

'Oh, no. I'm not getting into that territory. But trust me, at your age, *Sex and the City* will just scare you.'

Cupid scanned my small front yard, paying particular attention to the bushes. 'Did your rabbit come back yet?'

'No. I guess he's left me, too. I'm not having much luck with bunnies or boyfriends.'

'He'll come back,' Cupid said. 'Cheese puff?'

I resisted the temptation to ask Cupid whether he was referring to Jake or Harry Rex.

'A cheese puff isn't going to help me. Stop looking like a smug little Buddha over there. You don't have the answers, either.'

He came to sit beside me on the old wooden porch swing that came with the house. It creaked in welcome. Cupid sipped on his straw, staring intently at the orange staining the sky as the sun committed suicide on jagged rooftops.

'They're in the back of the book,' he said.

'What are in the back of the book?'

'The answers. You're not supposed to look at them. Not until you've tried to work it out yourself first.'

Below the rooftop horizon, the sun's power dimmed. Darkness would soon swaddle us, but in the intermission between day and night all glowed amber, and all was tranquil. The peace would be broken soon enough. By Cupid's mother telling him, and the rest of the street, it was time for his bath.

'Your schoolyard philosophy is surprisingly profound,' I said, 'but sometimes life just goes to sh – crap. Things are more complicated when you're grown up. There's no book with answers in the back. And questions don't have one right answer. They have lots of answers or no answer at all. Or else the right answer is staring you in the face, but it's of no use until you can figure out what question to ask.'

Cupid sucked the last moisture from the orange soda can, making a horrendous noise.

'You can say shit. I won't tell.'

'Why am I having this conversation with you? You're seven. How could you possibly understand what I want out of life?'

He closed one eye to peer into his soda can, to make absolutely sure it was empty. 'All I want is someone to sit with at lunchtime – no matter what. Even if Mommy makes me wear those stupid orange stripey pants.'

Maybe he did understand. 'Yeah,' I said, 'me, too.'

Cupid was clearly a genius.

'And I want to be sixteen.'

Or maybe he was just a boy.

'No, you don't. Virtually all sixteen-year-old boys are idiots. I remember. That's when hormones take over and you can no longer use your brain to do anything but think about sex, and it doesn't stop until you're . . . actually, I don't think it ever stops. Enjoy being a preteen while you still can.'

Cupid placed the can on the floor and picked up the cheese puffs. He picked out a smallish one and stuffed it up his right nostril. Then, with surprising precision, blocked his left nostril with a finger and blew the cheese puff back into the bag.

'Cheese puff?' he said, shoving the open bag within inches of my nose.

His eyes rounded, innocently enough, but I thought I caught the hint of a challenge in their blue porcelain perfection. It also could have been just a reflection from the last throes of the dying light. I wondered if he was trying to tell me something important. Then I wondered why I imagined a seven-year-old had anything important to say to me. Before I had an answer, the sun snuffed out, and Cupid's mother began bellowing for him to come inside.

FROM: Sydney Welles <s.welles@fbmm.com>
TO: God c/- info@godmademedoit.net
DATE: Thursday, November 17, 9.25 a.m.
SUBJECT: Of Priests and Men

Dear God,

I spoke to Father Giuliani about resigning and he was, as to be expected, very understanding about the whole thing, going so far as to agree with me that, perhaps, advertising is not the answer to the problem of child-abusing priests any more than shuttling paedophile priests from parish to parish or out of the country was.

It seems to be just more bureaucratic handling of the situation. When what really needs to happen is an internal change in the Church. I, for one, think you have to ease up the attitude on divorce, contraception, gays and women, if you want anyone to take you seriously. I also think you ought to allow Catholic priests to marry.

There are 48,000 Catholic priests in the country. Trust me, 48,000 men who believe in marriage, and who've had practice at not screwing around, would be a welcome addition to the dating world for single women everywhere.

Syd x

My exit interview with Larry had been a remarkably civilized affair, conducted in his office over three rounds of gin and tonic divided unequally between us. I had one gin and tonic. Larry had five. He no longer needed to be sober, now the Church account was secured.

'So, you're not pregnant?'

'No,' I said.

'Dying?'

'Only at the same rate as everyone else.'

'So, that stuff about taking six months off to work out what you want from life is true, then?'

'It's true.'

'Well, good luck. You'll need it.'

'Thank you for taking it all so well,' I said.

'Nothing to thank me for. This is a very stupid business with no redeeming qualities other than a few good laughs and sex with nice people. But the laughs are getting fewer and further between. As for the sex, nobody seems to do it any more. You don't even get to see anybody naked these days. I saw everybody naked back when streaking at parties was the thing to do. Whatever happened to streaking?

'Nobody drinks martinis at lunch or throws parties in their hot tubs or has sex on the boardroom table any more – or if they do they do it with a person they're allowed to have sex with, not someone completely inappropriate. Really, what's the point?

'It's all been downhill since the end of the 1980s. Why stick around if it's no fun? None of this is important. Not in the grand scheme of things. In the grand scheme there's only one thing that matters. If I could remember what it was, I'd tell you.'

'Why do you stick around?'

'Me? This is what I do. This is my life. I'm too old to change. You're not. Go fucking forth; find yourself. Find a new career if you have to. Have a life. Have babies – but don't bring the shitty little things in to see me. Come in for lunch, any time, without them. And come back to work any time you want. The door will always be open, any office in the network, anywhere in the world, as long as my liver holds out.'

'Thank you. I appreciate that.'

'Gives you something to fall back on if you wake up one morning and discover leaving here was the greatest mistake of your life.'

'Thanks, I'll keep it in mind. Well, good luck with the Catholics.'

'Don't worry, if the Catholics don't pan out, the Mormons are ready and waiting.'

'You're kidding?'

'Nope. Not kidding. It makes more sense for them to advertise than anyone else. No chance of advertising trivializing that religious experience. They did that themselves. They're a religion founded on a book someone found and claimed was the lost book of Abraham or some such biblical personage, which – since they can now read hieroglyphics – has been discovered to be only some ancient laundry list. It's a religion based on a meaningless text, and yet it's the fastest-growing religion in the country. You can't get better than that. They've had a publicity department since the 1930s. They have an unpaid army of door-to-door salesmen. They're all on Prozac, and they're all-American. Best of all, everybody ends up a Mormon.'

'What do you mean?'

'They convert you once you're dead. They convert everyone. Popes, presidents, prostitutes, everyone.'

'Are they allowed to do that?'

'Whether they are or not, they do it. That has to be the supreme irony of life. We think we have free will and independent thought, but the one inescapable truth of life is we're all going to be Mormons sooner or later.'

✝

Noah was waiting for me in the parking lot, on my way out. In a more than usually awkward way, he handed me a parcel. Inside was a black girl-shaped T-shirt in my size. It said: 'Friends Don't Let Friends Have Mullets.'

'It's sentimental, but . . .'

'Thank you,' I said. I gave him a hug.

'In theory,' he said, 'you're still my boss, so that was sexual harassment.'

'So, sue me. You're coming to the party?'

'Are you kidding? Larry said the agency is going to pay. Of course I'm coming. Everybody is coming. It's free.'

'You're a true friend.'

'Leave, before I have you thrown out by security.'

'I'll miss you, too,' I said.

'Hey, you'll never guess who Julie is seeing, as of last Friday night.'

'Okay, who?'

'Patton.'

'No,' I said. 'No.'

'Afraid so. And it looks like true love.'

'What does true love look like?'

Noah shrugged. 'I don't know, but it's one of those things. You know it when you see it.'

'I guess I'll have to see it, then. You going to stay on?'

'For a few months. There's that new assistant they've hired, looks just like that heiress – the one with the video. Then I think it may be time to go back to academia. Finish my dissertation – well, first, start my dissertation – and give my mother the opportunity to say, "My son, the professor," at least once before she falls off the mortal coil. It's your fault. You've inspired me. If you can leave a good job with no idea what you're going to be next – except poor – I can leave a mediocre job to live off my trust fund.'

'I don't know what to say,' I said.

I drove home from what was to be, for the time being at least, my last day on the job. I was still amazed at how easy it was to walk away. Somehow, that made it easier to think of going back as a possibility – one of many possibilities. Ironically, I'd quit my job and, instead of my world coming to an end, my life was full of possibilities that weren't there before. I could do anything – except perhaps get my head around Julie and Patton.

Pondering the possibility of true love between them, I

missed the turn I was supposed to make off Washington Place. I found myself having to pick my way home, slowly, through a maze of back streets.

On one of these streets I saw him, and, of course, when I saw him I couldn't help but pull over and get out of the car.

There he was, after all this time. And he looked exactly the same as when I'd seen him last. As sorry a creature as I'd ever laid eyes on.

My Harry Rex.

He was sitting on the well-kept lawn of a blue weatherboard house. And he was in love – completely besotted. Noah was right. You do know it when you see it, although, in this case, it was obviously unrequited.

She was the kind of bunny they put in the pet store window, along with the puppies and kittens, to lure you in. Petite and honey-coloured, with large, melted chocolate eyes and soft, soft fur, she was quite possibly the most beautiful rabbit I'd ever seen.

Her cage was formed simply. A sheet of chicken wire about four feet high had been curved around and joined in a circle, and placed on the grass. The top of the cage was left open. Though separated from her by the wire, Harry Rex's passion did not seem to be dampened by the impossibility of physical contact.

He ignored me. Ignored my pleading with him. Ignored my promises of a nice, new bunny hutch, squeaky bunny toys and as many pieces of toast as he could eat. I did not get a flicker of his attention, until I found a chocolate bar in my purse.

Harry Rex turned when he heard the rustling of the

wrapper. I broke off a piece and placed it on the ground in front of him, then took a couple of steps backwards. I figured he could be lured into the car by chocolate. After all, the same principle had worked on ET, who was a far more sophisticated life form.

Harry Rex hopped over to the piece of chocolate, sniffed it and looked at me before picking it up in his mouth. He turned and hopped back to the cage where he pushed it through the chicken wire. He did exactly the same with the rest of the chocolate bar, piece by piece, giving it all up for love. The object of that love, it must be said, scoffed down the candy as fast as he could bring it to her, doing so without any delicacy.

Once he was sure there was no more chocolate to be had, Harry Rex went back to ignoring me, mesmerized once again by the chocolate hog in the cage. I could see there was no way I could convince him to come with me willingly. He was giving up the promise of a cushy life to live on the outside of this girl rabbit's cage, when it was clear she wasn't the least bit interested in him.

Love sure does make you stupid.

'I'll come back and visit you,' I said. 'I'll bring more chocolate.' I figured I could at least help him to win over his girlfriend. 'Maybe some M&Ms?'

Harry Rex didn't even blink.

'OK, I'm going now,' I said. 'Bye.'

I turned back to take a final look at them. For a creature pining away from unrequited love, Harry Rex seemed remarkably content.

I sat in the car and watched them for a while. As I moved around in my seat to get more comfortable, I felt something in my back pocket. I was wearing, for the first time since it happened, the jeans I wore when I was kidnapped. I fished out the bumper sticker I'd picked up in the back of the van. It was a little worse for wear, having been through a wash-and-dry cycle, but it was still clearly legible. In almost red type on a now faded yellow background it said: 'Love Is the Answer.'

It was either something from the Bible or from the Beatles. Or both. The Bible and popular music are full of rotten advice when it comes to love.

As I continued to watch Harry Rex and his lady bunny friend, a new thought occurred to me. Maybe my rabbit wasn't quite right in his rabbit head, but if a beat-up old street bunny could believe in it, maybe love was grand after all.

FROM: Sydney Welles <sydneywelles@yahoo.com>
TO: God c/- info@mensa.com
DATE: Friday, November 25, 7.05 p.m.
SUBJECT: Love

Dear God,

Jesus said, 'Love each other, as I loved you.' He did not say, 'Call now. Sign up today. Believe in me and only me, and pay the fees in full, or you won't get into the good heaven.' That was some other guy on TV.

I'm with Jesus on this one. I'm beginning to believe that love is as good a reason for living as we'll ever find. Love, unconditional, brotherly or otherwise, is the one thing every major religion preaches – once you get past their advertised differences and unique selling points.

Love conquers all, love makes the world go round, love is in the air, love is all around us and love is all you need.

Love is the answer.

Only problem is nobody knows what the question is.

Love,
Syd

Charles Turner
22 Indiana Avenue, #1
Venice
CA 90291

Dear Charles,

In spite of the obvious drawbacks of your personality, I like you a great deal. For a while there, I even imagined myself in love with you. Of course, I'm not in love with you and never was.

You can't be in love with someone you've never met. That works only in Hollywood romantic comedies, and then only very badly. In real life, love is more than just a meeting of minds; other body parts have to meet, too.

However, I am in love. When I realized it – or rather, admitted it to myself – it scared me a little. Scared the crap out of me, actually. I behaved badly and may have messed things up beyond repair. But I've been trying to get my shit together and all I can do is hope that Jake will give me another chance.

I have my doubts, but Anna assures me that everything will be fine. She called me from her honeymoon in Spain to tell me this. She says men are stupid like that, and all I have to do is show up wearing something short or tight, and tell him he was right about everything whether he was or not. Then again, this is a woman who thinks any relationship issue can be solved with a well-timed blowjob. Actually, Anna could be right about that one.

What do you think my chances are?

Yours,
Sydney

PS By the way, if things don't work out with Jake, I'll give you a call.

Once I'd posted the last letter I'd ever write to Charles, I called my parents and, after managing to calm them down – it wasn't my designated day for calling, so they assumed the sky had fallen – I proceeded to bring them up to date on my life. Needless to say, there were still parts I left out for their own good, but the whole exercise was far less painful than I'd anticipated.

My mother was a little upset to find out I was no longer dating Matt – she watches his soap – but was interested in Anna's nuptials and in both Charles and Jake. She thought they were two different people, and nothing I told her could convince her otherwise. That's my mother; you can't give her too much information – or too much wine – all at once and expect her to keep facts straight.

My father didn't baulk at my newly unemployed state. He had no career advice to offer – he still has no idea what exactly it is I do when I am employed – but he went so far as to say that I must know what I was doing, and asked if I needed money only once. He had a lot to say, however, on the subject of God and religion – such a lot that I had to distract him with the promise of a visit at the end of the month to be able to get off the phone.

Both my parents asked me if I'd spoken to my sister. I said I had, so I had to call her, too. Buoyed by the relative success of those calls, I made a few more calls and as a result found myself, several days later, arriving home early one evening laden down with enough food and wine to throw a dinner party for six. There was good reason for that. The next evening I was throwing a dinner party for six. Now I have the time to talk to people again, I find that I still have a lot of friends. I'll need to throw several more dinners just to feed them all.

I'd also bought some cheesy snacks and fruit juice for Cupid, and a bottle of the most expensive single malt Scotch whisky at the wine store. I don't really drink the stuff, but I told myself I was going to start drinking it, as that was easier than admitting who I'd really bought it for.

I was a little disappointed not to find Cupid awaiting me on my porch. His company at the end of the day was something, I realized with mild horror, I now looked forward to. Afraid that I'd miss him if I took the groceries inside, I left them at my feet, on the porch, while I scanned the street for him.

I didn't have to wait long. Though, technically, it was Jake, not Cupid, who showed up first. His car pulled up in front of my house. The passenger door opened and Cupid hopped out.

The only thing not astonishing about the situation was that Cupid, once he spotted me, gave me the finger before scurrying across to his side of the street.

Jake got out of the car and after briefly glancing at me – standing on my porch with my mouth hanging attractively open – turned to Cupid, who'd stationed himself on the curb in front of his gate. Cupid waved at me from there, indicating he had to go inside.

Jake said something to Cupid I didn't catch. Cupid nodded.

'OK,' Jake said. He turned back to me. I was still standing on the porch, still wondering at the little scene that had been enacted before me, but at least now I'd managed to close my mouth.

As Jake started towards me, my heartbeat became erratic, my throat tightened, my breath got shorter and my limbs felt paralysed. If this was love, it was very similar to the onset of a panic attack. What if he'd received my letter and had come to tell me he didn't share my feelings? What if he'd received my letter and had come to tell me he did share my feelings? What if he hadn't received my letter? What if I really was having a panic attack?

Not being able to look him in the eye, I focused on his feet. As he climbed over the garden gate – it was still stuck – I noticed his socks didn't match. This, for some reason, made me feel better. I forced myself to take deep breaths. I was going to be cool, calm, collected. I wasn't going to ask about the letter. I'd wait for him to introduce the subject. I was not going to ask. I was not going to ask.

'Did you get my letter?' I wasn't certain whether or not I'd said that out loud.

Jake was smiling, but he was smiling the kind of smile that has its hands hidden deep in its pockets. I couldn't tell if it was friend or foe, but I tentatively returned it.

'I had an interesting meeting with my financial adviser today.'

That wasn't quite what I'd expected him to say.

'You have a financial adviser? Oh, stupid question. You obviously do as you met with him today.'

'Her. I met with her today.'

Little warning bells went off in my head. I had no idea why. 'The meeting went well?'

He nodded. 'Except that she's under the impression I'm gay.'

The world is an unconscionably small place that is good to Jake and wicked to me.

'She is? That's interesting. You know, I wasn't going to say anything, but, now that you've brought it up, I may as well just come out with it. It's that shirt you're wearing. It's kind of, well, lilac. Don't get me wrong. I like it. But people jump to conclusions so easily. Personally, I think it's great that you're confident enough in your masculinity to wear a shirt that colour. Really great . . . really . . .'

'Brigid mentioned she had a very reliable source. You, in fact.'

'Oh.' Shit.

'Why are you telling everyone I'm gay?'

I was drunk. I was stupid. I was jealous. I was a bridesmaid. Chief bridesmaid, a C-level job – the pressure got to me.

'I'm not telling everyone you're gay. I only told Brigid. It must have been Brigid who told everyone else. No discretion at all, that girl. Are you sure you want her taking care of your money?'

'She offered to set me up with someone. She said she'd told him all about me. Apparently, he's really looking forward to meeting me.'

'Of course he is. Any guy would be lucky to get you.'

'Thanks.'

'Do you know what I think? I think a healthy disregard for gender stereotypes is extremely sexy in a man.'

'Do you?'

'I was only trying to protect you. Anna's got this whole raft of cousins, all predatory redheads. At the hens' night, no penis within a half-mile radius was safe. And, you'd just broken up with someone: me. You were vulnerable –'

'I think you were jealous.'

'Was not.'

'There's a grown-up answer.'

I tried to think of a grown-up answer.

'Don't worry about it,' Jake said. 'Brigid also asked me if it'd be a good idea to introduce you to someone – one of her ex-boyfriends. There's one – out of several hundred – she thinks you'll like. I said to be sure to tell him you had syphilis.'

'You what?'

He smiled modestly. 'Let's call it even.'

'Syphilis is so nineteenth century.'

'It's making a comeback.' Jake stepped up on the porch and examined the contents of the three grocery bags sitting on it before he settled himself on the porch swing.

I knew then that everything was going to be fine. I sat beside him.

'There's something I have to tell you,' he said.

Then again, maybe I was wrong about everything being fine. I braced myself. 'OK.'

'A couple of weeks ago, I accepted a new assignment.'

'OK.' So far, this was not so bad.

'It requires me to relocate to Manhattan for six months.'

'Oh.' It was bad.

Jake's eyes told me that what he was going to say next was difficult for him to put into words. I hoped he wasn't going to tell me he and New York City's other recent acquisition were getting back together.

'I don't suppose there's any way you'd come?'

'You mean to visit?'

'No, I mean come with me.'

'Come to New York with you? For the whole six months?'

'That's the general idea.'

'You want me to quit my job, leave my home, my friends, my life, the right to turn right on a red light and this excellent climate, solely so you have company while you do your job on the other side of the country.'

'Yes,' he said.

'If things don't work out?'

'They'll work out.'

'You're asking me to give up my life for you.'

'It's a big decision, I know. You don't have to decide anything right this –'

'I'd love to go,' I said. 'Thank you.'

Jake seemed a little thrown by my answer. But, when it sank in, he had a smile for me, a smile worth moving across the country for – not literally, of course.

'Are you saying yes?'

I was surprised at how easy it was to say, 'Yes.'

Jake seemed to consider me from all angles. 'In that case, it's up to you whether we go or stay.'

'I don't understand.'

'If you'll move for me, I'll stay for you, if that's what you want.'

'You will? Really?' Maybe this relationship business wasn't as hard as I thought it was. 'That's very equal of you. But, I think I'd like to go.'

Jake reached out with his foot and tapped one of the grocery bags.

'If you're going to cook me dinner, shouldn't you invite me in?'

'You're pretty confident for a guy wearing odd socks. Are you sure you want to come in? I have syphilis.'

Judging by the way he kissed me, he was sure.

'What was that about?' I pointed at Cupid, who was still standing across the street, watching us. 'Why was Freddy Krueger Junior in your car?'

'I found him wandering around outside my house when I got home. He was lost. He recognized me and asked me to bring him home. It was as good an excuse as any to see you, after I got that letter begging me to take you back.'

'I didn't actually beg — Cupid was lost?'

'Yes.'

'He knows his way around this neighbourhood better than anyone.'

Jake shrugged. 'Must've gotten disorientated — it's getting dark. He's only what? Six? Good little kid.'

'Is it possible we're talking about the same child?'

I stood, unlocked my front door and pushed it open. Jake picked up two of the grocery bags and walked inside as if it were a perfectly natural thing for him to do.

Across the street, Cupid stooped to pick up something. There wasn't a lot of light left, but I could see it was a small animal he was holding, a small animal with rabbit-shaped ears. Cupid and the critter he carried seemed to be on good terms. He was patting it, and I could hear he was talking to it, but not what he was saying.

'Are you going to stand out there all night? Could you at least toss the Scotch in?'

I picked up the remaining bag and turned to the house. 'I'm coming,' I said, but I paused to look back across the street and wave good night to Cupid. He and his bunny-shaped bundle were gone, his tall front gate closed.

I'd have to give him the fifty bucks we'd agreed on tomorrow.

FROM: Sydney Welles <sydneywelles@yahoo.com>
TO: God c/- oprah@oprah.com
DATE: Sunday, December 4, 11.17 a.m.
SUBJECT: The Greatest Mystery of Existence

Dear God,

I've finally figured out that we are never going to figure it out.

Arguing over why we're here is a waste of time. If you had intended us to solve the mystery of existence, you'd have made us a lot smarter.

Hey, the only reason I even know what the Greatest Mystery of Existence is is because Larry told me. Of course, once he did tell me, it made perfect sense.

He found out ten years ago, while having dinner in Paris. Larry described his meal as a healthy portion of a cud-chewing mammal that, conveniently for the chef, had met its end by drowning in a rich cream sauce.

At the next table was an old man, also dining alone, who was both Portuguese and a marine biologist. He always ordered the stuffed cabbage, every time he dined at this bistro, every time he found himself in Paris. He had just turned seventy-five when Larry met him and could tell Larry which of the bistro's waitresses he'd tried to sleep with forty years ago.

Larry, when deep in his cups, sometimes wonders out loud if the marine biologist is still alive. Still studying a strange and wonderful fish covered in taste buds, which stands on the bottom of the ocean on three fins, tripod-like, finding its way around in the complete darkness by tasting the water. Still travelling the world and telling anyone who would listen, over red wine and stuffed cabbage, what was ruining the world: large corporations with no value for nature or human life. And still regretful there was so much yet to be discovered, so much he did not know, both 20,000 leagues under the sea and on dry land.

It wasn't until dinner was over, when their respective bills had arrived and Larry asked him how much would be appropriate to leave as a tip, that the old Portuguese marine biologist told Larry what Larry told me.

'The greatest mystery of existence,' he'd said, as he adjusted his glasses to examine his bill, 'is how much to tip where.'

It's true. If you can figure that out, the rest of life is easy.

Sydney Welles

PS See you in about 47 years, if it's true the average life expectancy for a person living in the USA is 77.1 years, and if you exist, and if I'm good.

# Acknowledgements

Thank you to Adele Lang and Tim Hallinan for helping me to start, Linda Hobrock for getting me through, and Araminta Whitley for organizing the happy ending. I also couldn't have done without Rebecca Watson, Valerie Hoskins, Lizzie Jones and, of course, Mari Evans and the Penguin team, Siobhan O'Connor, Claire Bord and Elisabeth Merriman. Thanks too to Andreas Smetana for being the world's most excellent photographer, the Ladies' Libation League (Culver City Chapter) for the cocktails, and Corey Mitchell for denying me the literary experience of starving in a garret.

# *Calling all girls!*

## *It's the invitation of the season.*

Penguin books would like to invite you to become a member of Bijoux – the exclusive club for anyone who loves to curl up with the hottest reads in fiction for women.

You'll get all the inside gossip on your favourite authors – what they're doing, where and when; we'll send you early copies of the latest reads months before they're on the High Street and you'll get the chance to attend fabulous launch parties!

And, of course, we realise that even while she's reading every girl wants to look her best, so we have heaps of beauty goodies to pamper you with too.

If you'd like to become a part of the exclusive world of Bijoux, email
**bijoux@penguin.co.uk**

*Bijoux books for Bijoux girls*

read more

# JULIA LLEWELLYN

**AMY'S HONEYMOON**

A five-star honeymoon in Rome…

What more could a girl want?

In Amy's case, a husband might come in handy…but, with the cost of a cancelled wedding to mop up and no chance of a refund on the honeymoon, she's jetting off to bask in the Italian sunshine on her own.

Except no one seems willing to leave her alone. If it's not nosy hotel guests, it's famous movie stars desperate to exchange suites. How's a girl supposed to wallow in misery when, under protest, she's dragged off to shop till she drops, or to film premieres or intimate picnics à deux?

But why was the wedding called off? Where is the absent groom? And can movie stars really fall in love with the girl next door? You'd be mad to miss out on this Roman holiday …

'A hilarious new novel' *Evening Standard*

www.penguin.com

read more

# LISA JEWELL

**VINCE & JOY**

> Remember having sex for the very first time?
> Remember thinking: *this* is The One?
> Remember life getting in the way...?

For Vince and Joy, *finding* your destiny is easy.
Following it, isn't...

From teenage love in an eighties holiday park to flatshares, relationships, career crises and children, *Vince & Joy* is the unforgettable story of two lives lived separately but forever entwined; and asks the question: how do you know when something is really meant to be?

'A comic writer who makes acute and funny observations about romance'
*The Times*

www.penguin.com

# ADELE PARKS

**HUSBANDS**

Bella secretly married Stevie, over a decade ago; they were at university, two big kids playing at being grownups. When it all unravelled and reality hit, Bella simply got up and left.

Years later, Bella meets Philip and, despite her vow never to marry again, she can't resist him. He is a catch. Funny, charming, interesting and kind. Only hitch is, she's still (technically, anyway) married to Stevie. And the moment to tell Philip never quite seems to arrive.

So Bella plans never to reveal her secret – after all, it's just a silly piece of paper, lodged at a registrar's office in Aberdeen, isn't it? She hasn't seen Stevie for years – probably never will again.

Except when Bella's best friend Laura introduces her new man to the gang it is none other than Stevie. Could things get any more complicated? Only if Bella and Stevie fall in love with each other again…

read more

# ELIZABETH BUCHAN

**THE SECOND WIFE**

**What if The Other Woman accidently gets her man?**

That's what happened to Minty. She stole her best friend Rose's husband Nathan and made him her own. But now she's got what she wanted – marriage, kids, a happy home – she's discovering a few things she didn't bargain on: like the cold shoulder from Nathan's *other* family; her husband's middle-age and growing distance; and the fact that first wives don't just go away.

Age also brings one or two other problems for Minty. Problems that will lead her back to the one person she really doesn't want to have to face …

*The Second Wife* is a tale of growing older, of making difficult choices – and of finding hope where you least expect to come across it.

'An irresistible story of love, loss and renewal' *Woman's Own*

www.penguin.com

read more

# MAGGIE ALDERSON

**CENTS AND SENSIBILITY**

**Stella Fain has a rule for men she likes: make them wait …**

But the gorgeous Jay proves an exception to the rule when he bowls Stella off her Prada wedges at a press junket on the Côte d'Azure. He might seem to have everything going for him, but Stella is about to realize there's only one thing worse than having a boyfriend with no money … and that's having one with too much.

Jetset lifestyles can be fabulous, but Stella's career as a journalist isn't something she wants to jeopardize for any man, no matter how filthy rich or gorgeous. And then there's her father – a six-times-married prime slice of Alpha Male with a grudge against inherited wealth … and Jay.

There's no denying money makes the world go round and diamonds are a girl's best friend, but they don't make the path to love any easier to tread. With or without the Prada wedges.


Praise for Maggie Alderson:

'A bubbly concoction of bitchiness, humour, glamour and eccentricity written with great verve and enthusiasm' *Sunday Mirror* on *Mad About the Boy*

'Fabulously glamorous . . . highly entertaining' *Heat* on *Pants on Fire*

www.penguin.com

read more

# MARIAN KEYES

**THE OTHER SIDE OF THE STORY**

The agent: Jojo, a high-flying literary agent on the up, has just made a very bad career move: she's jumped into bed with her married boss Mark...

The bestseller: Jojo's sweet-natured client Lily's first novel is a roaring success. She and lover Anton celebrate by spending the advance for her second book. Then she gets writer's block...

The unknown: Gemma used to be Lily's best friend – until Lily 'stole' Anton. Now she's writing her own story – painfully and hilariously – when supershark agent Jojo stumbles across it...

When their fortunes become entangled, it seems too much to hope that they'll all find a happy ending. But maybe they'll each discover that there's more than one side to every story...

'I whooped my way through this book; it had me in tears more than once and, very often, it had me barking with laughter' India Knight, *Daily Telegraph*

'Wildly funny, romantic and nearly impossible to put down. Elbow your way to the front of the queue to get a copy' *Daily Mail*

www.penguin.com

read more

# JANE GREEN

**LIFE SWAP**

Ever wondered what would happen if you got the chance to live the life you couldn't have?

Amber Winslow has got the kids, the hubbie, the suburban home in Connecticut, USA – and the feeling that somehow life is passing her by.

Vicky Townsley is features editor at *Poise!* Magazine in London, she's single, solvent and seriously successful – but she'd ditch it all for marriage, a country home and kids.

So when one day *Poise!* offers one lucky married reader the chance to life swap for a month with a glamorous, single journalist, Amber puts pen to paper ...

But neither Amber nor Vicky gets quite what they were expecting. And soon they find themselves asking: why does the grass look so much greener from the other side?

www.penguin.com

read more

# JANE FALLON

**GETTING RID OF MATTHEW**

When Matthew, Helen's lover of the past four years, finally decides to leave his wife Sophie (and their two daughters) and move into Helen's flat, she should be over the moon. The only trouble is, she doesn't want him anymore. Now she has to figure out how to get rid of him …

PLAN A
Stop shaving your armpits. And your bikini line
Buy incontinence pads and leave them lying around
Stop having sex with him

PLAN B
Accidentally on purpose bump into his wife Sophie
Give yourself a fake name and identity
Befriend Sophie and actually begin to really like her
Snog Matthew's son (who's the same age as you by the way. You're not a paedophile)
Befriend Matthew's children. Unsuccessfully
Watch your whole plan go absolutely horribly wrong.

*Getting Rid of Matthew* isn't as easy as it seems, but along the way Helen will forge an unlikely friendship, find real love and realize that nothing ever goes exactly to plan…

www.penguin.com

read more

# VERONICA HENRY

**LOVE ON THE ROCKS**

When Lisa Jones and her boyfriend George take on the run-down Rocks Hotel, they aim to do for Mariscombe what Rick Stein did for Padstow (even though neither of them is *quite* sure what to do with a red mullet ...) and set up a chic maritime retreat.

But renovating a hotel is about more than stripped wooden floors and Egyptian cotton sheets, particularly when the locals are shifty and unhelpful. Especially Bruno Thorne, the tall, dark and surly owner of the nearby Mariscombe Hotel, where life is one long holiday – for the staff, anyway.

Amid the sandcastles and surf, passions run high as ghosts of the past come out of the freshly painted woodwork. A little midsummer madness leaves Mariscombe's inhabitants floating on a tide of infatuation ... sending some of them rather too close to the rocks.

www.penguin.com

read more ⬤

# PENGUIN FICTION

*If you enjoyed this book, there are several ways you can read more by Penguin authors and make sure you get the inside track on all Penguin books.*

---

**Order any of the following titles direct:**

| | | |
|---|---|---|
| 9780141012186 | VINCE & JOY | £6.99 |

'The cream of pop fiction' *Glamour*

| | | |
|---|---|---|
| 9780141018263 | AMY'S HONEYMOON | £6.99 |

'A hilarious new novel' *Red*

| | | |
|---|---|---|
| 9780141015453 | HUSBANDS | £7.99 |

'Excellent, well-honed and acutely observed' *Daily Mail*

| | | |
|---|---|---|
| 9780141019888 | THE SECOND WIFE | £6.99 |

'A brilliant study of marriage' *Woman & Home*

| | | |
|---|---|---|
| 9780141021720 | LIFE SWAP | £6.99 |

'Green is the queen of the chick-literati' *Glamour*

---

Simply call Penguin c/o Bookpost on **01624 677237** and have your credit/debit card ready. Alternatively e-mail your order to **bookshop@enterprise.net**. Postage and package is free in mainland UK. Overseas customers must add £2 per book. Prices and availability subject to change without notice.

---

*Visit www.penguin.com and find out first about forthcoming titles, read exclusive material and author interviews, and enter exciting competitions. You can also browse through thousands of Penguin books and buy online.*

**IT'S NEVER BEEN EASIER TO READ MORE WITH PENGUIN**

*Frustrated by the quality of books available at Exeter station for his journey back to London one day in 1935, Allen Lane decided to do something about it. The Penguin paperback was born that day, and with it first-class writing became available to a mass audience for the very first time. This book is a direct descendant of those original Penguins and Lane's momentous vision. What will you read next?*

# *He just wanted a decent book to read ...*

Not too much to ask, is it? It was in 1935 when Allen Lane, Managing Director of Bodley Head Publishers, stood on a platform at Exeter railway station looking for something good to read on his journey back to London. His choice was limited to popular magazines and poor-quality paperbacks – the same choice faced every day by the vast majority of readers, few of whom could afford hardbacks. Lane's disappointment and subsequent anger at the range of books generally available led him to found a company – and change the world.

*'We believed in the existence in this country of a vast reading public for intelligent books at a low price, and staked everything on it'*
**Sir Allen Lane, 1902–1970, founder of Penguin Books**

The quality paperback had arrived – and not just in bookshops. Lane was adamant that his Penguins should appear in chain stores and tobacconists, and should cost no more than a packet of cigarettes.

Reading habits (and cigarette prices) have changed since 1935, but Penguin still believes in publishing the best books for everybody to enjoy. We still believe that good design costs no more than bad design, and we still believe that quality books published passionately and responsibly make the world a better place.

So wherever you see the little bird – whether it's on a piece of prize-winning literary fiction or a celebrity autobiography, political tour de force or historical masterpiece, a serial-killer thriller, reference book, world classic or a piece of pure escapism – you can bet that it represents the very best that the genre has to offer.

**Whatever you like to read – trust Penguin.**

read more
www.penguin.co.uk